THE LOST MILLENNIUM TRILOGY

Lieutenant Launa O'Brian.
Captain Jack Walking Bear.
They are the first time travelers, guinea pigs in an experiment that
cannot fail. From a future nearly destroyed by plague, they must
travel thousands of years into the past to the dawn of civilization.
Among tribes of primitive hunters, they will trace a fatal chain of
events—and alter history to save humanity from itself.

Book One: First Dawn

Ace Books by Mike Moscoe

FIRST DAWN
SECOND FIRE

SECOND FIRE

BOOK TWO OF THE LOST MILLENNIUM

MIKE MOSCOE

ACE BOOKS, NEW YORK

This book is an Ace original edition,
and has never been previously published.

SECOND FIRE

An Ace Book / published by arrangement with
the author

PRINTING HISTORY
Ace edition / July 1997

The Putnam Berkley World Wide Web site address is
http://www.berkley.com

Make sure to check out *PB Plug*,
the science fiction/fantasy newsletter, at
http://www.pbplug.com

ISBN: 0-441-00458-X

ACE®
Ace Books are published by The Berkley Publishing Group,
200 Madison Avenue, New York, NY 10016.
ACE and the "A" design are trademarks
belonging to Charter Communications, Inc.

PRINTED IN THE UNITED STATES OF AMERICA

10 9 8 7 6 5 4 3 2 1

PROLOGUE

SCREAMS AND SHOUTS grew dim and distant. Judith Lee hadn't heard automatic weapons fire for at least five minutes. She let out a long, slow breath; hiding here between a wall and some huge lab equipment had been the first relaxing moment she'd had in six months. Everything was finished. She was either right—or terribly wrong.

As a college professor, inhabiting the dusty halls of anthropology departments, she got away with thinking in terms of thousands of years, plus or minus a few hundred. But if she'd targeted Launa and Jack for the wrong year, everything—the time machine and six thousand years of history—was wasted.

Keep thinking like that and you'll run out of here screaming for somebody to shoot you. She glanced at Brent Lynch, squeezed with her into the cramped hideaway. "Shall we make a run for it?"

The old gentleman shrugged. "I doubt if I can do more than hobble, but I most certainly do not want to die here."

Since they most certainly were going to die—and soon— Judith slowly pulled herself out from the machinery that had hidden them from the mob. Her old joints ached, but, being five years shy of Brent's eighty, she went first.

As she wiggled out, a wire gouged her arm, drawing blood. Half out, she sat up, dabbing at the cut as she searched the wreckage. Bodies of Livermore personnel in lab smocks and uniforms lay scattered among those of the mob. None looked alive. *Such a waste. Do they really think this bunker holds a cure for the plague?*

She helped Brent out.

"How long do we have?" He spoke between gasps.

"The plague normally takes three to six days to kill. Your guess is as good as mine." Neither one spoke of the chance that he or she might be the lucky one in a thousand the designer plague left alive. Were the six million survivors who faced secondary plagues and lawlessness really that lucky? "My daughter lives ten miles from Livermore. I'd like to be with her." They probably couldn't walk that far, but Judith would not give up.

Brent smiled through gritted teeth. "Why not? I have no place else to go."

Judith felt the impact before she heard the shots. Chunks of her flesh and blood splattered on the wall in front of her, punctuated by bullet holes. She felt more relief than pain. Her last thought as she surrendered to the darkness was a prayer. *Please, dear God, let Launa and Jack change all this.*

ONE

CAPTAIN JACK WALKING Bear did his usual morning sweep of the valley around Tall Oaks. It looked as peaceful as Judith and Brent had briefed him to expect. Wisps of fog shrouded the planted fields and clung to the tops of the trees on the gently rising hill beyond. Goats grazed placidly.

Last summer he'd seen just how quick Kurgan horse raiders could change all that.

Predawn colored the clouds to the west in gold and pastels. He enjoyed a deep breath of the crisp air, a fine break from the cold drizzle of the last week. With luck they'd put this break in the weather to good use; Goddess knows, the wall needed shoring up.

Beside him, a blond head poked out from the deerskin flap that was the door to their home, followed quickly by the rest of his commanding officer. Lieutenant Launa O'Brian stepped gingerly, trying to avoid mud puddles. The leather jerkin and leggings showed off her lithe gymnast's body to good measure. He smiled.

"Who's working with us today?" Launa, as usual, was all mission . . . once outside their home.

"I think Antia and her pikes have construction duty, but the rain's made a hash of the duty roster."

"I'll be glad for whoever shows up."

A horse snorted; another whinnied. Both Launa and Jack

got busy doing a new set of full-circle searches. "Do we have a patrol going out this morning?" Launa asked curtly.

"Not that I scheduled," Jack shot back.

"Kurgans?"

"They're not supposed to go for winter campaigns, but I don't trust those bastards to read their own Ops manuals."

Jack listened hard. His life, and the lives of a lot of people, depended on him being ready when the Kurgans came calling.

The noise of animal and harness came from *inside* Tall Oaks!

Arakk, Bloodletter to the Wide Blue Sky, leader of the Stormy Mountain Clan, faced the sacred east. The sky was clear; no cloud marred its blue purity. Behind him, clouds out of season profaned the dawn. He ignored them.

Raising his long obsidian blade to the sun as it edged above the horizon, he called in a loud voice. "Father Sun, fill my knife with Your strength. Let my eyes see all that You see. Watch me slaughter the enemies of my clan."

Behind him came the sound of pounding hoofs. He did not turn; nothing would distract him from his morning prayers.

"Father, a slave escaped in the night."

For this, prayers would wait. Arakk turned to see his eldest son, Kantom, trotting toward him, leading two hands of horses. "They run," Arakk snarled, "we catch them. We beat them. They learn."

His son nodded. "It is the old one. He has run many times and been beaten many times. Last night he stole a horse."

Arakk grabbed the halter of the nearest horse and swung himself up. "No one steals a horse of the clan and lives. This time he dies slowly. Let his bloody body teach the others."

Kantom leaped from the tired horse he was riding to a fresh one, kicked it and led his father in pursuit. It did not take long to find tracks in the snow that dusted the good grass.

"He rides to the west, father."

"We follow him," Arakk growled. Always it was the west. Arakk had come to hate the west.

For seasons the clan had fled to the west from its strong enemies, seeking grass with no horses on it. Finally, they had found good grass, but it was not enough. Three moons ago he had sent Tyman and four hands of warriors to see what prey lay to the west. Or maybe Tyman had sent himself. Still, even if that puffed-up adder had done what Arakk half expected—charging into the next place of walkers and taken many heads—Tyman would have returned for his women . . . and to claim clan status for his band.

Arakk scowled. He still did not know what lay to the west. Next spring he must lead the Stormy Mountain warriors and their allies straight and swift to take more heads, more slaves and more pastures.

Once more, Arakk was trying to raise the cloak that hid the west. What four hands of warriors could not see, maybe one could. Danic had no fear of trees, like some steppe raised warriors. And Danic knew the honor his woman and young son received by feasting at Arakk's right hand would be short-lived if he did not return.

Arakk kicked his horse for more speed. It struggled to gallop faster, but failed. He pulled in another spare mount and leaped to it. When he kicked this one, it took off like an eagle. Beside him, Kantom did the same.

No one could escape Arakk's wrath.

TWO

JACK BOLTED FOR the center of town, spear in hand, not sure what he was headed for—trying to be ready for anything. In a minute he covered half the distance. The noise was to his left; he skidded as he turned. Grabbing a handhold on a log-and-wattle hut, he avoided a dip in somebody's overflowing cesspool. Two muddy streets over, he found what he was looking for.

Ten riders wound their way in a double column *out* of town. The helmets, weapons and clothing were Kurgan. Jack had peeled that gear off twenty dead horsemen last summer; he knew it well.

The riders were just as familiar. Jack identified faces he'd drilled for half a year. The leader glanced his way. *I should have known.* Antia!

"Halt!" Jack filled the word with the hard officer-presence the United States Army expected. The ragtag collection would be the despair of any Army recruiter . . . and most of the riders only half controlled their mounts. Jack reinforced his command by stepping in front of them and bringing his spear horizontal to block their way.

The word or the block had the desired effect. The troop came to a close approximation of a halt.

"Where do you ride?" Lasa, Speaker for the Goddess in Tall Oaks, stepped beside him and asked the question before

Jack could. Launa skidded to a halt on the other side. Nobody was going anywhere without riding over someone. The skittish horses didn't look ready for that.

"And why," Lasa finished, "do you ride in such clothing?" Jack had questions too, but Lasa had the floor. Here, six thousand years before he was born, a man kept quiet when a woman spoke.

Antia doffed her helmet and shook out her long raven hair. The daughter of She who Spoke for the Goddess at River Bend knew the Kurgans up close and personal. She'd been there when they burned her town and killed her mother.

"Taelon who leads the Badger People in the dark woods and who rode with the horsemen as a youth told me the horse people scatter their herds to feed them during the winter." She glanced back at those who rode with her, survivors of River Bend. "We go to visit one of their campfires as they visited us."

"See! See! Is this not as I told you?" Jack looked around for the source of that high-pitched, familiar voice.

"Shit, it's Hanna," Launa sighed. "Did everyone in this town know about this crazy sortie except us?"

Jack shrugged as Hanna waded through the crowd to Lasa.

"It is not enough that they spend every waking moment envisioning the horsemen coming to kill us. Now they go as death to walk among the horsemen. Death will return with them to walk among us."

Jack sighed, and grounded his spear to make sure he didn't do what he wanted to do . . . hit Hanna up beside the ear. It was good to teach the young to see themselves as skilled, capable, loved by the one they desired. But all the envisioning of yourself as winning the lottery didn't make those numbered balls fall any different. Nobody could make Hanna, or a lot of people like her, see that difference.

Launa nudged his elbow. "Let's back off. I think this is best left to local counsel."

He drifted with Launa to the edge of the crowd; they could hear. Most of it they'd heard before. Hanna wanted everyone to think nice thoughts. Antia wanted every horseman dead. Most people were somewhere in the middle, praying to the Goddess that the horsemen would just leave them alone.

Jack knew from the history books what these farmers did not. The attack on River Bend was just the first Kurgan campaign in a long war that would conquer Europe—and lock the world in a grim dance of domination and submission. Six thousand years up-time, a designer plague would kill that world . . . and the President of the United States would give Launa command of the Neolithic Military Advisory Group, and orders for the two of them to change human history from conquest to cooperation. Then, Jack had considered their mission a desperate long shot. Nothing in the last year had changed his mind.

"Step out of my path," Antia shouted. "No one can tell another the path for her feet."

So Antia had finally played her ace, the most sacred rule of the Goddess, and the one that might just lose them this war.

"But the horses you ride have eaten the grass of Tall Oaks for a season and more." That was the voice of Kaul, Speaker for the Bull. Jack looked for him. The other side of the crowd opened to make way for Lasa's consort. "You, too, have eaten from the bounty the Goddess shares with us. Wise Lasa has spoken the Words of the Goddess. Let all of us walk in peace and harmony. Where is the peace and harmony in what you ride to?"

"Our knives will give the horsemen the only peace they can know when we let the lifeblood out of them."

Launa snickered. "You rescued quite a princess there."

Jack shrugged. "She looked pretty helpless the first time I saw her." Roped together with nine other naked women and bullied by four armed Kurgans, Jack still wasn't sure how she'd escaped, but she had. Of the four Kurgans, Jack only killed two.

A commotion behind Jack got his attention. Taelon led in a group of hunters with a dozen deer slung across packhorses. Trying not to hunt out the area around Tall Oaks, Taelon was using the captured horses to range wide. He was also Launa's early warning system if the Kurgans did move during the winter.

Taelon listened attentively for a while, then threw his head back and laughed. "Little sister, you will clomp after the horsemen. They will hear you long before you see them. The cub does not hunt the deer, and you are not yet the wolf you want to be. You must learn more from me and Launa."

Launa shook her head. "Who says I'll teach her more?" she said.

Jack doubted they could avoid that. The voices boiled on for a few more minutes. Everything was in the stew now. It began to rain. Someone suggested they talk this over at the sanctuary of the Goddess. That just about guaranteed nothing would happen today. "Damn," Jack muttered, "how do we get a fire going under these people?"

"I want to know who's helping us mend the wall today?" Launa scowled as everyone headed elsewhere.

"I think we're looking at both of them," Jack said.

"Damn," Launa growled and turned for the outskirts of town.

Arakk grinned; the slave was as predictable as a thirsty doe going to water. He fled toward that place of abominations to the Wide Blue Sky the Stormy Mountain Clan had burned last summer. They spotted him as they came out of a tree line along a stream. He was halfway across a wide stretch of prairie, kicking his horse for speed. The tired animal could do little more than trot. Once again, father and son switched to remounts.

They topped a low rise as the rider and horse disappeared into a line of trees. Beyond them was the place. They raced for the ford closest to the abomination, and cleared the trees to see the man tumble from his horse beside one of the burned wooden tents. Kantom tossed aside the rope leading his spare mounts, lowered his lance and charged as a warrior should.

The slave heard them. He slashed the throat of the stolen horse with a stolen knife, then raised it in a defiant warrior's challenge. Kantom answered with a whoop and kicked his mount for more speed, aiming his lance for the slave's heart.

The man stood proud, waiting for death. Almost, Arakk could honor him.

Then, in a blink, the slave hurled a rock at Kantom's horse, sending the startled mount into a spasm of bucking—and ducked into a burned hovel.

Enraged, Arakk drew his bow, strung it without slowing, and nocked an arrow.

The man reappeared, knife in hand as he dashed for Kantom. The boy still struggled to control his mount.

"Son!" Arakk shouted as he let arrow fly. The shaft took the man in the side, but did not slow him.

Kantom jabbed him in the face with the butt of his lance.

The man recoiled from his attack and tried to flee. Kantom spun his lance around and hurled it. The flint point took the man full in the back. This time, he went down.

Arakk trotted up; the slave still breathed. "Drag him back to the camp. Let all see on his dead body the reward of a slave who runs."

The boy dismounted and looped his lasso around the man's ankle. "He is not dead, father."

"There are enough rocks between here and camp to make sure he is not breathing when you return to camp."

"Yes, father." The boy grinned as he mounted.

The man screamed in pain as Kantom kicked his horse and it took off.

Arakk watched them go, a frown forming on his face. Could the dirt-scratcher learn a warrior's way? This one almost had. Still, hands and hands of others went about their work with eyes downcast and did not raise a hand when they were beaten. Should this one worry Arakk?

He glanced around. Last summer they found this land that no horse clan claimed. The people dug in the ground or followed weak little animals. No man rode a horse or carried a lance . . . and they listened to a woman who strutted about as if she were a Mighty Man.

Arakk had taken heads, and made that woman a special offering to the Sun. Her heart and lungs he cut out, spreading them wide like the eagle's wings that are sacred to the Sky. She had still lived as he sacrificed her. Now the clan's mighty arm held these pastures, and slaves did the bidding of their masters . . . at least most had learned their place.

And when Danic returned, Arakk would go to the Mighty Men of the clans and raise high his totem. Many young warriors would follow him to the next abomination to the Wide Blue Sky.

There was pleasure in a well-built fire, in the smoke rising to the Sky. Come spring, Arakk would light a fire such as the Sun had never beheld.

It began to rain. He changed mounts and followed his son.

THREE

LONG HOURS LATER, it was pouring rain, but Launa wouldn't quit. "Quick, Jack, I need another stake."

The two roughly split logs she struggled to hold in place just might, if she could stake them down, keep Europe's first fortified wall from sliding back into the ditch they'd dug it out of two months ago. Another gallon of cold rain trickled into her eyes or down the back of her neck in the few seconds it took Jack to toss the stake her way. She caught it one-handed, wiggled it into place and hit it with a rock.

"Damn!" A splinter she hadn't seen bit into her hand. Now blood mixed with the rain. Launa adjusted her hand-hold and kept hammering. The stake offered some resistance; hopefully it had gotten past the yellow slurry the fine loess soil and rain was making of her wall. A grin started to edge around the scowl she'd worn most of the last month—then her feet slipped.

Launa didn't need to look down; the small ledge she'd perched on had given way. Half swimming, half crawling, she scrambled for safety over the logs as they followed gravity's urging. Jack managed to stay one step ahead of her.

Tears of frustration were lost in the rain on her face as she watched the mudslide and picked at the splinter in her hand. "Damn it, Captain, why didn't you include a bulldozer in our mission's table of organization and equipment?"

Jack snapped to attention. "Petroleum, Oil and Lubricant supply seemed questionable, Lieutenant. Intelligence says we're six thousand years from the nearest gas station," he deadpanned.

And Launa laughed, not because it was funny, but because the Book said officers laughed when they wanted to cry.

"Besides"—he put an arm around her—"a week before we jumped, that time machine couldn't throw a quarter-ton back six millennia. It looked like my modest lieutenant would be choosing between bringing bows and that dinky little bikini bottom."

Launa was glad the folks at the Lawrence Livermore Lab had managed to tweak their mad scientist's delight into some serious heavy lifting. Three stallions with full packs had come through time with them, as well as the half bikini the anthropologists said she should wear to meet the local female rulers.

Well, she'd met what passed for rulers here, and fought a battle or two. She'd gained allies, although Launa was never sure whose side Antia was on from day to day. Two months ago she had a good start on fortifying Tall Oaks to keep the Kurgans away from the farmers next spring. Then the rains came. Except for a few mounds where the grass had taken root, the wall was sliding back into the moat. Launa scowled; wouldn't anything go right?

"You know, your idea of planting thorn bushes in the ditch is working." Jack pointed along the bottom of the moat. "They're growing too fast for the mud to bury them. Some places they're so thick a mouse couldn't get through."

"Wasn't my idea," Launa snorted. "A couple of months back, this old guy showed up on the wall. He was one of the 'think nice thoughts and everything will be all right' type." Launa let her own fear and confusion layer her words thick with sarcasm. "While me and my cohort kept digging, he goes into this long rambling talk about when he was a kid gathering berries. Just as I'm about to tell him to get lost or get a basket, a light goes off. If the bears and deer only took the berries on the outside of the bushes, leaving the inside ones for a little kid to gather, horses would keep their distance too."

Launa remembered her baffled excitement of that afternoon. "So I start talking this idea over with Brege, and this guy says 'I am glad I could help you, my sisters. Let the gifts of the Goddess be our protection.' Then he just walks off. He won't fight with us, but he'll tell us things like that. What gives with these people?"

"I have no idea, and it gets worse every day."

Launa threw Jack a frown for a question. She didn't need something worse.

He talked to the ditch, avoided her eyes. "Something going on inside Kaul."

"So what else is new?" Launa snorted. There was something spooky about the Speaker for the Bull. "He's not backing out of supporting us?"

"No, not that." Jack adjusted the soaked skins that were supposed to keep him warm. "He's still with us. It just bothers him that we'll be killing horsemen without even speaking to them." Jack faced Launa square on. "These people have solved their problems for centuries by talking them out. It doesn't feel right to him to start killing without even trying to talk."

"Christ in heaven, or Goddess, or whoever's up there listening," Launa exploded . . . it was hard to know how to cuss these days. "The horsemen didn't talk to anyone in River Bend. They just started cutting heads off. And, God, what they did to the Speakers . . ." Launa didn't want to think about that.

Jack nodded. "He knows. It's just walking away from a path of the Goddess 'from of old.' "

"Jesus, Jack, my folks raised me Catholic, but they never let it interfere with what they wanted to do. Why do these people have to take their goddess stuff so seriously?"

Jack didn't try to answer that one. Launa wondered if anyone could. "Let's get cleaned up," she sighed. "God, what I'd give for a warm bath."

"My commanding officer's wish is my command." Suddenly Jack had one of those lopsided grins on his face.

And Launa couldn't help but grin back. Commanding officer, he called her . . . and meant it now. If her career plans had gone right, she'd be in her last year at West Point. But nothing had gone according to plan. Somebody had canceled the twenty-first century.

Here, long before either was born, Lasa spoke for the Goddess, and the forces that defended Tall Oaks took their orders from a lieutenant . . . even a combat veteran like Jack. They'd worked a few kinks out of the command structure, but it had been fine lately. Last summer, Launa had passed tactical command to Jack for their first battle. They had survived the victory; they would fight many more.

The rain streaking Launa's face smelled of salt. *Just how close is the Black Sea?* Tall Oaks was somewhere in the Danube River basin; exactly where, they hadn't had time to figure out.

Jack headed for their home, but Launa paused a moment to look out over the fields of Tall Oaks. Somewhere out there was her field of winter wheat. *May the Goddess, or somebody, bless it.* Because if She didn't, a lot of people in this town would take it as specific orders from on high to ditch these two troublemaking soldiers. Launa hoped the rains weren't drowning the seeds she and Jack had planted.

She glanced at the hills ringing Tall Oaks. Come spring, there was no question they'd sprout with the lances of a major Kurgan battle group.

With a shrug, Launa hastened after Jack.

It hadn't been planned that way, but the house the People had built for the two soldiers was right on the threat axis. In the spring, the Kurgans would hit this side of town first. Today, that meant Launa didn't have to wade through too much mud. As she got home, Jack pulled the deerskin flap aside.

Warmth swept over her.

"What the . . ." Her home had changed. It was still the four-by-eight-meter house, smelling of newly split wood. But now in the raised fireplace, a large ceramic pot-bellied stove edged a foot out into the room. Heat, wonderful heat, glowed from it and a clay chimney pipe. Atop it bubbled a bowl of water.

Launa whirled as Jack's arms closed around her. "What have you done, Bearman?"

"Something like that old man on the wall did, only the other way around," he grinned. "I was talking with Kaul as we recaulked the logs at the sanctuary of the Goddess. Somehow we got to talking about insulation. Notice anything else?"

Jack's gesture took in the rest of the house. The walls were no longer bare wood with mud and clay calking oozing through holes. Reed mats covered them and lowered the ceiling. They hardly moved. The cold drafts Launa hated were gone.

"The wood stove was a bit harder, mainly 'cause I only saw grandpa take his apart once on the reservation. Didn't need much heating in L.A. Anyway, people started talking, and a week later they've got one going. First one couldn't take the heat and blew up, but this one seems to work okay. Kaul told me once they got a few installed in the sanctuary, he'd let us have this one. But I think the hot water was Lasa's idea."

Somewhere in that long explanation, Jack had lifted the deerskin jerkin over her head. Now he was on his knees, undoing her leather leggings, his fingers working slowly down her thighs.

"Hum, that's nice," Launa answered a couple of things at once. "Think Judith will mind us giving away technology?"

Jack stood, cupped her throat with his hands and kissed her slowly. "Judith's toes don't have to stay warm here."

"Mumm," Launa agreed as Jack pulled her linen shirt over her head. She trembled, waiting for his hands to slide down her waist, loosen her belt, and let her leather loincloth fall to the floor.

Like a good tactician, Jack took the indirect approach. He dipped a cloth in warm water and began washing the mud from her arms and hands. Jack's hand massages were good for making Launa weak in the knees. She let herself plop down on the spare bed across from the hearth. In many houses, that was the man's bed. In this house, it was the couch.

Jack began wiping the mud from her toes. She could feel the caress of his fingers on her feet, and down her back—and in other places. The warmth of the house, the scent of earth and water, the touch of Jack all swirled in her mind, bringing memories.

On that warm autumn day two months ago, Brege and Merik had not knocked at the door. They just walked in naked. Launa and Jack had been naked too, celebrating their first morning in their new home . . . and very compromised by modern military standards. Brege laughed, and told the soldiers how the day was to go.

"We will plant a field to show the will of the Goddess."

Today, Launa reached for Jack, pulled him to her. She was clean enough. She wanted him.

That morning she'd wanted him too, but first he had to carry bags of seed and his naked need through town. But while he reddened in embarrassment, townspeople pointed at this first good omen. And it had begun to dawn on Launa just how different her new people were from the ones who sent her here.

The sun turned that day hot, and it was hard work for the men to draw the wooden plow. Brege insisted on taking a break before too long—and Launa discovered that seed was meant for more than the field.

Launa watched as Brege and Merik made love, so totally absorbed in the pleasure and each other that Brege hardly noticed Launa watching. Brege had paused only for a moment. "Do you not know how to play?"

And Launa had learned how to play—to love so full of herself and her lover that there was no room for *they* or shoulds or oughts. The Colonel and his lady would have disapproved, but Mom and Dad were dead . . . along with the world that spawned them. There, beneath the sun, open to the air and approving smiles, Launa learned new rules to play by.

Jack's hands caressed her breasts, drawing her from the

past to the present. *You play with all of you. Nothing held back. Nothing anywhere else. That's why you're naked.*

Jack's hands roamed lower. Pleasure began to explode through Launa.

"Come, my Bull. Come, speak to the Goddess."

Much later, as Jack snored softly beside her, Launa luxuriated in the warmth of her home. For an army brat, raised bouncing from one post to another, roots were special. That was what Tall Oaks had given her . . . roots. For them, she and Jack had given much.

The wicker chest at the foot of her bed held that part of their twenty-first-century trove they hadn't given away. Jack had shared out all the copper tools. Since Tall Oaks had no craftsmen to work the raw copper, silver and gold, nuggets of those metals were put away in leather sacks.

Ahead of their time, the bronze tools were hidden away too. But she and Jack carried bronze knives and axes; you could never tell when a little technological edge might keep you alive.

As best they could, they stayed to Judith's mission brief. No technological advances beyond those locally available.

Somewhere in the chest also was Maria's book—a treasure of healing herbs and medicinal properties of plants. Some day Launa would have to destroy that anachronism, but not until after she had memorized it and shared it with her newfound people.

Launa snuggled closer to Jack, comfortable in the familiar touch of his body along hers. In all the confusion of their mission, this much was clear: He was hers and she was his.

FOUR

NEXT MORNING, JACK and Launa broke their fast at the sanctuary of the Goddess. The place was as warm as their home.

The walls along the east half of the sanctuary had rammed earth risers along them. When the People met in assembly, the elder women sat there. Today, many of the sick and elderly huddled there under blankets. The clay floor was dotted with people weaving, making baskets and mats, working with leather. The matted walls rang with their chatter and laughter.

Blossom, Lasa's nine-year-old daughter, offered them mush sweetened with honey. "Father has words to share with Jack," she said as she gave them the bowls.

He and Launa found Lasa and Kaul in a group of spinners. As hands worked, so did mouths. Jack felt like he was joining a conversation that had started several hundred winters back and was still going, handed down from mother to daughter as they whiled away the short winter days.

Kaul leaned toward Jack. "I ride to Wood Village to invite them to our Winter Feast. Will you ride after me?"

With a raised eyebrow, Jack passed the request up his chain of command.

"Why not?" Launa shrugged. "It'll probably rain again today. We're not getting much done here."

It took the men a few minutes to bow out. Launa ended up with Kaul's hank of wool, helping Lasa tease out yarn. A half hour later, Kaul and Jack rode out leading a string of remounts. Kaul had made the run up to Wood Village several times; he set a brisk trot that limited conversation. Jack wanted to talk.

As almost anyone here was quick to point out, no one could tell another the path for her feet. Yet, somehow Kaul had kept the woodsmen up river, away from their families, cutting the trees that Launa needed for her wall as well as for firewood to keep the people warm. The alternative would have been to strip the nearby woodlot, upsetting the careful balance of birth, growth and death that was harmony to these people. Jack needed no crystal ball to tell him how Hanna would have interpreted that.

Yet, after the first storms of the fall drove the woodsmen out of the forests to sit with their consorts and children, practicing their woodcraft indoors, Kaul had talked them back into the woods as soon as the weather gentled. The flow of logs kept coming downstream.

Jack wanted to know how Kaul did it. Whatever way Kaul and Lasa spelled leadership, he and Launa needed to know it.

An hour later, Kaul called a break long enough to switch mounts. Jack took the chance to raise his question.

"Kaul, why do the woodsmen cut wood for us even when the winds blow hard and tree limbs could fall on their heads?"

Kaul laughed. "It is our way. When there is need, we work together to make what we must."

"Yet many of them are like Hanna. They would center their spirits on the harmony of the Goddess and remove from their thoughts anything of the horsemen less by thinking of them, they bring them here." Jack hoped he was getting the language right. These people didn't "think" or "understand," they "saw in their hearts."

Kaul pursed his lips as he settled his blanket on a new mount. "Maybe they do not follow after Hanna as closely as she would want them. And, a tree is a tree. Felling it is no different this winter than last winter. Here, in the woods, a man may do as we have from of old and not ask himself what will grow from it in the spring. Let you and I thank the Goddess for what She sends us, and for what these people do. And pray it is enough in the spring."

Kaul mounted, and Jack smiled. So that was how Kaul kept the wood coming. By wringing as much as he could out of the old ways and keeping the workers from looking too hard at the future. Come spring, the hard stone points of horsemen's lances would not be so easy to overlook.

They galloped on. Mud splattered them from the soggy soil they raced over, but the clouds burned off and the day became unseasonably warm. Jack enjoyed the ride . . . until the next rest stop. Kaul had been thinking.

"We work as of old, but the ways of the horsemen tear at us," Kaul mumbled to himself as he stroked the next horse he would ride. But his eyes burned with the fire of a man who knew himself, even if he didn't know the future.

"I seek a dream from the Goddess that will light a way for my feet in the dark that surrounds us. What She sends weaves too strange a pattern for my heart. I sit in the Sanctuary of the Goddess, listening to the words of the People. But the wall behind Lasa is not there. It opens on a campfire with many Horse People. They say their words and I do not understand them."

Jack swallowed hard. "The horsemen at River Bend did not talk before they started taking heads."

"Yes, I know. Yesterday, Antia wanted to ride out to the horsemen to see their blood on her knife. Could someone ride among them with words before they ride among us with lances? Hanna is right. It is our way to speak among ourselves. Will your soldiers take horsemen's lives with no words traded?"

"The ones who stand with us have smelled the fire the horsemen will bring among us."

Kaul smiled. "But do enough stand with you?"

That was the critical question neither Jack nor Launa could answer. Jack's rough census of Tall Oaks counted about three thousand people, half of them too young or too old to carry a spear. Of the fifteen hundred women and men Launa considered potential soldiers, maybe two hundred practiced with the legion. That might be enough, if too many horsemen didn't come calling.

Until that day, there was no way of knowing if they were enough. And then it would be too late.

The stop at Wood Village was brief, hardly longer than it took to change horses. As soon as Kaul announced that the wise women had declared that four days hence would be the shortest day of the year, everyone started packing. At first light tomorrow they'd hike back. Kaul made no mention of restarting work after the Winter Feast; Jack suspected that would be negotiated later.

They chose a different route back; Kaul wanted to see how the deer herds were wintering. A half hour out from Tall Oaks, the sun was getting low; Jack had a serious case of get-home-itis. Then he yanked his horse to a halt.

"Those aren't deer tracks. They're horses." He pointed.

Kaul nodded. They searched the prairie ahead of them. Nothing visible. Jack led out at a walk, keeping his horses to the cover of the treeline beside them. Whoever had ridden this way before had done the same.

"Could they be some of Taelon's hunters?" Kaul asked.

Jack shook his head. "Taelon takes two or three hands of horses with him." Jack made a more careful survey of the steppe. He spotted a beaten track maybe two hundred meters out from the trees and pointed them out to Kaul. "There is an old trail where many horses passed. This is only four horses, maybe one rider. They are fresh." Jack spotted droppings. "Very fresh. Today."

Kaul frowned. "Let us follow with care."

Danic had ridden forth from Arakk's camp with the praise of the Mighty Man of the Stormy Mountain Clan ringing in his ears. It was an honor for Danic's woman and child to eat at Arakk's tent. At least, that was what Danic told himself.

For a hand of days now, he had searched the west for the next place of huts and weak women. He might have spent as much again and found nothing, but three hands of horses leave a trail even a blind woman could follow.

Danic was no fool. Who rode here had made two strong men and more than six hands of warriors vanish with not one voice left to sing a song of vengeance. He kept to the trees, leaped to a fresh horse, and looked every which way, as fast as his head and eyes could turn. He would flee at the first sight or sound.

But no one or no thing showed its face to him. He walked his horses for half the day until the smell of smoke on the wind told him he was close to what he sought. Tying his horses in a thicket, he moved silently through the woods, then crossed a stream to overlook an expanse of open fields.

As at the other place, wooden hovels, not proud tents, met his eyes. There were many of them, too many to count. That did not bother him. These people would die like the others, scared rabbits with no fight in their hearts.

But what he saw made him think again.

Across the field stood mounds of straw or dirt. Many hands of people shot with bows at the targets. Danic squinted, trying to take the measure of this; it smelled of strange.

The bows were as long as the archers were tall; a horse rider would never use such a bow. Then his eyes grew wide. An archer paced off the distance to retrieve his arrows. He walked hands and hands of paces, far too many. No arrow could fly as far as these arrows flew. But they did!

What did they sacrifice, and to what god did they offer it that their arrows should stay so long in the air? Arakk must be told that the clan's warriors would feel these arrows long before their lances could drink the blood of these animals.

Closer to the hovels, people stood in rows, one side with spears, the other with knives or axes. They fought, one against the other. More often than not, it was the knife wielder who yielded before the spear—but not a spear jab. A slice with the long pole to the head, foot or arm would end the fight. The wood of the spear was more deadly than the stone tip!

These were not the frightened rabbits at the other place

who waited trembling while Danic laughed and slit their throats. Arakk must hear Danic's song of warning.

Quickly, he recrossed the frigid stream and raced through the dark forest. Who were these people who rode horses, shot far-flying arrows and used spears against knives? What would the Stormy Mountain Clan face in the spring? What god stood with these farmers against the Sun and Wide Blue Sky?

Danic's thoughts tumbled through his mind even before he pitched face forward on the trail, his legs pulled out from under him.

FIVE

JACK HAD SPOTTED the four horses in the thicket and picketed his own beside them. Whoever he was trailing was good, but this close to Tall Oaks, there was little doubt where he'd gone. Jack found the barest hint of a trail.

It was Kaul who set the trap, stretching twine across the game path to catch whoever came this way again. Kaul hid among leaves. Jack climbed a tree. They had not long to wait.

A young man, blond of hair and in Kurgan leathers, soon hurried down the trail.

Kaul yanked the string tight, and the man stumbled. Jack was on him before he could regain his balance. A whack with the hilt of his knife rewarded Jack with a groan and a cooperative lump of unconscious humanity. Using solid leather rope, captured last summer from the Kurgans, Jack quickly trussed the spy.

"How will he walk?" Kaul asked.

"If he can not walk, he can not run away. His horse will carry him."

Kaul shrugged and headed up the trail to collect the horses. "I want to talk to him," he said over his shoulder.

Having finally got one alive, Jack wanted to talk to him too. "You're mine. You're going to tell me what's really going on here."

The prisoner moaned.

At dusk, Jack and Kaul rode into Tall Oaks. Solidly tied, belly down across a horse, the Kurgan was awake. If Jack was any judge of linguistics, he was cursing them roundly.

They dismounted in front of the sanctuary of the Goddess and turned the horses over to troops from the legion.

"What've you got there?" was Launa's first question.

"Picked him up just outside of town, too busy putting distance between him and Tall Oaks to look where he was going. What was the drill today?"

"Damn! This afternoon was the first decent weather we've had in weeks. Everybody was out, pikes drilling, archers shooting."

"At long range?" Jack raised an eyebrow.

"Several at two hundred and fifty meters. Think he saw?"

"I wouldn't trust any other assumption," Jack said.

"Damn, damn, damn. Could we just slit his throat?"

"I haven't heard of capital punishment around here, have you? And Kaul wants to talk to him. So do I."

"Five will get you ten he won't tell us anything."

Jack wouldn't take that bet.

Many of the elders were already at the sanctuary for supper. Word passed quickly and more soon arrived. As Jack and Kaul took their prisoner through the door, Kaul's eyes brightened. "Taelon, I have a horseman for you to talk to."

Taelon didn't look too excited, but Kaul hustled their Kurgan over to the old hunter. "Welcome him in the name of the Goddess and tell him we mean him well."

"I will try." Taelon pursed his lips and spoke haltingly.

For a moment, the prisoner listened. Then he snarled at Taelon, spat and began shouting.

"What does he say?" Kaul asked his old friend.

Wiping spittle from his cheek, Taelon shook his head. "His words say nothing to me."

Launa nudged Jack. "I thought Taelon was supposed to have spent a year with the horsemen when he was younger."

"See how much of your high school French you remember in twenty years," Jack whispered back. Which wasn't quite fair. Launa spoke fluent German, French, Spanish,

Arabic and Russian, picked up as her father followed his orders around the world. Her gift for languages was one of the reasons she was here.

"And Taelon might be trying high school French on a German," Launa finished, no slight taken.

The elder women took seats on the benches along the walls of the eastern half of the sanctuary; the men settled on the floor at the western end. Children moved among them, offering herbal teas before taking a place at the back of the room.

Even though everyone wasn't seated, Lasa hastened to invoke the Goddess. Kaul, Jack and Launa were still standing with the prisoner in the center of the assemble. While everyone else listened to Lasa's prayer, the Kurgan began shouting. Jack had not heard the people use invectives or curses, but the intent of the prisoner's bellowing could not have been lost on the council.

"Let us take him to our room," Kaul said and led the way to a small deerskin door toward the rear of the sanctuary. Through it, Jack found Lasa and Kaul's private quarters: simple, spartan, clean.

When Launa pointed for the man to sit on the floor, he refused. Jack took the guy's legs out from underneath him, gentle like, knowing Kaul was watching, and settled him on the floor. "I'd like to hog-tie this character so the more he struggled the more he'd choke himself, but I don't think I better."

Launa cast a glance over her shoulder at Kaul. "I think we better not."

Jack shortened the rope between the Kurgan's arms and legs so he'd have to sit or lie with them stretched out in front of him, then patted him on the shoulder. "Stay, fellow. You aren't going anyplace before we get some answers from you."

The Kurgan spat at Jack . . . and missed.

"Real nice people," Launa observed.

As Jack hastened from the room, he saw Bomel, Lasa's firstborn son, drawing a steaming mug. Jack smiled at the boy—he'd been the first kid to help Jack the day they walked into Tall Oaks—then hastened to his place.

As so often was the way with these people, he need not have hurried. Nothing had happened while Jack and company were busy. The room had sat quietly, everyone lost in thought or meditation or whatever these people did to avoid making a decision.

Jack shortened his own leash after that mental snide remark. These people were the only allies he and Launa would ever get in this crazy lost war they were trying to win. Respect was something he couldn't afford to lose, either for these people, or from them. Still, the speed these people made decisions could drive a patient man around the bend, even a soldier who'd learned the hard lesson of waiting in the ancient school called war.

Jack settled in his place beside Kaul at the head of the men. As soon as Launa reached hers with Brege and Antia seated in front of Lasa, the Speaker for the Goddess stood.

"What shall we do with this horseman whom the Goddess has brought among us?" she asked, then sat.

No sooner was she back in her chair than Hanna was on her feet. "He is our guest. Have we forgotten the duty of a host to greet a stranger with food? He is cut and his skin is bruised." She shot Jack a venomous glance. He smiled back in injured innocence; he'd followed the Geneva Convention . . . and then some. She turned back to Lasa.

"Whenever *strangers*"—her inflection there left no question she meant Launa and Jack—"come among us, we offer them hospitality that they may share with us their songs. That is our way from of old." She finished, hands on hips.

Antia didn't even wait for Hanna to sit before she shot to her feet. "He did not come to hear our songs. He came for our heads, as he came for the head of my father at River Bend. I say we cut his head off."

The room broke into a roaring babble, and Jack cringed. Hanna and Antia had one-track minds going in opposite directions. The people needed to find someplace in between them, but the two extremes, as usual, dominated the debate.

Taelon rose slowly to his feet. He waited for the side discussions to die down, then cleared his throat. "Hanna is right; when someone of the People comes in pilgrimage with the Goddess, we share what we have, one with the other." He paused while a wave of nods worked its way around the assembly.

"But when a wolf comes to sniff your herds of sheep or goats, you do not offer it a lamb. You send one of your hunters to track it, or you invite we of the Badger People to join you in the hunt. That horseman is a wolf, sniffing the ground, looking for a way to tear our throats out. We cannot let him do that."

From the thoughtful nods slowly flowing around the room, Jack could see that agreement was fairly easy on what they couldn't do. As usual, agreement on what they should do was a bit harder to arrive at. Jack leaned back wondering how long these folks would toss this hot potato around.

A scream from the back of the room told him they'd lost control of the schedule.

As soon as the deerskin flopped closed behind his captors, Danic attacked his fetters. With his wrists and ankles tied together, he could not get his teeth at the leather knots. He worked first one, then the other; there was no play in them.

Light warned him that someone was coming; Danic relaxed.

A young man of an age for his first battle entered the room. Danic had seen earthen vessels such as this one carried when they burned the other place of animals. This cup steamed with some kind of drink. Danic had not eaten since morning; his stomach growled. Still, when the youth offered him the cup to drink, Danic only tasted it, then turned his head away.

It was not the drink, but the cup Danic wanted.

The man said something, gently as if speaking to a freshly broken pony. Danic wanted to snarl, but he swallowed his anger and waited, playing hard to get as any two-year-old filly.

The youth set the cup down and backed away, eyes fixed on Danic. The horseman played his game. Glancing first at the cup, then at the youth, Danic wiggled a bit farther away from both.

Go ahead, fool. Believe I am too proud to drink while you watch. But, oh, I want to drink. You can master me if but once I drink what you bring me. Maybe next time I will drink from your hand.

I will bite your hand off, Danic snarled, but deep within himself.

The fool retreated through the flap and let it fall closed behind him.

Danic lunged for the drink. Hands around the cup, he let the liquid in it slosh out as he brought it down hard on the clay floor. It cracked. Danic held his breath. Would the little noise he made bring back his captors? Would the little fool want to see if he'd taken the bait like a dumb animal?

The deerskin stayed in place.

Danic pried the cup into pieces. As he had prayed, several of the shards were sharp. At the other place, last summer, a woman had thrown a pot at one of his friends. He had dodged it easily, but the pot had shattered on a wooden beam; the flying pieces, sharp as flint, had cut his friend's face.

They laughed at him for letting a woman draw blood on him. The woman died very slowly. Danic smiled at the memory of her screams as he worked against his bindings.

The first sharp edge dulled. He tossed it aside and attacked his fetters with a second shard. It cut leather and skin; the bindings grew slippery with his own blood. Still, the leather thinned; Danic pulled hard. The length holding his wrists together gave way to his power. With joy in his heart, he quickly cut the cord that bound his ankles together.

Free, Danic armed himself with the most dangerous-looking shard and jumped to his feet. He paused behind the deerskin flap, peering around its edges. Men sat on the floor in disorderly lines, like lancers beginning their charge, enthralled by whatever was being said. The youth was among them, taking a drink to a coughing man near the door. Good.

Danic paced the walls, pushing against them. Had they been felt or hide, he would have cut his way out, but these walls made of trees did not give at his shove or offer him anything to cut. No, the only way out was through the door he had come in.

Again, Danic studied the assembly beyond the deerskin. No one stood like a Mighty Man, telling the warriors what they would do. Women talked. And when the men talked, they sounded no better than women. If Danic had not seen what he had seen in the afternoon sun, he would think these rabbits no better than those they had slaughtered at the other place.

He must do something. He chose a warrior's way. He would dash through these birds and scatter them with a shout.

Danic threw the skin aside and ran for the door. Men turned or looked up at him in dumb amazement. Danic waved his potsherd like a long knife, shouting a battle cry. Men rolled out of his way, or scuttled backward on their hands.

SIX

JACK TWISTED WHERE he sat. The Kurgan was loose, charging through the men in the rear of the room like an Army fullback going for a touchdown through a dazed Navy defense. Jack rolled to his feet and ran to block the exit. "Stop that man!" he shouted . . . in English, of course.

Behind him Launa yelled, "Stop the horseman!" in local.

Men stood. The rush of the Kurgan slowed. A high-pitched scream froze everyone.

The press slowed Jack. A good head taller than those around him, he could see what they could not. A hole opened in the mob. The Kurgan turned circles in the space, widening it, dragging Bomel with him, a sharp potsherd at the boy's neck.

"Please, do not hurt my son," Lasa called from the front of the sanctuary. Men fell back from the Kurgan and his hostage, thinning out toward the door as some men took the opportunity to leave the mess.

Jack headed for the door too, shoving men right and left. Behind him he could hear Kaul saying, "I want to talk to him."

"Only after we catch him again," Taelon observed.

"Don't let him get away," Launa ordered.

"I'm trying! I'm trying!" Jack shouted, knocking men

sideways, down, or any other way that got them out of his way.

The Kurgan got to the door with Jack only a moment behind him. However, pursuit was slow getting started; the Kurgan shoved Bomel at Jack as he yanked the boy's knife from his belt and hurled the potsherd at Jack.

Jack took a second to disentangle himself from the boy and make sure he was all right. Settling him on his feet, he shoved Bomel toward the kennels. "Get the dogs. Let them chase after the horseman. Bring horses, too."

Recovering, Bomel shakily trotted off.

Jack looked around for his erstwhile prisoner. He spotted him pelting down the main street. Behind him, a man and a woman of the legion gave chase, the woman falling behind as she waved at Jack, shouting, "Here is the horseman! Stop the horseman!"

Jack took off in pursuit, with Kaul, Taelon, Launa and a half dozen others hot on his footsteps.

Tall Oaks' city layout was orderly, at least around the sanctuary of the Goddess. Houses stretched out in rows with proper cross streets . . . for about five blocks on either side of the sanctuary. Then it became a jumble.

The runners ahead of Jack hooked a hard left just where that jumble began and took off cross country. Jack had caught up with the woman as he got to that turn. She, he, and a major part of those trailing after them skidded as they went into the turn—and almost fell over the man who'd been first chasing the Kurgan.

The Kurgan had grabbed a post off a garden fence, and poleaxed his pursuer as he rounded the corner.

While the woman took care of the downed man, Jack trotted on for a few more houses. He spotted no runner. Launa came up beside him.

"Think he's gone to ground?"

Jack glanced around. The night was chilling, with no cloud cover to keep in the day's warmth. The moon and stars were out. He couldn't read a newspaper by their light, but he could certainly see movement. He didn't see anything. "Looks like it."

Kaul and Taelon told the searchers to spread out and keep alert. Jack closed his eyes, considering what he would do, a stranger in strange surroundings, afraid and hunted. To his left a pig grunted; another squealed. Jack opened his eyes just in time to see a muddied form bolt from a pig wallow.

"There he goes!" Launa shouted. Both of them took off after the Kurgan. Behind Jack, he heard a German shepherd yap, taking up the hunt. *Good! Frieda was in it now. The fellow would not shake her as easily as humans, not covered in pig shit.*

Jack was gaining on the Kurgan as they reached the edge of town. The beat of horses' hooves echoed from somewhere behind them. Lungs on fire, Jack kept up the chase. This guy was his. He was going to get him back.

The fleeing Kurgan leaped up a small rise, all that was left of the wall, then sprawled forward. A scream shattered the chilly night air. Jack slowed.

They were building the wall to keep the Kurgans out. Instead, it had kept this Kurgan in. A tendril of the briar had worked its way up the slumping wall, putting down roots here and there. Not much, but enough to catch the foot of a man running by moonlight . . . and send him pitching forward.

Right into a stake. This two-inch-thick bit of wood had failed to hold the crumbling wall in place. Now it stood straight up, two feet of sharpened point, driven through the belly of the Kurgan and out his back. Moonlight turned the blood black.

Jack swallowed hard as his stomach went into free fall. It could have been him down there, if the Kurgan's luck had been better and Jack's worse. Launa, Kaul and Taelon joined Jack, out of breath, maybe just as chilled by the view.

"It is a death wound," the old hunter said, "but a slow one."

Hanna and Lasa joined them. The Speaker for the Goddess exchanged a worried glance with her consort. Jack didn't need words to tell him the problem. One of the People who was mortally hurt might be given the mercy blow by one of the Speakers or a wise woman. However, to have the blood of this Kurgan on anyone's hands would be . . . inconvenient.

Surrounded by his enemies, the Kurgan struggled with his pain; only a whimper escaped his lips. Taelon looked from face to face, then slid carefully down the ditch to squat beside the dying man. The Kurgan looked up at him, rage in his eyes, and stretched to reach something lost in the briar.

Taelon rummaged in the bushes and came up with Bomel's stolen knife. He pressed it into the Kurgan's outreached hand, and held that hand down. The hunter used his own knife in his other hand to quickly open the wounded man's jugular.

Taelon spoke to the convulsing body. "To feast by the fire of the Sun, a warrior cannot go emptyhanded. I gave him a knife to die with."

"If we had given him food and drink, he would not be dead," Hanna shot back.

Bomel joined the circle, Frieda on a short leash. "I *brought* him a cup of tea. He used it to cut his bindings and held a sharp piece at my throat."

Hanna turned on her heel. "I do not care what you may say," she snapped as she stomped away. "You will never make me kill. I will never have the lifeblood of another on my hands."

Lasa shook her head. "None are so unseeing as she who has eyes but will not use them."

Kaul gazed down on the Kurgan. "How do we open eyes that are tightly closed? I wanted to share words with you, oh dead horseman. What does your body say to me?"

Launa came up beside Jack, put an arm around him, hugged him. "You okay?"

Jack's glance slipped from Kaul to the body and back to Kaul again. He shivered. "I guess so," he said, but he was back in Wyoming, training with Judith and Brent. The two scholars had insisted they think beyond survival skills and tactics. "How do you get a people to take up arms?" Judith asked.

"How do you get people to want to fight—to risk their lives?" Old Brent had stretched the question.

"When your life is threatened, you fight." Launa gave the cadet answer, and seemed embarrassed by it.

Jack had shaken his head. "My grandfather wondered why he fought the Japanese in the Pacific. All he got for it was a reservation. They spit on my dad after his first Nam tour. He wondered why he should go back." Jack's father had not returned from that second tour to hold his newborn son.

"But it goes beyond that." Judith took the discussion in a new direction. "The people of the Old European culture see themselves and their world as one. They won't make distinctions between themselves, and deer—and the Kurgan invaders."

"I think I see the problem." Launa had spoken slowly, unraveling the problem as she went along. "Even if we say the Kurgan invaders are like a flood, destroying all, it may have no impact. The flood is a natural part of their world. The Goddess sends it for good and bad and you just have to accept it. The Old Europeans will think of the Kurgans the same way."

Brent had nodded. "Right. They must distinguish themselves from the Kurgans before they can fight them."

"How do we do that?" Launa asked.

Back then, Launa had been proud of herself for recognizing the problem, but nobody came up with a solution. Now, watching Kaul watch a horseman die, and Hanna stomp off blindly, Jack doubted they were any closer.

SEVEN

ARAKK GREETED THE cold sun with an upraised knife. The point of the finely worked obsidian in his hand brightened as the light of the winter sun edged above the steppe behind it—a good omen on this, the shortest day of the year. The Sky was Wide and Blue. Its power flowed into his blade, filling it, strengthening it. The chieftain of the Stormy Mountain Clan sucked in his breath. Good. This blade had much to do when warmth returned to the land.

Two days' ride to the north, the water-giving snow was up to the top of a man's boot. The land would be lush and green when the snow melted. Here, a dusting nourished the grass, yet left the blades open to the horses that grazed upon it. This also was good. This was as he remembered it in his father's day.

In his left hand, Arakk held the totem of the clan, a sun-bleached horse skull on a pole. He drove it into the ground; it was a good omen that the earth was soft to receive it. The totem sank deep to taste the earth and grow strong at its teat. Arakk glanced at the totem, the fist of grass and a skin of water that proclaimed their right to pastures was not there.

Arakk smiled, remembering when he had first ridden his pony behind his father, carrying high the clan totem. Now Arakk's son carried it into battle. There was much to please the spirit of Arakk's father.

Arakk's eyes followed the rays of the Sacred Sun as it brought light to the day and the grazing herds. Now it took both hands to count the families of the clan. Each herd was the property of a strong man who could lead a double hand of warriors. A good number, but there would have been two more if Tyman and his two double hands of warriors had ridden back from the west.

And now, to that Arakk must add Danic's name. He should have returned by now. That was one of many questions Arakk would find an answer for—because the Sun was pleased with him. The herd grew. The clan needed more pasture.

True, few of the young boys and women added to his clan from the cleansed place had lived through the cold. They sickened, coughed out their lives and died.

He scowled. These were not Horse People. He remembered the smell of the acrid smoke last night when the men burned the scalps they had taken. Warriors did not hang on lances the hair of men no better than women. Yet, with the spring, Arakk would lead his warriors against the next strange place. They must burn it and offer the two-legged animals there a chance to ride with the clan.

Arakk turned back to the tents. There would be feasting and drinking and smelling of smoke today. And there was one slave girl who had not grown too thin. She was a strange one. She pleased no man. Tonight his whip would break her to saddle.

EIGHT

JACK KNEW LAUNA was anxious for the Winter Feast. She beat him out the front door. Dawn's light just creased the eastern sky.

"What'll it be like?" she asked. "Growing up Catholic; I know there's more to Christmas than presents. But what will a Festival of the Winter Solstice be like four thousand years before a Child is laid in a manger?"

Jack shrugged. "I don't know who will be at the sanctuary. Any grandmother can lead a family's celebration. Ballda's family is taking up the soldiers' longhouse." They laughed. Bellda was the retired Speaker for the Goddess. Hanna was her daughter.

"Bet they try an exorcism on it," Launa giggled. "Think we ought to search it tomorrow for bugs or booby traps?" They were still smiling on that one when they arrived at the sanctuary.

Today, evergreen boughs decorated its walls. The platforms on either side that normally held the elder women's benches were covered with food—cooked, baked and stewed. The aroma alone made Jack want to let his belt out a notch, if it had notches.

Two magnificent goat cheeses had been carved into the likeness of an aroused ram and a pregnant ewe. Crushed nut meat covered them as fleece. Artistry had also gone into the baked breads. Jack saw likenesses of grains, fruits and vegetables. The bread-stick men were fully erect, and a clitoris had been made quite prominent on the split atop the loaves of bread. *Nothing bashful about these folks. The Goddess can't miss the point.*

The benches were spread out on the floor with women, men and children sharing them together. Today, in the warmth of the now insulated room, Lasa sat her chair in a gaily colored linen skirt. Her hair flowed gracefully, parting to highlight breasts the years had been kind to. Kaul greeted them, bare as he would have been on a summer day, the waves, horns and swirls of his tattoos gleaming. He urged them to stand beside the Speakers.

Beside Lasa, a table held statues of the Goddess in her many guises, as well as clay images of grain, peas and animals. For as long as these people could remember, the products of their fields and herds had been enough for their joy.

Launa nudged Jack. "If I'd known about that, I'd have brought a clay image of a wall. Food alone is not going to get them through to next winter."

Jack nodded and smiled at the many familiar faces. Warm smiles were reflected back at him, many of them from the legion, more who were not.

This was a different Christmas from any he remembered. Neither his stepfather nor mother was religious. Christmas was a time for wrapping as many presents as stepdad would let them put on the credit cards. The only gift Jack wanted was an envelope with an airplane ticket in it—a ticket to spend summer with his grandfather on the San Carlos Indian Reservation.

There, the old Apache showed the city-raised rich kid what life was really about. Each summer Jack learned more of land and air and water; then one winter night, a phone call came. The wise man who taught Jack how to survive broiling heat and bitter cold couldn't survive the empty life of a reservation Indian. Too drunk to take care, he'd frozen to death.

Jack shook away the memory; he was here to change that. It felt a bit out of place, being empty-handed. *Well, we've already given out our presents.* The longbows he'd shown the craftsmen how to make were feeding these people well. *Did these folks count it a gift to bring Brege and company back alive from River Bend with words they had never heard before?*

Jack counted the gifts they'd brought, and recalled the world they'd left. It had cheered when a man landed on the moon and ignored epidemics that killed millions.

That crazy world was gone, leaving Jack and Launa to change its history, to somehow stem an invasion now so these Old Europeans might have a chance to build a world more on cooperation than competition. *Merry Christmas, folks, Santa wants a present too. It's not much, just your life, your liberty and maybe your very souls.*

Lasa invoked the Goddess in more formal prayer than Jack had heard before, probably an older version of the tongue. Lasa offered up the clay symbols of life for her people and consigned them to the fire. The old woman who had built the new stoves opened the doors for the offerings, and smiled at Jack as she closed them.

Now that Jack stood this close to Lasa, he could not miss the shine in her face, almost a radiance. Maybe it was just the warmth of the room or seeing so much skin after the winter cold's enforced modesty. But Jack remembered that look, that smile. Sandie, his first love, had had it when she carried Sam. Jack shuddered, remembering the chaplain's sad eyes when he brought the news that a drunk driver had killed his wife and son. Jack swallowed hard; Lasa had to be too old for motherhood.

As the Speaker finished, a drum began to beat and a pipe wailed. Jack felt a shiver go up his spine even before he saw Antia and Brege lead a dozen of their troops forward, quarterstaffs at present arms. The drum slowed; the pipe became low, plaintive. Jack furtively eyed Kaul and Lasa. They held their bodies straight, their eyes fixed on the soldiers. This could not be a traditional part of the Solstice feast.

These two squads had spent a lot of time on their own. Jack had noticed them standing around, looking furtively his way when he looked their way. He'd shrugged, aware of the limits on his power to command here. Besides, Brege and Antia were as hard charging as they came. If they took a squad off the line for something, they had a good reason. Jack settled back, preparing for the show the troops had so scrupulously kept from their officers.

Typical of the People's drill, this was one part manual at arms, two parts dance, and a final twist mystical. There were no shouts, no cadence calls. Indeed, there were no words spoken. The drum played, now soft, now loud, now fast, now slow. The pipe, a reed fashioned into a type of recorder, followed the drum. Beneath it all, the troopers gave voice, not in words, but in tones that left Jack feeling the hunter and the hunted. Jack let his mind bathe in the onslaught of color, sound and emotions. He did not watch so much as experience.

Hands came up, the troops fell to their knees; they lived in the presence of death. He trembled at death's company and mourned its hold over life. Again Jack smelled the dust, the sharp tang of blood, the stench of death at the Battle by the Tree. In the warmth of the room, Jack shivered.

Grounded spears beat in slow rhythm on the floor, then faster and faster until the beat went wild. In a mad clash of wood on wood, the soldiers shot to their feet; death fled, and life returned. Was it only Jack who heard the shouts of the horsemen, the screams as they died and the cheer of the scouts when they knew they would live?

Dancers crisscrossed the room, mingled with the watchers, bodies swaying as they searched, searched. Blood surged in Jack's veins. The beat took his toes; he tapped a tattoo to it. Wide-eyed children, caught up in the emotions, joined the dances; Jack wanted to. Beside him, Kaul and Lasa sat like clay statues; Launa was pale, trapped in a flashback. Jack sat.

The drum changed again, the players returned, children padded along with them and were let in. One more time the rhythm quickened. Troops faced out, eyes sharp, spears leveled. What did they see? Each heart decided for itself.

I see the lance. Do you?

For a long moment, no one moved.

Then Lasa let her breath out slowly and stood. "It is not easy to measure what yesterday held. We may only guess what tomorrow will bring." Then quickly her solemn face twinkled to a smile. "But celebrate with me a promise for the future. Let our daughter Brege stand with me."

Brege and her consort Merik came to share the dais with Kaul and Lasa. The Speaker beamed. "Today we celebrate the gift of new life. The promise that, despite the dark around us, the warm sun will return, bringing life to Mother Earth. Celebrate with me. With the spring and summer new life will blossom within our daughter and me. A daughter and granddaughter will be given to us by the Goddess." The people cheered. The room bubbled with hope at this sign of the Goddess's favor.

Jack and Launa hugged Lasa and Brege, then stepped aside for the others. As Kaul took them by the arm and led them to a bowl, Launa bent close to Jack's ear. "Let the old ladies take this as their omen from the Goddess and quit eyeing my belly."

Jack gave her a hug.

At a bowl of warmed wine, Kaul dipped out mugs for each, then guided them to a quiet corner in the back of the room. As they settled by a stove, Kaul lovingly eyed his consort. When he raised his mug in toast with Jack and Launa, Lasa softly blew him a kiss. Kaul smiled back, but the endearment died somewhere between his lips and eyes. Jack's first swallow caught in his throat as Kaul began to speak. "The Goddess sends us guidance when we ask . . . even if it is hard."

Then Kaul shivered and seemed to throw off his mood. "There are those like Hanna who see you two as an ill omen that must be cast away. Others see my consort, dressed for spring festivities at our Winter Feast, and say you bring good. Many a sick child or old one I did not expect to live through this winter is healthy in homes warmed by the words you shared." Kaul sipped his drink.

Jack studied the Speaker for the Bull. He'd seen the look before: the shadow behind the eyes, the catch in the voice. In the desert, the driver of their Bradley was haunted by dreams of death. He asked for a transfer he didn't get. When the orders came, he went. To his great surprise, he lived through the war. Two days later he died on a mine as he ran to help a Bedouin child. Then, Jack had wondered how a man could go forward with death at his elbow. Now Jack saw the same strength in Kaul.

"Even Hanna, whose belly now swells larger than my consort's, and who often wonders how it is that Launa's belly stays so flat, can marvel at the new life in two others. This will be Lasa's last child. In five summers, she will step aside and let another woman Speak for the Goddess."

"Must a speaker have children?" Launa asked, the curious cadet still full of questions.

"Our Lady is three, Maiden, Mother and Hag. The Hag is the bringer of death, necessary, but the people need life first. To ask a maiden for the wisdom to Speak for all is too much for a young woman. No, a mother Speaks for us all." Kaul looked tired. He sat on the floor, warming his hands at the stove.

"After most women have had two or three children, it is enough. With the stone seed, they can enjoy their years without becoming burdened. Strange that Hanna should choose to have a child now." Jack had heard that Navajo women knew of a seed that acted as an oral contraceptive. Apparently, the People knew of something like it. *Why'd Hanna quit using it?*

"But She who Speaks for the Goddess must show at due times the fruitfulness of Our Mother." Kaul smiled at something fondly remembered. "Lasa enjoys children. We looked forward to our years together, watching them grow up, grow wise. I will miss that." Kaul took a long drink, emptying the dregs from his cup. Launa's nostrils flared; she had heard it too. Jack waited for his friend to tell why he would not be there to watch his children grow wise.

"It is wise to tell a child that nothing is settled by hitting her playmate. You soldiers are wise to prepare to face the Horse People if they come to Tall Oaks as they did for River Bend. Yet, Hanna is wise. Something is missing."

"We see horsemen, but say nothing to them. Even when

they come among us, they will not share their words with us. Before we spill each other's blood, someone must try to find a way across the chasm that separates us." A youngster brought Kaul a full mug. He smiled at the boy, exchanged cups. He blew on it, waiting for it to cool. Jack kept still. He wanted to say something. Beside this saddened man, he felt lost, nothing.

"Now that Lasa is with child, I will not be needed at the spring festival. A pregnant Speaker may rightly excuse herself from the more enjoyable celebrations of new life—if she asks."

"Why would Lasa?" Launa broke the silence among the three.

"The rivers are low now, and will stay low for several moons. But with the coming of spring, the belly of the river will swell. No one may travel at such a time."

"But you must travel before then." Jack wondered where they were going. Just as Kaul knew he must travel, Jack knew with the same wordless conviction that Kaul would not travel alone.

Before Kaul could voice an answer, a young boy pulled on his elbow. "The Lady asks for you. She has gifts for you and the strangers. She says we have to wait for our gifts until they have theirs." The child's high-pitched voice was as plaintive as any youngster's whose Christmas must wait until 6:00 A.M. With a smile, Kaul let the youngster drag him.

Launa held back, worry and puzzlement in equal measure on her face. Jack took a deep breath; it was like this, being a soldier. You waited and waited, not knowing what to do. Then all the pieces fell into place. The tough decisions almost made themselves. Soldiering was easy—only the dying was hard.

Lasa's eyes followed Kaul as he came to her. She must have known what he had shared. Now Jack saw the hint of moisture in the corners of her eyes—the terror that she did not let her body show. Jack had seen that look on wives sending majors or colonels off to war. It took years of love and duty to grow that discipline.

As Kaul stepped on the dais, Lasa smiled, and she meant it. "The People have gifts for you who have given so much to us."

For the next half hour, families or groups shared with Jack and Launa. Many had come together to work on one present. Half of the hunter families had made a soft, water-repellent deerskin cloak for Jack. The other half had done the same for Launa. One collection of families gave Jack a tunic with spectacularly colored thread work. Another had a longer tunic for Launa. There were boots, stockings, kilts and shawls, all gaily decorated with dyes or needlework. Jack received a finely tooled leather belt, like Kaul's.

Launa held up a brightly colored, fringed and knotted bikini bottom. "I'll wear this when the weather gets warmer," Launa promised the gray-haired man who gave it to her. Jack suppressed a smile. Launa really was loosening up.

In the enjoyment of the moment, Jack almost forgot Kaul's heavy words. But there was a sad twist to Kaul and Lasa's smiles as parents threw aside cloaks and showered children with their presents. The Speaker and her consort seemed intent on creating a memory. Jack did his best to help. Only after the meal was shared and children taken in tow for home did Jack take quiet station next to Kaul. "I ask again. Why must you travel before the rivers swell this spring?"

Kaul pursed his lips, collected a cup of now cool wine and returned to squat next to the stove. "When my friend Taelon was young, he and his brother wandered far to the east, over the plains. They fell in with some horsemen and spent the winter where three rivers come together, beneath the yellow sand.

"In a dream, I have seen myself there. I must go there now. Taelon no longer remembers the words he learned in that long-ago time, but in my dream I speak to the Horse People. If he learned their words then, I can learn them now. There are many questions I ask. The Goddess gives me no answers; maybe they will."

Jack stood to attention. "When do we leave?"

The scowls he drew from Launa and Kaul were only the first shots in a long war.

NINE

YOU LEARNED LEADERSHIP at the Point. You learned not to challenge a subordinate in front of the troops. Commanders settle disagreements in the privacy of their tents. Launa repeated the lesson over and over again during the rest of the feast, a mantra that locked her temper down rock hard. She said not a word to Jack until the door flapped shut behind him in their own home.

"Just what the hell do you think you're doing, soldier?"

Jack stood, his back to the deerskin door. His eyes met hers without a flinch. "I'm going to make sure Kaul gets where he's going." Jack's voice held the same determined calm Kaul's had.

"In case you've forgotten, we've got a mission to accomplish," she snapped, her voice not quite breaking. "There are only seven billion people counting on you and me to stop this invasion. We're not going to help them by charging a couple of thousand kilometers into enemy territory. Captain, you've done some shit-for-brains stunts since we've met. You don't need to top the last one."

Jack paled. *Maybe I've finally gotten through.* This mission was hell. Launa hadn't always had a grip on her emotions, but neither had Jack. Still, one of them always kept his or her head screwed on right. Somehow, they'd managed to keep on course.

He opened the wood stove and began blowing on the red embers. One by one he fed bits of kindling to the growing fire. "Launa, Kaul must prove to himself, to Hanna and God only knows who else, that there is no other option except war to the death."

"Okay, but why do *you* go with him?"

"You heard him," Jack snapped. "The winter encampment is far, probably on the Dnieper River, two or three major river crossings and a thousand klicks from here. What good does it do if he's picked off on the trip by a wandering troop of horsemen?"

Launa could see the logic. "The People *have* to know how he dies. If Kaul doesn't return, nobody knows."

Jack broke a stick and fed it to the fire. "So much is riding on Kaul. I took plenty of prisoners in the Iraqi desert. We didn't take a damn one last summer. Even if we'd caught that Kurgan again last week, I think he'd have killed himself before he'd have been recaptured." Jack looked into the fire, as if again seeing the dying. "Once the killing starts next summer, it won't stop until one side is down to women and children," he whispered, then stood to face her squarely.

"Kaul's right. God or the Goddess alone knows where we're headed. If he's willing to risk everything to make peace, a peace we all better hope he can negotiate, I'll be damned if I won't do everything I can to get him there." Jack turned away, but Launa saw the gleam of tears in his eyes.

She went to him, hugged his back, rested her head on his shoulders. She wanted to feel what he felt, but she didn't dare. Too much depended on them. "Okay, Jack, if Kaul has to have an escort, I'll take the troop out."

Jack whirled in her arms and took two steps back. "No!"

"Why not, Jack? Why can't I do it?"

"You can't. I've got to go."

"Why, Jack? Why? God damn it. And don't give me any women-in-combat bullshit."

Jack's mouth dropped open. "No. No, that's not it." Jack sucked on his lower lip, then let out a long breath. "Launa. I've watched too many people die. I know that. Kaul is not my grandfather. He's so much more. Time passed Grandfather by. Kaul lives at a crossroads. I need him." Jack paused as the fire crackled, yellow light burnishing his face.

"Kaul's heart holds a key to a door that I can't even find. We've got to lead these people someplace the human race has never been. The bastards always win. We've got to find a way for people to work together to beat them. Oh shit, it's not that simple. You and I have sixty centuries of learning how people can kill each other. We can defend Kaul. But without our baggage, maybe Kaul can see what you and I can't even dream of."

Launa opened her mouth. Jack held up his hand. "Yes, I don't want to lose him. If it's going to happen, I want to spend every moment I can with him. I understand maybe every third or fourth word he speaks. But next year, or the year after that—probably for the rest of my life—I'll be waking up mornings and saying, 'Oh, so *that* was what he was getting at.' "

"And that is why you go?"

"Yes."

Launa turned her back on Jack. She didn't want to see him. She needed to think. If she gave him a direct order, would it make any difference? At the Point they had both learned "Duty, Honor, Country." But here, "No one could tell another the path for her feet." In class, an all-volunteer force sounded great. Right now she'd give her right arm for a draft board, and a couple of MP's. Would stockade time sway Jack? Kaul? Anyone in this crazy place?

Should she even try to change Jack's mind? *What had Judith said?* "Don't assume that primitive means stupid. Let the Old Europeans use their heads. Trust the options they come up with." *Judith, did you have any idea how crazy these people are?*

Launa didn't know what Judith would do, but she knew what Launa O'Brian, Second Lieutenant, United States Army, was going to do. She turned back to Jack and cut her next words from the same rock he had used. "If you're going, I go too."

Jack scowled at her and shook his head.

Launa ignored him. "Your head's up your ass, Captain.

Judith told me you were supposed to be my keeper. Right now, you need a keeper."

She hoped her demand would bring Jack up short. Knock some sense into him. Jack said nothing, just stood there. Launa turned on her heel, marched the few feet to her bed, threw off her clothes and climbed under the blankets.

Jack added a few logs to the stove and closed the door. Then he slipped into the bed they'd never used.

Launa lay awake, alone. She fumed, letting her anger keep her warm. Point by point, she went through her options like a classroom exercise.

As much as she despised Hanna, the woman was probably reading the People right. Most could not kill, not even in their own defense. They likely couldn't believe they'd ever need to. Launa had studied the atrocities of Hitler, Stalin and Pol Pot, with shock and disgust. How could people let themselves be herded to their deaths? Now she had met men and women too rational to understand the killer's insanity.

They'd better learn fast.

Kaul was trying. The counsel was sacred to the People. If the Speaker for the Bull was murdered in counsel by the Kurgans, the shock might be what these people needed. *Okay, for the good of the many, one must die.* Launa cringed at the thought; Kaul was no expendable stranger. She might not love him like Jack did, but her world would be a lot emptier without him.

Where do I go from here? Kaul's negotiations with the Kurgans would not be on CNN. If he vanished with no one in Tall Oaks the wiser, his sacrifice was for nothing.

If Launa remembered her history right, the Japanese kamikaze of World War Two had a fighter escort—to get them through American interceptors and report on their achievements. Jack was offering to be that escort.

Maybe she should let him go—alone—while she pushed the defense effort here.

Launa let that roll around in her mind. The look in Jack's eyes as they talked haunted her. She ticked off the number of deaths that had touched his life—father before he was even born, grandfather he had come to love, wife and tiny child. That didn't count what he'd seen in the desert. Was Jack in any shape to escort a kamikaze and not become one himself?

Launa pulled the covers close. They had a while before they could travel. Things could change. And if Jack looked like he could handle the job, she could always send him alone.

TEN

JACK WAS NO stranger to war, the hunkering down, locking away any part of you that was soft. He'd known war, but before the hostiles were over there. Now he shared a roof with the opposition, and the war was waged over and over again while the moon waxed and waned three times.

Launa greeted him next morning with a silent glare. Jack could almost hear the order, but Launa never voiced a command he could disobey. While the weather slowly warmed, a bitter, icy silence grew between them.

Brege waged her battle in the open. She was against anyone going, for reasons a daughter needed no logic. How many times did Jack find her crying in Kaul's arms? "Do not go, Father."

Each time Kaul shook his head in silence.

Taelon opposed Kaul for the sheer waste. "Old friend, you are a dead man the day you walk into their camp."

"You walked into their camp, and back out again. I will too." Jack heard no conviction in Kaul's words.

"You will not," Taelon growled. "I have seen the blood lust in their eyes. I was an animal that amused them. But you will talk to them as an equal, as a man with a full heart. They will cut your heart out. Do not do it, my brother. Enough will die this new year. Do not make your blood the first."

Lasa looked at her consort, a silent tear pleading with

Kaul to honor Taelon's wisdom. Yet no word slipped past her lips. Jack respected the iron resolve that held the Speaker. As was their custom, she allowed those around her the freedom to seek the way of the Goddess for themselves. As much as she must have wanted to, she did not invoke the Goddess to speak her own heart.

Kaul placed a hand on Lasa's shoulder, another on Taelon's. "Someone must try to find a way around that blood. In my dreams I see us on a log, carried along on a river in flood. It is easy to go with the current—easy, but dangerous. Who knows what awaits downstream to overturn us? This raging torrent is strange to everything we know. It carries us to a land we have never walked. A land so strange I cannot see it even in my dreams."

He turned to Launa and Jack. "I mean nothing ill toward you and your way, but the way of death is not our way. You may be right. Tomorrow, there may be no other path for us. But today, while Lasa speaks for the Great Goddess to the People, I will not let my friends and sisters take this new path without doing everything that I can to find another way."

All his words spoken, Kaul stood alone, vulnerable, yet splendidly complete in himself. Jack wanted to shake him, hog-tie him until the rivers flooded and he could not travel. Jack mourned Kaul as one already dead even as he swelled with respect for him. Kaul was wrong in what he did, but he was right in why he did it.

Jack chose the fifteen best riders as an honor guard to escort Kaul. He had many to choose from.

Launa had organized the legion for tactical efficiency. First, second and third Pike Cohorts were their heavy infantry. The best archers and slings formed two cohorts to support the pikes. Jack drew mainly from Taelon's hunters to fill the ranks of first and second Axes. These men would repel individual knife-wielders who got in among the pikes and repair breaks in the line. The plan had been coming together well until the wall turned to mud.

Last autumn, each cohort had been busy drilling, digging

ditch, building wall, tending crops and bringing in the harvest. Launa had talked of introducing competition between cohorts, then dropped the idea. Everyone who joined the legion turned to with a will; there was no need to urge them on.

Launa did announce that those who showed the greatest skill with pike, bow, sling or axe would have the first chance to learn to ride. Jack had agreed with her until one woman showed them how wrong they were. Sara fumbled every weapon she tried, but she was always around the horses, feeding them, currying them. And when she thought no one was looking, she rode. Sara was the best rider in the entire town.

Jack remembered the laugh he and Launa shared as they tossed the Book away. These people did things their own way.

He wished Launa would laugh with him now. All he got was silence.

Jack included Sara in Kaul's honor guard.

The day after Jack selected the escort, he, Kaul and Taelon gathered with them at the horse corral to outline the expedition's course. Brege, Merik and Launa showed up for the meeting.

"If you go, we go." Brege stood tall as she made one last attempt to stop her father's magnificent gamble. The words spoken, she calmly stepped back in ranks with her two comrades as if she challenged authority every day.

Kaul frowned. "You are with child. You cannot ride."

Brege shook her head defiantly, the long ponytail down her back coiling like an angry snake. "It is many moons until my time. I ride every day in practice. I will go with you."

Kaul ignored her.

"Father, do not do this. But if you make this journey, you make it with me at your side."

"I see no wisdom in any of this." It seemed to Jack that Kaul would finally lose his temper, but no. In a twinkle, Kaul was again logical. "We cannot look like a war party when we approach their camp. I must go alone. Taelon goes with me, but he will not cross the last river. Jack, I do not need your three hands of lances. I will go with my friend Taelon." Kaul folded his arms across his chest; he thought he was finished.

Jack glanced at Launa. Brege's declaration had been the first public announcement that Launa was going too. Her eyes were locked on him. Now was the time to back out.

He shook his head. "Maybe Taelon did go alone among the horsemen many years ago. But this summer at the tree, we saw how the horsemen greeted a hand of travelers. If you are to speak your heart at the winter camp, you must get there. I and my lancers will get you there."

"And we will go with them," Brege whispered.

"I will talk with your mother about this."

What words Kaul and Lasa passed between themselves were known only to them. Lasa had said no one could tell another what to do, and no one did. No one could find in their heart the words that would change another's resolve. As the spring equinox approached, no one had changed anyone's mind.

The day was March windy as Launa reviewed her troops. The ground was slowly thawing to soup as the pikes tried to drill. In the chill, each cohort was still at around forty. Launa hoped warmer weather would bring more out. She and Jack, Kaul and Lasa had done their best, still Launa hated all the unknowns. So much was riding on their next battle. Launa wanted a big margin for error. Kaul just might give her that margin, but at what price?

Launa wasn't sure what she'd hoped for when Brege made her last desperate try to stop her father. Now there was just more in the pot to lose on one throw of the dice.

And the splendid people Launa had chosen to lead the legion were willing to make it worse. Organizing the legion into cohorts with officers was supposed to give her better tactical control. Launa wondered if she could control anything—Jack, even herself. Now that it was common knowledge that Launa was going with Jack, every officer in the legion wanted to go too.

Launa managed to face most of them down, demanding that they have their troops better trained when the spring weather allowed more drill time. That worked for most of them. It didn't work with Antia.

"I will ride with you." The daughter of She who had Spoken for the Goddess at River Bend did not walk away with the rest of the cohort commanders.

Launa looked hard into Antia's eyes. "This time we ride around horsemen. It will not be like the Battle at the Tree."

Antia nodded. "But you will see far into the land from which the horsemen come. I would see that too."

That gave Launa pause. Had Antia really been listening to the little war college lectures Launa had been giving her cohort commanders and any soldier willing to listen? Most of the time Antia seemed intent on flaking flints for spear points or axes. Maybe there was hope for this one. "You should stay with your cohort."

"And you should stay with the legion. Cleo can train my cohort as well as I."

Launa gave up. "You will ride close to me."

"Yes."

Tuam, consort to Taelon, was another matter. She had been a witness at River Bend and stood with Launa and Jack at the Battle at the Tree. When she approached Launa, the soldier had no idea how she could refuse her a place in the guard beside her husband.

Tuam said nothing except, "Walk with me."

Launa did. The wind that blew around them took their warmth, and almost Tuam's words.

"I will stay with Lasa in Tall Oaks. You should stay too."

Surprised, Launa gulped. "I go with Jack . . . I mean Kaul."

Tuam fixed her with hunter's eyes as she might a wolf that crossed her path. She waited for Launa to give way. Launa looked straight back. *I know what I'm doing.*

Tuam waited for a long moment, then shrugged. "I watched Jack lay the trap for the horsemen at the tree. There is a wisdom in your eyes that sees what others do not. Many here can hunt a wolf, but none a man. If both of you go and do not come back, what eye will have the wisdom to set the next trap?"

"We will come back." *With me in the troop, they will. With Jack alone, they will not.* This Launa believed.

Tuam shook her head. "The heart is powerful. I was glad to stand beside my man when we faced the horsemen last summer, even if death had come for us. Lasa will not say this, but she prays that you can bring her man back to her." Tuam turned away.

Launa watched her go. So the burden Launa carried was larger. And Tuam was right; Launa's heart was involved. If she was Jack's keeper on this trip, it was time to focus. Launa stalked off to check weapons and some war booty. With a bit of luck, it just might save their lives. If Jack hadn't been tripping over his heart, he would have thought about it first.

ELEVEN

ARAKK'S KNIFE FLASHED in the warmth of the noonday sun, then swooped to drink blood. This was the day when the Sun unbalanced the moon. From now on, the day would stretch longer and the darkness shrink before the all-powerful Sun. Today was a good day to offer sacrifice.

A horse or a bull might have done for an offering, but war lay ahead of the Stormy Mountain Clan this summer. Arakk chose one of the taller slaves taken last summer. Their leaders had not taken well to the honor of feasting in the tent of the Sun. Elders slipped a brazier with smoking seeds into this one's tent and broke his fast with fermented mare's milk. The sacrifice had breathed more smoke during the morning and came to the noonday feast with a smile. He did not have time to cry out when one elder grabbed his feet and another his arms to splay him out on the wooden altar.

Arakk slit his throat before he could make a sound. Arakk's son, Kantom, held a bowl to catch that blood even as Arakk slashed open the sacrifice's belly and cut deeply before plunging his hand in to grasp the still-beating heart. Arakk and the clan leaders smeared the blood from the heart on their faces and chests. Kantom took the basin among the warriors that they might streak their cheeks and dip their lance points, a foretaste of what was to come.

"When the moon is full, I and my band will ride to the

great winter encampment. We will tell them of our mighty deeds and lay my claim for the lands I have taken and will take this summer. By this blood I swear all will know the boundaries of this clan's pastures."

The warriors made their cries and shook their lances. Arakk smiled proudly as blood dripped from his cheeks. This was good.

TWELVE

COLD WATER DRIPPED down Jack's back. He tried
again to adjust his rain cap so the water dripped from it directly to his deerskin cape. The locals did it instinctively;
Jack would have given much for a standard army-issue poncho.

Last dark of the moon, the wise woman said, was the
spring equinox. The festival would come with the full moon.
Kaul chose to leave between the two. Jack guessed it was
early April.

He held Windrider's reins and a horse for Kaul, waiting
for him to emerge from the sanctuary. Wordless, Launa
stood by him with Star, and mounts for Brege and Merik.
The escort waited on the outskirts of town. Most of the people
stood here to say farewell to Kaul.

Kaul, Lasa, Brege and Merik stepped from the sanctuary,
a family tableau bound today by tension more than love.
Several older women joined Lasa, huddling in wool cloaks
and shawls for warmth. Hundreds of voices greeted them.
Kaul raised his hands. "You know the danger that awaits me,
as I know the dangers that stalk you." Some heads nodded;
others stared straight ahead.

Kaul turned to Lasa. "I pray that the Goddess will be gracious to you as you pray for wisdom for me." Every head in
the throng could give assent to that.

Jack walked the horses through the crowd. They mounted in silence. From his horse, Kaul faced Lasa. "The journey is long, my friends. We have said our good-byes to those closest to our heart. Let me say good-bye to you all now."

A noisy babble of "Good-bye," "Farewell," "Take care," "Go with the Goddess," engulfed the riders. Kaul gave Lasa a smile.

She stood silent, tears running down her cheeks, no blessing for their going this morning. One of the women behind Lasa whispered, "Go with the Goddess and know her ways." Kaul nodded sadly and turned away.

They halted only once on their way to the waiting escort. Samath blocked Kaul's passage. "Do not do this thing for my heart, friend of my youth." The carpenter's eyes glistened with tears.

Kaul stopped, then walked his horse up to Samath and laid a hand on the woodsman's shoulder. "I walk this way for my heart and no one else's, old friend. Remember that, you who mark my memory, when spring comes round if I am not among you."

Tears streaked both men's cheeks. Samath stepped aside.

The escort stood to horse: fifteen loaded with packs, twenty-two spare mounts plus the twenty-two under the riders. Jack was leaving only twenty-five mares and the best of the captured stallions behind. If he lost this detachment, Tall Oaks would have few mounted scouts. If he and Launa were lost, more than the town was at risk. Launa was right; he was stupid.

Or was he? He was trained to take risks when the return was worth it. If they were going to find a way around so much of the brutality that lay ahead of the human race, it would be through the wisdom of men like Kaul. Jack just wished there weren't so many damn unknowns in the gamble he was taking.

Taelon led them across the ford below Tall Oaks and straight out onto the steppe. The clouds burned off as the day warmed. The journey might have grown pleasant if its purpose had not been not so somber. The steppe was green with winter rains. The moist vegetation held down the dust.

On the second day they passed to the west of the battle tree. The next afternoon brought them to a major river; it didn't look big enough to be the Danube. They had seen no evidence of horses so far.

With the sun low, they crossed. The nonswimmers followed Launa and Jack's example, holding tight to their horses' manes and letting their mounts tow them across, but the cold was something else. On the far side, Jack built a sauna out of saplings, blankets and hot rocks.

He was starting to think the trip might be easy as he slipped into the impromptu sweat hut. Kaul chanted softly. Before Jack could say anything, Taelon quieted him. "You have made a sacred place. I think Kaul is beginning his death song."

Jack blinked. Sacred place? He just wanted to get everyone warm. Taelon saw his puzzlement and put his lips to Jack's ear.

"You bring earth and air, fire and water together as never I have seen. Surely this is a sacred place for your people."

Jack remembered his grandfather's sweat lodge. Jack was too young or too white to be admitted. Grandfather had promised him next year, but that had been the year that never came. Wordlessly, Jack nodded, learning now what he had not learned then.

The following morning dawned foggy. Merik, Sara and Tomas, a hunter from River Bend, volunteered to ride distant scout for the guard, ranging ahead to look over the next rise. Before midmorning, Tomas rode back to report a herd of cattle and horse over a ridge to the east. Jack mentally put on his soldier's helmet and got down to the serious business of being a cat at a dog show. He assigned people to ride flank and point.

Rather than burning off as the sun rose, the fog got worse with the rising temperature. It played hob with visibility and Jack's security efforts. He couldn't see half his outriders and had to assign additional troopers to ride halfway between the them and the main body. That did not leave much of a main body.

Launa trotted up beside him, glanced around and grimaced. "Now you've got the troops scattered to hell and we still can't see worth a damn." Jack glared at her; if she didn't have a better idea, she could at least not ride him. He said nothing.

That night, Merik and the distant scouts did not rejoin. Jack also found out that Antia had somehow managed to attach herself to them. He shot Launa a searing look, but she managed to be looking the other way. Jack fell asleep gnawing his lower lip, wondering what Antia would come up with.

Early morning light saw the escort leaving the lakes and fog behind. Ahead stretched the breathtaking vista of the open steppe. Grass-covered, low rolling hills stretched forever. Jack felt tiny in the face of this vast emptiness.

The openness also presented a tactical problem. If he could see forever, so could horsemen. Beside him, Launa sat Star quietly. Jack turned to her. "Didn't Judith say there's a treed steppe somewhere to the north of us?"

Launa closed her eyes as she tried to remember their briefing. "Right. But they couldn't agree exactly how far south it was at any particular time. Shall we find out?"

"I'd rather have trees for cover than be bare-ass naked out there," Jack answered.

"That's one of the smartest things you've said in a long time. Think the scouts'll find us if we move north?"

"I hope so," he snapped, trying to cover how dumb he felt for misplacing some good people. "If they can't, they'll have the good sense to go home."

Launa said nothing. He would have felt better if she'd come up with a blistering rejoinder. Her aloofness was wearing heavy. Jack led due north. By late afternoon, when they found scrawny trees, they had seen neither horse herds nor scouts.

They had pitched camp and lit a small fire when Merik and Sara rode into camp. Jack stood as Antia and Tomas followed with over twenty horses.

"You found us," Launa said, greeting Sara.

The young woman's grin was as wide as the steppe. "I listened to you talk of going around problems, to come from the direction the enemy does not expect. I knew you would go north."

"And the horses?" Jack snapped.

Antia grinned. Tomas shrugged. "We have only one spare horse. We need more. These strayed from a herd."

"And who follows after you?" Jack had enough problems without a pair of freelancing troopers.

Sara stepped between the men. "I rode far behind Tomas, until he was out of sight. I saw no one."

Tomas launched into his own defense. "I led the horses up a stream and did not take them out until we were far from where we rode in. Once I lost a deer I was tracking when it did that. No one could follow our tracks."

Jack took two deep breaths. Antia avoided his glance, apparently willing to let Tomas take the blame, though Jack would wager all the gold he'd brought through time that Tomas hadn't come up with this one on his own. He forced himself to relax. "The deer probably did use a stream to hide its tracks. I know my grandfather's people used that trick when they stole horses. But, boy, you took a big risk of bringing a horde of angry horsemen down on us."

Tomas blanched in the firelight.

Kaul joined them, his face an alarmed frown. "I have come to talk to these people, not to steal their horses."

For a moment Jack felt as if he'd been kicked in the stomach. Then he saw another opening to stop Kaul.

But Kaul went to his own pony. "This is the horse the People of Tall Oaks traded for two summers ago. I will ride it. If this is the only one seen when I enter the winter encampment, no one will tie me to the missing horses. Jack, you must make sure that no one sees us during the journey there."

Damn! Too quickly the shepherd spotted a way to hide the lost sheep. Jack looked around at his small troop. "Okay, friends, let's get some sleep. Picket the horses in close tonight and post a watch. Horsemen also like to steal horses. Let us not lose ours to them."

THIRTEEN

ARAKK CHOSE THE best of the prizes they took when they cleansed that place last summer. He would even include the fairest and most docile of the women slaves he had taken. She would find the long ride difficult, but she and all the other booty would impress the Mighty Men of the clans. Surely this would attract more warriors to ride with the clan's totem when he rode against the next place this spring. The Stormy Mountain Clan was strong. Yet the west had shown it had teeth. Maybe the next place would not be as easy as the last one. Bitter experience had taught Arakk to be cautious.

At the winter camp he would lay his claim to pasture in the lands he had taken. He would claim his right so strong that none would question. He would also invite many to join him, to take slaves and prizes from those who had no right to them, who rode no horses, who carried no lances. Such pretensions by those who only walked the land could not be permitted. Still, he must state his case wisely to the other clan leaders. One of them might move to claim the green pastures his strong arm had taken. He would have to be as crafty in victory as he had been in weakness. Yes, but this would be much more enjoyable.

Pounding hooves jarred Arakk from his reverie. Two riders approached his camp at a gallop. Arakk turned from his own double hand of warriors to face them. Brave Tassin slipped from his mount and stood before Arakk. He had been riding hard, but he needed no time to catch his breath as he composed himself and folded his arms across his broad, bare chest. "Someone took ten horses from my herd, and ten more from Karne's." He spoke without preamble.

"Where did you pasture them?" Arakk suspected he knew the answer, but he needed time to take the full measure of these words.

"As we smoked on at the last council of strong men, I moved my horses north to taste the spring grass."

"That moved them closer to the river where the Stalwart Shield Clan feeds their horses on both sides." Arakk stroked his beard.

"Yes," Tassin hissed.

"Did you follow the horse tracks?"

"Yes. I lost them in a stream. The thieves are crafty."

Arakk turned away to stare at the wide horizon. Were the other clans ready to take honors on the Stormy Mountain horses again so soon? No Mighty Man would boast of such a deed against a clan that had been named woman and walker only five summers ago. Some young buck must have done this. How to make this carry a lance for the clan?

The herds were growing. The horses roamed wide for their grass. If he saw his horses on another's rope, he would apologize that it had wandered onto another clan's land. This would show for all to see that the Stormy Mountain Clan was stronger and needed more pasture—their own land to the west. Arakk turned back to his underling.

"Tassin, stay with us this night. I have several slave girls that can make it enjoyable, and if they do not, your whip is as sharp as mine. Tomorrow, choose horses from my herds for yourself and your warrior. Then ride with me to the winter camp. If you see your horses there, I will make them carry a pack for us, even if they do not wear your halter again."

"Ah, Arakk, you were always the sly one." Tassin pounded him on the shoulders.

As they strode to his tent, Arakk's woman called to her slaves and used a switch to speed them in placing a meal before him and his guest. This was the way he remembered it in his father's day. This was the way it should be.

FOURTEEN

IN THE DESERT with the 24th Mech, Jack learned that waiting to die could be boring. Sarge Townsend had been good. He'd kept them busy, too busy to think, almost too busy to be scared. Now Jack was in charge. As he rode deeper into enemy territory, he practiced what the old sarge had taught. Stay alert. Stay ready. What Jack couldn't do was keep from thinking. Was he doing the right thing?

He'd almost gotten used to Launa not talking—but Kaul? Jack was on this crazy ride to catch whatever last thoughts Kaul might share, yet he was saying nothing.

About the only thing going right was the horsemen. They cooperated by staying elsewhere.

The terrain went to hell. Small streams gouged the land. They spent most of their time finding places to go down steep draws only to come right back up. "At this rate, it'll be the twentieth century before we get there," Jack growled. He estimated they only covered five miles that day. That was not enough. "How long do we have before the rivers swell?"

"Any time." Taelon shrugged. "We could travel faster. The land is more open to the south."

Launa nodded. "But it will have many people riding it."

"We could scout ahead of you," Sara offered.

"And I will not collect more stray mounts," Tomas promised.

Part of Jack wanted to hide under a rock. He tossed Launa a raised eyebrow. "We need to know more about the horsemen. How many. Where they wander." *Come on, Launa, talk to me.*

She snorted and went to one of the packs. Opening it, she pulled out a leather helmet and threw it at Jack. "I knew this would happen. Recognize this from last summer? I figured we'd get close and dirty with horsemen sooner or later, and these weren't doing us any good back at Tall Oaks."

Jack winced at her reproof.

Launa stood, hands on hips. "We got enough of this for everyone. At a distance, in this gear, maybe we can pass for horsemen. Our scouts had better keep them at a distance." She finished handing out helmets, then stomped off to her bedroll.

Jack watched her go. She didn't like what he was doing, but at least she was doing her best to get them back alive. Then he mentally kicked himself. *Why didn't I think of bringing horseman gear? Launa's right, I've got my head up my ass. Start thinking, soldier.*

At first light, while the others ate, Merik led the scouts out of camp. Waiting for them to get a half hour lead, Jack went looking for Brege. She looked uncomfortable when he found her.

"Do not you watch me too as if I were a clay jar that may break. I will send you running like Merik," she snapped.

Jack wasn't aware he had looked at her any differently. He prayed his luck with horsemen would be better than his luck had been with women lately. "How many more moons?" Jack remembered that as a safe question.

Brege patted her belly. "Five. She hardly shows. This daughter will be born with a halter in her hand. She rides well. Do not worry about me. Worry about my father."

Jack did. Kaul remained silent. Was Kaul lost in his search for words to say to the horsemen, or in his death song? Whatever he was doing, Jack missed him almost as much as he missed Launa's friendly partnership.

All that day Jack led the column northeast. It was clear

and cool; quickly they rode out of the forest. The few trees did little to break up the power of the vast sky.

The scouts were late returning again that night. Merik was last; he had missed their track and rode in from the north just as Jack was getting worried. All three scouts had seen herds. Tomas, the northernmost, had seen two.

"But they stay far from the trees," Tomas assured Launa.

For a moment, Launa stared at Jack, saying nothing. Then she cocked an eyebrow. "We can travel fast here where the trees are few. I'm willing to accept the risk."

Jack nodded. "If we keep our scouts out ahead of us, I don't think we'll get surprised."

Kaul picked up a handful of dirt and let it sift through his fingers. "The land is dry. The clouds are few and thin. I smell little water here." Kaul pulled his blankets around himself. "We shall see."

The next day, scouting pairs swept out a couple of rises ahead; then one would report back. They saw several herds to the east and south, but alerted, Jack kept the main body out of contact. He was so concentrated on his right flank that he forgot to pay attention to his other. Late afternoon, Launa rode up to him.

"Look to the left, a little behind us," she said softly.

Jack turned to look at her but let his eyes travel far behind. A half dozen riders and twice as many horses rode out of a draw to the north. Several carried lances. A couple were children. They led horses heavily laden with long wooden poles. A man with a lance waved. Jack bit his lip and ignored him.

"Troops, forward at a trot. Ho." Heads came up quickly. As Jack brought his hand down, all broke into a trot. In ten minutes, they topped a rise and Jack looked back. The horsemen trotted along, straight across their track. He breathed a sigh of relief, but did not slow the troop until they were halfway to the next shallow ridge. Jack added another line to his intelligence notebook. Those bastards can show up anywhere.

Shokin, Mighty Man of the Stalwart Shield Clan, frowned. Surely the leader of the other band of Horse People had seen his wave. Yet, he rode away. Why?

Always when bands crossed trails they talked, shared meat and smoke. Yet these were strange times, and many warriors rode a land that was strange to them.

Happy little Cor galloped up to him. Like a good son, he waited to be spoken to. Still, he waved the sapling he had cut, reminding his father silently of the promise to make it into a bow by tonight's fire. Shokin smiled at this young warrior-to-be. *How strange will be the steppe you ride?*

Shokin kicked his horse. They had much land to cross before tonight's fire. He would let the strange riders go their way.

Jack rested his troop that night on the banks of another wide river. If he guessed right, this was the Southern Bug, the last major river between them and the Dnieper. With morning light, they searched north for a crossing and found a ford late in the afternoon. They had to swim, and the water was biting cold. Again Jack built a sweat lodge and again Kaul sat in it, surrounded by others, yet turned in upon himself. Quietly, the Speaker chanted to himself. He did not join them for supper.

As the others gathered for their meal, Jack stared into the fire, letting his thoughts whirl. Launa walked over to stand beside him.

"You look worried."

He smiled, appreciating her closeness. "I am."

"About where we are going, or how we get there?"

"Both." Jack let out a long breath and sat back away from the fire and the others. "This winter camp sounds like a place Brent mentioned. The Scythians had a city just below the first rapids on the Dnieper. When the Russians excavated the site, they also found a much older area. They didn't have the money to explore it, but I think that was where Taelon was."

Launa squatted down. "It's nice to know something about where we're going."

Jack leaned back, enjoying Launa's closeness, both in body and mind. "Yes. But how to get there? The fastest way is down the Bug to the sea, ride around the bay to the

Dnieper, then follow it up for about fifty klicks to the rapids."

Launa smiled ruefully. "We'd probably run into a customs agent or two. What's the best route for smugglers?"

"Stay with the trees until we hit the Dnieper, then follow it down to the first rapids. That's four times as long."

"Is there a third?"

"Ride straight across the steppe. We're about two hundred and fifty kilometers from where we want to be. We could make it in three days of hard riding."

Launa sat, her back to the tree Jack leaned against, her hands behind her head. She stared at the sky, as if the stars held some answer. "The scouts might help, but traveling fast, we'll outrun them. How do we improve our odds?" she murmured.

Nothing came to them before they went their separate ways to their bedrolls.

Kaul watched the others slowly fall asleep, only the rumbling of his stomach keeping him company. He walked away from the camp to stand on a knoll. Behind him the river sang its song. Ahead of him the steppe rolled away, leading where he could only guess.

Kaul had eaten nothing for three days. Tonight he would see the moon down and the sun up—waiting. He raised his hands to the moon, beseeching the Goddess for a vision to guide him.

Never in his life had Kaul so wanted a vision. He had tried to compose his death song; it would not come to him. He walked toward the vultures with no chant on his lips. That would be a terrible way to die.

He fixed his gaze on the moon, let his eyes follow her as she rose higher and higher into the night sky. She was waning now, turning Her full face away from Her people. That was the way of the Goddess, to hold a man fully in Her arms for a time, then turn Her back on him for a time. Always She came back and always She went away. Although Her face was almost full, still Kaul felt as if She already had left him.

The night passed. From time to time, birds called. A wolf

howled mournfully to the moon. Maybe Kaul slept where he stood. Maybe he dreamed.

The Goddess turned Her face full to him. She smiled.

Beside Her, a horseman stood with arms folded on his chest. He was different; he did not wear his hair in one or two horse tails. It flowed freely down his back and shoulders, all except two forelocks he wore braided, one on each side of his face. He neither frowned nor smiled at Kaul, but pointed with his left hand. Horses raced across grassy plains. They bucked and pranced, gamboled and played. Suddenly, the grass was brown. The horses fell to their knees and turned to bones.

The man of the Horse People pointed again. Children ran toward him and Kaul across a field of flowers. The flowers turned to stone. The children stumbled and fell. In the wink of an eye, only their bones were left.

Kaul opened his mouth to say something, but the horseman was gone. The sun rose in front of Kaul, a swollen red eye, gazing down on a yellow landscape. Here, close to the river, the grass was green. What was the grass like where the sun awoke?

The others were waking; Kaul joined them. While they ate their meal, Kaul relived his dream, marking every color, every form, every motion. This dream he would meditate on. He paid no attention to Jack when he began talking. Only when Taelon spoke did Kaul take notice.

"I remember many little streams and marshes around the great river we are seeking." The hunter's eyebrows furrowed into a deep frown. "But the horsemen just rode to it."

Launa scowled, as she did so often on this journey. "Let us ride to the east, keeping scouts out ahead. Let us see what the day brings."

With no better guide for the day's journey, they broke camp. Kaul eyed the stream they followed away from the mighty river. It was but a trickle. Once there had been marshes around it, now only damp mud. The grass was winter brown, not spring green.

Jack ordered the horses watered and the waterskins filled.

"The steppe is supposed to be arid, but this is past dry," he muttered within Kaul's hearing.

That evening, the scouts reported three herds, all near the river.

Kaul broke his fast when the others ate supper. When it was eaten, he stood beside the fire.

"Now I begin to see the root of the sorrow between the People and the horsemen. As long as memory, the People walked to the north or east, along the Great Mother of Waters. When the family had too many mouths for the Earth Mother to feed, or we could not agree among ourselves about something that was strong in our hearts, some of us walked away. Each time we walked, we came closer to the land of the horsemen. Some of their young men have wandered to us, just as Taelon in his youth wandered to them. Yet much land lay between us. There was no bad blood." Kaul fed a stick to the fire, watched for a few moments as it crackled. The fire quickly ate the dry wood.

"Feel Mother Earth." Kaul lifted a handful of dirt, let it slip through his fingers. "It is not the fire that makes it yellow. She is dry. The grass should be green after the spring rains. It is still winter brown. What food is there in such grass for a horse?" He looked around the fire.

"I have met few horseman. You have." Kaul eyed Jack. The soldier squirmed as he returned the gaze. "Could you count their ribs as you put your spear into their heart?"

Jack nodded.

"My heart told me before you did. We had no floods these last many years. It is good for us. But when less rain falls out on the steppe, it means death to the horsemen."

Sara pursed her lips. "But if the Great Mother does not give water to those who live here, why should they take blood from us?"

Kaul could give her no answer. He sat back, pulled his blanket around himself and prepared to sleep through the night.

Breakfast was silent. Kaul's dreams showed no path away from the cliff that yawned before them. Jack took Kaul aside.

"Now we see the root of the blood between the People and the horsemen. I cannot bring rain where the Great Mother does not send it. Can you? They are dying here and would kill you and take your land to live. We have learned much in this journey."

Kaul nodded. Jack rushed on. "There is no need for you to continue. You have no wisdom that will feed them. What words can you say that have not already been spoken in their council?"

Kaul frowned in thought as he walked to his horse. There was wisdom in every word Jack spoke—wisdom and life. But Kaul's belly told him that path to life was a false trail. Patting his mount's forehead, Kaul stared into its wide brown eyes; the horse blinked. Kaul turned back to Jack. How to make the stranger see what was clear to anyone born of the People?

"You are wise in all you say. But my heart cannot walk with you. Many times I have entered the Sanctuary of the Goddess with no words in my heart for the troubles that walked with our people. Many times I have heard the People in council say first one word, then another. I listen with my ear and my heart and soon, word by word, we build a bridge. I have lived that way." Kaul scratched his mount behind its ear.

"Standing here, I see no path from death. Why should I expect the horsemen to see a path? But together, with all our hearts, we will find a way." Kaul clenched his fist, let his voice rise. "We always have. I must share their words." The horse stomped its foot, snorted. Kaul turned back to soothe it. "I understand the troubles in your heart. My stomach might follow you." Kaul's voice sank to a whisper. "But I must not."

With a sigh, Kaul leaped on his mount. He pulled on its reins, then patted its neck to calm it. Finally he turned back to Jack. "You need not follow where I go. Take the escort back. I am almost there. Let me go on alone."

Jack let his breath out slowly, emptying himself. He'd tried. *Damn, I was close.* Was Kaul suicidal? Could he take Kaul back by force? Jack hated the helplessness that ate at his gut. His modern education named the problem a zero-sum game. If the Kurgans win, we lose. If we win, they die. In the wet years, families and herds grew; life was good. Now there was not enough to go around. Famine, hunger, pestilence and war stalked the horsemen and the People. It was nature's way. Mother Nature could be a bitch. There was no time to waste on philosophy.

"Listen up, troops." In a moment, everyone stood beside their horses. With a glance at the sun, Jack pointed southwest. "We ride until we come to water. It may be three days or more, so drink your fill. The water we carry will be for the horses."

Merik, Sara and Tomas got first call at the creek. Minutes later, the scouts led out at a gallop. Ten minutes later, riding close to Kaul, Jack led the rest at a trot. To keep the dust down, he spread them out in a line abreast. No horse trailed another. Every hour, he ordered a short stop to change mounts.

The sun beat down, a gleaming ember, giving little heat, yet blistering skin. The wind blasted him with sand. No matter how Jack deployed the troop, the wind always had sand in it, a fine grit that found its way beneath clothes to rub skin raw. Faces and hands, chapped by wind and dust and sun, dried, then cracked, then bled. Troopers, normally wide-eyed and alert, now rode slumped, pulling in on themselves and their private agony.

Jack let them slump. They rode until dark, made a fireless camp and rode out at first light. The first day, the scouts saw nothing. Jack wasn't surprised this far from water. The second day seemed to go like the first, only more dull, more painful.

At noon, Jack called a halt. He dismounted, poured water in his helmet and let his mount drink. Down the line, others doled out water. Launa was watering her horse when she casually said, "We got company coming up our six o'clock."

Jack's heart skipped a beat as his head snapped around, but he tried to stay as cool as Launa. Ten kilometers behind them, a dust cloud hung over the crest of a low rise. As far as the eye could see in any directions, the land was flat. Jack was a fly on a dining room table—with no wings. "Prepare to mount."

Precious water already in a helmet was shared out. With worried glances, the troop waited for Jack's next order.

"Mount up." Jack led off at a trot.

The oncoming horsemen were specks atop the ridge. Jack figured them for thirty or forty horses, maybe eight to ten men, a bit to the right of his track. Jack led his troop at a slight angle to the left and held them to a trot for an hour as the horsemen overtook them at a gallop.

As Jack sweated out the approach, several horsemen leaped from one horse to another. Jack scowled; none of his troops had ever made such a transfer. He was considering trying one himself when Launa grinned, pulled a mount in tight, worked her way up on her knees, and jumped. For a moment, she was off balance; Jack feared she'd go down. But Star sensed Launa's problem. Rider and mount worked it out together. Launa settled in her seat with a broad grin. "I don't have to worry about aching balls."

"But you got big brass ones," he called back.

Her grin got bigger.

Jack had two kilometers between them by the time the horsemen drew even. One man rode in the lead; red hair and beard flowed over his shoulders. His helmet glinted with boar's tusks. Behind him rode a man holding high a horse skull totem. Eight other warriors in no tactical formation scattered out behind them. A woman trailed the pack, leading five horses but doing a very poor job of riding.

The leader waved a lance; Jack waved back. Something was called across the steppe; he ignored it. The two groups rode on, separating more and more as the horsemen galloped.

Jack waited until the racing warriors were only a dust cloud on the eastern horizon before he ordered a rest break. With a low cheer, the troopers tumbled to the ground. The mounts were flecked with sweat. As soon as their riders were off them, the horses rolled in the brown grass and dust. Jack ordered a double issue of water and grain for the horses and allowed a half-hour break for the riders before he led the troop out at a walk.

They rode until dusk was deep. Again there was no fire. Troopers dismounted slowly, walking like arthritic old ladies. But there was spirit in them. "Now I know why horsemen are in such a hurry to get off the steppe. There's nothing to burn for a fire." Tomas drew laughs from the others.

"There is when you're with a herd. You can always burn dry horseshit. That's why horsemen stink." Merik got a laugh too.

Jack grinned at their humor. The scare of the day had not taken that from his troop. As for himself, this game of cat and mouse deep in enemy territory was pure hell. Oh, for a good platoon of tanks under this open sky or a company of light infantry hidden in the jungle. Boy, did he miss modern tools like personal radios or decent maps and a compass.

Launa laid her bedroll near him that evening. "You handled that well," she said.

"You're a pretty good horsewoman yourself."

She rested her hand near his. "That old wrangler at the CIA ranch would have been proud of me today, wouldn't he?"

Jack took her hand in his and squeezed. "When that chief called to us and I had to ignore him, I thought we'd lost it." Jack might have said more, done more, but his exhaustion took him. His next memory was being wakened for last watch.

"Bet that chieftain was making a beeline for the winter camp," Jack said next morning between bites. Breakfast was again dried meat, eaten at the trot.

Launa mulled over his idea. "You're probably right. Should we follow him in?"

Jack shook his head. "Let's pass to the north, and come down on the camp." It sounded logical. But later in the day, as they shared out their last water to the horses, Jack wondered. He called a stop when it was totally dark. No trees made promises on the horizon, and the scouts were not back.

When the sun lit their fourth day on the steppe, the escort

rode into a rolling land, cut by dry streambeds. Here and
there a few dead trees dotted the washes. At mid-morning,
Merik rode up behind them. "Sorry we lost you. Three herds
trapped us yesterday. We hid like rabbits."

"Many horsemen ahead?"

"Many. Many herds as you come close to water."

Jack rubbed the exhaustion from his eyes, tried to think.
"We need water."

Merik nodded. "Then you must go to it through herds."

Jack swore under his breath. To have come this far only
to have water bring them to grief. Then he scowled. Water
was the root of the whole problem.

FIFTEEN

LAUNA RUBBED AT her eyes, trying to clear the dust and exhaustion from them and the deadly numbness that soaked her brain. They'd had a few surprises, but none they couldn't manage. And, Goddess bless her, even Antia had pulled in her horns, staying close and causing no trouble after that horse raid. Jack's grief at losing yet another father figure hadn't kept him from being a decent commander. *If he just doesn't do anything more stupid, we may get back alive.*

Today had been rough. Four days with only the water they carried, and the horses were getting hard to control. They could smell water; it took all the troopers had to keep their mounts from charging straight in.

Each stream, no matter how tiny, had its own herd guarded jealously by lance-wielding warriors. Jack had led the troop through a zigzag course, looking for an opening, but giving each herd a wide berth. *Nothing wrong with that man when he decides to soldier. Now if he'll just stay on the ball.*

As night fell, they still had not gotten a drink. Searching in the bright moonlight, she matched the land that fell away before them to the map in her head. The Dnieper itself probably lay beneath the distant cloud bank ahead. Tendrils of fog snaked out to cover the plain before her. She scowled; those offshoots would wrap themselves around the escort as they groped their way to the river. If her troop stumbled into a herd in that fog, it would be the death of them all. Launa shivered; danger lay like a stone knife against her heart.

At her elbow, Taelon squinted. "I see where we are." He pointed to the south. "Those are hills of sand. Far beyond them is the great salt water. Ahead of us is the river, and beside it, the winter camp." The hunter turned to the north. "There, beyond the rocks, I know a place we can rest."

Launa gauged Jack's growing tension by how he gnawed his already bleeding lip. He was at the edge. "Lead us," he ordered.

Taelon led to the north. Jack rode beside him, keeping him below the ridgeline so they were not silhouetted against the night sky.

Launa glanced around, looking for the best place to put herself. The scouts were exhausted, slumped, half asleep. Launa drifted to the rear. An hour later, a rider fell from his mount. Even then, it took a long minute for him to wake up. Launa helped him catch his horses. Sara joined her; the two whispered back and forth to keep themselves awake. They helped two more sleepers that night.

At first light they crossed a rocky escarpment and were soon in a marsh. It stank of damp decay, but to Launa, it smelled heavenly. Taelon led them straight into the fens before pausing to let them drink their fill. Then they rode on for several hours until Taelon turned and headed straight into a lake.

"Can we go there?" Sara asked, wide-eyed.

Launa shrugged and followed. The lake was shallow, never rising above their horses' knees. Suddenly, they were on dry land. An island rose behind trees that had made it invisible from the shore.

Jack ordered the dismount and checked his horse's hooves for water damage. Launa did the same, then led Sara on a quick survey. The island was low, with a clear spring flowing from its middle. Grass was plentiful and green. The other side was also screened by trees. She returned to Jack and reported tersely, "Looks good to me."

The troops quickly unloaded the horses, let their mounts

drink, then staked them out or hobbled them near browse. Before another hour passed, the squadron tumbled into bedrolls. A silent Kaul stood watch.

That night, marsh mist hid their first fire since launching themselves onto the steppe. As they roasted fish, young spirits rose. Launa ignored the jokes and laughter, waiting for what must come next. She watched Jack watch Kaul, trying to measure the craziness behind Jack's eyes.

Kaul tossed a stick on the fire. "I will go with tomorrow's sunrise. You should begin your journey back then."

"No." Jack set the single word between them like a wall.

"Why not?"

Jack looked around at the escort. "These people and their horses must drink their fill. We cannot leave until they are rested. You must not enter the camp until we have begun our journey home. You must wait three days."

Kaul returned Jack's gaze, then shrugged. "As you say."

The days passed quickly as the scouts quietly celebrated their victory of slipping through the enemy's land unscathed. The island offered hunting and fishing. Sunny and clear weather warmed their refuge. Only the company troubled Launa. Kaul stayed quiet—a monk contemplating eternity. Jack grew more moody. Hardly a word passed between them.

On the third day, Kaul rode out with Taelon to see the path to the ford and the winter camp. Jack went with them.

Launa watched them go, suspecting the mission objectives were about to take a new twist, wondering what she would do. Sara stayed with her through the long hours as they awaited the mens' return. Launa appreciated the quiet company of the unassuming woman.

Shortly after noon, the men returned. Kaul dismounted wordlessly and returned to the small knoll that had become his hermitage. Jack watched him go, grimaced and went to his own equipment. Methodically, he checked his weapons, testing each point, each binding. And Launa went off to do the same.

After supper, Kaul drew the copper knife Jack had given him. As he turned it over in his hand, it caught the fire, sparkling like hope. Kaul handed it to Jack. "New friend, I return this to you. I take no sharp edge to their camp."

Jack took it, then drew the ancient stone blade Kaul had given him. "Would you have this back now?"

Kaul accepted the knife, ran his finger along its edge, held it up to the night. "When once I looked into its dull sheen, I saw strange things about you. My eyes still cannot see all the strangeness that surrounds you." Kaul flipped the knife in his hand, then offered it again to Jack, ancient hilt first. "Take it again into your keeping. Many must see it in your hand. If my journey leads only to death, you must use this blade to go before our people on a different path."

With that, Kaul turned away, walking alone toward his private Gethsemane. He spoke his final words without looking back. "I will be gone when you awake in the morning. The moon is enough light for me. You should leave at sunrise."

Taelon nodded. Jack just grunted.

Launa went to bed promptly, intent on waking up very early. She awoke to Sara shaking her. Tomas crouched beside her.

Launa searched the camp. Kaul led a horse toward the water. Jack was not in his bedroll. Launa squinted through the dark to where Windrider was picketed. Jack was there. Launa squeezed Sara's arm and continued to survey the camp. One tree away, Brege sat up in her bedroll, watching. The same with Antia. *Is the entire camp awake?*

With no backward glance, Kaul mounted. Launa heard his horse splash into the water. As soon as he was lost in the swirling fog, Jack led Windrider forward. And Launa moved to intercept. "Captain, you can wait and we can discuss this later, or we can argue now and he'll hear us. Your call."

Jack pursed his lips—and stopped. Brege, Merik, Taelon and half the camp soon stood around them, listening as the fens swallowed up all sound of Kaul's passing.

Launa waited for a hundred count after Kaul was gone, then turned to Jack. "Okay, Captain, what's on your mind?"

Jack's eyes flashed in the light of the full moon. "I will

follow him, Lieutenant, establish an observation post above the winter camp and observe."

"And attempt a rescue if possible." Launa added what he would not. His silence confirmed her suspicion. "By yourself. For God's sake, man!"

"Yes." Jack looked away.

Launa scanned the camp. There was a reason the Army did not want lovers in the same foxhole. Her head and her heart warred as she tried to figure out how to handle this new mission objective. She measured Jack, hard eyes, hand resting on knife, legs tense, ready to do what? *In for a dime, in for a dollar. I'll give you a little more rope, Jack. For Lasa's sake.*

Decision made, she turned to Taelon. "You watch over this camp. See that everyone is ready to ride at any time. Use your hunter's eye to set up traps. Something worse than bear may come after us when we return." She put her hands on her hips, looked from face to face. "Sara and Tomas, you ride with me and Jack. The rest of you, stay here with Taelon."

Brege stepped forward. "I ride with you."

Launa's temper snapped. "No! For the daughter under your heart and the father we follow, you will stay."

Brege flinched, but stood her ground. "Then take Merik."

Launa sighed. There were reasons for the goddamn Prussian drill that hammered obedience into soldiers' heads, even if Launa did hate it. There were reasons why for centuries only men went to war. Life was simpler if one sex stayed home and tended the fire. Simpler, but not necessarily smarter. Some time when she had a day or two to call her own, she'd sit down and figure all this out. Today was not that day.

"Merik, get your horse."

Launa grabbed five helmets and vests for her chosen band, then added a sixth. Antia had her horse and kit ready to ride.

As first light turned mist from black to gray, Jack led them out. Once across the lake they swung left and followed a stream. The swamp grew rocky. Giant boulders forced them to twist and turn. Finally, the stream cascaded into the great river. They walked their horses down a cleft.

It was cold close to the river; Launa gritted her teeth to stop them from chattering. The sun had yet to break above the gray rock walls rising on either side. An hour later, they passed the last of the rapids and the land opened up. Launa could see half a dozen herds; there were few outriders. The camps did not seem to be stirring this early. Were they still on a lazy winter schedule? Jack kneed Windrider to a trot, and the five followed. Launa saw the ford, but no sign of a lone rider.

Two dozen warriors appeared on the far shore of the river and crossed. Launa marked where they rode, even as she held her breath. But they ignored the small party and set out straight for the steppe. This large party exchanged shouts and waves with a smaller group that was making for the ford from the south.

Jack urged them on, and they followed, reaching the ford before the oncoming group. "Who'd have expected so much traffic this early in the morning? Reminds me of Seattle," Jack mumbled.

Launa laughed, grateful for the break in the tension. She wished she could have passed the joke to the others. Except for Antia, they looked pale with fright. Sara's teeth were chattering. It was cold, but not that cold.

On the other side, they followed the path over a bank and past a stand of trees. Once out of sight of the other riders, Jack led them off the track, into trees. They climbed a steep hill, urging their horses up until Jack signaled a halt. By now Sara was shivering uncontrollably. Launa pulled her blanket off Star, collected Jack's and wrapped Sara in them.

"She needs body warmth." Tomas included himself in the wrappings, holding her close, giving her his warmth.

Launa smiled. She wasn't the only one following her heart into hell. Who was the best person to share a foxhole with? She turned to Jack. "Where are we?"

"If I remember the reconstructed map Brent showed me, we've made it. See the sand dunes along the Dnieper?

There's the small river that flows into the bigger. Behind us should be another stream."

"Where's the camp?" Antia asked.

"About halfway around this hill. By God, we have made it," Jack said, his voice mixing equal parts of elation and surprise.

"Right," Launa agreed dryly. "Now all we have to do is get out again. I don't mean to sound negative, Captain, but I haven't been so scared in traffic since I flew a single-engine Cessna into O'Hare."

"How'd you manage that?" Jack sounded impressed.

"That's a long story, and you don't really want to know. Let's just worry about getting out of here."

Sara grinned sheepishly. "I'm sorry. I do not know what happened to me."

Launa gave her a hug. "Do not worry. It happens to me all the time when I get wet on cold mornings. Jack is always having to warm me up." Tomas took the chance to give Sara another hug, then included Launa as well.

Antia scowled. "What do we do now?"

Launa glanced at Jack. He looked away, then back to them. "We move through the trees until we see the camp."

Launa broke from the hug. "Let's ride, people."

SIXTEEN

ARAKK SPENT HIS first night at the winter encampment in prayer. He checked his horses before returning to the tent that had been given to him by the Mighty Man of the Clans. Satisfied that his ponies were well pastured, he was returning to camp when he spotted Shokin, leader of the Stalwart Shield Clan, striding toward him.

Before Shokin got to Arakk, he stopped, squinted toward the river and pointed. Arakk turned. Coming around the hill was a single rider. He carried no lance. The lone horse he rode must be the worst of the herd.

Arakk trotted toward Shokin. With his hand on his knife, Arakk stood beside him.

"Who is that?" Shokin asked.

"It looks like one of the farmers. My son sat his horse better in his second summer."

Shokin grunted agreement. "Where are his weapons? No warrior would ride without his lance."

"They are animals, fit only to be hunted down."

"Yet this animal has the courage to ride into a camp with more hands of warriors than I can count. There is a strange smell on the wind. I would use my hunter's eyes today."

Arakk froze his face to hide a scowl. If Shokin were not here, Arakk would have run the farmer through with his lance. But Arakk needed Shokin. The Stormy Mountain

Clan could not look to the Stalwart Shield at its backside while it went to meet the farmers. Also, Arakk wanted more warriors with his totem. Shokin must not refuse to let his warriors follow Arakk.

The stranger rode up, then slid easily from his horse, almost like a horseman. He stood before them, straight as an arrow, hands falling easily to his side. There was no knife in his leather belt, no bow or quiver. The man was as unarmed as a slave girl. Even Arakk's woman had a knife in her boot. Yet the man stood with his shoulders back and dared to look both Mighty Men straight in the eye.

Arakk wanted to kill him where he stood.

Yet there was the matter of Shokin. And the question of what happened to Tyman and Danic.

The stranger raised his hands, palms open to them. Arakk cowled. Did the fool not know they had already seen he was defenseless? The farmer spoke. Arakk could understand none of his jabbering. He did not listen to slaves' words, but silenced them with his whip. They should speak like Horse People or not at all.

The man fell silent, apparently aware that his words held no meaning for his listeners. He moved his hand to his face; two fingers pointed at his eyes, then he swept his hand to point at Shokin's head, his hair flowing freely except for two braided forelocks that were tied with blue leather thongs.

The warrior frowned in puzzlement. "The man thinks he has seen me before."

"Have you?"

Shokin shook his head. "I have never seen the likes of him, except for the slaves from last summer's raiding with you."

"Then let us bring this animal before the Mighty Men. I have a slave girl that can speak their grunts and tell us what this mare is bawling about." Arakk grabbed the stranger by the arm and pushed him roughly ahead of the two warriors.

The man tried to walk beside them, as if he were an equal and not their property. When he tried, Arakk shoved him again. He did not fall. When he realized his place was before them, he walked with such presence and grace that Arakk's disgust rose as rapidly as his temper. The stranger led the way into camp as if he were the Mighty Man and they were the slaves.

SEVENTEEN

LAUNA WOUND HER way through a birch forest. The bare trees afforded great visibility—not what Launa wanted. Horses and cattle grazed on the plain below. Launa worried they had missed the encampment.

Then it came in view. Jack edged higher up the hill to a rock outcropping. They tied their horses and crawled out for their first good view. It was terrifying and breathtaking.

Hundreds of circular huts dotted a slight depression below them. The huts were in no order, just scattered everywhere. People scurried like ants among them. Here and there, horses and riders raced about. The distant strains of strange music came to them along with the scent of roasting meat and the stench of open latrines. In the middle of the camp, four large conglomerations of tents and huts marked off the four corners of the world and the four corners of an open space. Tall poles with totems stood before each structure, facing a grassy court.

A crowd gathered in the common around a smoking fire. Half a dozen men, in helmets and holding lances, faced a single man. He stood bare-chested, bareheaded, empty-handed. Launa could not make out faces, but she knew Kaul's stance.

Someone knelt, groveling between the one and the many. Probably a translator, a survivor of River Bend trying to put

Kaul's wisdom into whatever strange tongue the horsemen spoke. Launa doubted the language of these people could hold Kaul's faith in power as a trust for the good of all. How could these butchers conceive of a person's innate value flowing from her very existence, rather than her strong arm? All the words tumbled through Launa's mind that she had heard Kaul struggle with, even as she struggled to understand the new twists he brought to the wisdom of the great thinkers she had studied in school.

Then Launa kicked herself mentally. What did she know of the Kurgan language? How could she guess the depths of their philosophy? Had she fathomed what lay in Kaul's mind when she first saw him? Judith had warned her never to underestimate these people. Launa had learned to respect Lasa and Kaul; she must do the same for the enemy. Still, she doubted this frightened slave had mastered the new tongue with the precision and depth necessary to give the horsemen a taste of the wisdom that stood before them.

Apparently the chieftains found the experience disagreeable. One stomped up to Kaul, shouted something and struck him. Kaul stumbled back, but did not fall. The chief rained blow after blow on the man of peace until he fell to his knees. Other warriors descended upon Kaul. It looked as if they dragged him away to a tent, but Launa couldn't tell at this distance. The five scouts turned away.

"So much for diplomacy." Launa hated her words, but they said it all. "Words do not slay wolves," she translated. Sara nodded. Antia snorted.

Merik stared dumbfounded. "They will listen to him in council."

"They had their council with those six," Jack whispered.

"Six men do not make a council." Merik's voice broke as he spoke.

"More likely, the one who hit him was the council," Launa told him. Merik stood open-mouthed as she walked away.

"What do we do now?" Sara asked.

Launa turned and frowned at Jack. "There are too many

horsemen for us to cross the river by day. We wait for night. Then go. Right, Jack?"

"Right," Jack answered absently. And Launa knew he didn't mean it.

As the afternoon wore on, Jack grew more edgy. Finally Launa came up behind him. Rubbing his back, she tried to massage the knots out of his muscles. The task was impossible. "Shall we find a trail down to the camp?"

Jack turned to her, his tormented eyes wide. "You want to?"

Launa stepped back, and prepared for the fight of her life. "I've come this far. Don't assume I'll go farther. I don't know if we can rescue Kaul." She rested one hand on the hilt of her knife. "I will not let you endanger the rest of us. If necessary, I'll frag you." Without an impersonal grenade, she'd have to use her knife.

Jack nodded, then grinned sheepishly and sat down. Resting his back against a tree trunk, he looked up into the clear blue sky. "I know I've put everyone at risk. Maybe you're right and I'm seeing my grandfather. Maybe I'm right and we at least have to tell Tall Oaks how he died—and save him if we can. You've come this far. You've let me put the assets in place to make a rescue." Jack looked her straight in the eye. "Thank you."

He turned again, gazing out over the plain. Drawing his knife, he tested its bronze blade, then began whetting it on a stone. "On the flight out to Livermore, I said I'd let you take charge. I didn't do too bad for a while. You let me have the command at the tree last summer, and you've followed me on this. I appreciate that. Now I'm turning it back over to you. You decide if we can make a rescue and when. That okay?"

Launa chuckled. "You've led twenty people a thousand klicks behind enemy lines. We're outnumbered a zillion to one, and now you want a change of command. Gee, Colonel Custer, I can't tell you how much this lowly lieutenant appreciates the chance you've given me." Launa grinned to take the sting from her words.

Jack laughed with her. "I guess it is that bad. You don't want it?"

Launa sobered quickly. "I've got the command, Captain."

"I thought you'd take it." He picked up a stick, in no apparent rush to move out. He toyed with it for a minute, then sighed. "This is all so crazy. There are times when I feel like I was born here. You know what I mean?"

Launa nodded and sat down across from him. She knew very well what he meant.

He threw down the stick. "Then there are times when my brain flips. I can nearly hear a click. Then I'm thinking and looking at things like a modern soldier. It almost hurts to make the change." Launa held her breath, waiting for him to go on. She had suffered through the same changes.

Jack spoke slowly. "I can go on for weeks, living quietly like these people; then something will happen and I'm off, hard charging with the old ways. This trip"—Jack sat up straight—"as soon as we started getting ready, it was like I put on a suit of armor. I was going to kill or be killed, and I became the soldier all over again. What will happen for these people when they have to become . . . ?" He stood up.

Launa glanced up at him. Jack couldn't even say the words that made these farmers into killers. But then, neither could she. She offered him her hand and he helped her up. "I can't say what it's like for you, Jack, but when I have to become a killer, I go back to my roots. When I can live, I live with these people. I think it's better to let the twenty-first-century part of me do the killing. It doesn't hurt as much."

Jack stood beside her for several moments looking downhill, still holding her hand. "I guess you're right." He turned, looked at her. "I'm glad we're talking again. Now, shall we go check out the approaches to the camp?"

Sara went with them. The rest stayed with the horses. The three followed a game trail downhill. It twisted past rocks and washouts. In the dark, the trail would be tough. The full moon and lack of foliage might help. As they approached the camp, Launa raised a hand in caution. "Watch out for kids, young lovers, that sort of thing."

They managed to work their way to within two hundred meters of where the trees ended. For several minutes they watched the bustle of the camp as people went about their chores. It didn't look that different from Tall Oaks. When some children ran into the woods to gather sticks, Launa led her troopers back uphill.

On the way to the rock, Launa spotted a game trail heading off to the right. They checked it out. As Launa expected, it took them to the west edge of the camp. "We'll use this."

The three returned to the rock just as the evening sky began to slip from blue through pastels to black. The air was crisp, holding promise of cold before dawn. The woods filled with night sounds. With a soft whisper, Tomas called them to the lip of the rock where he watched activities in the camp. "A bonfire is roaring. I can't see what's going on around it, but something is happening."

Jack and Launa exchanged glances. She remembered tortured screams around such a fire at River Bend. Antia looked away.

The evening had turned to flicked ebony when the drums started. High-pitched, undulating wailing blended with them. The bonfire spoiled Launa's night vision. She could see nothing of what went on around it. Away from the fire, everything was shady night.

They hadn't long to wait. A piercing scream shattered the calm night. A choked groan escaped Jack. Launa shuddered.

"What are they doing?" Merik didn't sound like he wanted an answer.

Launa rested a hand on his shoulder. "If you wound a deer when hunting, do you hunt it down?"

"Yes. It is in pain."

"These men wound and stand aside to watch the pain."

As the moon rose higher, the night was shattered time after time by screams torn from the throat of the man they loved as a grandfather. At River Bend, Launa had not known the tortured souls crying their life into the cold night air. Tonight she did. She wished herself anywhere but here. She wanted to flee, but knew she could never get far enough away to silence Kaul's agony.

Merik jumped up, knife drawn. "We have to do something," he choked.

Launa stood slowly, facing him. Sara and Tomas joined her. Jack rose to stand beside Merik. Antia stood apart from all of them. Launa had expected this. She had hoped it would be otherwise. Slowly her hand edged toward her knife. The words she shot at the two men were as hard as the stones for her sling. She prayed words alone would be enough to stop this senseless waste. "We wait here. In the morning, before first light, we will try."

"It will be too late," Merik sobbed, pleading.

Jack put a hand on Merik's arm. "To go there now would be death for all of us."

Merik spun, his drawn knife only inches from Jack's stomach. "I thought you would come with me."

Slowly Jack shook his head. It seemed to Launa his whole body shook. "My heart cries out to go with you. But my eyes see and tell me only death awaits such a dash." Jack's words were hard, but his voice was soft with understanding.

Launa watched a tear work its way down Jack's cheek. Slowly she released the breath she had held, eased open the steel door she had slammed shut on her heart. She'd been ready to fight the man she loved, to fight him with words— blades if need be. No matter what the cost, she would not let Jack endanger the escort and all of Tall Oaks.

Launa let her breath out, but swelled with pride as she watched Jack. No matter how torn he was between what he wanted and what he knew was right, the discipline of their duty to others held him.

The knife wove unsteadily but stayed deadly close to Jack's vulnerable belly. "If we wait, he will be dead." Merik's voice broke. "We have come so far to just stand here."

Jack let out a long shudder. "Yes. I brought us here. I risked our lives, and more than you can ever know." His words became hard as obsidian. "But we wait here. Kaul had to go there. We could not stop him. Now we must wait and hope there will still be enough life in him for us to save tomorrow."

Merik seemed to deflate under Jack's gaze. He dropped his knife as he turned away from them. Launa heard him crying softly. Tomas and Sara went to him, surrounded him in a hug, consoled him. Launa moved to Jack. He was cold as ice in her embrace. "I didn't want to do that," he whispered.

"I know, but you did." She pulled him closer, tighter, never wanting to let go.

"Will there be anything left in the morning?"

Launa could not answer that.

The night passed slowly; the scouts locked in their private thoughts. Over and over again in her mind, Launa tried to plan the day ahead of them. No matter how many times she did it, there were just too many variables. She gave up. *If I wanted to play it safe, I would've stayed home.*

When the moon was halfway down, Launa called them together. "Water your horses. We ride fast today."

Preparations complete, they stood ready to lead their horses downhill. Launa swallowed hard and issued her first life-or-death order. "Jack will enter the camp alone. We will stay in the trees on the west side of the encampment. Jack, my love, we will wait for you there. If we hear shouts in the camp, we will try to create a diversion, maybe stampede some horses through the camp." She paused, took the most difficult breath of her life, and finished. "We will not enter the camp. You're on your own." *Now if I can only follow my own orders.*

Jack looked at her for a long moment, then nodded.

They made their way downhill, moving slowly, as quietly as the horses would allow. At the fork in the trail, Launa came to Jack, hugged him, wiped her own tears. Then, taking Windrider's halter, she led the other four down their trail. Jack stood, watching them go, then turned to take the path of his own choosing.

EIGHTEEN

JACK STOOD ALONE in the woods, Launa's sounds fading away. He took several breaths, tasting the fresh morning air. With each breath, he inhaled clean newness, exhaled the stale horrors of the dark. The morning had reached that time that comes just before the dawn. It can be the worst moment of a long and terrible night, or the best of a long and terrible day. Jack remembered such mornings in a desert, six thousand years away.

The young man who had borne his name then had been angry steel, shackled by duty to a place not of his choosing and longing to be elsewhere. This morning Jack stood at the end of a path he had chosen. He moved now with a gentler resolution. There was no anger in his blood, just sadness. These people had changed him. There were times now when he did not understand himself.

He thought of Launa. He hadn't wanted to bring her; he didn't want to leave her now. Her love strengthened him, yet tore at him. Fear for her safety never left him. Maybe the barracks Lotharios were right; soldiers were meant for sex, not love. Maybe in that world there was a reason lovers should not fight side by side . . . but not in this one.

Jack respected the insights he had been taught and recognized wisdom in what he saw here. He prayed to live through this day. Maybe then he would have the time and smarts to sort it all out. Now was a time for action. He squared his shoulders, rotated them to unkink the tension of the night. Then, at a crouch, he silently glided down the trail.

In moments, he stood behind a tree, scanning the encampment. The moon was still up; he had enough light to see. The round huts were formed from willow staves with skins, felt and reeds woven between them. They seemed solid enough for the winter winds; he hoped they would hold out the sound of his passing. With a deep breath, he stepped into the open. The ground was pounded dirt, only here and there a clump of grass. He saw no sticks or twigs to betray his passing. Moving swiftly, quiet as an Apache, he passed from shadow to shadow. He advanced in running bounds, pausing to catch his breath in a shadow, looking, listening.

Near the common, he slowed, listened more intently, moved more carefully. The camp was silent, no dogs, chickens or geese. He mouthed a grateful prayer for the pride these people took in horses and cattle. Finally, he crouched beside one of the large structures, part tent, part hut. Searching, he heard a low groan. He could see nothing from where he hid.

Jack stood and, as if he owned the place, swaggered into the open. No guards. The fire's embers did nothing to dispel the morning chill. Its cold glow cast shadows, invoking the ruddy specters of the souls it had watched give up their lives. By that light, Jack saw a square frame. A man hung spread-eagled. Jack ran to his side—and almost cried out in shock.

Jack had seen much in the desert. He'd pulled what had been his friend off a mine field, one leg dragging by a strip of flesh. His young eyes had seen things he only understood now as they came back to him in nightmares. But none of the happenstance of modern war could prepare him for the malicious sport that had been played out on Kaul's body.

The flesh of arms and legs, chest and back had been flayed in small patches. Each one must have created its own moment of agony, then grown dull as another portion of skin went under the knife. In the shadows, it took a moment longer for Jack's eyes to absorb all of Kaul's nakedness.

Jack gagged.

Kaul was no longer a man, at least not a man as Lasa had need of him. On the ground, scattered in small pieces, were testicles and penis.

Jack wanted to weep, vomit, call down an artillery barrage, a nuclear-tipped missile on these butchers. His hand went to his knife. Did he cut Kaul loose as he had planned, or slit Kaul's throat to free him from the agony of slow death?

Kaul moaned again; his eyes opened. Terror showed in them, then recognition. "Why are you here?" he croaked through blood-covered lips.

"I've come to take you home." In that moment, Jack knew what he would do. Quickly, he cut the bonds at Kaul's legs. Stripping off his own loincloth, he slipped it on Kaul, as much to protect the wound as to cover the obscene void at his groin. *Why hasn't he bled to death? No time for that.* Jack slashed the leather bonds that held Kaul's hands. The man collapsed into Jack's arms. Clenched teeth stifled a scream of agony. Sweat beaded Kaul's brow. Carrying him like a baby, Jack began the long journey to the west edge of camp.

First light was brightening the eastern sky as the moon set. Jack had light to see, and made the most of it. He took no time to pause in the shadows, listen for the enemy. Jack ran as fast as his burden would let him. He struggled to keep a steady hold on Kaul, to jar him as little as possible. Jack's legs began to knot. His arms screamed. Kaul's gasps urged him on.

Jack kept the brightening sky to his back and tried to maintain situational awareness. He thought he was doing fine. Then he rounded a hut and nearly ran down two people in leather hides and leggings.

Jack froze where he was, letting Kaul slip to the ground. Jack tried to ignore the man's stifled cry of pain as he pulled his knife with his right hand. He faced the two, desolate, knowing he could not kill them before they raised the alarm.

He had come so close. Jack made a thrust for the closest. He leaped back, eyes big. The other circled wide. Jack knew he was done for even as he wondered why they had not raised a shout.

"You have come for the wise man?" A boy spoke the language of the People.

"The Goddess protect you." A young woman of maybe fifteen blessed Jack as he turned his knife on her.

"Sweet Jesus." Jack froze, renewed hope rising even as he doubted his luck and hoped the Goddess would not take offense at where he gave thanks. "Come with me," Jack offered, keeping his words few, fearing his accent would raise their fear.

The boy looked to the west and shook his head. "My sister lives. I cannot leave her here alone."

The woman put Kaul's arm around her shoulder. "My brother died from the cold and the whip this winter. I am Killala. There is nothing here for me. Better to die running." Her words were bitter, harsh with their want of hope.

The boy nodded sadly, turned and walked away without a backward glance.

Jack had no time for second thoughts. "We must run." This time he did thank the Goddess, if silently. It was much easier carrying Kaul with the woman's help. The jostling took its toll. Kaul fainted, his head rolling limp as they ran. Jack increased the pace.

Once when he started to turn right, Killala pointed left. "Arakk rises early to pray."

Jack went left.

A few moments later, Jack froze in mid-step. Off to his right, someone coughed and hacked. While Jack listened to spitting and a shared laugh, Killala fell to the ground at the sudden stop. Jack clapped a hand over Kaul's mouth, stifling a yelp as the man came awake. Half dragging the two, Jack put a hut between himself and the noise.

When he peered around the corner, thirty meters away were two men, warriors with lances, talking as they walked toward the center of camp. Jack didn't need to understand a word they spoke. They pantomimed well the eternal signals of young men bragging the night after a drunk. They passed, unaware of the three. Jack figured he had five minutes, more or less, before they got to the common. He and the woman redoubled their speed when they dared start up again.

An eternity passed before the huts became fewer and farther between. Jack searched the woods. Where was Launa?

Five riders broke from the forest. Jack gasped a prayer and tried to run. Kaul moaned. Jack felt Kaul's blood on his arm.

"Can you ride behind my consort?" he asked his comrade in flight.

"I will have my own horses if you ride where I show you."

"Will they chase a horse thief?"

"Ha!" She laughed scornfully. "You take their god-sacrifice and their sport and worry they'll chase us because I take horses." Jack saw her point. "But do not worry. Kakaz is old and his son rode out yesterday."

Launa thundered up, the Goddess on horseback. She led Windrider around beside Jack. Tomas and Merik jumped from their horses to hold Kaul while Jack mounted. They handed him up gently, sickness and revulsion showing on their pale faces.

Antia and Killala exchanged greetings as if they had parted only yesterday. In a moment Antia pulled the woman up behind her and together they raced for a nearby herd. Killala called one to her, leaped on it and quickly cut out three more. The horses followed her willingly.

Jack surveyed the situation. It was better than he had any right to expect. "We head for the river."

"Can Kaul survive the ride?" Launa gulped hard.

Kaul stirred in Jack's arms. "Take me to the island."

Jack rode for the ford.

There must be a gracious Goddess or God somewhere, Jack mused as they crossed the ford at a trot. They had seen no one. On the plains were herds and outriders, but none close to the river. Then, of course, the celebrating on Kaul's flesh must have kept everyone up late last night. Jack remembered how the raiders slept in after the butchery at River Bend.

Jack led the group out onto the plain, following a well-beaten path. Near a rock outcropping, he used the hard ground to turn north and back to the river. It was cold; Kaul shivered. Launa took a moment to dismount, then caught up again and tossed Jack her horse blanket. He wrapped Kaul in it.

The sun was halfway up the sky when Jack's mount splashed into the lake. The island looked deserted. For a moment Jack feared he'd misplaced his camp. Then bowmen dropped from trees and spears rose from bushes. Taelon had prepared well.

Brege ran to her father, then froze, hand in mouth, as the blanket came away when Jack handed him into Taelon's strong arms. "What have they done?"

Taelon looked from his friend to Brege. "You saw River Bend. What did you expect? Your mother is wise with herbs and dressings. Have you brought any?" Taelon's words to Brege were hard with a hunter's knowledge of blood and life. But Jack had been close enough to hear the catch in Taelon's throat as he received his friend, to see the startled flare of nostrils and eyes. Taelon's heart was shaken, even if his words were hard.

While Brege fled to her bedroll, Launa took Taelon aside. "I want all the escort sent away. I don't know how bad Kaul's wounds are, and I don't want everyone seeing them." She glanced at Jack. He gave her a nod. Taelon turned without a word and strode off, signaling for the troop to join him.

And Jack realized Launa had chosen the hunter for a new second in command. Jack wanted to be close to Kaul, and Launa was letting him do that. Taelon was a good topkick. Still, it felt strange to Jack to find himself out of the chain of command.

Before he could think too much on that, Brege returned with a small leather bag. She pulled out different jars, stoppered with pieces of wood. Every time she looked at her father, she trembled. Launa knelt beside her. "What will you do?"

"I have seen mother rub these ointments and poultices on cuts, and I know which to use. I have sewn deep cuts." Brege stopped, looked at Launa. "We need to wash his wounds." She pulled a basket of bark from her kit. "Make tea from this. Mother puts these seeds in the tea if someone is very hurt."

Jack nodded. "Let's see how good a nurse I can make." He picked up the offered items. One looked like willow bark; the second might be poppy seeds. "I'll get the water boiling and boil enough for cleaning too. Launa, don't let her clean his wounds with this swamp water or we'll lose him."

While water warmed, Kaul lay unconscious in his daughter's arms. A worried Launa came over to help Jack tend the fire. "I hope she's got the right herbs and ointments," she whispered.

"Do you have Maria's book?" Jack stacked wood around the ceramic pot. The fire snapped and spat. So did Launa.

"No, goddamn it, I did not bring a twentieth-century book to the heart of enemy territory six thousand years before it was printed." She stood with hands on hips. "And I have not memorized it. When in the last twelve months have we had a peaceful moment of daylight for me to curl up and study, my ass of a captain who got us into this mess?"

Jack wasn't quite sure what he'd done wrong in the last five minutes to deserve this, but he suspected he'd done enough in the last week to cover the rest of their lives. He looked up at her, "I'm sorry. Thanks for waiting. You saved my ass. Seeing you charge out of the trees was . . ." Jack ran out of words.

Launa stood for a moment, as if testing his words, then stooped down beside him and let out a long breath. "Seeing you come out of the camp with Kaul, I learned how to breathe again."

Jack leaned forward and gave Launa a quick kiss. "I'll try to be a partner worth waiting for."

"Yes." She patted his shoulder as she stood. "Now all I have to do is get us all back alive." She returned to squat beside Brege, watching Kaul's labored breathing.

It was an hour before Jack was ready to clean Kaul's wounds. As ordered, Taelon had scattered the scouts. Several watched around the island or were picketed to covering trails. Some were sent as far as the edge of the caprock to see what was going on. Launa sent Sara and Tomas with Killala to check out the freshly stolen mounts. Only Taelon, Brege and Launa were with Jack when he removed the breechcloth.

Brege stopped, a cloth halfway to the steaming water. Taelon muttered something Jack didn't need translated. "Oh, my friend." Taelon wept.

Launa swallowed, took the cloth from Brege's hand and began to clean Kaul's groin of something that made his wounds glisten. "What is this?"

Jack reached for a dried flake of the substance. It felt oily. He sniffed and offered it to Taelon who shook his head. "Butter," Jack half guessed.

"Butter! They cauterized the wound with boiling butter?"

Taelon's face darkened. "They did not want him to die too soon."

Jack felt like throwing up—like killing someone. He vastly preferred the latter. "Taelon, do you have a large feather?"

The hunter nodded and left them. Jack studied the seared flesh. Nowhere did he see blood oozing. "I hope those bastards do this often enough that they've got the procedure down solid."

Taelon returned. Jack trimmed the feather and cut both ends of the nub. "Somewhere I read that eunuchs pissed through a goose quill." He searched in the ruin of what had once been Kaul's manhood, found what he hoped was the urethra and squeezed it open. As gently as possible he pushed the quill in. Kaul screamed, but Taelon and Launa held him. Jack's own genitals tingled in sympathetic agony, but he went on. A second later, Jack's first medical procedure was rewarded by a trickle of urine through the feather and onto the ground between Kaul's legs.

Jack took two deep breaths as he studied his handiwork. "At least he won't die of renal failure. Now let's handle those cuts. Brege?" Jack's question brought Brege back to life.

"Yes." She rummaged in her sack and held up a large pot.

Launa took it. "Bring your father some tea, then we will clean him." While Jack dribbled the liquid between Kaul's lips, the women washed his flailed skin. Kaul winced, but only once did a moan escape him. Brege was not the only one to shudder.

"Mother would sew cuts, but these are so many, and they are not deep. What would she do?" Jack had no idea. Neither did Launa nor Taelon. They kept cleaning. Sometime during the process, Kaul passed out without a sound.

When they finished washing and dressing Kaul's wounds, Brege cradled his head in her arms, singing softly, as though to an infant.

Launa took Taelon and Jack aside. "I want to put distance between us and the encampment as fast as we can."

Jack nodded. "Don't forget the spring floods. It may not be raining here, but it must be raining somewhere upriver."

Taelon frowned. "How can Kaul travel? Yet you are right, you must travel. Kaul and I will stay. The rest of you return."

Launa closed her eyes as a long breath escaped her. Her words came in a whisper. "Kaul came. He saw. He was cut. That's the message to Tall Oaks. Yes, I can leave Taelon and Kaul here to make their way home as best they can." She opened her eyes, focused on Jack. "But how many would stay behind? You and Brege for sure. Merik and others as well. How badly would my command fragment?"

Jack grinned sheepishly. Launa scowled.

"With twenty archers, I stand a good chance in a fight. Six of us were death for twenty horsemen last summer. How many could this force stand against? I intend to keep my troop together. We all came. We all go."

"Shall we make a travois?" Jack offered.

Launa shook her head. "That would slow us down and leave pretty obvious tracks. Think we could sling something between two horses? Our moderns should carry Kaul's weight easily. One of those horses Killala cut out today is as big as my Star."

Jack nodded; there was no question a lot of people were going to be in hot pursuit. "We've used up a lot of food. I think we can convert a couple of pack saddles."

"Good." Launa turned to Taelon. "I want us out of here this afternoon. We will ride by moonlight tonight and not stop until tomorrow night. I will aim almost due north until we hit the trees, then follow them to the west."

Taelon sent riders to call the pickets back to the lake when the sun was half down. Most outposts had seen nothing. The farthest, who had manned a lookout at the caprock, reported riders scurrying across the lower plain, but most had turned south.

Launa pushed them north all night, stopping only to change horses. Windrider and Big Red had little trouble carrying the hammock slung between them. Star and the other horse Killala called the Brute were another matter. Jack couldn't control the animal. Killala took over the reins and managed to keep the big horse under control. The pair with Kaul set the pace, and that pace was slower than for the ride in.

After the first morning break, Jack waived Killala in close. "You were in the camp. Tell us what Kaul did."

She nodded; Launa, Taelon and Antia drew near.

Killala rode in silence for several minutes while she searched for words. "When they killed our people at River Bend, I was made to follow after Arakk, the man with the red beard. I did not please him." Her eyes flashed defiantly.

"Neither did my brother." Killala's eyes fell. "He grew sick from the cold and beatings and died. They would not even let us bury him. They will answer to my knife for his blood." So Antia had a soulmate.

"Arakk sent me away after that, to Shokin who leads many warriors. Shokin is not so . . . twisted as Arakk. My life was better. It was with Shokin's women that I came to the winter camp. I was washing clothes when the word passed from mouth to mouth that a man from the west had ridden into the camp." Beside Jack, Kaul mumbled. Jack pulled Windrider farther from his stablemate and stretched Kaul out more comfortably. He quieted.

"The woman who tells me what to do and hits me if I do not struck me and told me to finish what I was doing. Then she went off to the place of totems and killings to the man-thing they say is more powerful than the Goddess. I finished quickly; who cares if there's still shit on his pants?" Killala flashed a bitter grin. Jack smiled back. Slaves learn quickly to do the minimum. He had not seen that attitude since coming through time.

"I went to the totems. This man stood tall and proud. He spoke of the gifts of the Goddess and the need for all people to share those gifts with each other. He said he came in search of a way for farmers and horsemen to walk in harmony. One pretty young girl from River Bend, who went to Arakk's bed easily, tried to make your friend's words into words for the Mighty Men. She did not speak well. I would not expect her to know any words that did not help make her pretty or spread her legs." Killala spat. Jack suspected life had been easier for those who could bend. Killala did not look easily bent or broken.

"Could you have put Kaul's words into the mouths of the horsemen?" Launa asked.

Killala frowned, then laughed. "I would have done better, but no. How do you say harmony to men who will settle their differences with knives when they are out of their heads from what they have drunk or the smoke they have breathed?

"When Kaul spoke of calling everyone together to talk of the needs of the people, the one who walks first in all things struck him for calling the people to rise up and kill him." Killala shook her head. "He did not understand, but how could he?" Jack wondered if she spoke of Kaul or the chieftain. How could Kaul know that the way he solved problems was sedition to a despot? It had not mattered. People of the knife could not hear the words of someone who carried no blade.

"The Mighty Man shouted to the clans that since this man came like a woman, they would make him one that night." Killala shivered. "I knew what they would do to him. I made up a drink to take the sharpness from the pain. They caught me, beat me and gave me the early work. That is why you found me. I tried to help him in the name of the Goddess and She smiled on me." Killala shrugged, and for the first time Jack saw the way she winced as her body moved. How badly had they beaten her? Carrying Kaul and riding a horse all night must be agony.

Taelon grew redder and redder as Killala told her tale. Now he exploded. "Kaul walked the way of harmony with the Goddess. The horsemen know nothing of that way. Now I know the path for my feet. Many will follow when they see the marks of the horsemen's knife on Kaul's body. We will have blood for blood."

Brege had ridden beside her father, worry etched on her face. Now she turned paler still. "How can he be mother's consort? He cannot Speak for the Bull. Dear Goddess, where is Your mercy? Oh, father!" Tears fled down dusty cheeks.

Jack felt for Kaul's ancient stone knife in his belt. His fingers traced the weathered carvings in the wooden handle, the leather bindings. In the depth of his soul, Jack felt something begin to grow. He wondered what it was.

In the desert, he had learned the patience needed of those whose profession was death. He had learned to wait for whatever was coming his way. He had enough problems to handle right now. He could wait for any more to show their face.

"Killala, you said Kaul was from the west. Did the mighty man know that?" Launa asked.

Killala's face grew solemn. "Arakk who wielded the knife on Kaul's skin, four of his warriors disappeared at River Bend. He sent four hands in search, and to look on Tall Oaks. He kept asking Kaul what he knew of them." The woman shuddered. "Even under the knife, the wise man told him nothing."

The troop rode on in silence. The two sides had met, and like flint and steel, sparks had flown. The horsemen were afire now, ready to roar down on the west, destroying all they touched. Jack would have to stop that fire. As a peacetime soldier, he'd spent time on emergency fire duty. Often, he'd worked on the second fire, the back fire that would burn out the wild fire.

Jack glanced at Kaul; the Speaker for the Bull shivered. Some how, some way, Kaul must get back, his words, his wounds would spark that second fire in the hearts of his listeners in Tall Oaks. Jack urged more speed from Windrider and Big Red. He would have given much for a medevac chopper.

Launa wanted to make Kaul comfortable. He was covered by blankets, but the dust got into his wounds, aggravating them. Every hour when they stopped, Brege washed him, laving the dust from his raw flesh. She used a lot of water. Her small pots of ointments and poultices were emptying fast.

By evening, they had seen only one herd, and that at a distance. "Can we stop yet?" Brege pleaded.

The sun was down; Launa would have preferred to ride until dark, but Brege needed light to tend her father. Launa called a halt, and almost fell from her mount. The last three days had been long. Taelon set the watch. Launa helped Jack and Brege settle Kaul into a bedroll. Brege again washed Kaul's wounds; she let no one help her. Launa slept beside Jack until Taelon pushed her out of her blankets in the predawn light.

The next morning Kaul's fever rose. Everyone shared their water with him, but Launa could see the worry on their faces. They had barely had enough water to make it the last time. Would their water hold out for the slower trip back? Was she making the right decisions for her first command?

Launa kept the outriders close through the second day. They'd seen no horsemen and she didn't want to misplace anyone this far from home. By dusk they rode among trees.

As they made camp, Killala came to Launa. "I went with a wood-gathering band last summer. We are near a lake. May I search for it in the morning?"

"Yes." With the thought of water, Launa breathed the first hopeful air she'd tasted in four months.

NINETEEN

ARAKK LED HIS band of warriors away from the river by the great winter encampment. The Mighty Man of the clans himself had told Arakk of a ford near the mouth of the next river that he should use, and use quickly. The rains would come soon.

Arakk had much to be proud of. When he sent the torch to the clans, many warriors would come. So many that for every one of his, there would be another. That was good.

When they burned the first place few had ridden with them, only Shokin of the Stalwart Shield and Orshi of the Broad Sky. Less than ten hands of warriors had followed his totem. Shokin would not come this year, but many more would. Yes, Arakk had much to be proud of.

Still, Arakk was in a foul humor. Where had the man from the west gone in the night? True, a slave was missing, and the boy who should have worked with her had said nothing, even under the knife. He had said nothing and was dead.

Was the magic of this mother god thing strong enough to stand against the power of the Sun and Sky? Impossible! The man from the west had not sprouted wings and flown out of the camp. He had bled under Arakk's knife; he could die. He might have been a brave warrior if he carried a lance.

Still, warriors who should have ridden with Arakk had

turned their backs on him, making signs to ward evil. And Shokin would not lead his warriors under Arakk's totem.

Arakk would look for this farmer as he traveled back to his camp and when he burned the next place this summer. If he found him, he would send his head to the Mighty Man. This would show the people where the power was. Arakk growled as he looked around himself and kicked his horse to greater speed.

TWENTY

NEXT MORNING WHILE Jack helped Brege prepare Kaul for another day, Launa told the troop that Killalla thought water was near. That got a ragged cheer from dry throats. She spread the riders in a wide line as they rode. At mid-morning a shout came from the right; they had found the water. Launa didn't have to issue orders—everyone galloped for the shout.

After helping Brege and Merik settle Kaul beneath a tree, Jack finally took time to scrub away the dust of the steppe and filth that had butchered Kaul. Clean and watered, the troop was in higher spirits than Jack had seen since leaving Tall Oaks.

The sun faded behind clouds that afternoon; a cold drizzle dampened spirits again. Launa made camp where she found a windfall for Kaul to sleep under. "That'll keep him dry and warm. It worked for me on my little hike through the Rockies."

Now they could laugh at Jack's blunder that had put her stark naked and alone in the mountains . . . and a target for an AK-47. Jack built a lean-to to keep the rain off them. Launa smiled and spread her blanket beside his. He found a rain-soaked rag and washed her clean as he peeled her dusty clothes off. He wondered if either of them had any strength left, but as she returned the favor, her touch ignited a hunger that exhaustion could not stint. Their passion warmed them under the shared blankets, driving away the drip of water, the threat of death, the winter cold that had seeped into their hearts. When Jack collapsed, spent, Launa pulled him close. "Welcome home," she whispered.

"You're the only home I ever want. I never want to go to war with you again."

"Nor I you." That was the last Jack heard until Tomas woke them with the dawn.

By morning, the rain was steady. Launa increased the pace. No words were exchanged, but Jack could see the worry in Launa's and Taelon's eyes. They had a very sick man on their hands, and several rivers between them and home. A war party probably rode somewhere behind them. The rainy season had lousy timing.

Jack's heart sank as they approached the Southern Bug. It had been big a week ago; now it was huge. Launa sent Sara and Tomas to test the water. They walked their mounts through shallows for a mile, then got a wild ride in midstream. Still, they made it to a beach only two miles down from where they entered and waved back encouragingly.

Launa looked at Kaul's litter, then at Jack, one eyebrow raised in question. Jack nodded and took charge. "The next five head over. If anything goes wrong, make sure you carry the song of what you have seen to Tall Oaks. The rest of you, help me make a raft for Kaul."

In the rain, with the flooded river spreading well past its normal banks into the trees, it was a nightmare job. It took time to find three downed trees, more time to trim the worst of their branches, even more time to wrestle the logs into the water side by side. Jack sent another five across, then five more.

As Launa started to tie logs with leather ropes from the packs, Jack took them from her and kissed her. "Your turn. Take Brege and Merik across now. Taelon and I can finish up here and get Kaul on the raft. Take Windrider. Leave me a pair of the ponies Antia stole. They'll do fine for towing us through the trees and into the river." He spoke quickly, knowing he had to say it all before Launa's temper tripped in.

"You want to make sure one of us gets across."

"Honey, word has to get back, and one of us, too. That wall's not going to get built. Someone's got to figure out a new defense." Launa nodded calmly, the hot-tempered young woman nowhere in evidence. *God! She's learning to command!*

"I'll wait for you on the other side" was all she said.

The trust in her voice kept Jack warm as he tied logs together and to two dry pieces of down wood that would serve as cross supports. Taelon cut two long birch poles; Jack found a flat stick for a paddle. They laid three packs across the raft and gently settled Kaul on them. He moaned softly as they moved him, but hardly seemed aware of what they did.

Taelon brought the two small horses, sat on the front of the raft and urged the ponies to pull. As they towed the raft through the trees, Jack walked alongside, pushing it away from brush and tree limbs. The cold water was past Jack's knees when they reached the end of the trees. He swallowed hard; in the hours needed to build the raft, the water had risen. It coiled and rolled like a snake. He straddled a log and poled.

The current grabbed them, stretching the logs lengthwise to the river's flow. The lines to the ponies got crossed; Taelon let one go. The other horse tried to make headway alone and lost. The halter pulled at its neck, then pulled off. Taelon found himself holding empty reins as the raft picked up speed.

Jack considered jumping off and pushing the raft, but it was moving at close to five miles an hour. He poled as best he could and was just making it into mid-channel when he came even with the scouts on the far bank.

The raft was three logs wide; the roiling waters floated them like demons dancing to different tunes. With a report like a pistol shot, a cross support snapped in two. The center log smashed against Jack's leg as he straddled the outer one. He cried out in pain.

At his cry, several scouts started back into the water. Launa stopped them. Jack waved encouragingly just as something else snapped behind him . . . followed by a splash.

Jack twisted around. The rope binding the front of the raft had parted, throwing Taelon into the water. He clutched one of the logs. Unbound, the raft began to splay apart. One of the packs Kaul rested on sank into the water between the spreading logs. Jack lunged over Kaul, reaching for the three logs with his bare hands. Kaul screamed as Jack landed on top of him.

Jack struggled to hold the logs, to keep them from spreading wider. The twisting waters twirled the raft broadside to the current, almost tipping them into the muddy water. Jack held on. The current now worked for him, pushing the logs together. He tightened his grip as they took another rollercoaster plunge. The two outer logs dipped; the middle one rose to smash Jack in the jaw. Dazed, he tasted blood, but held the raft together.

Jack tried to edge forward. As he rolled off Kaul, both men groaned. Jack concentrated on finding a good handhold. The stump of a limb gouged his leg.

Taelon pulled himself along one log. The broken rope had snagged in a crack. Taelon grabbed the leather and began to work his way forward, clutching it in his teeth.

"I will tie this end again," Taelon gasped.

Jack grunted. Raindrops pelted his back and streamed down his face. He blinked to clear his eyes. Remembering the scouts, he searched the bank. Through blurred vision, all he saw was river. With a prayer that Launa wouldn't do anything dumb, he laid his head back down. The river took that moment to bash him again with the log. Jack lay still, concentrating on riding the bucking logs. That was enough to do.

Taelon crawled up beside him. "I could only tie two of the logs together. There was not enough rope."

Jack nodded and rolled over, shivering as cool gray day turned to cold black night.

*   *   *

Launa had smiled at Jack's wave when his raft came even with the scouts. It was like him to encourage the troops even when he was in danger. The next instant, she suppressed a scream, fist in her mouth, biting knuckles until she drew blood. The raft dipped and began coming apart. What price did the men pay as Jack threw himself across Kaul to hold the raft together with his bare hands? Then the rain got serious again and she saw no more of the riverborne tragedy.

"What can we do?" Sara cried. She had been ready to charge into the water. Now she stood, water streaming off her, looking at Launa for an order. They all did.

Launa gripped her heart with both hands, struggling to keep it from coming apart like the raft. She wanted to throw herself into the water and follow Jack. She took a deep breath and let it out slowly as she studied the river. The floodwaters lapped against the steep bluff; there was no path. She stared desperately into the thickening rain and made her decision. "We will go downriver, but watch it from the top of the bluff."

That was easier to say than do; trees and brush blocked the view. Launa balanced her push southward with stops to check the bank for a wrecked raft. Any way she worked it, she didn't like the results. She guessed the current at ten miles an hour. Jack was going away from her much faster than she was following. Yet, he might have been washed ashore. Night forced her to make camp long before she wanted. She slept fitfully and got up long before dawn to keep Brege company beside the fire.

Dawn was lost in rain showers. She led the scouts downriver as fast as the trees would allow. Twice she sent detachments downhill to investigate the river. She hastened on, leaving them to catch up as quickly as they could.

"There's something down there." Tomas pointed. A tangle of trees looked like they might have captured the raft.

Mud made the trip down slippery, even with Launa, Sara and Tomas roped together. Launa carefully climbed over the debris, looking for tree limbs hacked off clean by axes. She found none.

Bitterly disappointed and angry at herself for wasting

time, Launa attacked the climb up with a vengeance—and the rain-soaked bank crumbled under her. She rolled into her two companions. They might have all been impaled on the snags below, but Tomas managed to grab a limb.

Covered with mud, Launa took her time to untangle the mess she'd made. Slowly they worked their way back up to the rope she had lost her grip on; then she tied it around herself and let the scouts haul her up. The other two followed her lead. By the time she finally stood among the scouts, the other detachments had caught up.

Riding south, Launa examined her options like they had taught her at the Point. She was going into territory actively patrolled by the enemy. While the horsemen probably were not alerted to their presence, the escort had followed a roundabout track. Fast messengers could have carried the Word ahead of them. Launa should assume the worst.

Her own people were tired, worn thin by all they had been through. How much more could she legitimately expect from them? She shook her head; not much.

The strategic picture was bleak. Tall Oaks lay open to attack. True, the horsemen probably would not move until after the spring floods. But, the wall was not being built in this weather. Somebody was going to have to figure out an entirely different defense for the town.

And unless the People were told what happened at the Horse People's encampment, they would be just as dumb and open to the fire sweeping down on them as they were before Kaul's magnificent sacrifice. As Jack said, somebody had to get the word back. Then again, with her and Jack doing the planning, the casualties for the defense would be a lot lower this summer.

A coldhearted son of a bitch like Patton would order the troop home right now. But she was no Patton. Her man was out there as well as Lasa's consort. How could she face the woman without Kaul? It was bad enough being marooned six thousand years from everything she had known. She would not lose her comrade without doing everything she could to find him.

"Tomas, are all the rivers in flood?"

The young man turned from where he had been peering at the river. "Yes. This is the time when rivers swell, sheep give birth, the earth grows fertile. No one travels." He shrugged. "Except us."

That took one burden from her shoulders. There was at least one major river between her and Tall Oaks. Even if she ordered it, the escort could not make it home.

For a moment, the enormity of the situation swept over her like the raging river below. She was separated from Jack with a continent to find him in. If he was swept to the mouth of the river, God Himself couldn't tell her where he'd go. Launa shut that thought out. She would follow the Bug until it opened on the plain. If she didn't find him by then, she'd double back, checking the river to make sure she hadn't missed him, then head for Tall Oaks. The thought of her and Lasa facing the horsemen without their men beside them sickened her. God, for a Search and Rescue chopper and a couple of handheld radios.

A helicopter: She brought Star to a halt. Jack had flown out to check on her every night of that stupid survival hike. She'd used the most primitive signal—smoke. Surely Jack could make a fire. If he was alive, she would find him under smoke. Besides, Jack would need the fire to keep warm and cook.

With a little more confidence, she urged Star on. Jack would get the raft off the river long before they reached the sea. Jack knew what he had to do. She'd do what she had to.

Gray morning brought sight to Jack's eyes. He was seeing double unless he kept one eye closed. Sometime during the night they had collided with a gigantic old tree. Its knurled roots still clutched chunks of the earth that had failed it. The tree floated like a stately procession, disdaining the rush and hurry of lesser flotsam.

Jack was grateful for the smoother ride. He didn't know how many more hits his head could take. The dull ache he felt lying down turned to excruciating shooting pains when he moved.

"Stay." It was Taelon's voice.

"Still on the river?" Jack gritted his teeth and sat up. His vision grayed, but he sat still until it cleared. To his right was the bluff, but it was losing its cover of trees. That was not good, a small voice whispered. He tried to remember why— the steppe, the horsemen. He struggled to turn around, to study his surroundings. This time he did black out.

TWENTY-ONE

THE NEXT TIME Jack woke, he took his time getting up. It was amazing how much you could see flat on your back if you really tried. In the tree next to them, two squirrels chattered. Sometimes there were four squirrels; he was still having trouble focusing. A collection of birds flitted through the branches, as if they rode a tree ark every day. Jack wondered what else might be in that tree, and decided not to worry; nobody else was. On the other side of him, Taelon, huddled in wool blankets and skins, fished contentedly. Fished!

Jack rolled over carefully, clutching the blanket. Taelon smiled in his direction. "Fair morning."

Jack winced as pain shot through his head. He lay back and stared at the sky. "Fair morning," he lied. "Catch anything?"

Taelon shook his head. "I have nothing to offer my cousin the fish, so he shows no interest in my hook."

Jack nodded, regretted the action, and between lightning strikes in his skull asked, "How is Kaul?"

"Better than you are." At Kaul's voice, Jack turned his head enough to get a better view of his friend. Sunk among two packs and buried under skins, Kaul managed a smile. The cuts on his arms flamed angry red; some dripped pus. Time was running out for him, even if his humor had not. Jack gritted his teeth, took a deep breath, and slowly sat up.

By tightening his stomach and leg muscles, he kept enough blood flowing to his brain to avoid anything worse than another grayout.

Jack kept one eye closed to avoid doubling his world. He had all the troubles he needed without multiplying them. Picking a lone tree along the bank, Jack watched it drift by. Their speed was about three miles an hour. He stared downstream. There were trees to the right, an island. Every mile he stayed on the river was another mile between him and Launa.

Jack reached for his knife; it was still there. "Taelon, we must get to that island."

Taelon surveyed the scene. "Yes." He picked the biggest log and settled Kaul along it. It sank deeper, barely supporting Kaul's weight. Blankets and packs drifted away as Taelon and Jack cut the log loose. Taelon hung on to the forward end. "I and my brother used logs to cross rivers by kicking beside them. I can do it again."

Jack pushed the log along the tree. At the last grip, he kicked off with all his remaining strength. Lying half on the log like it was a surfboard, he paddled for the island. The cold shock of the water invigorated him.

Once away from the tree, the full power of the current took hold. Jack and Taelon paddled desperately for land as the river clutched at them in its race for the sea.

They passed the beginning of the island, a forever distance away. Jack increased his strokes. Feeling the power in his arms draining away as they were swept past the center of their goal, Jack put everything he had into his strokes. *If we don't make it here, we're dead men and Launa is going to be awfully lonely.*

That thought gave his adrenaline another boost. There was no use holding anything back. As they were swept past the end of the island, Taelon reached up, clutching at a trailing willow strand. He caught it; for a moment he held. The log pivoted on him. Jack's end swung in. Then Taelon yelped as the thin branch cut deep and slid through his bleeding grasp.

Desperate, Jack slipped from the log. He sank up to his

chest; then his feet found ground. The water pushed against him, pushed the log. Jack pushed back. He took a step, then another, driving the log against the current. Taelon quit trying to paddle slipped from the log and found the water up to his neck. For a second, Jack feared Taelon could not stand, but he did. Inch by inch, they moved the log forward.

The thought hit Jack; the log was low in the water, giving the current more to push. "Kaul, I'm going to pull you off. Float on your back. I'll hold your head up."

Kaul rolled himself off the log. Jack grabbed for his chin, caught it and lifted Kaul's head free of the water. Taelon shoved the log away from them. Towing Kaul was easier going. Taelon's body blocked the current, making a path for Jack.

Later, they traded places, Taelon holding Kaul and Jack taking the lead. Jack lost track of how often they did that. The water beat at them; its cold robbed his muscles of strength, leaving them knotted.

Finally, Jack was only up to his waist in water. Now the island became more a breakwater and less a goal. Jack turned, reaching for Taelon. Together they struggled forward with Kaul between them. They shook with exhaustion. Brush gouged Jack. Tree limbs seemed to reach out with malice to snag his aching flesh. Finally, mud squished between Jack's toes. He looked for dry land, found a moist mound and lunged for it. The three fell, collapsed in one unconscious pile.

His chattering teeth brought Jack awake. He struggled to his feet, seeing too many trees until he closed one eye. Sapped of strength and warmth, he lurched forward, hunting for a refuge. Two trees were down ahead of him. Leaves covered the ground. Returning to his friends, he roused Taelon. The two picked up Kaul; he was ice cold to the touch. They carried him to the den beneath the downed birches. Jack settled next to Kaul, trying to rub warmth back into his flesh without opening his wounds. He couldn't. Jack settled for holding him close. The smell from some of Kaul's wounds made Jack gag. Had gangrene set in?

Taelon cut saplings, adding them to the canopy above

them. He gathered fallen leaves, piling them around Jack and Kaul before taking his place beside Kaul, adding his body heat to Jack's. Under this leafy blanket, Jack began to warm.

As darkness came and Jack drifted toward sleep, he remembered something Launa had told him after her survival hike. She's promised him penance for what he did to her. Boy, was he doing it. But could he survive this? He wasn't sure. As sleep took him, he thought he heard the *thump, thump* of a helicopter.

The next morning, Jack remembered the chopper. He had ridden out to keep watch over Launa. She hadn't been too mad at him to signal with her fire. Ignoring the screams of his muscles, Jack leveraged himself up and stumbled from the lean-to, one eye closed, searching for a few dry twigs. Taelon produced flint and stone from his pouch.

Leaves, protected from the night's rain in their nest, dried by their shared warmth, should have caught fire. Hour after hour, Jack and Taelon took turns striking sparks, trying to catch fire to the leaves; some smoldered, but none caught. In mid-afternoon, Taelon found some dry moss on the underside of a fallen tree. He brought it, with punk wood for kindling. For the next hour, Jack redoubled his struggle to bring flame from this collection. Time and again a small glimmer would catch and die. Jack fought to keep desperation at arm's length.

Toward sunset, Taelon dropped a sodden something on the far side of the fire that Jack had once more failed to start.

"What's that?" Jack asked as he took a deep breath, searched his soul for patience and began again.

"I don't know." Taelon shook his shaggy head. "I don't know how long it's been dead. But it's three days we've been without food. We need to eat if we are to keep our strength."

"Raw?" Jack struck flint to stone. Sparks flew. One of them caught on a strand of moss. Softly Jack blew on it. The strand next to it caught, then the next. Hope glimmered in his soul as Jack nourished the fire like a mother with a new-born.

Taelon hacked at the carcass; a stench filled the clearing. "I'll cut muscle; it lasts longer than the gut." Jack suspected Taelon had eaten worse, but he doubted the USDA would approve.

"Should we cook it?" Jack was dubious as he took the strip of gray meat Taelon offered him.

"We'll cook it over the fire you're tending." Taelon flashed a sardonic smile. Jack nodded, cut a small chunk and placed it in Kaul's mouth. He chewed slowly on it. Jack blew on his fledgling fire and put tinder close to it, praying it would catch. Then he began to gnaw on his meat. It didn't taste all that bad, if you liked aged rare meat.

Taelon cut a half dozen strips before it got too dark. Jack's fire finally caught. The last three strips were roasted over the fire. *God, it tastes good.*

Having spent all day starting a fire, Jack found they had little dry firewood. *Why didn't Taelon spot my mistake?* Neither was thinking very well. It didn't matter why they made mistakes; they needed wood. But stumbling in the dark was dangerous for men so weak. They piled what wood they had on the fire. Jack felt warm for the first time in days, and slept.

He awoke sometime in the night. The fire was out. Now one burned in his stomach. He knew he should throw up what he'd eaten, but he couldn't muster the energy. He felt himself slipping away, either to delirium or unconsciousness. He no longer cared.

In the morning, Taelon tried to rouse him. Jack felt something trickle down his chin. A stinking slime had collected beside him. He knew he must get up. His head throbbed. Every muscle knotted. His stomach revolted, but only cramped. Analytically, Jack knew he had to do something or die. He resigned himself to death as darkness came again.

Jack's head was agony. Taelon was holding it up, forcing water down his parched throat. Jack spit it up. Taelon began again. The water was warm, with just a hint of something in it. Behind Taelon, a tiny fire smoldered. Jack sank down into oblivion again. Maybe this would be the last time.

I'm sorry, Launa. I didn't do as well as you. Maybe I should have taken that survival hike after all, Somewhere in his dream world, a naked Launa glided toward him through the brush.

Around noon, Launa reined in Star, but there was no way to stop the battle between hope and despair that tore at her. The trees along the bluff were few. It was easier to keep an eye on the river, but it was clear they were passing onto the steppe.

"We must turn back." Antia pulled up beside her.

"Not yet!" Brege shrieked, then shut her mouth, looked away.

"It was bad enough that Jack risked everything to enter the horsemen's camp. We cannot put more stew into this broken pot."

Launa rounded on Antia. "Jack risked much to cut you loose from the rope of slavery. Will you risk nothing now?"

The two women eyed each other. Launa waited to see if Antia would settle this with knives, like a horseman, or with words like the People did. Killala rode between them.

"I still have the welts of the horsemen's whips on my back. I would not want to put on a slave rope again."

Launa glanced away, let her eyes rove the flooded plain. What did she owe her troops? What did she owe herself and Jack? What did she owe people yet unborn? Was it time to give up this wild chase? Just thinking that drove the breath from her lungs.

The sun broke through, giving her the best view in days of her surroundings. The flood stretched to the east for miles onto the plains. On this side of the river, she could see two rising smoke plumes: one far out on the plain, obviously hostile, and one closer to the river. A trickle from what might be a third fire wafted from a clump of trees on a drowned island. She studied that one, frowning, then turned to her troops. "This is as far south as I will lead the escort."

"No!" Brege pleaded.

What if they'd come this far and quit within sight of Jack's smoke signal? "I want to see who sits at two of those fires, the one near the river, and the one on the island, if it is a fire. Who will go with me?" *This wasn't the way they taught leadership at the Point, but, damn it, even Travis drew a line in the sand, gave the troops at the Alamo a chance to quit.*

Beside Launa, Sara turned to looked at each trooper. Iron bands around Launa's lungs kept her from breathing until Sara walked her mount in front of Star. "We ride with you."

Fighting tears for this gift these people gave her, she kneed Star. "Let's go."

Antia and Killalla did not stay safely behind.

Launa veered away from the first fire; a herd grazed around it. Isolated by a fairly deep channel, the island presented more of a problem. Worse, there was no smoke rising from it now. Feeling responsible for getting the scouts off the steppe before nightfall, Launa called a halt.

Sara paused beside her. "Let Tomas and me cross to the island. We can search it and catch up with you before dark."

Launa closed her eyes, desperately wishing she could see the future. Not the future six thousand years from now, but tomorrow and next week. Like every other human born to woman, she couldn't. She gave a quick nod, and the two were off.

Sara and Tomas charged the water well up from the island. The channel ran fast. Launa watched them, sitting her horse with the calm she had been told a leader must show before her troops. Inside, her heart, lungs and guts roiled in agony.

Launa glanced around; none of the scouts turned for the northwest, so she dismounted, grateful for a consensus that allowed her to wait here. She'd forgotten to breathe. She tried; it wasn't easy forcing air into her lungs. Breathe one, breathe two, she counted, trying to match a cadence.

The pair made it to the island. Once there, they rode along its length, peering into the birch thicket. They had covered most of the island, and Launa was preparing to give up the last shred of hope, when Sara started waving her arms.

Tomas slid from his horse and dashed into the brush. Launa did not wait for more. She leaped on Star and charged the water, Brege right behind. She heard Merik shouting orders, holding part of the scouts back, sending others into the water. Launa didn't care.

The swim across the channel wasn't as bad as crossing the Bug. She let the current take her, pointing Star toward the end of the island. By the time Launa was ready to urge her mount from the water, Taelon was standing with Sara.

"They're here!" Sara shouted.

Launa threw Star's reins to Sara and dashed into the woods. "Jack. Jack!"

"Here!" Tomas called. Launa burst into a tiny clearing. Beneath a lean-to, under a blanket of leaves, lay a bruised Jack. The stink of every kind of death hung in the air. Jack lay in filth. Kaul, beside him, was a welter of weeping sores.

Launa wanted to throw up. She wanted to grab Jack and hug him and shake him and love him. Now was not the time; she had to get them off the island before dark. Launa ordered the scouts to carry the invalids to the beach. "Sara, ride beside me, keep Jack's head above water. Merik and Tomas, do the same for Kaul."

After all the agony, the crossing was easy. Back on dry land, Launa wanted to get upriver before sunset. "Tie Jack and Kaul to their horses. We need speed."

Taelon shook his head. "These men need rest and healing."

"Damn it, I know." Launa screamed in English.

"I know a place a day's ride, maybe two, from here." Taelon ignored her blast, though the English could not have hidden her meaning. Launa was grateful.

"Lead us."

They were off at a trot.

TWENTY-TWO

ARAKK SCOWLED AT the river in flood before him. It had begun to rain as he crossed the second river from the winter camp. With only one more river to cross, he had ridden hard, but the rivers had risen faster than he could ride. The flood stretched across the plains. Arakk could not even see through the mist to the far bank of the river.

Arakk thought back to the camps he had seen between these two rivers. There were several tents that had made him welcome, that had not humiliated him too badly when first he brought the Stormy Mountain Clan among them. Now they would feast him, looking forward to hunting, plunder and slaves in the spring.

Arakk remembered one clan that hunted the tree people, herding them like cattle before they skewered them on their lances. If he had to spend a moon or two until the river fell, it would be pleasant practice to join in their sport.

Arakk led his warriors off to the northeast.

TWENTY-THREE

TAELON LED NORTHWEST, out onto the steppe. Launa gritted her teeth at the risk, but took it. She had tied the two men's hands and feet around their horse's necks and bellies. The scouts moved at a fast walk, but the pace jarred the two casualties. Semiconscious, they moaned at each step.

Launa saw no herds. Now was the time to claim any luck the Goddess was willing to send their way. They were in trees before dark. As they made a quick camp, Tomas started a fire. While Sara made a broth, Launa examined Jack and Brege tended Kaul, scraping her jars, searching for a last drop of medicine.

Jack looked bad; there were bruises all over his face and body. One leg was deeply gashed. Angry red lines ran up his leg from the wound—blood poisoning. At least none of his head bruises felt squishy to the touch. Taelon said he'd been keeping one eye closed a lot—concussion. He'd been vomiting and had diarrhea. Taelon admitted self-consciously that Jack had been sick since he had shared a carcass the hunter had scavenged—food poisoning, too.

Desperately, Launa wished her first aid training went beyond using the nice stuff in a tank's first aid kit that they hadn't brought with them. Taelon helped her make Jack comfortable, clean him and feed him the soup Sara brought. Beyond that, there was little to do. That night, Launa held

Jack close, trying to keep his cold flesh warm, and cried herself quietly to sleep.

Before dawn, Taelon led them deeper into the trees. "There is a cave I knew. A tribe uses it. In my youth, an old woman knew of herbs; she had a daughter. I pray the tribe is still wise in the ways of plants and herbs."

Launa nodded. With modern medicine, Jack's problems would be a minor inconvenience; now they were life-threatening. Not only did she have to rely on what this century could offer, but she had to pray she could find it. Concentrating on Jack's problem, she almost didn't register the full impact of Taelon's words. "These hunters do not like horsemen."

"Yes. But if we ride fast, they may hear my words before their arrows fly."

Again Launa knew she was taking risks. She prayed it worked. There was one thing she could do to increase her chances. "Everybody, get rid of the helmets. We are in trees, let us not look like horsemen."

Helmets went into bags. Taelon nodded. "I had forgotten."

Launa managed a smile. "A good commander remembers the small stuff."

They kept the horses to the fastest walk they could, hardly stopping to rest. The sun was down when Taelon led them through a dense wood to the foot of a hill. Halfway up, a rock outcropping marked a cave. In the gathering dusk, a large fire painted the opening. Taelon dismounted.

Launa searched the area. "I do not see anyone."

"They heard us coming and hid. I will go to the fire and see if anyone comes to talk to me."

Taelon had picked up some firewood at the last break. Now he took it uphill. Squatting down, he warmed his hands and fed the fire. He glanced around the dark. A bent woman shuffled from the cave and settled beside him. They talked for several minutes; then she laughed and called out. A gray-haired man in a bear cloak stepped from the cave; men slipped from trees. Taelon greeted the man in the bear cloak; they embraced.

"Launa, bring Kaul and Jack up."

Launa cut the bonds that held Jack to Windrider. "Tomas, you take charge of the horses. Sara, help me with Jack." The two women carried Jack. Brege and Merik brought Kaul.

They laid the men down by the fire. By its dim light, the old woman examined them. "Bad, very bad, the men who did this. I must get my things." She limped into the cave, returning in a moment with a woven basket. From it she took two small pots. One she handed to Launa, pointing at the gash on Jack's leg. "Wash it, then put this in the wound."

Launa moistened a cloth from a skin of water they had drawn from a clear spring. Tomorrow she would boil water; this would have to do for tonight. Semiconscious, Jack winced when she touched his wound. Sara moved to hold him down, but he had already sunk back into a stupor. Launa finished with the rag. The pot contained a poultice that smelled of wintergreen. She applied it thickly, then turned to the woman.

"Have I done this right?" She got a nod and gave the pot back to the woman, who began coating Kaul. It did not go nearly far enough.

"Tomorrow, you will come with me into the woods to find more." She stood up. "These men are too weak to sleep in the night air. Carry them into the cave."

Gently, six people each picked up Kaul and Jack. Launa held Jack's head. They followed the wise woman into the cave where a second fire gave light. The woman led to the left. Drawing aside a curtain of skins, she pointed the way into a small alcove. The two men were gently laid on a bed of reeds. The woman clapped her hands. Two younger women ran from the fire, warm rocks held out in front of them with sticks.

Launa sent Sara back to the horses to get linens and blankets; then she and Brege stepped inside the niche. It was pitch dark. A moment later, the gray-haired man brought a clay bowl with a flaming wick.

Between the heated stones and the three women's body

warmth, the alcove warmed. Sara returned and helped Launa carefully cover Jack with linen, then blankets. After Sara left, Launa settled next to Jack prepared for a long night. When the next batch of warm stones was slipped past the curtain, the wise woman sprinkled them with something. They gave off pleasant-smelling fumes. Launa found herself growing lethargic. She tried to find a comfortable sitting position.

When Launa awoke, the curtains were open and morning light streamed into the cave. Jack slept fitfully. The wise woman motioned Launa and a just-waking Brege to come with her.

As they left, the woman let the skins fall back in place, darkening the sickroom once more. She picked up three baskets, handing one to each woman. "Your men will sleep. We must gather roots and leaves to make ready for when they awake."

Launa and Brege walked on either side of the wise woman as she shared her wisdom. "I am Glengish. I know the wisdom of the glens and brooks, the gifts the Goddess gives to free us of ills. Let us pluck them fresh, so that having been close to the Goddess this morning, they may bring more of her power to the sick."

On the edge of a meadow, Glengish pointed out several plants. Launa was surprised; one of them was parsley, the stuff restaurants put on her plate and she ignored. The other was a green-leafed plant that smelled of mint. The small red berries caught Launa's eye. Glengish pulled it up and handed the root to Launa. This was where the wintergreen smell came from. Launa had always gotten it from a bottle of alcohol or a tube of muscle rub. She shrugged; Maria had just started teaching her the plants of Wyoming. Now Launa was learning again in the moist woods of Europe. Glengish dug several roots in the meadow, found more in the woods, finally collected the last along a creek.

As they returned to the fire by the cave, Taelon brought a deer and began skinning it. He left the mess beside them. Glengish smiled a thank-you and stripped a handful of fat

from the deer to warm in a pot. Sara brought the five ceramic jars the scouts carried. Glengish delighted in their
hardness. Launa showed her how it could be put directly in
the fire to warm water. The wise woman did not understand
that, but was content to use four jars for her work and leave
the largest one for boiling.

Glengish used a pestle and stone to crush the parsley and
a root together. "This will clean the wounds. That is why my
mother called it woundroot."

"The warmed water is for washing the wounds. Could we
add those to it after it has bubbled?" Launa didn't know
what boiling would do to the medicinal properties of the
root, but the water had to be boiled. Enough river water had
gone into Jack's wounds to muster an army of bugs. Launa
felt as nervous and ignorant as she had before her first battle—and hated it.

Glengish pursed her lips thoughtfully. "Yes. I do not
know why you heat it, but I know you do not intend to scald
your man."

Launa accepted the approval. She was a battle commander, not a combat surgeon. And even though it was Jack who
lay sick, she could not be everything for him. She watched
as the woman added the other herbs to the melted fat to
make a poultice for the wounds. Later, after the water had
boiled and been taken from the fire, Launa helped Glengish
add the mixture of greens. Then the woman pressed nuts,
dripping their oil into the water.

Glengish stirred the concoction, then called to a young
woman. "Make a broth, slight of meat, but rich in barley.
The men will need it if they awake soon. Also, mix some
bark tea to take away their pain. I will tell you after I care
for them if you need to add sleeping seeds to it."

The young woman nodded and obeyed.

Glengish and Brege picked up jugs and headed for the
cave. Launa collected the last two and, like a soldier marching into battle, climbed after them. She was as ready to fight
for Jack's life with these new weapons as she was with her
knife.

Glengish drew aside the skins. Both men groaned with the

light, yet neither surfaced to wakefulness. Brege and Launa cleaned wounds, dipping their cloths in the large jar of boiled water. After a moment, Glengish took an extra cloth and helped Brege. With the skins drawn aside, fresh air as well as light entered the nook. The stink of the wounds began to dissipate.

Still, Launa's nose was all she needed to know the men were in trouble. Jack's pulse came slow and uneven. His sweat stank, and his wound was warm to the touch. Launa moved quickly to clean him and settle the cover back over him. Glengish stopped her. "That gash festers. We must drain it."

"Let me clean this knife in fire."

Glengish frowned at Launa's words but did not stop her. Launa heated her bronze blade and returned when it had cooled.

"Hold your man. He will not lie still for this."

Launa took Jack's shoulders. He twisted in her grasp as the wise woman sliced into his leg. White pus drained while Launa held him still, shocked at how weak he was in her grasp. Glengish wiped the wound clean, washing it again with the boiled water, then applied a poultice. Jack stiffened, then seemed to faint away. Launa again checked his pulse.

Glengish nodded. "You know much of the wisdom I will pass to my children. Your mother was a wise woman." Launa saw no reason to explain that a crusty master sergeant had taught her scout troop their first aid.

As Jack settled into a deep sleep, Launa called to Tomas. "Bring me my sleeping blankets. I will trade them for Jack's and wash his."

In a moment, Tomas was back with Launa's as well as his own, which he offered to Brege. As soon as he had the used ones, he excused himself. "I'll wash these." Launa smiled her gratitude.

As the man left, Glengish fixed Brege with a stony gaze. "When is the baby due?"

Brege glanced up, then away, unable to meet Glengish's eyes. "Not for a long time, four or five moons."

"And how long have you been bleeding?"

Launa sat back. For the first time in too long, she examined Brege. There was blood on her leggings. Brege swiped at it. "It is nothing. Just blood from my father."

"Then you will not mind if I examine you."

"No!" Brege's eyes darted about as if she were a rabbit seeking a place to flee.

"Shall I call men to hold you down?"

Brege's eyes flared at the threat of involving men in this most personal of a woman's experiences; then she surrendered. "Where would you have me?"

"I have a place, deep in the womb of the Goddess." The two women turned and went deeper into the cave.

Many minutes later, Glengish returned alone and fixed Launa with a disapproving glare. "How long have you let that child take no thought of herself?"

Launa accepted the rebuke. The Book said the commander was responsible for his troops. Of course, the Book hadn't been written yet to cover a command and control lash-up like this one. "That woman has a will that does not easily bend to another's. This is her father. He did as he would, and she did as she would." Launa would have loved to add "I was just along for the ride," but didn't. For the last five tragic days, she had been in command—nobody had been in control.

Glengish grimaced. "The woman is proud, but her pride may cost her the child she carries. She has heard the wisdom of my words and will stay away to care for the life within her." The wise woman turned to leave. "We will care for these two."

For the next two days, as fevers rose, Launa and Glengish bathed Jack and Kaul, cleaned them, breathed the same fetid air. Others kept clean blankets and warm rocks coming. Brege was nowhere to be seen. When Launa had a moment to whisper the question to Sara, she shrugged.

"Merik and the men built a hut for Brege and him. Brege does not come out of it. We take her meals to her. I have never seen one with child so unhappy."

Launa was surprised at how happy she was caring for Kaul and Jack. Both were unconscious; she tended for them as babies. Yet a closeness grew in her for these men, one her love, the other the man she admired more than any other she had met in her life.

She respected Kaul for what he had done, and she loved Jack for the loyalty that carried him in Kaul's footsteps. Her heart, not her head, thought for her, but she could not condemn herself for it. This was not the land and time of her birth. The rules had not yet been made. The Book had not been written. These years were pregnant with possibilities. She felt the urgent need to give birth to them.

Every day, Glengish and Launa went in search of more herbs to make into ointments and poultices. Once a day, Launa smelled the fresh air, felt the gentle wind, tasted the cool water. Glengish insisted on this. "How can we bring new life from the Goddess to these who struggle with death, if we do not taste of life also?"

On the third day, the wisdom of Glengish's holistic approach won. Jack's fever broke. His first words were "I'm hungry," followed by "Where am I?" and finally "I love you." Launa was content to be a close third.

Kaul improved as well, though he did not join the lucid.

With Jack awake, Launa examined their tactical situation. Before she asked, Taelon offered to take a detachment west to see the next river. He, Sara, Tomas, Antia and Killala with several of the hunters left early and returned at nightfall.

Taelon immediately came to Launa in the sickroom. "The river is high, bigger than the one that almost killed us. We cannot pass while its belly is so swollen."

Jack gave Launa a weak smile. "I guess we stay. If we can't cross, neither can the horsemen." He was asleep in a moment.

Taelon looked down on Jack as one might at a son, then motioned Launa from the room. Outside he squatted by the fire. "The river is in flood, but that is not all we saw."

Launa sucked in her breath and waited.

"As we were returning, two hands of riders came in view. They gave chase and, though I had to push Antia myself, we fled into a thicket the hunters knew. Killala said she knew one—Arakk, the red-haired chief who was at River Bend and again at the camp. He demanded from Kaul to know where his warriors were and let out much blood when Kaul would not answer him."

"Such a one is near here?"

Taelon nodded.

Launa sat back on her heels. If Arakk came hunting, could they take him? She didn't know. But if there was a swollen river between Launa and Tall Oaks, the same river was between Arakk and his target. Launa weighed the odds and placed her bet.

"Taelon, say nothing to Jack or Kaul about this. But warn the hunters that horsemen may come into their woods. Warn everyone to be watchful for horsemen."

"I have already. The hunters do not fear the horsemen in the woods. This is their home, and they know how to lay traps for horses. I think they would like to have them come here."

Two nights later, Kaul's fever broke. Glengish frowned as he slipped into his first calm sleep, her eyes settling on the flat place of Kaul's blanket where a man should bulge. "Does he know what has been done to him?"

Launa shook her head.

Glengish pursed her lips. "His body will heal better if it is not vexed by a mind with horrible knowledge. I will make a potion steeped in certain seeds. Let him sleep a while longer."

Three days Kaul slept under the drugged teas they dripped into his mouth. Glengish studied his wounds each morning and evening. Finally she shook her head. "It is time for him to awake. Let us give him only water tonight."

Next morning Launa was busy spooning soup down a very hungry Kaul. Jack looked better too, but made only one try at sitting up. Glengish warned him to lie still, and he did.

It was Launa who drew back the blankets and cleaned Kaul's wounds on that first morning he was in his senses. As she bathed his groin, his nostrils flared. He made a feeble search for what was not there.

"I had hoped it was only a fevered dream." His choked

138 · Mike Moscoe

words wrenched at Launa's heart. She bit her lip, desperate for some word of comfort.

Jack reached across the space between them, took up Kaul's hand from where it had collapsed. "I could bring out your life, wise one. I could bring out your heart. If what I brought out was not a man, I know not the meaning of the word."

Kaul stared at the cave roof. After several long minutes, he began to mutter. "My father said that a man's work may be more than a man can do, but not too much for a man to try. I have lived ready for death to take all that I am. But now, for death to take this and leave me breathing." Kaul began to weep.

Launa went to him, held his head in her lap, washed the tears as they fell. Jack lay back on his bed, watching her. Launa rocked back and forth with Kaul, feeling his grief, blending her tears with his, softly keening his loss.

Glengish had removed herself from this scene, leaving it to the three. It was some time before she returned.

Days moved quickly as the men recovered. In a week, Jack could walk in the woods with Launa as she gathered herbs.

The next week, Launa cut two quarterstaffs and tossed him one. "Ready to give me a workout?"

Jack made a swipe at her. She parried easily. He stumbled and fell avoiding her thrust. Jack laughed. "Remember how mad you got the first time we worked out and I suggested you take it easy because the altitude in Wyoming might cause you trouble?"

"Yes."

"Well, I won't be a bit upset if you go easy on me."

She did.

It was harder on Kaul. The cauterized scar between his legs made walking stiff. Both Taelon and Glengish feared if he did not exercise, he would lose the suppleness he needed. In agony, Kaul walked the woods with Launa.

"How is Brege?" Kaul asked.

Launa had expected that. "She bleeds."

Kaul blanched; Launa hastened on. "Glengish feared for her baby when she tended you long hours. Glengish sent her to bed and now all goes well with mother and child."

Kaul breathed a sigh, then attempted a smile. "Glengish sends me to walk and my daughter to bed. Someone should tell that old woman to mind her own spinning."

"And what would you do, my proud Speaker . . ." Launa stopped too late. She had meant to remind him of his strength.

"I will do nothing. What I did was nothing. It was worse than nothing. There was a man there. He knew of the riders who died before the tree last summer. He wants blood. And now he knows to come to Tall Oaks for that blood." Kaul's words went from slow, to rushed, to slow again, like a clock that only guessed the time.

Launa stepped in front of him, stood nose to nose. "What you did was brave. You faced the killers in their own council. You challenged them to grow, to change, to find a new way. Yes, they did not. I knew they would not, and your heart must have told you the same. But you were man enough to try. You were man enough to say the words that needed to be said. Now you will be man enough to say the words that remain to be said."

Kaul looked down at his flat loincloth. "Am I man enough to do anything now?"

"Yes you are, goddamn you." Launa knew her temper was long gone and she ought to take ten deep breaths and think carefully on what she said next. She didn't.

"The People will have to kill many horsemen before this is over. We need you to show them the way to be men who can kill and men who can love. You have tried to show the horsemen there is another way—they wouldn't listen. Now someone has to show the People there is another way, or they will die. They will listen to you. And following after you, they can find the way that Jack and I have not." Launa knew she was saying too much. Today the sky shone blue; the air smelled warm. The earth was coming back to life. She wanted that life.

"Kaul, you have never asked where Jack and I came from.

With you we have journeyed far from Tall Oaks, using horses and logs. Jack and I have traveled from tomorrows so many seasons away that you cannot count them." Launa waited for a reaction.

Kaul nodded. "There are many strange shadows around you and Jack. So they are shadows of tomorrows yet to be seen."

Launa searched Kaul's face, but saw only acceptance of her story. "The people who sent Jack and me here never found a way to face the horsemen. We learned to kill them, and doing that, we became too much like them. In the end, they killed all except us. We came to you to find another way. And you showed us." Launa's memory raced over the last months. At the Point, they taught her how to make decisions. These people knew nothing of modern methods and procedures, yet Kaul had naturally followed a process all the experts would have given high marks.

"Kaul, you listened to Antia. When her words failed to light a path, you sent others to bring more words. The council listened to everyone, and then chose a path that let people walk different paths together."

Launa remembered Samath building the soldiers' long-house, the old man suggesting berry bushes. Even people who were against the soldiers had helped. She had received presents at the winter feast from Hanna's adherents. In high school she'd been at bull sessions between military advocates and the peace movement. One group sworn pacifists, the other sworn to defend all, yet the two sides could hardly talk to each other. They damn near went to war. It seemed funny to Launa at the time. Now she knew the flaw and the alternative.

"You not only listened to those close to you, you listened to strangers like Jack and me and even traveled far to include the Horse People in your words."

Kaul looked at her, puzzled at her words. "But that is the way of the People."

Launa stamped her foot. *How do you make a saint see his goodness?* "Would Hanna let her ears hear what you heard? Your ears listened to Jack. Your eyes saw the difference between the wolf that hunts the sheep and the shepherd who hunts the wolf. Your heart heard. Your heart can show the way. Not from death to death until all are dead, but from death to life until all may live. Do you think we followed you across the steppe because we wanted a pleasant ride?"

Kaul grimaced at her sarcasm.

Launa had to smile. "We need you. More than water and sun, we need you. You can show us what none of our wise men saw. After all we have traveled, you cannot walk away from us."

Kaul stood thoughtfully for a moment. Then his face broke into a soft smile. "Glengish says I must walk. Will you step from my path so I may do as the wise woman said?"

For the next hour, Kaul shared his delight in birds and butterflies with Launa. With each step, he grew more alive.

Each day, after Launa worked out with Jack, she would collect Kaul for his walk. Each day, the workout grew harder and the walk longer.

The day Glengish released Brege and Kaul for travel, Taelon put the question to all the hunters. Would they travel to Tall Oaks? If they came, he offered them food, good hunting, and a chance to kill horsemen when they came for blood. The council went long into the night. Next morning, the troop started teaching the hunters to ride. Several older folks preferred to walk. The brisk pace they set did not slow the mounted.

The trip passed quickly. The swollen rivers didn't slow them down; the hunters knew the trails and fords. Launa's spirits began to rise. She was getting her troop back in one piece. There had been times when she'd almost given up hope.

TWENTY-FOUR

WHEN THE WORD came that the river was tame enough to ride, the chieftain announced a feast in Arakk's honor. All that day they hunted the deer, even giving chase when they spied one of the giant cattle at a distance. That one eluded them, but many deer were killed to roast over a glowing fire and much fermented milk was placed before Arakk. This was good.

The last two moons had been good, and the memory of this time would wash away the recollections of other days. Still, Arakk wondered about one thing.

When they hunted the tree men, they had seen a hand of riders, riders who disappeared into the forest like shadows. Such was not the ways of the Horse People.

Hanging over everything was a strangeness, like a thunderstorm out of season. When the spring came and the clans gathered to cleanse the steppe of the next collection of huts and walkers, Arakk would call on all his skill and cunning. He would have many warriors. He would lead them with the craft of a fox.

TWENTY-FIVE

THE SUN WAS low when Launa signaled a halt for a break. Jack was glad. His leg hurt like hell. His hands hardly had the strength to grasp the reins.

Glengish and her people huddled for a moment, then announced their intent to make camp for the night.

Taelon yawned. "I will sleep tonight with these hunters. But the rest of you may want to be home in Tall Oaks."

As exhausted as Jack was, he still felt the hunger for home. He only hoped he could stay on Windrider long enough to make it.

Launa did a quick eyeball check of her troops. "They look ready to press on. Think you can make it, Hon?"

Jack nodded.

Beside him, Brege shook her head and slid from her mount. Merik was at her side in a moment, fussing about her in the way Jack remembered of expectant fathers no matter what the age. The expectant mother swatted at him. "Nothing is broken. My back is killing me. I am tired and tomorrow is soon enough." Nevertheless, when Glengish came, Brege went with her for her nightly checkup.

Launa ordered a trot. Beside Jack, Kaul gritted his teeth. Whether he grimaced because of the pace or what lay ahead, he said nothing.

A half moon lit the way when they waded the stream

below Tall Oaks. Launa dismissed the troop, but Sara hung back. "I will take your horses." Tomas stayed with her.

Jack half dismounted, half fell off Windrider. For a moment, Kaul's eyes swept the town; then he too struggled from his mount. Jack was glad to hand Windrider over to Sara. She and Tomas led the horses away, leaving the three alone.

They stood, unsure of what to do next. Kaul cleared his throat. "I will go to Lasa. Tomorrow morning, please come to the Sanctuary?"

"Would you like us to go now?" Launa made the offer, but Jack heard the catch in her voice. What could they say to Lasa?

Kaul's eyes sank to his feet. In the dim light, Jack saw tears. "Tomorrow is soon enough." He whispered and walked for home and the woman he loved.

Launa came to Jack, took his hand, squeezed it as they watched Kaul go. Only when he disappeared behind a house did Launa turn and pull aside the deerskin flap of their home. "Oh, to sleep in my own bed."

Jack sighed. He could agree with that.

The house was cold. They slipped out of their clothes, filthy from the ride's dust, and quickly slid between blankets and soft skins. There was no need for the second bed tonight. Launa held him close, almost painfully tight. She made no move for more, nor did he. The thought of Lasa's bed haunted Jack. The unfulfillable yearnings of that Penelope at the return of her brave Ulysses drained Jack of desire.

In short time, exhaustion gave him rest.

The pain in Jack's leg woke him at first light. For several minutes, he listened to the early-rising birds. Shakespeare had Juliet tell time by the lark's first chirps. The things premodern people knew that he had yet to learn.

He lay flat on his back, holding his leg straight out. It hurt less that way. Launa wasn't the only one who needed to read Maria's book on herbs. There was so much to do and so little time to do it. Jack tried to master the fear rising in him.

He had been sick. He *was* sick. His mind was confused; he couldn't concentrate. He missed important things. *The horsemen are coming and I'm not worth a damn,* he thought.

"You awake, love?" Launa rolled on her side, facing him. He felt her warmth along his bare flanks. Another day, his need would have been urgent. Not this morning. Her touch might yet kindle passion, but her fingers did not rove his flesh.

How many had been castrated with Kaul? Jack yearned to feel the power of his sexuality . . . and feared it would never rise again. "I guess I'm awake."

Launa lay back down, her eyes on the ceiling. "We've got a lot to do today. I need to survey the wall, see how far it's come. I'll have to inspect the legion, check them out. If the wall's not done, we'll have a difficult ratio of space to forces."

Jack listened to her rattle off the problems. Damn, she was good. She'd better be; if the horsemen didn't give him time to get in shape, she'd have to tell him what to do. But even he knew what was first today, and what she was avoiding. He waited for her to slow down. "Launa, we've got to see Lasa and Kaul."

She sighed. "I know. How long do you think we can wait?"

"I've heard people walking by already. Folks are up."

"I guess we should be too." Launa took several deep breaths, then pushed the covers aside. They took their time dressing, each lost in thought, and finished at the same time.

"God, I hate visiting widows," Launa whispered as Jack pulled aside the deerskin door.

"Only this one's man isn't dead."

"He just feels that way." Launa squared her shoulders and marched for the center of town. Jack hurried to catch up, trying not to limp; already his leg hurt. Launa must have noticed; she slowed. He was grateful and angry at the same time.

At the longhouse, several elderly people gathered around the stoves, warming themselves. Blossom met them. "Mother and father are still in their room."

"We will come back later." Launa turned to go, but the girl shook her head, large brown eyes fixed on Launa.

"Mother told me you would come and you should go to her." The girl led them across the long room to the small doorway. She pulled aside the white deer skin with painted blue swirls.

Jack stooped and followed Launa into Lasa's bedroom. A large bed stood against the far wall. In it, a couple huddled together under several blankets. Jack stood silently with Launa, but their coming had been noted. Lasa and Kaul sat up, their backs ramrod straight against the wall behind them. The blankets settled, covering their waists. Their eyes were red; both had wept. Yet Lasa and Kaul sat as proudly as reigning monarchs. They hurt, but faced the world not with defiance, but a stronger power—they and the world were one, and right, and nothing could change that. It made Jack shiver.

They gazed at each other, no one willing to break the quiet. Finally, Lasa gestured. "Would you sit?"

Launa and Jack shared the offered bench. Lasa nodded at Jack. "Kaul told me how you entered the winter camp to bring him out. I thank you with all my heart for bringing back my man."

Jack nodded back. Before he could say anything, Kaul threw back the covers and began pacing the floor. Last summer, Jack had become used to seeing Kaul naked in the hunt or before a crowd. Now, watching him striding so powerfully naked, not only of clothes but of his manhood, the images of power and weakness were juxtaposed. Jack was confused, as if he were watching a rabbit make war on a lion . . . and win.

Kaul stopped pacing, held his arms out to his consort, confronting her with what he no longer had. "They did not bring back a man."

Lasa swallowed, her face pale. "That is not true."

"Yes, it is. In the dark, we could pretend like children. But the light comes. You can see as well as I can—as well as anyone. I have nothing that Speaks for the Bull."

Lasa shook her head, a quick, angry shake. "How can you

have a heart that takes in so much, eyes that see so far, yet be so blind?"

"It was not my eyes they took." Kaul words were gentle, meeting her anger with soft bitterness.

"But it is your eyes and your heart that I need." Lasa blinked back tears. Kaul went to her, sat beside her, held her head as she sobbed softly against his chest. Beside Jack, Launa reached out a hand to him, took his, clasped it to her heart. Jack swallowed his helplessness, awkward before this tragedy.

For a long time, Kaul held Lasa, rocking gently back and forth. Long after her sobbing stopped, Kaul spoke low. "He who Speaks for the Bull, he who would be consort to She who Speaks for the Goddess, must bring joy and pleasure and children with her. That is something I cannot do."

Lasa pulled back to sat by herself in the center of the bed. Kaul stood and backed a step away from the bed. "Most beloved of consorts, I would that I could be of service to you."

"Kaul, it was in service of me that you went forth. It was in service of me that you return so injured." Lasa spoke her words softly, but nothing hid the hard strength that flowed in them. "From last night until the day I return to the Goddess, I will miss the service you can no longer render. But, I have need of your other services."

Kaul blinked; his brow questioned.

Lasa smiled, half pain, half love. "Most beloved of consorts, these strangers say that a new path awaits the People. After gazing upon you, my heart knows that is so. But to walk a new path is to face many crossroads. How will I know which way to go at each of them?" Her smile became sorrowful. "I am no fool to think that the Goddess will put words in my mouth. I will need the words of farseeing eyes, of great hearts, if I am to find the new path of the Goddess. I need your eyes, I need your heart, here, close to mine." Her hand went to her breast.

Kaul gnawed his lower lip. He glanced at Jack and Launa, then back to Lasa. "As ever, my love, your words are full of wisdom. If I could, I would follow after you. But all I need do is walk the streets of Tall Oaks, and questions will rise. We face death, my love. It is not a time for half the People to doubt that the Goddess walks with you."

Lasa nodded. "And why should they? The weather is still cold and you have been hurt. You need not prance about in nothing, like a boy seeking to impress the first girl of his heart. Dress warmly. The spring celebration is done. I sat most matronly by myself and burned with hunger for your touch as others reminded the Goddess of the fertility we needed."

"And what of children?"

Lasa reached for his hand and guided it to her swelling belly. "We both knew this little one would be my final gift to the Goddess. Five springs from now, when we are well along this new way, another woman may sit in my place. But this little one that kicks so strongly already has a father. She has no need for another. A man is not a father just because he plants a seed. A father hoes the field, nurtures the seed, helps it grow straight and tall." She smiled up at Kaul. "This little one has need of her father to bounce her on his knee, to hug her, to show her the path of wisdom and power in the Goddess. No one can make you less a father for this last one under my heart."

"We will have to place this before the People sometime."

Lasa turned to Launa. "The horsemen are coming soon?"

"When the bellies of the rivers are no longer swollen, they will come." Launa spoke as if she saw death already.

Lasa threw back the covers, slid from the bed and stretched, innocent in her nakedness. Watching her, Jack felt a stirring. God, she was beautiful in her pregnant radiance. Her breasts must have been small in her youth. Even after nursing four children and swelling for this fifth, they were as firm as many of the young girls Jack had seen last summer. Her figure, even with an expanded belly, showed solid muscle. For so long, Jack had seen the woman of command. Now he saw past to the woman who commanded. She pulled Kaul to her, kissed him, letting her passion flow in her fingers as she played with his buttock.

Kaul kissed back. "As ever, my love, you feel good to the touch."

"Good. You have loved me in many ways, and you will continue to love me, and I you." Lasa reached for a robe and covered her passion. Jack swallowed male awareness of her beauty like a callow boy. Robed, she turned to Launa and Jack. The lover was gone. The imperium now addressed them. "The horsemen come to guest at our table. We will prepare a feast for them. I understand they like death. We will place a heaping bowl of it before them."

While the four ate a hasty meal, Lasa sent word to the cohort leaders to gather at the east end of town. Before starting for the meeting, Kaul put a long bearskin cloak on over his loincloth. It fell to his knees, fully covering his middle.

They made slow progress as they walked for the edge of town. People greeted Kaul with shouts, asking about his journey. He shrugged gently. "I am back. Let us assemble together."

From everywhere, townspeople joined them, including many who had held to peaceful thoughts through the winter. When they reached the edge of town, Launa greeted her cohort commanders. Lasa and Kaul climbed a mound that should have been a wall, and Kaul signaled for silence.

"The brave escort traveled with me to the winter camp of the horsemen. I entered alone, as I was pledged to do. I shared words with the men who speak for the horsemen. I told of the many gifts of the Goddess. I invited them to gather their people in council and search for a way that we might live in harmony." In the crowd, heads nodded, confident that matters had gone well.

Kaul shook his head. "Before I could finish talking, the speaker for the horsemen struck me on the mouth." Kaul pointed to the healing cuts on his face. A shock wave swept through his listeners. "They tied me up and took a knife to my skin." Kaul raised both his hands above his head, and his cloak fell down his arms. The healing wounds of legs and arms stood out stark in the morning light, red scars cutting swaths through the blue of his sacred tattoos. The crowd fell into a stunned silence.

"They did not want to hear my words, only my screams of agony." Kaul brought his arms down. Flint-hard eyes swept the people. "They have no ears for wisdom, only for blood. My heart says they want our blood. I say give them their own."

In the crowd, people turned to each other, talked. Jack caught few words in the rumble.

Samath stepped from the throng and climbed to join Kaul and Lasa on the mound. People grew quiet. Jack held his breath.

Samath's eyes swept the crowd. "You all know the words I shared in council. All winter I prayed to know the way of the Goddess. All winter I centered my heart on the good and joyous gifts She sends to us." Samath turned to Kaul, rested a hand on his shoulder. "I sent Kaul forth with my prayers, and I know they entered the horsemen's camp with him." Samath reached out for Kaul's hand, drew his arm out of the cloak. His fingers softly traveled the tortured flesh.

"What they did to Kaul, they did to me. Now I see that my eyes saw more from my wants than with clear vision. I was wrong. Lasa, I say there is only one path for the people to follow. What must I do?" A cheer swept through the crowd like fire. Jack allowed himself a smile. They'd paid a damn high price to get this second fire going. Maybe it was worth it.

Then he swallowed hard as Ballda, who had once Spoken for the Goddess, hobbled to the foot of the pile, waving her cane. As she turned to face the crowd, Hanna came to her side.

"No, no, no!" Bellda scolded them as she might a child. Though her voice was but a whisper, everyone fell silent. Not one word was lost. "We cannot walk in this way. I will not live among those who will tread this path. It leads only to death." Out of breath, she fell silent. Heads in the crowd nodded. Jack trembled as this flood swept out to douse his fire. Could she?

Lasa shook her head. "No one may tell others the path for

their feet. We must not drag you down our path. Yet neither should you stand in ours." She who now Spoke for the Goddess looked from face to face, then to the earth and sky as if silently seeking their guidance.

Beside her, Kaul cleared his throat. "There is the village we built for the woodcutters."

Samath nodded in agreement. "We built it strong. The houses should be comfortable. It would serve well this wise old woman and those who follow her."

"Let it be so," Lasa intoned with the authority of the Goddess.

Masin stepped forward, shaking his head ruefully. "My heart wonders at the wisdom of my consort, but I will go with her. We will need some heads with less gray hair to help us."

"Let all who wish go with you. You go with our blessings." The Goddess was still in Lasa's voice.

Hanna, ponderous with child, an immovable boulder, addressed Lasa but turned to face the crowd. Jack suspected she was less intent on speaking to Lasa. "My daughter will be born in the home of her ancestors. My home is here. I will not be cast from it." Her words were sharp as nettles.

Lasa seemed struck dumb by Hanna's refusal to go. She looked to Kaul. He bit his lower lip, at a loss.

Jack found words on his tongue. Should he share them? Was it his place now? When no one helped Lasa, he spoke into the tension. "Let all follow the path the Goddess shows to their eyes and heart. For a winter all have walked their different path in harmony. Can we not do it in the warmth of the spring the Goddess sends us?"

A broad grin spread across Lasa's face. "Yes, we can. Let us walk in harmony where we will. Those who choose to go may go. Those who choose to stay will stay. Those who would meet the horsemen with arrows and spears may prepare. All, I fervently hope, will pray to the Goddess that She will be gracious."

Hanna tensed beside Jack. The look of anger she cast him did not strike him as all that peace-loving. "It was easy," she hissed, "to walk together when there was yet hope we would walk the way of peace. I prayed Kaul would be blessed with peace. Yet I hear that your bloody deeds of last summer went before him, poisoned the horsemen against us before he arrived."

Jack wondered who in the scouts had been talking to whom. He hadn't ordered secrecy. How careful had they kept the secret of the full extent of Kaul's wounds? Since Hanna had not announced it, he guessed it was still known to only the right few.

The woman stepped closer to Jack, her voice rising. "Now even Kaul says we have no way but the path of blood. I say no. I will always say no. We must not, now or ever. Enough blood has already been spilled." Beside Hanna, Ballda moaned, seemed faint. Hanna turned her attention to her mother. The People opened a path respectfully for them to pass. Slowly, haltingly, with the older woman leaning heavily on the younger, they went.

Launa turned to Lasa. "Oh, Lady, we have worked through the winter to train the legion to stand between us and death. Please do not let any who have trained through the winter go away."

Lasa let out a deep breath, her eyes on Hanna. She glowered back. When finally Lasa spoke, her voice was the most tentative Jack had ever heard it. "I see the wisdom in your words, you who carry the spear. Yet it goes against our most ancient wisdom. I see well that we must walk a new path." Lasa wrung her hands. "But there are some ways that are more sacred than life. If we forget how to walk with each other, how can we walk any path?" Lasa shook her head. "No. Let each look into her heart and decide the path for her feet. I will not use rope to tie the feet of our people. I would be no better than the horsemen."

Hanna snorted. "I am glad our Speaker still remembers some of the ways of the Goddess." She turned and left. Quite a few people went with her, including at least two legionnaires.

Jack knew Lasa was right. He also knew time was short. Six thousand years from now, he had wondered why the Old Europeans did so poorly when they faced the horsemen. He prayed he wasn't seeing why. Lasa interrupted his thoughts when she signaled for Launa and him to join the three on the crumbling wall.

Disappointed at his weakness, Jack struggled up the mound. Launa got there first and turned to face the People, her people. She swelled with pride; she was home. So was he. He tried to taste that joy as Launa began to speak. "The horsemen will come for us soon. My heart tells me they will come before the moon shines again as it did last night. Once I knew how we would fight them, with wall and pikes and arrows." She looked to where the wall crumbled, filling the ditch. "The rain was not kind to our wall. I must look at what we have and count those who remain with the legion. I will meet with those who lead the cohorts and we will walk the wall together."

The assembled people accepted that. The crowd dissolved, people going their separate ways in small groups. Jack listened to snatches of conversation as tongues busily digested the news. He heard more confusion and uncertainty than he liked.

As the women walked the perimeter, Jack hobbled along. He didn't feel much like a soldier and he didn't see much he liked. In most places, the wall had simply melted into the ditch. The one good sign was the brambles. They had survived the mudslides and thrived. In most places they might be enough to discourage horses. The wall petered out close to the west edge of town.

Launa shook her head. "Both ends of town are wide open. The river is the only defense to the north. Think it's enough?"

Jack shrugged, unable to organize a clear thought.

Launa squatted and began drawing an outline of Tall Oaks in the dust. "I had planned to trap the horsemen between a wall on each side of the main street and two walking walls of pikes. Now we have no wall. Jack, any ideas?"

He frowned as she handed him the stick, struggling with the mush his brain had been since he surfaced from fever and concussion. "The best we can do now is keep the horsemen out of town. We will kill many, but it will not be as it was at the tree last summer. When the horsemen see they cannot kill us all, they will turn and flee. But they will come back."

Launa nodded. "That will have to do. For this defense, we will need as many bows and slings as pikes." Launa stood. "Brege, you lead the archers and slingers. Pick from Antia's pikes those who can use a bow or sling until you have an equal number. Tell Das we must have the better bowmen from his axes. We must count on arrows and stones to drive the horsemen away."

Launa scratched her head and turned to Jack. "Time's short. It's not smart to change an army's organization just before a battle. But it's stupid to stay with an obsolete battle plan."

Jack nodded. What more could he say?

But Launa didn't seem to be listening. Her eyes had gone vacant as she gazed over the field. She squinted to the east, examining the hills the horsemen would ride over. "Lasa, I see something. Perhaps we can yet set a trap to kill all the horsemen." Launa stooped and rapidly drew in the dust.

Jack shivered at what he saw. Launa's plan looked beautiful. Lines and arrows flew in the dust, a good sandbox exercise. But this was no history class at the Point. Real people would have to make this plan happen. Jack knew these townspeople; they lacked training, good communications and combat experience. How many plans that looked great on paper brought wreckage and death in execution? Launa knew how to lead a small unit. Jack began to seriously sweat her first major battle.

Lasa knelt at Jack's elbow, the grin of a tigress tasting first blood on her face. Jack shivered at the risks Launa was taking and raised his objections as a good executive officer should. Lasa liked the plan. What Lasa liked settled the issue.

The rest of the day was bedlam as the tiny army restructured itself for a different kind of battle. Several, not as many as Jack feared but more than he wanted to see, went with their parents or grandparents to Wood Village. For every one of them, ten eager recruits presented themselves.

Jack shook his head. "It's bad enough changing the emphasis of trained troops. If we drop our trained people into the middle of this new batch, we risk losing them all. I suggest the legion stay as it is."

Launa watched Antia issue spears to the new people. There weren't enough; many brought hoes and scythes, hammers and axes. "Maybe we could form a second legion. We'd have to draw commanders for the new cohorts from the first legion."

Jack scowled. "And I guess we could use a few green troops to fill the holes in the first legion, especially if they're good with a bow."

New minted captains and sergeants found themselves showing the recent volunteers what to do with the poles they were issued. People who had held to peaceful thoughts all winter went through the first lessons of thrust and parry with the short spear. By mid-afternoon the new troops at least knew how to hold their weapons. Now they needed time to train, to practice, to learn new skills—time and luck.

As much as they needed time, they took a break for one special moment. Kaul called the escort together for a cheer from both legions.

When the troops made to rejoin their cohorts, Launa called Sara front and center. "You rode at my right hand through much danger. Now I make you my eyes. Everyone, greet her as *Commander* of Scouts."

Sara beamed.

Launa clapped her on the shoulder, then turned to the gathered escort. "You have ridden well. Now, I give you back your horses. I send you out again. I place your eyes where the rivers run low and horsemen may pass. Our lives depend on your seeing when they come and bringing that word to us."

The scouts nodded, solemnly accepting their charge.

Launa turned back to Sara. "Bring your command up to twenty. I will talk with Taelon and Kaul on the best places for you to stand your *watch*."

Launa elbowed Jack and grinned. "I'll send the scouts out with the captured stallions. When the new mares come in season, only our Arabian quarter horses will be around to fight over them." She sobered. "And we won't have to geld any."

As the formations broke up, Tomas hung back. He waited patiently for Launa to recognize him, then stood at something close to attention. "The scouts will see, and come back to say what their eyes have seen?"

Launa nodded.

"Will the scouts draw blood?"

"It is more important for me to know what comes to us than it is for one scout to kill horsemen."

"I understand." Tomas nodded. "Yet, I will have the blood on my pike of those who took my father's head. That day at River Bend, I was hunting. At the winter camp I ran for your sake. I will run away no more. Let me stand with Antia's pikes."

Jack saw the pain behind Sara's eyes, the lump she swallowed, but she held her tongue. Launa glanced at Sara, then turned back to Tomas. "No one can tell another the path for his feet. Sara, find another to ride in his place."

Jack doubted she would find another to stand in her heart.

That day lasted far past sunset. When finally Jack got home, he undressed quickly and fell into bed. He lay facing the wall, away from Launa. For several minutes he lay in peace.

"Honey, does your leg hurt?" Launa's fingers played along his back. That usually started something, but Jack's thoughts were of Kaul, pacing the room, naked and stripped of so much. How could Jack enjoy what his friend would never feel again? Unbidden, his mind's eye saw Lasa, passion glowing from every inch of her bare skin. He felt his erection grow. Confused and guilty, he tried to send his thoughts anywhere else.

Launa pulled him over. "Jack, the horsemen cut Kaul. I love him and Lasa as much as you do. They'll see this through. And so will we." Her fingers traced their way down his chest, to his belly, and arousal. Assuming it was from her effort, she threw back the covers. "This is more like it. I know the blood poisoning drained you, but I want you. You just lean back and enjoy."

Jack did. But in the dark, he kept seeing Lasa.

TWENTY-SIX

SARA LED TWENTY scouts out from Tall Oaks the next morning. Pride was in her breast. Cheers rang in her ears. She had her "orders" . . . and her problem.

As a child, she had played hide-and-seek with the other children of River Bend. To be found then meant giggles and laughter. Now she played a game of hide-and-seek. But to be found by the horsemen meant death.

And the problem was greater still. Her duty was not to hide from the horsemen; she had to find them and send word to Launa of where they rode. The scouts must be the hunted and the hunters at the same time. Sara had not been a soldier long, but she had ridden beside Launa enough to know this would not be easy.

Out of sight of Tall Oaks, Sara ordered her troop to scatter. Four would go to each of the five places the wise hunters thought most likely for the horsemen to cross the swollen rivers. Four rode to each crossing so that every three days one could ride back to tell Launa that nothing had happened. Sara had not asked why. Even she knew that if no one rode back in three days, it would be a signal as bright as a fire on a dark night that something had happened and no one lived to tell of it.

Sara chose River Bend for her team.

Two days of hard riding later, Sara stood atop the hill

overlooking what had been her home. Sure that no living person shared this place with her team, Sara studied the valley that had given her birth.

The river was wide, but not as wide as it had been.

The fields of River Bend were green. Last year's crops, never harvested, had sown this bounty. The horsemen would pass this way again if they had any wisdom.

She struggled to see the land as Launa would. The horsemen would come from there; she looked downriver, just as they had come last year. *They would go . . . where?*

Sara found the path the twenty horsemen had followed out of the valley when they rode to see Tall Oaks. Yes, they would probably use it again.

She had a problem. To stay on this hill, where she had a good view of everyplace, would put her in the wrong place when the horsemen rode out of the valley.

Would the horsemen leave her alone on this hill or on the steppe, across their path to Tall Oaks? *No.*

What to do when the horsemen find me and mine? Where to hide when death races on my heels?

Sara turned around slowly, studying the familiar with strange eyes. There it was, the woods and marsh where her friends and she had spent many hours fishing and hunting. Over half a day's walk from River Bend, to hunt there meant to spend a night. Happy memories tugged at her, and tears. Most of the friends of those nights were dead . . . and what of Tomas?

Blinking moisture from her eyes, she knew what she must do. "Stivo and Gos, take axes, baskets and antlers. We go to prepare a hiding place for when the horsemen seek our lives."

Launa grinned as the legions began morning P.T.; it wasn't the cool morning air that made her shiver. These were *her* people, come to fight *her* battle under *her* command. They were the fingers; she was the hand. She had never been more excited . . . or terrified.

It seemed every time she blinked another day was gone. True, the days grew longer, but that offered no encourage-

ment. They were getting closer to what she guessed was
June . . . the month Hitler launched his invasion of Russia.

Even as she crammed another minute's drill into already
packed days, subsistence made its demands. Cohorts had to
nurture the winter crops as they ripened. Spring crops had to
be planted. Launa's casual mention to Lasa over supper that
horses would trample much of the crop around Tall Oaks
ended up causing more trouble. Lasa asked people, including Second Legion, to go to Wood Village. Half of the spring
planting was done there.

And it didn't help when holes started appearing in the
ranks of both legions at muster time. Each cohort had a full
strength of four fifteen-person squads, sixty all told. But few
squads stayed at fifteen. Men and women would go missing
one day and show up sheepishly a few days later. Others
never showed up again. Launa needed to talk with Kaul. She
grabbed Jack and headed into town. She didn't have to keep
the pace down too much for him to keep up.

She found Kaul with Lasa outside the longhouse. Hanna
was with them.

Talk was fast and animated as Launa approached. The
spring day was warm; both women were down to mostly
bare skin. The flush of their anger went almost to their pregnant bellies; their voices rose with more emotion than Launa
had heard in a long time. Lasa turned her back on Hanna to
greet Launa.

"Little Blossom, bring water. Our visitors must be
thirsty." Lasa's ten-year-old girl was off at a run. Kaul rose
to greet her. His neck showed red, too, but he was covered
with a linen poncho. None saw how empty his breechcloth
was.

Hanna glared. "What brings killers to talk to the
Speaker?"

Launa stopped in mid-stride. She hadn't heard such a slap
this side of the time jump. "I will come back," she stuttered.

"What do you have to share with Lasa that is not to be
shared with all? Will you not only take blood from the People, but their words as well?"

Jack started to say something, but Launa put a restraining

hand on his arm. "It's okay, honey. When you grow up army, you get into these types of talks. I can handle it now. I just wasn't expecting it."

Hanna glowered at Launa.

With hardly a pause, Launa sat. Hanna was playing to her strong suit; this would be fun. "The danger is clear. The horsemen will come soon. You have heard the words of those taken as slaves at River Bend. You have seen what they did to Kaul when he would talk to them. Have you no fear of being burned by their fire? Even your consort walks with us."

"He is no man of mine. He lives under another roof." Hanna spat the words.

Launa had wondered if divorce was that simple. *Hope it's easier on Samath than it was on the Colonel's wife.* "Could you not find it in your heart to walk together in the way of the Goddess?" Launa jibed at her.

"That is no way of the Goddess," Hanna jabbed back. The child in her womb kicked at that moment. Lasa stared at the omen, patted her own swollen belly. Her child lay still.

Hanna seized the advantage. "To kill and kill is not the path my mother led the People in."

"And you would take us down a path that leads only to death," Launa shot back. She was getting tired of Hanna. "Look at what the horsemen did at River Bend. Listen to Killala. Is that what you want for your child?" *Are you so spineless, you'd be a slave, and your children as well? Christ!*

Hanna shook her head with a jerk. "To walk with the horsemen does not mean to die." She turned to Kaul. "You say the rains come late and little to the plains. Let us show them how to plant crops. Let us walk with them and show them the many ways of the Goddess. If they make us walk farther than we want to, well, my legs are strong and I can do it. Is that so much to give so I and my children can live without blood on our hands?"

Beside her, Jack shook his head. "At River Bend, the People went out to greet the horsemen. The horsemen killed them." Jack spoke softly, as if cool words might cool tempers. "Kaul went to speak to them without even a knife. He bears their scars."

Hanna turned on Jack and snorted. "They wanted to speak to him of the ones you killed. Blood flows from your hands. It swells like a river. I say take grain and fruit to place before the horsemen. They hunger. Feed them. We have plenty. With their help, we can have more." She pulled herself to her feet and turned to Lasa, pleading. "Turn away from the path of these killers. Trust the Goddess. We can walk in peace with the horsemen. They will learn our words, and our ways. It may take years, but they will walk with us." Hanna searched Lasa's face for acceptance. She found none. Disgusted, she turned to go.

A light went on for Launa. "Do you share these words with the legionnaires? Is it because of you that some come no more to practice?"

"Yes." Hanna glowed proudly. "Not everyone wants to become a wild animal. I do it and I will continue to do it. People will see that Lasa leads us not in the way of the Goddess, but into a hole that will be the death of us all." She turned her back on them and stalked away.

And Launa's mouth closed with a snap that almost hurt. *Oh, my God. I've been in that hole. It's an underground bunker at the Lawrence Livermore Lab.* Launa felt a chasm open beneath her feet. She struggled to keep her balance, to keep from tumbling into a hole she'd never climb out of.

As if from far away, Launa heard Jack speaking to Kaul, "We came to ask if you know why some of the legion did not come to drill. I now see why. We will return to practice."

The little girl arrived with water. The four shared a drink. Launa hardly touched it. With a light touch on her elbow, Jack steered her away from the sanctuary.

The walk back to the drill field was slow, for once not because Jack needed it, but because she did. It took her several tries to get words around the thoughts spinning through her head. "Could Hanna be right? Is all we're doing leading to that underground bunker in California, to the whole world dead? Hanna's right; the horsemen will learn the People's language. Is a defense that fails worse than no defense at all?" Launa paused to let her eyes slowly scan the green fields, the hills. "Is surrender better than resistance?" She shuddered to a stop.

Jack nodded. "I've lived with that fear since our first night in the Neolith."

Launa scrubbed at her eyes. He had? She thought she'd covered every contingency. She'd never considered that everything she was doing was wrong.

Jack took a deep breath and folded his arms across his chest. The invalid was gone; a warrior's words snapped out at her. "Lieutenant, Hanna may be right. She may be wrong. I don't know. I do know the horsemen are coming to kill *my* people. I'm a soldier. I won't let that happen. It's that simple."

Launa heard his words. They plummeted into the maelstrom that was her mind and struggled, like attack helicopters in a hurricane.

Jack reached out to rest an arm on her shoulder. His hand locked onto her, almost painful. "Nobody gets a guarantee for what they do. Not you, not me, not Hanna. You and I know something she doesn't. We know the horsemen will kill and pillage these people for the next four hundred years. We know that what they leave behind looks nothing like what we have seen here. We know that even the goddess they worship two thousand years from now will be a bloodthirsty mockery of the one Hanna speaks of. Maybe she's right. Gandhi's idea of passive resistance brought down quite a few governments. Hanna would like to try it. But I don't recall them ever bringing down a ruler who enjoyed drinking people's blood."

Jack was right. Someone like Hitler would have shot Gandhi out of hand. And a horseman would slit Hanna's throat without a moment's pause.

"Remember, boss," Jack finished, "we've only got one chance. Which do you want to bet on?"

Mentally, Launa tossed a coin. *Am I right? Am I wrong?* She didn't bother looking for heads or tails. It wouldn't matter. Her hand went to her knife. "Let's get back to drill, Captain. We've got few enough people for the job."

* * *

Day after day, Jack watched fletchers make arrows and young children collect stones. Grandmothers wove shields and practiced carrying them with their grandchildren. They marched in ranks beside mothers and fathers, sons and daughters who drilled with pikes or spent hours shooting with bow or sling.

Launa introduced bodybuilding, and extra hours went to exercise and lifting stones, strengthening limbs beyond what was needed for herding or farming. Jack also spent time working out; slowly his strength returned. Without antibiotics, recovering from blood poisoning was a long and tedious process. He was finally up to running two miles a day, but he still couldn't pull the bow for a shot of more than 250 meters. For what Launa planned for him, he wanted better.

Aware that they were not the only competition in town for the hearts and minds of these people, those who stood together against the killers gathered in the evening. Over dinner, Jack listened with tears in his eyes as Antia, Killala and other survivors sang new songs with new words that Launa gave them. Now the people learned words for *murder* and *slavery, pillage* and *rape, attack* and *defend.* Eyes that had been soft and gentle became hard. Day by day, the line grew more solid between those who would fight fire with fire and those who could not. They had failed to build a wall around Tall Oaks. Now one grew within it.

Jack pondered what lay ahead. It is not easy to kill. He had fought in the desert with the fervent prayer that his enemy would wave something white, a handkerchief, underwear, anything, so Jack would not have to kill. Many Iraqis had, but others he had killed. The gentle people of Tall Oaks faced an enemy that gave no quarter, and had not shown Jack that they knew how to surrender. How could he help these farmers kill without a second's pause?

Jack took Kaul aside and carefully, using oblique words, shared his concern. The wise man nodded. "Launa told me you have traveled from our tomorrows. My heart is saddened that they drip with so much blood." *So my C.O. forgot to mention she'd cleared Kaul for classified information.*

Kaul pulled thoughtfully at his beard. "Two summers ago, my heart could never have listened to such words as she spoke, as you have shared. Yet my eyes have seen so many strange things since then. My blood runs cold as my eyes try to see how the horsemen would have us live."

Kaul looked hard at Jack. "You have our gentle heart. It was wise to send us one such as you. On the day that is coming, too gentle a heart may be death. I will sleep on your words."

But Jack could not leave the problem with Kaul. Jack had known the struggle to live with himself after a close brush with death, or becoming death itself to others. What could he offer these people when the bloody business was done? He remembered nightmares. What would haunt these people's sleep? He wondered as he waited. And each morning when he looked into Launa's eyes, he saw the same shadow. Were they doing the right thing? Was Hanna right?

His nights were too exhausted to leave room for nightmares now. Launa's need for him grew more urgent. He breathed a sigh of relief when the images of Lasa faded until only Launa shone through. He hoped she had not noticed.

Day after day, the legions worked and trained. Whenever a horse was seen in the east, every head would be raised until the rider was identified. Jack worked and waited . . . wanting more time . . . wanting it to be over and done with. The days grew longer, and the rivers fell.

TWENTY-SEVEN

SARA BLINKED, SQUINTED hard, and then ducked low behind the ridge line. Horsemen were crossing the river below River Bend. "Stivo," she called in a low voice, then started counting.

Behind her, a youth dashed from the clump of trees that was their camp. As she had taught them, he crouched low as he approached the tree. "You called?"

Having counted every finger on her hand five times, Sara made a mark in the dust, as Launa had taught her, and started counting again. When she made the second mark and still had more horsemen to count, she stopped.

"Stivo, pick three of the fastest horses and ride for Tall Oaks. Leave now. Ride all night. Ride as long as you can all day. Tell Launa I have made two marks in the dust and there are still many many horsemen to count. Now go."

Stivo dashed off.

Gos joined Sara. "So they have come, and they came back to River Bend. You are wise, Sara."

"Yes," she hissed. "But am I wise enough to keep us alive?"

It was not easy keeping an eye on the horsemen with only three people. Sara placed Gos with the last three spare horses across the path the twenty had taken out of River

Bend. If the horsemen went that way, he would gallop immediately for Tall Oaks.

But the horsemen did nothing that day. Noon came, and they still had not broken from their camp outside the ruins of River Bend. Late in the afternoon, many horses, some ridden by women and children, joined the camp and the number of tents grew.

"They bring their families this time," Arto muttered at her side. "Should I ride to tell Launa?"

Now Sara knew the wolves that gnawed at Launa as she led the escort in search of the lost men. Launa needed to know that the horsemen brought their families this time. But Sara had only three people to keep watch over them. What would she do if there were only two of them when the horsemen broke camp?

"No." Sara shook her head. "Two of us must watch the horsemen if they ride for Tall Oaks. I can send no rider now."

Arto nodded. Sara prayed that she had chosen wisely.

Next morning, Sara took her turn, riding out on the steppe to watch the place where the horsemen would go if they rode for Tall Oaks. At mid-morning, four hands of warriors splashed across the river. They led no spare mounts; to Sara they looked like no threat. Still, she got a ridge between them and her, ducking up only once in a while to make sure they still rode as they had.

After shadowing them for a while, Sara grinned. If they rode into the valley after the next one, she wanted to be there to watch. The bones of the horsemen who had tried to take Launa and Jack's heads lay where the death birds had cleaned them.

She was about to dismount and check over the ridge again when she glanced back. Six horsemen trotted up the valley behind her. "Uh-oh." Sara kicked her horse to a trot.

Unlike the twenty in the next valley, these could cut her off from the river and the woods that would hide her.

Sara guided her mount close enough to the ridgeline to glance into the next valley. The twenty had not changed direction. Launa had warned her that the horsemen might wander around like goats with no thoughts. Still, the six behind her could hunt her if they chose.

"Ride slowly, girl. We must not let them see fear," Sara ordered herself as she had heard Launa do many times.

For a while she thought they would not bother her. She was approaching the next rise, one shared by three valleys, when she checked behind her. Six galloped for her.

There was no way to know if these dumb-as-goats horsemen were after her, were just racing among themselves or thought they chased a friend. It did not matter; Sara could not meet them. She kicked her horse to a gallop and edged to the right, away from the river and toward the valley with the twenty.

She did not have far to go. She crossed the next rise in full view of the twenty as well as the six, but there was no way around that. As soon as she was out of sight, she pulled her horse's head around and pointed it to the left. She raced for the river, legs tight around the heaving chest of her horse.

Backward glances, stolen beneath her arms as Launa had taught her, showed the hill empty. She ran not knowing if six, twenty or all of the horsemen would ride over the hill and down upon her. She prayed to the Goddess none would.

The Goddess was gracious; Sara's next rearward check showed only six mounted men on the hill. They crossed farther away than she had. They *had* tried to cut her off; she had fooled them.

But the Goddess did not smile enough to get them off her trail. They spotted her and kicked their horses for chase. She was well ahead when she took a path into the familiar woods.

Riding slowly, Sara searched the ground. She had begun to fear she had taken the wrong game path when she came to a branch across the trail. She dismounted, tossed the marker into the brush and carefully guided her horse to the right side of the path. Mounting quickly, she kicked her horse to a brisk trot.

The path twisted and turned. When it crossed with others, Sara tried to leave clear signs of which way she went. She easily found the second place she and Gos had prepared.

She went around the next twist in the trail before dismounting. Leaving her horse, she doubled back. It took only a moment to bring a special branch back tight and tie it in place with a leather rope. The spear points still glistened on shafts long enough to go through a man, big enough to make a deadly hole. Another moment passed quickly as Sara stretched twine across the path at knee level and attached it to the release for the rope.

Her father, may the Goddess greet him, had shown Sara how to make a small trap like this for hunting. He had once killed a bear with a large trap like it. Today Sara fled an animal more fearsome than a bear.

"May the Goddess grant that this works."

Sara had often uttered that prayer. It felt strange to pray it when a man's death lay at the end of it.

"But it will be my blood if it is not so."

She quickly mounted and trotted farther down the trail. If her traps did not stop the horsemen, she would need to be someplace else quickly.

A scream, high-pitched and short-lived, told Sara her pit trap had claimed a horsemen. She did not halt, but guided her horse through more twists in the trail. The smell of water grew strong; she was close.

She grabbed her horse's neck and held on tight as it slid down the steep bank beside the stream. Pausing to let her mount drink a little, she weighed her choices. To turn right would lead her upriver. "Maybe they will lose my trail."

Better still, maybe the first trap had taken the heart out of the chase. She could hope.

A shout and a long, high-pitched scream told her they had not abandoned the hunt, at least not after the pit trap. Sara pulled her mount's head from the water; it had drunk enough. She guided it left.

The high bank and the brush hid the trail from view. *However, there should be one place.*

"Yes." She had hunted here before. Standing on the bank, she had a good view of the trail. Yet the trees near her would hide her from the deer—or horsemen—using the game path. She dismounted.

One more choice yawned before her. Did she use the longbow or a horseman's bow? Launa did not want the horsemen to know of the longbow. At this range, the short bow would reach. Still, Sara had watched the power of the longbow at short range. In her quiver were arrows with large, jagged heads. A short bow would put them in a man. The longbow would drive them through.

Whoever was so stubborn as to stay on her trail when two of his friends were dead would not be easily stopped. Sara chose the longbow—and prayed Launa would be gracious.

Sara chuckled at herself; strange how the Goddess and Launa were looking so much alike to her inner eyes. "Hope Lasa doesn't mind." Then again, if she didn't live through today, Sara would not have to worry about Launa or Lasa.

From up the trail, Sara heard wailing and cries . . . someone was dying slowly. She waited for what would happen next.

She had not long to wait. A horse and rider galloped into the clearing she covered. Sara pulled an arrow back to her ear and let fly. A second rider came in view.

Sara grabbed another arrow and put it to bow in time to see her first quarry transfixed by a shaft through his chest. His tumble from his horse drove the arrow sideward and backward. He screeched in agony.

Sara let fly at the second rider and pulled her third arrow from her quiver. Her second arrow pierced the man's belly. He bellowed his pain and jerked his mount around, searching for his tormentor.

A third rider entered Sara's view, but he reined in his mount. Sara sent her third arrow for the wounded rider. This time she took him full in the back. He slumped from his mount and slid to the ground. His horse bolted back down the path.

Sara readied her last deadly arrow. Another man had joined the first. They shouted at each other, then turned and followed the bolting horse.

And Sara slumped against the closest tree; her stomach heaved and she was violently sick. She wanted to curl up on a bed of moss and cry until the world quit hurting. Instead she checked the killing place once more.

Someone moaned. The fight was not over. Sara slipped down the bank to kneel by the stream. Lifting water to her lips, she cleaned her mouth and spat it out. Another moan brought her attention back to the death she had fled from.

Sara climbed the bank and slowly paced off the distance to the two men who now wore her arrows. The one who took two arrows was closest. The two long shafts would not let him lie down in death. They held him up; his chin, covered by a young man's thin beard, slumped forward, but did not reach the ground. He did not move.

A groan drew Sara's attention. The other man, his chest horribly torn by the arrow shaft as he tumbled from his mount, struggled to sit up and pull his knife at the same time. Sara grabbed a nearby lance and drove it through his throat. He died, teeth gritted in a bitter snarl.

Sara cut her arrows from his body, then from the other. She wanted to leave this place, ride fast and far. But she had a duty to the Goddess. No hunter left a wounded creature to die alone and in pain. The blood of two more men dripped onto the earth. She could not leave them.

Quickly Sara trotted through the woods, careful to keep to leaf-strewn places that made no sound, hard ground that left no tracks. It did not take her long to come to the nearest trap.

The tree limb had snapped back; the rider had been in the middle of the path. One spear had pierced his belly, the other his shoulder. Both were death wounds . . . neither fast. His face still glistened with his tears. A horseman had slit his throat.

Sara listened to the woods and heard nothing that did not belong there. She quickly covered the distance to the second trap. She need not have bothered. One of the wooden stakes she had placed in the bottom of the pit had taken the falling rider under the chin, driving up through his skull, almost tearing his head off his shoulders.

Sara was sick again.

Weak as her knees were, she did not allow herself to collapse, but ran as quickly and carefully as she could from that place. At the stream, she hurled herself on her horse and kicked it for speed as she pointed it downstream. Heart sick

and gut torn, she still guided her mount carefully, leaving little trail for others to find.

As she rode into camp, Gos came to greet her. "We saw
many horsemen go your way. We worried for you."

"You need not have" was all the answer Sara gave him.

That night was long, filled with dreams of horsemen who
snarled at her through slit throats and heads half torn off.
Then her father came to her, his head comfortably cradled in
his elbow. "You have done well, my daughter. Sleep now."

She did.

TWENTY-EIGHT

LAUNA PROWLED THE archery range like a good sergeant, encouraging here, chiding there. The subject of her attention at the moment was a young man who had spent all winter thinking gentle thoughts. But his eyes were clear and his arm was strong. Today his arrows flew beyond the 200-meter targets and didn't hit a thing. The man clenched the bow tight—and missed by twice as much.

"No one can hit something that far away!" he snapped in frustration.

Launa refrained from damaging his ego further by doing it herself. "You do not have to aim so carefully as when you shoot for a lone deer. When Jack and I hunt at this distance, we shoot for the herd. On the day the Horse People come, you will not aim for one man but for a group of horsemen."

He drew another arrow and aimed for a clump of hay 250 meters out.

"Wait for the wind to gentle." Launa spoke softly. "Remember, the horsemen will ride for you. They will be closer to you when the arrow arrives." Launa wished they had some way to simulate a charge. *You can't play laser tag with arrows.*

Somewhere behind her, Jack raised a shout. "Scout incoming, riding hell for leather."

A shudder went through those around Launa that could

have been measured on the Richter scale. She refused to let her troop see the anxiety in their C.O.'s heart. Patiently she waited while the youth let fly and watched as his arrow buried itself in the dirt next to the target. "Good."

Then both turned to join everyone racing for the east edge of town. The rider was mobbed, but the people respectfully opened a path for their commander.

The scout stood beside his lathered horse. "The horsemen make their camp at River Bend. Sara counted two marks in the dirt and more. She will send a messenger if they move."

Launa tried to remember what she had taught Sara about a covering force. Her scouts were mice at a cat convention. If Sara got too close, a wandering band of horsemen could catch her and cut her to pieces. Yet if she held too far back, the mobile horsemen might slip past her. "Jack, using light cavalry to screen light cavalry is dangerous. You got any ideas?"

He scratched at an ear. "That's the risk you take. If he's got dependents this time, his center of gravity will maybe move slower. Still, outriders are a problem. Just 'cause we didn't see any at River Bend doesn't mean he hasn't gotten smarter and won't use them now."

Launa wondered how Jack could stay so calm. Would she be more sanguine after a few battles? "Thanks for the help," she grumbled and turned to Brege. "Sara is wise. We must gather the scouts to her so they can screen the horsemen's advance to us. Get this man three fresh ponies. Brege, who can ride swiftly to carry the word to the other scouts?"

"Merik?"

"No. He leads a cohort. Get Tomas. Tell him he must again be eyes and not a spear tip."

Brege grinned. "He will not like that."

Launa laughed. "Tomas is a good soldier. He will do as he is ordered."

Launa squelched her own desire to ride up to River Bend and get a good look at her opposition. Did he have families with him this time, or was this just another raid? In another age, she could have made her surveillance in a chopper, or maybe a heavy cavalry recon. But she fought a different kind of war with different kinds of forces. She gave her questions to the breathless scout and sent him on his way.

A few minutes later Tomas rode by. She waved at him. He shook his fist . . . but was laughing as he did it.

The crowd dissolved as people returned to work and Launa went back to the archery range. Around her, bows were held tighter. Muscles strained as arrows reached out a few extra meters. When it was too dark to shoot, people took up their spears and practiced with them. Only when it was too dark to do anything else did the people go to their evening meal.

Launa had a working supper at the sanctuary. Lasa's time was near, and they wanted to make it easier on her. Brege was also large with child, but it would have been death to remove her from command of First Slingers. She obeyed her mother and Glengish, resting during the midday and no longer running with her cohort. But she would not give up her place in the line. Merik finally begged Kaul to take his place commanding Second Pikes so he could stand beside his consort. "Taelon commands the Second Archers beside you."

Kaul looked to his consort for the decision.

Lasa sighed, and sent her man to stand in another's stead. "If Launa can fight with her man elsewhere, so can I."

Launa wondered if she should countermand Lasa. She did not like juggling the command of her units with the enemy so close. But these people were militia, defending their homes and families, not cold Prussian steel to be ordered about. With a sigh, Launa kept silent. She hoped she was doing it right.

That night, her need for Jack was stronger. The scent of death must be doing something to her hormones. She took him by storm, hardly giving him a chance to get to bed. His strength was returning, and he gave as good as he got. Whatever the shadow was that had come between them, it was gone now.

Sara was grateful for the company when Tomas rode into camp with three scouts from the crossing north of her. She could get down to seriously covering the horsemen when Stivo arrived with three more from the south. Half the scouts were with her now.

Stivo also brought questions from Launa; Sara smiled at the first one. "Are there women and children this time?"

Tomas volunteered to take the answer to Launa. With a shrug, Sara let him go. She could not ask him to stay, to use his wisdom of the lands around River Bend to watch the horsemen more closely. He had made his choice. She must let him walk the path of his choosing.

TWENTY-NINE

WHEN ARAKK DECREED that the Clan and those who rode with it should rest a ten day at the place of last year's cleansing, he expected to rest. Instead, all he got was trouble.

First two young warriors with shit in their pants galloped into camp, screaming they had been attacked by hands and hands of warriors. The next day, Arakk and the wise and strong men of the Clan rode out to view the bodies. Half the dead lay in animal traps, but the other two had died like warriors. Even though one's throat had been cut, his head was still on his shoulders.

Search as the wise hunters did, they could not find the spoors of many warriors, nor of even one. Under stern questioning, the two warriors admitted chasing a lone rider into the trees. They saw no one after that.

Arakk led a silent band back to camp.

Two days later, sharp-eyed Tassin came to Arakk as the sun set. "Hunt with me tomorrow."

"We have plenty of meat."

"There is no meat on the bones I will show you."

"I will ride with you and your warriors."

Next morning, as soon as Arakk's devotions to the rising Sun were done, he rode forth with Tassin. Silence rode long with them as they trotted from one rise to another and another. Though the steppe was green and the day warm,

Arakk's patience grew short. He had many strong men to deal with before he rode forth to cleanse the next place. And one never knew when some young or old fool would threaten all Arakk had done by starting a blood feud with one of the bands who rode with the Stormy Mountain's totem.

They paused at a ridge overlooking a shallow valley marked by one tree. "What we have come to see is before us."

Arakk frowned. The grass was spring tall and full. "I see nothing."

"Ride with me." They trotted for the tree and past it. Tassin signaled a halt where grass grew up through the bones of a man. His head had been taken; he had died a warrior's death.

"Who is it?" Arakk asked, his eyes searching the bones.

"I do not know. The totem, medicine bags, jewelry have been taken from all of them."

"All of them?" Arakk looked up.

"Come with me."

As they walked their horses up the other side of the valley, Tassin pointed out more bones, some of horses, all picked clean, all with nothing to say who they were in life. Arakk tried to clothe the bodies with flesh again, make them tell him their tale of death. Near the ridge top he found almost two hands of dead.

"Here they made their stand," Tassin said.

"They fled from someone who killed many of them, from there to there." Arakk pointed with his whip from the first body to the many who lay close.

"Yes." Tassin nodded. "But what could be so strong that twenty warriors would flee it? So mighty that it could slay twenty strong warriors and leave none alive to bring the bloody lance to his clan brother for revenge?"

Arakk stroked his beard. "Do you think we need look no further for strong Tyman and the Swift Arrow Band?"

Tassin scowled and nodded. "Someone ambushed these twenty last year. Someone led six into a trap not two sunrises ago."

"Maybe the two young warriors deserve more honor for escaping the trap than we give them." Anger boiled Arakk's blood. "The Mighty Men have declared there is no honor in making war against we who have no pastures. Someone does not give the honor to the Mighty Men's words that they should. Who would dare?"

Tassin shrugged. "Shokin and the Stalwart Shield Clan do not ride with us."

Arakk nodded. "Let us lead many warriors to plunder and slaves."

"Yes." Tassin grinned, waiting obediently for Arakk to tell him more or no more.

"Then we will teach Shokin to fear the lances of the Stormy Mountain warriors." Arakk returned Tassin's grin, as if each of them already saw new skulls dangling from their saddle blankets. "But until then, let no young warrior go chasing into traps. Let us hold contests outside the camp. Let us show all who follow our totem who is mightiest among them."

"Race you to the camp," Tassin shouted and kicked his horse to a run.

Arakk had expected the challenge. He was off before the words were out of Tassin's mouth. Across the plains their horses flew, neck and neck, together. As they entered the camp, they were separated by less than the length of a man's arm. But it was Arakk who had the extra length. They laughed as they gave their horses to boys to care for and went into Arakk's tent to share the smoke.

THIRTY

FOR THE NEXT four days, Launa watched her legions drill with the intensity of demons. They made her proud. While tension rose as eyes searched the hills for any sign of scouts or horsemen, still the ranks of the cohorts grew solid. No more did anyone fail to take their place in the line.

Launa sent youths to set up observation posts on the hill. They were the ones who spotted a lone returning scout. Sisu, the brown-eyed eight-year-old she had found wandering the hills above River Bend, rode breathlessly to Launa with the news. Half an hour later, Tomas raced up to where Launa worked with Antia's pikes. He turned his horse over to another and jogged to Launa.

"Sara says the horsemen bring their families," he began without preamble. "They have the travois like you showed us. Some women ride and carry bows. Many walk. Some of them are short and dark-haired, like us. Most are tall and have light hair. The man who rides first has hair red as the setting sun. Killala names him Arakk. Now, can I have a spear back?"

Launa laughed. "Give this man a spear. He has done well." She turned to go, then remembered the most important question. "Are they still camped at River Bend?"

"Of course." Tomas twirled a spear, then thrust wickedly

for his shadow's gut. "If they came here for us to kill, I would have told you that first."

Four days passed before another scout rode in at sunset. The horsemen were on the move. Three days later, Launa canceled all practices. The observers on the hill had spotted riders approaching Tall Oaks. These wore helmets.

Jack watched as Launa meticulously went down her prebattle checklist. Immediately, she ordered Tall Oaks to what she half seriously called "Defcon 3." The youngsters pulled back from the observation posts on the hills, but new posts were set up on the outskirts of town. The kids were given drums to beat if they saw more horsemen than they could count on their fingers and toes.

All military preparation was made to disappear from prying eyes. Both longhouses were appropriated so the pike cohorts could take turns drilling with spears against knives or axes. Slingers who needed further honing spread out in the trees by the river. Launa had her plan, and it was all coming together. The one loose cannon, she told Jack, was Hanna and her people.

On the second day of the masquerade for the horsemen's scouts, Jack headed into town with Launa to spend the heat of the day with Lasa and Kaul making final preparations. "We've got to get Lasa to put Hanna's people under house arrest. We can't have noncombatants wandering around the battlefield. We've only got seconds to get the stones and arrows into the killing zone. My archers and slingers can't waste time sorting out stray friendlies. If it's out there, it dies." Launa's words were deadly calm. Genghis Khan would have been proud.

Jack scratched at his beard. "I don't think clear fire lanes are going to persuade Lasa to toss out one of the Goddess's most cherished rules. Two weeks ago she wasn't ready to clap Hanna in irons, and I haven't heard anything that makes me think she's changed her mind."

Jack could smell blood in the air. His mind had clicked. He was a captain in the United States Army once again. It wasn't just that he and Launa were speaking English, he was back to thinking in it. He had felt the change the last few days. Rationally, it seemed like the best way to face what was coming. But his heart tasted sour.

During the rest of the hike to the sanctuary, the soldiers went through their options. As soon as they turned the corner onto the main street, Jack knew they had wasted their breath. Hanna was there before them, seated on the porch with Kaul and Lasa.

"I hear that the horsemen have finally come. Is your heart glad? Have you killed anyone yet?" Hanna didn't waste a moment.

"No." Launa was polite. "These seek to learn about us. We will show them nothing. Will you go out to offer them bread?"

Hanna seemed taken back by the question. "We can't even see these people you call scouts. How can we offer them anything?"

Launa raised an eyebrow, but said no more. A young girl brought water. Launa and Jack shared a jar, then sat still, waiting for Hanna to leave, unwilling to discuss classified matters with a known security risk.

No one else spoke. Another day, Jack would have been comfortable enjoying the warmth of the sun on his skin, the taste of air as he breathed. Today, too much of the frantic twenty-first century coursed through his veins. Apparently it beat in Launa's heart too. She broke the silence.

"It is not too late to go upriver to Wood Village."

"I did not go before and I will not go now." Hanna patted her swollen belly. She could not be more than days from delivery. "My daughter will be born in the home the mother of her grandmother built."

"And what will you do when the horsemen come to Tall Oaks?"

"The people who walk after me would have you not go out to meet the horsemen with stones and arrows. We would have us all go out with baskets of bread and fruit." She looked to Lasa.

The Speaker for the Goddess shook her head. "You will

not tell us how to walk. Those who choose to meet the horsemen with bow and sling may do so."

Hanna glowered. "You stand in our path." The two women stared at each other. Both were pregnant with child and possibilities, neither willing to move aside.

Finally, Hanna shook her head. "The dreams of those who petition the Goddess seem to guide us all in the same way." Hanna squirmed, trying to find a more comfortable position. Jack remembered Sandie's last days carrying Sam, and his heart went out to Hanna; she must be miserable. "We will come to the Sanctuary of the Goddess. We will sing songs of Her marvelous gifts and center our hearts and thoughts on the true way of the Goddess."

Jack's heart bounced back to him. He wondered how those who put their bodies between the horsemen's lances and the sanctuary of the Goddess would feel about this prayer meeting. When they had watched their friend or consort die in their arms, would they feel grateful to those who prayed far from lances and arrows?

Jack sighed; Hanna and her followers had not come up with any creative approach to the problem that now faced the People. How could the ways of the People resolve an issue where one person's solution cut out the other's options? Hanna had chosen to step aside, to avoid the confrontation. At least Launa didn't have to worry about policing the rear of her battlefield.

Jack would share a word with Das about keeping some spare axes and pikes near the sanctuary. They would serve as a last defense as well as a security force to keep their "friends" there. Jack stopped himself; he hadn't come up with any new solutions either. He and Hanna were both just applying the same old timeworn ideas to this new problem. Jack scowled.

No one had an answer for Hanna. One was not necessary. Jack heard hoofbeats; every head turned. Sara galloped up to the sanctuary and leaped from her horse. "The horsemen are here. They camp in a draw on the other side of the hill. I think they will come for us tomorrow."

Kaul helped Lasa to her feet. Hanna watched the Speaker

for the Bull like a hawk. Despite the warmth of the day, he
wore his linen poncho. Jack had seen old men wear this gar-
ment. Last year, Kaul had been down to his belt and tattoos
in this weather. Did Hanna wonder at his change? If she did,
there was no process for her to raise a question. Again, the
simple ways of the People faltered when confronted by
problems that went far beyond their experience. All Hanna
could do was watch and wonder.

Lasa turned to Kaul. "Have any hunters returned today?"

He grinned. "Taelon led back five horses laden with
deer."

"The Goddess smiles." Lasa did too as she pronounced
this good omen. Ignoring Hanna's scowl, Lasa continued.
"Let us proclaim a feast this evening. Let all who wish come
and celebrate life." She turned to Hanna. "Will you join us?"

"No." Hanna spat her reply. "You say the horsemen are
hungry. We will gather by the river, and share in their
hunger." Hanna turned with angry dignity. But the waddle of
a woman so late in her pregnancy failed to carry either anger
or dignity.

Kaul watched Hanna go. "It is just as well that her people
will not share this meal. I have thought much on how hard it
will be for people to kill people. I think I can help them."

"Have you had a dream?" Lasa asked.

Kaul shook his head. "Since the winter camp, I have not
been touched by the Goddess. I wonder if they also cut that
from me."

Lasa reached out to hug her consort. Jack could offer no
solace. The change was coming for him. It was not a time to
feel another's loss. The time for killing was upon them.

Arakk studied the filthy place. He saw few people. Between
where he stood under the shade of a beech tree and the first
hut, only a handful of people stirred the dust with their
sticks. On the distant hill he saw several flocks of goats, but
none blighted the slope he stood on. Among the huts he
could see some people, but not many.

Arakk frowned. The last place had been half the size of

this one, yet it had buzzed with people like a beehive full of honey for the taking.

"Could the animals have run away?" Sharp-eyed Tassin spoke the concern Arakk was beginning to feel.

"There are still many for our sport. What have you seen?" He asked Tassin who had led the first hunters Arakk had sent to study their prey.

"Only what you see now. Never do we see more people than I can count on both hands. Never anyone with a lance or bow."

Arakk stroked his beard. Except for the lack of people milling about as at a festival, it was as the last place. Maybe it was no different. Still, something about this prey did not smell right. "You have sent no one near the town?"

"Those were your words to me," Tassin quickly answered.

"Send some now. Young warriors with eager eyes."

Antia was glad that Lasa had proclaimed a feast for tonight. She often wondered if these people of Tall Oaks had the stomach for what was galloping at them. Her mother at River Bend could not have foreseen what the horsemen would do to the People. For her lack of sight, the Speaker at River Bend had given up her life in a terrible way. Now all knew the twisted way of the horsemen. The Speaker for the Goddess at Tall Oaks and her people had to know what the horsemen would do tomorrow.

Last year at River Bend, Antia would have killed all the horsemen if she could have. Now, with other pikes at her back, she might.

When she finished the last drill with her cohort of pikes, Antia invited Cleo and three of their best pike-wielders to bathe with her in the river. "We cannot come to a feast smelling of sweat, like a horseman."

The three from Tall Oaks laughed as at a joke. Cleo had been with Antia at River Bend. She knew the stink of the horsemen up close. Four horsemen paid with their blood for the games they played on Cleo and Antia's bodies.

At the river, the five washed and laughed and talked of

women's things. Antia might have missed the warning had not one of them been talking on about how she and her lover would spend the night after the feast. Antia looked away—and caught the sway of a branch. There were eyes beneath it.

The boys of the People might spy on young women as they bathed, but they would not watch for long. There were pleasant games to be played in the water. Antia waited for the boys to join them. When they did not, she slipped over to where her clothes rested on the bank. With her body between her hand and prying eyes, she slid her knife into the water.

Kozan saw the women first. He could not believe his luck. Not only had he and his friend been sent to spy closely upon the quarry, but they had found women naked. He would bring all five to his chieftain, and then he would have his sport. The two boys drew their knives. One raven-haired beauty drew his eyes. Kozan felt himself hardening. Maybe he would not wait to take this one until he presented her to his chief. With a signal from him, both of them leaped down the stream bank and ran for the women.

The horsemen were so predictable; Antia grinned. Show them a bare ass and they would grab for it. Antia had her back to the two strangers when she heard their whoop and splashing as they came toward her. They were almost to her when she whirled, joyful cry of the successful hunter on her lips, knife in hand. She took the near one full in the gut. He stopped in mid-shout, eyes wide in surprise. The stupid man must have thought no woman could lay a finger on him. Driving her knife up into his heart, she shoved him against the other. Both men went down in a red froth.

The second horseman was too dazed to even shout. Antia slit his throat before he uttered a word.

The three women from Tall Oaks had not even had time to scream. They stood, up to their knees in water, too startled to say or do anything. Cleo knew what to do. She helped Antia guide the still-twitching bodies over to the bank.

One of the other women found her voice. "What do we do?"

Antia grinned proudly, pulled aside her first attacker's breechcloth and took her knife to the now-pliant flesh. "These are mine. They are the gift I take to the feast."

All that afternoon, the smell of deer roasting over the open fire filled the plaza. Launa chuckled. *Wonder what the spying horsemen made of this party? With luck, it will also make some tummies growl among Hanna's followers.*

As the sun sank lower, over half the town turned out, overflowing the plaza and filling avenues and side streets. For the first time, Launa saw a major portion of Tall Oaks' three thousand children and adults in one place. But not all.

True to her word, Hanna and her followers fasted. They gathered, several hundred strong, on the other side of town. But the people with Launa had no time for them. They laughed, shared stories and joked. At Launa's suggestion, Lasa mixed water with the wine, and only three wineskins were brought out. The atmosphere was sober but congenial, almost covering the underlying tension.

The food was just being laid out when Antia stomped up to Lasa's table. Holding something in a sack, Antia turned to the gathering, the grin of a sated tiger on her lips. "The horsemen are not content to just look. Two attacked as we bathed. I killed them, and bring these to you."

Antia emptied the pouch on the table. Launa suspected what would be in it; a quick glance proved her right. Launa's main worry now was how her troops would take this bloody trophy.

Several turned green. Many stared wide-eyed in dismay. Confronted with the harsh reality of human slaughter, Launa could see second thoughts draining the fire from their souls.

Before their reaction could find any voice, Kaul jumped up on a table where everyone could see him. In the spring warmth, among those who walked the soldier's way, he wore only a loincloth. The setting sun reddened the scars on his body. He glanced around; the people grew silent.

"My friends,
I have lived among you all the days of my life.
You honored me, as I honored you.
In your name,
I went forth to share our words among the horsemen.
I shared your words that they might know the happiness
and harmony of the Goddess
and walk with us in that joy.
I walked among them, a man of peaceful words,
But I found no one to listen to peaceful words.
The men I found had no use for peaceful words.
They could not believe
that a man could bring words and not a knife."

Kaul reached for his loincloth. Launa held her breath. With one swift pull, Kaul stood naked before his people. Was it the last rays of the setting sun or the ruddy glow of the fires that seemed to make blood flow again from the ugly scars of his healed groin? Again shock swept the assembly. Groans of revulsion sparked a roar of anger at anyone who would do such a deed to their Speaker. Kaul turned so all could see the handiwork of those who camped near by. Stoically, he waited for quiet.

"With their knife,
they took the manhood of one they would not hear.
With their knife,
they would have taken the life
of one they would not hear.
I stand before you,
a man who bears the marks of those who await us
*   tomorrow.*
I stand before you
to say that they must die,
as wild animals who know no mercy.
Tomorrow,
if for a moment, you doubt that one of them must die,
Remember what you saw tonight, and take away that life
before it takes away your life,

or your consort's life, or your child's life.
Remember my words. Pass them from young to old,
from mouth to ear as long as the seasons turn."

Launa shivered, but she did not tremble alone. A tremor ran through the gathering. Lips drew tight against gritted teeth. No one now questioned Antia's right to take what she had taken. Hands went for bows or slings or pikes. The fire within them leaped high, consuming all that was soft or tender in these peaceful people. Tomorrow, this second fire would meet the horsemen's flames. Launa wondered what would remain when next the sun set.

THIRTY-ONE

"When will my man return to me?
When he comes, what will he bring to me?
Will he carry meat for our people?
Or will his brothers carry him back cold meat to me?"

THE WOMAN'S VOICE was husky, haunting. Launa didn't need a song to remind her of the tomorrow's unknowns. She'd made her plan. She'd drilled her troops. How many times in the last month had she gone over the battle plan, working out kinks, allowing for surprises? By all rights, tomorrow should see the bloody massacre of the horsemen. But in the back of her mind she could hear the calm voice of her instructor at the Point. "No battle plan survives contact with the enemy."

Launa shivered at the unknown. Jack put his arm around her, rubbing warmth back into flesh gone cold. It was good to feel the warmth of his touch. Tomorrow, one of them could well be cold dead meat. And Launa realized that being a veteran of meeting engagements and an escort mission had not prepared her for a night of waiting, wondering, trembling with fear.

Launa shook her mind out of that line and ordered it elsewhere. How were her troops taking this? She searched the faces listening to the hunter woman's song. Like her, they stared blankly into an unknown future. Unlike her, they had not lived it. Unlike her, they did not question if their actions would spawn six thousand years of suffering and death.

Turning in Jack's arms, she looked into dark eyes. Firelight danced in them. It offered the only warmth about the man she loved. His quick smile had vanished. The creases around his mouth and eyes were hard. He was Apache, unquestioning on the eve of battle. *God, how does he do that? Can I ever do it?*

Across the fire sat Antia and the other survivors from River Bend. They had sung the first song after Kaul's story. They sang the new words *attack, pillage, rape, slavery, defend.* On the haunted faces of these refugees, the people of Tall Oaks saw their possible future. Hands stroked bows, spears, pouches full of stones. They would have another future.

Launa clenched her jaw. These people saw tomorrow's battle as a fight for their lives. She knew it for so much more.

Again Jack's hands moved to warm her. He nuzzled her ear. "You worry too much, Lieutenant." His hands roved, pausing to distract here or there. She wore the fringed bikini bottom the old man had given her at Christmas. Tomorrow she might die in it. Tonight, Jack's fingers roamed what she bared.

She let out a slow breath. Around her, couples sought shadows. Who was to say theirs was not the better way to spend the night before battle? She drew him to her. Tomorrow would come soon enough. She would have plenty to worry about then.

Arakk, Bloodletter to The Wide Blue Sky, leader of the Clan of Stormy Mountain, sat his horse. Ahead of him lay the prey.

Behind him the sun warmed his back. That was a good omen. Behind him, warriors, a double hand of double hands of warriors from the Stormy Mountain Clan and as many more from other clans brought their shaggy ponies up the hill and spread out along the crest. That also was good.

A soft nicker from behind drew him around. Arakk's young son, Kantom, sat his horse. His beard was only beginning to grow, yet his hair was pulled back in two long horse tails as befit a warrior. At his waist a quiver with bow and a hand of arrows he had made himself was belted to his felt pants. Unlike the others, Kantom grasped no lance. Instead he held high the totem of the clan, a sun-bleached horse skull. The fist of grass and skin of water that proclaimed a recognized claim to pastures did not dangle beneath it.

Arakk smiled at his son with pride, remembering when he too had ridden behind his father, carrying high the clan totem. The two warriors that had not returned from scouting the village had been Kantom's friends. Arakk would have to let his son take a price if the two were dead. The thought that these animals could have drawn first blood brought Arakk's eyes back to the place.

A few people scurried from hut to hut. One pointed to the hill where his warriors sat their ponies. Arakk grinned. Their fires had burned late. Did they now sleep? He had come here to keep watch through the night and pray up the Sun. He had listened to their whimpering songs. Did they make offering to their weak woman god thing?

He would offer their leader as eagle to the Sky. Their babies he would give to the flame. He would cleanse this place of the stench of their strange ways and make it clean for Sky, Wind, Sun and Fire. He drew his stone knife from his belt.

"By this blade, I will make this land my own," he called. Behind him, the Clan's warriors drew their knives, echoing him.

He walked his pony down the line to where Tamer and Siskar sat their mounts. Each had brought a hand of double hands of warriors from the winter camp, young warriors from other clans, eager for blood, older men, eager for slaves. "You lead your warriors around the filthy place. I will drive them to you. Let your horn take any who would run away."

Siskar accepted the wisdom of treating these ground squirrels like warriors. It would make for better songs. He saluted, fist to chest. "None will escape your horns, Oh *Baskaki*."

Arakk acknowledged the high honor they named him. As yet, no title was properly his. When the sun set, he would have that honor—and more. All clans would recognize his claim to this pasture.

He let his horse prance back to the center of the line. In one deft motion, he stood upon its back, for all to see his command. He waved his lance. "Let the lances drink. Let the arrows drink. Let us all drink the blood of our enemy."

Some of the older men who still led their own double hand waved high the bleached skulls of foes they had taken in single combat. The young men shouted, hoping to find an enemy of sufficient honor that they too could take such a trophy today. As one, they broke for the village.

Arakk rode beside his son, keeping a slow pace for the totem. While it flew high, no one dared pass it without his command. To his left, Tamer and Siskar led their warriors off at a fast trot. The long horn moved to circle the quarry.

Ahead, people who had come out of that place turned and ran back to their huts. Arakk laughed; these animals were more alert than the last. Maybe some who had escaped the plunder last summer had carried tales to these. Let them know fear. Let them know what it is like to die on the lance of a true warrior.

The horn spread. Confident that the horn would catch all who tried to flee, Arakk motioned his son to lower the totem. Young warriors whooped with glee and galloped for their play. These walkers would make great sport.

Arakk and his double hand slowed to a walk. There would be plenty of these weaklings left for their enjoyment. The sacrifice of the leader and the one who called himself her man would be Arakk's. There was no need to rush.

Arakk's father had passed to him much wisdom. Arakk had not used it in the place they burned last year; he had not needed to. But the last few days gave him pause. Arakk had also thought long on the strange man who had come from the west to the winter camp. He had vanished with no trail. Very strange.

Today, Arakk would use all he knew, sending the horn and holding back his double hand that they might see where the bravest deeds were needed and ride to do them. The young men would hear nothing of such talk. Arakk's band was drawn from the strong and wise warriors of experience . . . and his son.

The charging horde was still many bow shots away from the first buildings when several hands of men and women in two lines ran out from the huts. At the same spot, each one turned, one line right, the other left, and, still in lines like quail, spread out in front of the charge. Many of them held a bow that was as tall as they were. Arakk had never seen such a bow.

They stopped as one. Some nocked arrows and a few began to shoot. Others swung slings. Arakk laughed. So stupid to waste arrows or even stones before any target was in reach. What honor was there in letting a lance drink such blood? He would order the lances burned after this day.

In the dim light of the hut, Launa went down the row of armed women and men. Archers clutching longbows alternated with slingers. Although many of the archers were drawn from the hunters, her thirty light infantry were split equally among the sexes. Like a good officer, she checked each bow, each sling, each quiver and pouch. Today her first battle command would go just as she planned it.

Her new-made soldiers had a distant set to their gaze. What thoughts spun behind their eyes?

She reached the end of the line. All was in order. All was as it should be. Stefen smiled nervous encouragement. Launa took a deep breath.

"The horsemen come," a high-pitched young voice piped from the doorway.

"Have they reached the outer marker?" Launa tried to keep her voice calm. The manual taught cadets to do that.

"No." Sisu's voice broke.

"Then wait, little one. There will be time enough."

Launa returned to her place, first in line. She tousled

Sisu's brown curls. "Hold tight to your shield. You know how to carry it high."

He nodded, his dark eyes serious, their sparkle gone to solemnity. She remembered him the way she had found him, huddled, alone, in the brush outside River Bend. His eyes had snagged her heart. She was vulnerable to him as only an army brat could be, only someone who had spent her childhood waiting for the visit from the chaplain that made her an orphan.

Launa took a deep breath and rested her eyes on the hut across the street. Brege stood in its doorway, heavy with child, her hands gripping her sling tight. Did she see again the split body of She who Spoke for the Goddess at River Bend? Today Brege stood between that death and her mother.

At the door of the next hut into town stood Antia, leader of the heavy infantry. A wicker shield rested on one arm; in her other hand were the fourteen-foot-long pike and the five-foot thrusting spear. After all their practicing, Launa still wondered how many of these people could jab a spear into another human being's gut. Antia looked at the charge and grinned, like a big cat sniffing its prey. Her mother had been Speaker for the Goddess at River Bend. Yesterday's kill had not slacked Antia's lust for blood.

The horsemen reached the large outer marker Jack had set. It was time. "Forward at the double." Launa stepped off on her left foot, just as the Book said. Green troopers followed. Beside her, supporting her belly with one hand, Brege struggled to keep the pace. At the chosen point, Launa did a column right, deploying into line. Brege stepped aside; Merik led her troops to the left for the full length of their array.

On the plain, the horsemen saw them. Launa heard whoops and cries as ponies were urged on. "Column halt. Left face. Archers and slingers, deploy."

Archers took two steps back, slingers two steps forward. Both weapons now had room. Launa was proud of her plan.

The forward element of the charge approached the first archer's marker. Jack had measured off two markers for the archers, one at 300 paces, the closer at 250. The slingers had a single marker at 200 paces. Several skilled slingers could reach 250 and intended to do just that. For a cooperation-based society, there was unseemly competition among the ranks.

How many times had Launa planned this battle? Again, she did the deadly arithmetic. Light cavalry charged at 200 meters a minute. Long bows could reach out 300. The horsemen's short bows were good for only fifty meters. For seventy-five precious seconds, the horsemen were in her killing zone and could not touch her troops. The sixty archers and slingers arrayed here could get off seven or eight aimed rounds during the critical seconds. She estimated the opposing force at about one hundred. The morning air was dead calm.

She had the bastards. None would live to use his bow. Certainly none would close to use a lance. Like the battle last summer at the tree, like Agincourt so far in the past and the future, she had them.

She smiled at the enemy's disarray. They were not making a disciplined charge. From point to trailers, the horsemen spread over 200 meters. She had twice as long to kill them.

Launa lofted an arrow before the lead target got to the first marker. She was nocking her second when the first took out a man as his pony raced past the distant post. To her right, old Ballen, as cool and experienced a hunter as Taelon, joined her. Other archers waited for the second marker. As the horsemen charged past it, a storm of arrows and stones reached out. Warriors fell; Launa grinned. It was as she had planned.

To her right a shriek rose, and died as suddenly. A long cry followed on its heels. Launa turned, another arrow half out of her quiver. Hanatha stood, hands to her mouth, her sling slipping through her fingers. Tonnolan slumped to the ground, his bow falling from limp hands. A rock was buried in his skull.

Launa had put the archers *behind* the slings just so nothing like this could happen. Hanatha had followed the sheep for years. She knew the sling; she had killed a wolf. How could she have let go at so wrong a time? Launa clenched her teeth. Hanatha had practiced with pike all winter, only returning to the sling when Launa shuffled her troops. Also, Hanatha had never faced men who wanted her body for sport.

Along the line, eyes were on the fallen, not the horsemen. The hail of arrows and stones ceased. Launa swallowed hard as her eyes swept the incoming horde. Horsemen raced for them. She moved down the line to rally her troops.

"Come on, soldiers. Heads up. We have horsemen coming. Shoot."

Ballen looked to the archers on either side of him. "You heard the Lady. Just as in practice. They are a bigger target than the deer, and they are coming at you." He laughed as he drew a bead. "They make it easy."

Brege stepped forward. "Death comes for us all. Let us be death to these riders. Shoot, my sisters and brothers. Shoot."

Arrows reached out again. Horsemen and horses fell. The screams of wounded horses mingled with war cries. The noise of battle did not cover the soft whimpers of Hanatha. She knelt beside Tonnolan, held him as convulsions came, closed his eyes when they ended. The other slingers looked on, helpless.

Launa stepped forward to fill the gap in the line made by friendly fire, herself the rock to replace Tonnolan. Horsemen were already inside the 200-pace mark; they had to die. Her smile was gone. Things were not going as she planned.

Arakk reined in his mount. This day was not going as it should. None of his warriors were within three or four arrow flights of the bowmen, yet he could already see a double hand of warriors in the dust. To his left, the riders of the horn were also stung by long-flying arrows. War cries filled the air as youths kicked their ponies. It had been a long run from the top of the hill; some ponies faltered.

From the huts, another line of women and men came forth. They carried spears, twice as long as any lance Arakk had seen, and large woven shields. Beside them ran children with shields on their arms. The young went to stand next to an archer or slinger, ready to protect them from arrows. Here and there a crone buzzed about the children. They carried shields too and stood in the line with the young. The spear-carriers did the same. Never had Arakk seen the likes of this.

As he watched, the charge of the warriors of the Stormy Mountain came to a standstill. The courage of their upbringing urged them on. A hailstorm of arrows urged them back. Brave Lurgan, leader of his own double hand and most honored of archers, put arrow to bow and kicked his pony forward. When he let fly, it fell to ground short. Lurgan fell, an arrow in his eye.

Arakk gnashed his teeth, pulling hard on the reins, twisting with his pony, searching, searching for the place to strike, to avenge this insult. Brave Easos shouted and pointed to the right. There was a space between the river and the huts. Easos led off, and Arakk's double hand of warriors followed. They would slip into this place and come up behind those who dared to stand against the horsemen of the Clan. They would take many worthy heads this day.

Jack soothed Windrider. The horse stomped its hooves, eager to join the battle whose noises came to them on the wind. Behind him, twenty more archers stood by their horses. Tension was tight in their eyes as they waited for Jack's orders.

He took a deep breath and waited.

Launa had gotten what she wanted. She was in the thick of the battle; he was well beyond its edge . . . and would stay there until the right moment. And that was the question that ate at his gut. *What was the right moment?*

Jack sought a balance. He had to hold back far enough to stay unengaged. Some wandering band of warriors on the edge of the fight could not stumble on him. Still, he had to keep close enough to know when the time had come to close Launa's trap.

"God, what I'd give for a radio. Even flares would be nice."

Jack heard the noise of riders. Someone was flanking Tall Oaks on the river side. Jack signaled his men to silence. It was tempting to commit his troops to stop them, but that was not what Launa had planned for him. Jack let them pass.

THIRTY-TWO

IN THE SANCTUARY of the Goddess, Lasa sat her chair. Wise Glengish stood beside her. Those hurt would be brought here. Those who could be cared for would be washed, their wounds cleaned and dressed with the herbs gathered in the last three days. Jack had shared with her yesterday the horror of wounds too bad to heal. He had not surprised her. Lasa had watched her mother tend a man mauled by a bear. She had prayed, then taken a knife and let out the hunter's lifeblood so that he might again have peace. Lasa knew death. But she feared she had never seen as much of it as she would this day.

In front of her stood Hanna and several hundred of her followers. They sang songs that praised the peaceful ways of the Goddess and those who walked her paths. Last spring, Lasa would have sung those songs the loudest, but this spring day she was silent. Did a quiet voice inside her whisper she was wrong? Or was that voice angry because none of these risked the sharp arrows that now flew over the fields of Tall Oaks?

The doors and windows of the sanctuary were open. They brought light and warm spring air. Now they also brought the shouts of the *battle*. Such a strange word, hard for the mouth to form. Launa had given Lasa many new words. Lasa prayed there would be no need for more after today. A

shadow passed across the plaza before the longhouse. She
went to the door. It was only a small cloud before the sun.

Standing in the doorway, Lasa heard screams from both
ends of town. Her place was here, yet people were in pain.

Launa had often talked of plans, of the need to work by
them, and of the need to change them. Lasa's heart told her
it was time to change one. "Glengish, collect cloths, pots of
herbs and water to wash wounds. Then come after me."

Lasa did not wait for the woman to give her counsel, but
started walking to the west. She heard noise as she approached Samath's shop. Passing his street, she froze.

Two horsemen rode carefully through the berry bush as
another topped the mound that had been the wall. Samath's
son, Hass, stood in the street. He drew back his bow and
shot the first. As he reached for another shaft, the second
horseman put an arrow through Hass's chest. The young
man fell, clutching at the wound. The raider grabbed his
lance and charged.

Lasa turned to run. She did not see one of the logs that
Launa had had scattered around the streets to slow racing
horses and trip them. She fell, half on her belly, half on her
side. A shooting pain took the breath from her. Sprawled in
the dust, she turned to meet her death.

As the horseman passed a doorway, Samath screamed and
dashed out, swinging his axe at the rider's stomach. The
raider fell from his horse, bowels and blood spewing everywhere. As the craftsman brought his axe down on the fallen
raider's head, the last horseman crossed the wall, taking aim
at Samath. That one's horse stumbled as it stepped from the
wall. The first arrow went wild, narrowly missing Lasa.

Samath raised his axe over his head and charged the
horsemen. Coolly the invader nocked a second arrow. He
was drawing it back to take aim when Das rounded a corner,
arrow already nocked, and let fly. The last rider took the
arrow square in the chest. Knocked back by the force of the
hit, the rider's arrow sailed high and elsewhere.

While Das and two axemen took station by the wall,
Samath knelt beside his son, held his head, wiped away the
blood that frothed his lips. And Lasa saw past them. In a vi-

sion she saw Kaul lying on another field, an arrow piercing him. The vision passed, yet its promise drove her to action. Lasa picked herself up. "There is a young man hurt. Tend to him," she called to Glengish as she ran to the west, toward her heart.

No longer was Launa sure her archers and slingers could stop this charge. She was glad for the company of the heavy infantry when they joined the line. Antia deployed her troopers, but took station next to Launa. Little Sisu stuck to Launa like a shadow.

The horsemen learned quickly. An arrow flew at 45 meters a second. At 200 meters, the raiders had four seconds to see it coming and dodge. Horses weaved. Riders ducked. Arrows missed.

But this tactic had its price. Launa aimed at four riders who had bunched up. They dodged her arrow, crashed together and went down in one pile of screaming horseflesh. One rider didn't get up, and, though busy elsewhere, Launa watched out of the corner of her eye when raiders put two horses out of their pain.

Arrows that missed riders hit horses. Launa steeled herself against the pitiful cries of the wounded beasts. Nothing had prepared her for this. She felt as if she were murdering innocent children. But walking horsemen were less a threat. And more raiders were walking.

"Slingers, aim for the walkers. Archers, shoot for the horsemen." Troopers moved to obey Launa's orders. Even tear-stained Hanatha rejoined the battle.

The charge stalled 150 meters out. At that range, the raiders had time to dodge arrows and stones. Many removed the shields they had slung on their backs for the charge and used them to ward off rocks and arrows.

"Why won't you bastards go away?" Launa checked her supply of arrows. She had used up one quiver; half her arrows were gone. If her people shot themselves dry, they were dead.

"Hold on to your arrows, archers," Launa yelled. "Don't

let fly unless you have a good target. Slingers, let them feel your stones. Sisu, get us more stones."

As the little fellow took off running, the slingers stood taller, glad for the chance to redeem themselves. The archers gathered in twos or threes to rest and talk.

Launa noted that the horsemen did the same. Whenever five or six of them got together, she ordered a volley. With arrows coming from all angles of the line, more horsemen sprouted feathers. The survivors learned to keep to themselves.

Good, Launa thought with a sneer. *The battlefield's a lonely place. Don't you bastards want to be someplace else? Learn to retreat, you sons of bitches.*

They didn't.

Launa wiped sweat from her forehead, her eyes searching high in the sky for the sun. It was still low. It couldn't be more than 0900, probably more like 0800. What she thought had been hours was more like half an hour. Around her, people took deep breaths and leaned on their pikes. One group laughed. Launa wished she'd heard the joke. This was crazy. She remembered from her textbooks that ancient battles often went in phases, the warriors taking breaks. Raw combat could only be maintained for a few minutes; then people took a breather before working up their courage and resolution to lay on again. Launa wondered how long this would last.

Across the field, one horseman set an arrow to bow, yelled and broke from the rest. Kicking his horse, he raced for Launa's troops. He dodged rocks. It wasn't until he drew his bow and shot that he presented a steady target. Ballen let one arrow fly. The warrior fell shrieking, the shaft in his eye. The horseman's arrow fell short.

Encouraged by him, three more warriors followed close on his heels. Archers and slingers took them under fire. It took a moment for realization to dawn on Launa, but only a moment.

The raiders rode for her.

One man had four arrows in him. He kept coming. Looking straight at Launa, he took aim. She pulled a blunt-headed arrow back to her ear and watched it pierce him. He didn't even flinch. There was no time left to run. He aimed straight for her heart, sneered, let fly and slumped from his mount.

Little Sisu must have seen what was happening. He dropped the sack of stones he had brought forward and ran for Launa. He got his shield in front of her in the second the arrow was in flight.

Launa would never forget the little one's scream as he skidded to earth in front of her.

The battle hung suspended. Launa dropped her bow, falling to her knees beside the child. The broken arrow pinned the wicker shield to his tiny body. Blood gushed from the wound in his chest, flowing like eternity onto shield and grass and dust.

Launa, the woman, someday mother—no longer the warrior Goddess—shuddered helplessly as she gently rolled him over, cradled his head. Brown eyes going dull looked up at her.

"I'm sorry." Sisu coughed, gasped for breath, blood dripping down pale cheeks as a rasping whisper poured out his young soul. "Forgot to hold . . . shield away . . . didn't mean . . ." His head rolled limply on her arm.

The battle looked so different from her knees seen through powerless tears. Launa tasted exhaustion. All across the field, enthusiasm had fled. The killing continued, but in a desultory fashion. Occasionally a raider ventured closer. An arrow or stone reminded him to keep his distance. He did.

Launa gave herself over to a wail of mourning for a boy who had died under a man's load. Ballen came, stood beside her, rested a strong hand on her shoulder. Antia and two others stood, backs to her, shields between her and the enemy. Someone wept with Launa. It was not Antia.

Lasa ran, gasping for air. Clutching her belly, supporting as best she could the new life she carried, she ran to the life that was more dear than her own. As she rounded the last row of houses, the battle lay before her. Kaul and Taelon commanded here. Launa had spoken of the importance of an even line to hold the horsemen away from the town. That was not what Lasa saw.

The horsemen were clumped near the river. Most of the archers and pikes stood there. Close to her, the line of defenders was ragged. That did not seem to matter. Horsemen and pikes stood resting. Few slingers or archers shot. Lasa would have thought that nothing had happened here, but in the fields, bodies littered the green. Horses screamed; men groaned. Lasa looked wide-eyed. Kaul stood with Taelon, talking as he might on any spring day while they considered the planting of several fields.

Lasa drew breath. Her heart returned to her breast. Kaul saw her and trotted toward her.

At that moment, something changed. Two hands of riders sped away from the others. It looked as if they would leave the valley. Yet, as they drew even with Lasa, they turned, racing for the line where she stood. It took a moment for the archers to realize their danger. They shot, but the horsemen dodged, racing for them at an angle. Many times Kaul had told Lasa how hard it was to shoot a deer that bounded away from him at an angle. Now Kaul drew an arrow.

The horsemen had bows in hand. Some fell, but many still rode when one of their arrows took a woman in the neck. Kaul turned, shouting for more archers and pikes to come. A horseman took aim at Kaul's back. Lasa screamed. Taelon, running toward the line, saw what Kaul did not. He shoved his friend as the arrow reached him. Kaul fell, an arrow through his arm.

Taelon bellowed, pulled back his bow and shot that raider from his mount.

A second horseman put his lance through a slinger as a woman thrust her pike in his belly. A third took two arrows in his shield, and dodged a pike thrust as he flailed about himself with an axe. A slinger went down under his blows. Two children slipped under his reach. His mount smashed out the brains of the girl, but the boy's knife slit wide the horse's belly. As the horse collapsed, the invader took the boy's head off with his axe. But three pikes cut through him, pinning him to the ground.

That horseman was the last with the heart to charge the line.

Lasa sank into the dust beside her man. She had twice seen his death. She wanted to weep. She held back tears to tend him.

"Do not worry about me, my love. Help me up." Struggling with the baby, herself, her consort, Lasa got Kaul to his feet.

Kaul pushed the arrow through his arm. Holding it in his uninjured hand, he waved it, red with his blood, at the invaders. He and Taelon shouted defiances and suggestions of what their mothers and fathers had been. Lasa wanted to laugh. She regretted the horsemen did not speak the People's tongue. Still, as one, the raiders turned and took flight.

Then she felt a pain, followed quickly by another. They were sharp. It was time. This child would be born into a new age. Why should she not be born in a battle? While pike, archer, slingers went forward to bring death to those who had no horse, Kaul came to her.

The third pain shook her. She smiled up at Kaul. "Our daughter comes."

Launa felt Ballen tighten his grip on her shoulder. It seemed an eternity had passed. "Lady, I smell trouble." He pointed with his bow. The shield wall opened. Launa saw a dozen or more young warriors on foot. One of them harangued the rest.

Tenderly, Launa arranged Sisu in peaceful repose. She stood, her flesh going hard again. Death would not win from all what it had stolen from this child. Launa wiped tears away. Sisu's blood covered her body. Now it striped her face.

Twelve raiders afoot rushed for the line.

"Greet them with arrows and stones," Launa ordered in a voice of flint.

Warriors began to fall. It seemed all would. All should have. But one thin youth with a large shield twisted, dodged and zigzagged as he ran. By charm or magic, an arrow never fell where he was, or else his shield held it at bay. Nothing halted his dance toward them.

With a shout of vengeance, Tomas lifted his long pike and charged. Archers and slingers froze in mid-aim, fearing to strike one of their own. Launa bit back a scream. The short spear was for hand-to-hand combat. The pike was for stopping charging horses. But the young man who had lived while his father died ran to meet his fate.

The warrior was good. As Tomas charged with his pike, the warrior charged too, his long knife waving. At the last moment, the clansman sidestepped the pike. He grabbed it as it went by, pulling Tomas to him. Tomas had no chance to dodge the knife that slashed open his belly. He sprawled in the dust, whimpering in shock as his blood reddened the brown.

Before the raider could raise a victory shout, Antia was there, death with a short spear. She held the weapon as Launa had taught, like a quarterstaff. With its butt, she parried his thrust. Around and around they circled, now thrust, now parry. He was unsure of how to fight this stick. She, careful, bided her time for an opening. When at last he overextended, she brought the butt down on his arm to a crunch of bone. Just as quickly, she swung the tip at his head. He groaned and slumped in the dust beside Tomas.

Antia used his own knife to hack off his head. She used his pigtails to swing the trophy back at his comrades. A groan escaped the clansmen. A shout went up from the townspeople.

Now was the time.

"Come after me!" Launa shouted, her voice harsh. On wobbly legs, she stalked toward the enemy. Her pace was slow, deliberate. With trembling hands, she nocked an arrow, took her time to aim and shot. The enemy had to be pretty far gone too. Her target forgot to dodge. He screamed, clutched at the arrow in his chest, staggered and fell.

All along the line, slingers, archers and spear carriers advanced. Clansmen backed away.

THIRTY-THREE

ARAKK'S BAND SLIPPED around the line of archers and slingers, disappearing into the trees that lined the river. Easos led them in through the second opening to the town. Arakk grinned; there was no one to see them enter. They would charge these animals from their own stinking huts and skewer archers on their lances before the bowmen knew what was behind them.

The horsemen slowed as they entered the town. Logs and branches lay scattered on the ground. Their ponies stepped carefully around them. Easos had almost reached the main street when a woman darted out from a hut. She carried a long stick with an antler on it. With a defiant cry, she snagged Easos's shoulder and pulled him from his horse. A horseman put an arrow into her at the same moment a shaggily dressed man appeared and brought his axe down on Easos's chest. Easos's and the woman's screams mingled as one.

Suddenly, everywhere, there were women with poles and spears and men with axes. Some appeared in doorways. Others ran from the next streets. In the blink of an eye, half of Arakk's band was on the ground, fighting, screaming, dying.

Arakk had no time to watch. Someone tried to snag his son from his horse. The chieftain put an arrow in her, then lost his bow as he twisted away from an antler. Someone with a knife got close to his horse. Arakk let his mount kick out and heard bone crunch.

A spear jab narrowly missed him. He grabbed for it and began a tug-of-war. Arakk shoved it away when a man with a long-handled axe went for his son.

Arakk's lance thrust caught that one unaware. It was good to see blood on his lance again.

For a moment, the fighting paused. Arakk looked around him. Only his son and Olak still sat their horses. This was not possible. These rabbits were his for the slaughter. Now they gathered, a solid wall between him and his goal. Long spears came down. Axes twirled in the sun. Those he had ridden here to cleanse from the steppe edged forward, their eyes burning with the killing rage.

Olak backed his pony to stand beside Arakk. "We will not get in here, and there are too few of us now to slaughter the archers if we did ride among them."

"Yes," hissed Arakk, angry at the wisdom in those words. He clenched his fist, but did not hit Olak for what he said. Instead, Arakk yanked his pony's head around and kicked it to a run. The two followed his son out of the village, chased by the spears and jeers of those they should have killed. Arakk snarled back empty insults as he sped for the Clan's warriors.

They were few, and they were riding or running from this foul place. Far out, only two double hands fled back from the horn. Neither Tamer nor Siskar rode with them.

Arakk called to rally the clan. Riders fled by him. He controlled his urge to strike them from their mounts. Others joined him, shouting war cries. They milled about. One moment, angry, they wanted to drink blood. The next, too galled by arrows and stones, they wanted to flee.

Arakk considered hurling the Clan against the band of archers and slingers, but the defenders held together as they walked from the town, and he was not sure his warriors would charge them again, even if he led.

Suddenly, between the warriors and the hill, four hands of riders emerged from the trees along the river. They spread out and dismounted. As the fleeing warriors approached them, arrows from these cut them down. Arakk growled low in his throat. The Clan had ridden here to spring a trap. Now his warriors were dying, caught in a trap of someone else's making.

Jack deployed his dragoons to close Launa's trap. Originally, he suspected Launa just wanted to get him out of the center of the defense. If things came unhinged, one of them had to live to fight another day. Once Launa had put the idea of annihilating the horsemen to Lasa, there was no use arguing. After what they had done to Kaul, Lasa wanted blood.

Now, much to Jack's surprise, the trap was working. No horseman would live to tell the story of Tall Oaks and the longbow. *Launa, it was worth the risk.*

The survivors of the repulse before Tall Oaks galloped back the way they came. The first few loners were easy pickings. Jack shouted for Trass to take his hunters farther to the left. The wreckage of the flankers needed mopping up. "Let none live."

Trass gave Jack a hard, solemn nod that sealed the fate of those given to him to kill.

Jack turned back to the main event. Launa's deployment had proven brilliant. She and Brege led half of First Legion in defense of the east edge of town. Taelon and Kaul, with the other half, held the west end. The recruits of Second Legion, leavened with Das's axemen, patrolled the wall and river. It was a good thing.

Jack had expected leakers around the edges, but not a concerted flank attack. Whoever was calling the shots for these dudes was good—too good. Throwing a wing out to flank the town was smart. The Mongols would use that tactic in A.D. 1200 but Jack was surprised to see it this early. It would be better if this one died.

Ten horsemen had held back from the charge. Was this guy savvy enough to keep an uncommitted reserve? Jack figured he had an ID on the C.O. among the three survivors of the riverside sneak. Too bad for him. Jack hadn't brought a West Point education back six thousand years and halfway around the world to have some local genius charge off the Russian steppe and outfight him. The People of Tall Oaks were his people, and they were going to live.

Jack's squad picked off a few more stragglers, then waited patiently as the enemy chief rallied his last twenty-plus for a charge. Trass polished off the flankers, but they in turn drew him too far off for support.

Jack looked down the line at his nine shepherds, tightly gripping their bows, awaiting whatever was coming. This morning they had expected to die. Now their homes and loved ones were safe. They had watched the horsemen die in their pastures. Odds of one to two didn't frighten them.

Jack, however, knew he faced a dilemma. If he spread out to cover the front, he risked defeat in detail. If he closed his troops up to support each other, horsemen could escape around his flanks. Lousy tactical situation, but he'd known that when he took the job.

Launa and her archers advanced from the village. If old horsefeathers wasn't careful, his light cavalry was going to be ambushed by infantry. That would be one for the Book when Launa got around to writing it.

A horseman fell to the advancing archers. Arakk threw down his bow. There was no time for arrows now. There was no longer time for anything. He couched his lance and kicked his pony. "Follow me, son."

Beside him, Kantom lowered the clan totem, signaling the charge.

With tight, angry eyes, the Mighty Man studied the archers between him and the hill. The one at the end waved to the rest. They moved to obey. That one would die.

"The tall one leads them," Arakk shouted. "He is a true warrior. Honor the lance that drinks his blood." The lances came down. All warriors rode for one enemy.

"Ride on my right," Arakk called to his son. "The Mighty Men must know of these arrows that reach out with demon arms to kill warriors too soon. You must live to bring my words to the clans. Let them come here in numbers too many to count."

"I will, father," Kantom called back.

Arakk aimed his lance for the one who led this tiny band between him and life. Beside him, riders fell. The distance was impossible but still his men fell, arrows in chests or horses.

Arakk slumped over his horse's neck, mumbling a prayer, asking forgiveness of his mount's spirit for using it as cover, even as fear rose in him. *Was their mother god stronger than the Mighty Sun?* He switched his lance to his left arm; he would ride to this man's right, a shield for Kantom. Arakk aimed his lance for the man's heart.

More horsemen fell. The thunder of the charge grew quiet. In the end, only his pony's hoofbeats and those of his son's pony pounded in Arakk's ears. He was within a bow shot now. If he had kept his bow, he would have this man. The target on the ground pulled an arrow back to his ear and let fly.

Pain shot through Arakk's side. He gritted his teeth; nothing must cause his lance to waver from that man's heart.

This warrior had no honor. He danced away. Arakk moved the aim of his lance point to follow him. It would not go. His arm would not obey. Slowly the lance sank toward the ground. Arakk tried to drop it, but could not let go. His breath came in gasps. The lance struck the ground, knocking him from his seat. Darkness came as he rolled on the ground.

Pain shot through Arakk's head. A veil of red covered his eyes. He clutched for his knife, found it, drew it. To move was agony. To a warrior, what was pain? He rolled over. Across the plain, he saw the dead. But farther still, his son raced on, galloping for the hill.

"Ride, Kantom, ride," he tried to shout. It came out a croak. Still, Arakk could laugh in his heart. The deeds of the Stormy Mountain Clan would live on in the songs of the Horse People who came in numbers too many to count to cleanse this blot from the Wide Open Sky. The mother god would yet weep.

But now the warrior without honor drew an arrow to his ear and aimed for Arakk's son. Arakk hurled his knife at that one. It struck him. Arakk collapsed with a smile on his lips.

Jack flinched as he let the arrow fly. A stone knife took him full in the back, then fell to the ground behind him. He'd been hit, but with the handle end of it. A quick glance showed the fallen chief a dead heap behind him. The arrow missed wide; Jack pulled another from his quiver. Only two more left.

The rider was opening the distance fast. Jack quickly took aim and let fly. On that man and Jack's arrow the secret of the longbow, and a world's future, hung. He watched the arrow as it flew, studying its flight for wind drift. It took the rider full in the back.

He slumped on his horse . . . and kept riding.

Jack's next shot missed behind.

The range was opening fast as Jack strung his last arrow. The angle would be high, the odds of a hit slim. Jack prayed he could at least hit the horse.

His arrow took the mount in the right hindquarter. No killing blow there. At best it would slow the animal, make it easier for them to chase it down. Jack turned to yell for the horse holder to bring him Windrider.

The fleeing horse kicked once, then twice, trying to rid itself of its pain. The arrow stayed in its flesh . . . but the weakened rider lost his battle to stay on. He tumbled from his horse and rolled like a rag doll. He did not get up.

Jack let out a sigh of relief—and turned, on guard, as a scream from behind him made him jump.

The chief lay in the dust, his back broken by his fall, struggling to reach his lance.

Jack picked up his spear and trotted to him. Here was a warrior his Apache grandfather would have respected. Here was a man who would die with his weapon in his hand. Here also was the ancestor of the man who had sent biological warheads at Europe without realizing he condemned the whole world to death. Jack sank his anger into the spear jab that slashed the man's throat.

Jack's eyes swept the field. Horses screamed in pain. Raiders lay in crumpled heaps. Here, one coughed blood. There, another cried out. Near Jack, one sat silently as his lifeblood gushed from a neck wound. In the distance, a small band afoot fought its last battle with Antia's spears. They went down. The battle was over. The battle was won.

Jack's knees went weak. He leaned on his spear for support. His hands slipped on blood and he almost fell. A sigh, half sob, shook his body. He lived. He had met the enemy; they were dead, and he lived. The second fire Kaul and Launa and he had ignited had burned out the Kurgans—here, today. This battle was theirs. He shivered; history said it would be a long war.

Across the littered battlefield, Launa walked toward him. He waved his spear. She wearily waved hers, then jerked it back front.

A warrior dragged himself to his feet. He lunged at her with his lance. She batted it aside. For a moment they stood like statues, he defenseless. Was she disarmed by his helplessness? Again he brought his lance up to strike. Launa drove her spear point into his chest. He crumpled. Launa paused, looking down at the heap of human flesh.

Jack wondered what nightmares would come in the dark. The heat and sand of the desert gave him his first taste. Today would not be his last.

Launa covered the final distance to him, giving fallen riders a wide berth. For a heart-stopping moment, Jack feared she was wounded. Blood covered her breasts and stomach, legs and arms. Her face was smeared in tears, dust, dried blood. She came to him, dropped her spear, embraced him.

"Are you hurt? Launa . . ." What words does a man use to his beloved when she looks like a bloody demon from hell?

"Sisu's dead. He saved my life." The words were mumbled to his chest. It took a moment for them to register.

"Oh, Launa," Jack whispered, remembering the morning above River Bend. He had brought in Antia and her sisters. Launa had found Brown Eyes and his friends. He hugged Launa close; the nightmares would be bad.

"Damn Tomas. He used his horse pike to go hand-to-hand

with a bastard." Launa pushed herself away from Jack, shook her fists at the world. "The SOB deserved what he got."

Jack swallowed. Not Tomas who had ridden into hell with him. He pulled Launa back. "You don't mean that."

"I don't." She shook. "I don't. But why didn't he do like I taught him? He'd be alive now." She huddled close. Quiet tears fell on his chest.

Jack's tears could wait.

His eyes drifted over the battlefield. Across it, men and women he had lived with for the last six months stood in shock, staring at what they had done. Of what would they sing tonight? Here and there, other blood-speckled couples held each other.

A small number, the survivors of River Bend by the belts they wore, went from horseman to horseman, making sure they were dead, finishing those who weren't quite. Jack knew what they did was a mercy, but ascribed no virtue to their action.

And it came to Jack. What had he let loose? The horsemen were dead. But what of their killers? How much had he changed these people? What had he taught them? He had sneered at the horsemen as evil incarnate. He had come to protect these people. Had he protected them, or infected them himself?

Launa stiffened beside him. "I'm sorry, Captain, for getting emotional on you."

Jack shrugged off her apology as well as the questions that haunted him. "Why? You led your troop. You won your battle. You drove what was left to me. You planned the battle. You fought it according to your plan, as near as any battle ever is."

Launa looked across the battlefield, slowly shaking her head. "It didn't go at all like I thought it would."

"It never does, honey." Jack stooped, slung an empty quiver over his shoulder, picked up his bow. He was tired. Lord, was he tired. All he wanted was to go home and sleep.

Behind him, hooves thundered. He unlimbered his bow in a hurry, snatching an arrow from Launa as he turned.

It was Sara.

She reined in beside him. "The horsemen made their camp in a canyon. Only women and boys guard it. Killala says she sees people from River Bend there. We need help to take the camp."

Damn, Jack winced. *Hadn't he already done enough?* "Dragoons, mount up. We ride to free the slaves taken at River Bend." Trass and his ten cheered. Jack's ten mounted up. Once on Windrider, Jack looked down at Launa. "Want a ride, Lady?"

Launa looked at the hill. Somewhere behind it were the slaves she would have charged to her death to free last year. Jack knew what her answer was. She reached out. He pulled her up behind him.

THIRTY-FOUR

JACK CALLED TO Antia. "We go to the enemy camp to free the people of River Bend. Follow after us."

She waved and took off running.

Jack eyed the battlefield. He was riding for another. More blood. He groaned. And sparked an idea. "Launa, get me that lance, the one with all the feathers. The last guy to charge me was waving it." Launa was down and back up in a moment.

As Jack followed Sara, he tried to figure out what to do with the enemy base camp. He'd just seen one disastrous offensive. He didn't want to repeat the favor. In truth, all his thinking since coming through time had concentrated on defense. Without a tank and a couple of weeks of bombing to soften up the bad guys, Jack wasn't too keen on sticking his nose where it wasn't wanted. Pending a chance to look the terrain over, he'd use arrows, lots of arrows, followed up by careful infiltration. Maybe at night. Night couldn't be too long from now. He hunted for the sun. It was not yet noon. *Damn!*

The camp was in a draw. The horsemen had pitched their tents beside a stream among tree-covered hills. It was not well protected. Jack's archers could take the high ground and shoot down on them. Brent had said these guys liked hilltops. Maybe they hadn't learned yet, or maybe they weren't expecting trouble.

Sara's scouts were out of sight. The arrival of his twenty dragoons created a stir in camp. People ran to greet them, only to fall back in shock. The two sides eyed each other. They saw riders with longbows and no helmets. Jack saw women in long dresses and young boys in leggings. Both sported short bows. One woman took two steps from the rest and shouted something.

Killala broke cover, running from the bush that concealed her to stand in front of Jack and Sara. "She asks who you are."

Launa slipped from behind Jack. He dismounted and raised an eyebrow to Launa.

"I think a man better talk for us," she said.

Jack turned to Killala. "Tell her I am the war leader for the town of Tall Oaks."

"They have no word for town, but I will name us a clan." Killala cast strange words across the space between them. Shock turned to anger at her words. Arguments broke out among the women. Killala shrugged. "They don't believe you."

Jack waved the lance he'd brought to prove his credentials. "Tell them I took this from the dead man who carried it."

At Killala's words, the women went silent. Even Jack could understand the bitterness and doubt in the next words the woman sent stonily across to them. "She would look on the lance."

Jack held it out, point to the women. "Tell her she may have it."

A young boy ran warily forward. He didn't look any older than Sisu. He stopped a little beyond the reach of the lance. Disdainfully, Jack tossed it in the dust. The boy reverently picked it up, then dashed for the woman. She fingered its feathers, then clasped it to her breast. A high-pitched keening slowly turned to a long moaning wail. Others joined her mourning. More stood stunned. The woman turned back to Jack and screamed something.

"She says the lance will drink our blood. Arrows will greet you when you come for them."

"Call them back. I wanted to offer them a chance to lay down their knives and either return to the steppe or eat at our table." Jack knew his voice sounded desperate. He'd seen enough killing. He glanced at his troops; they didn't look very enthusiastic for more killing either.

Killala shook her head. "The words she has used are those of the war band. I have never heard a woman use them."

"What do we do now?" Sara asked.

Jack groaned. "I need to sit down."

Sara pointed to a stand of trees. More scouts appeared to take their horses to water. The dragoons deployed, backing up the scouts surrounding the camp.

Jack collapsed once he got in the shade of a tree. It was hot. Sara offered a waterskin. Jack tried not to drain more than half before offering it to Launa. She did drain it, using the last drops to wash the blood from her face and hands.

Jack sat up. "I say we go in after dark with ropes and take as many prisoners as we can. Maybe tomorrow morning we can talk some sense into them."

Launa frowned. "Think we can get Antia on board with that? She had the blood lust up last time I saw her."

"If she doesn't like it, she can go hand-to-hand with me. I've seen enough killing today. Women and children are not on my legitimate target list."

Launa looked at the distant camp, her eyes unfocused. "Yes, we've seen enough blood today."

An hour later, Antia rode up with almost a hundred mixed pike and archers. She immediately deployed her new arrivals in a line and made ready to charge. Jack trotted out to put an end to that nonsense. Launa followed on a borrowed mount.

Jack reined in, but before he could open his mouth, muffled screams came from the camp. He glanced over his shoulder. Black smoke rose from the camp's center. Jack spun Windrider around.

"What's going on?" Launa shouted.

"I don't know, but I think my plan just fell apart." Jack kicked Windrider. Behind him, Launa shouted the charge.

Jack rode like a bat into hell, expecting any moment to be met with a swarm of arrows. Nothing came.

The smoke rose, billowing above the camp. Even as he galloped among tents, he saw no one. Slowing, he trotted into the central space and halted, unable to believe what his eyes saw.

Scattered across the yard were hundreds of bodies. In front of him, a young woman's hand twitched as it came away from the knife in her throat. Beside her, three small bundles of clothing . . . children . . . their heads half off their slashed throats. Jack's breath escaped in a shudder. He wanted to cry out. *No!*

Ahead of him, three women stood, holding torches. At their feet lay the bodies of children, blood still gushing from their throats. At a word from the middle women, they threw down their flaming brands, pulled bloody knives from their belts and drove them into their own throats.

Jack blinked back shock. His stomach revolted as his skin went cold. He swayed on his mount, his head spinning, his brain refusing to process any more.

Screams pushed him again to action.

Behind the dying women, two tents burned. Travois poles leaned against the tents, adding heat to the fire as they burned.

Jack leaped from his horse. One young woman lay with a lance in her heart, the lance he had taken from the chieftain and given to the boy. Jack used it to knock aside the poles. They fell, leaving a space of burning cloth. With his knife, he cut through, pushing aside felt even as he smelled his hair burning.

Inside the tent was bedlam. Women and children stood or knelt. Hands tied behind them, they struggled to get as far from the flaming walls as they could. Three burned already, their clothes torches that threatened fire to those close to them.

Jack screamed "Come," and pushed with his bare back against the flaming tent to widen the hole. Faces turned to him, hope gleaming through their tears. Those who could ran for the opening. Suddenly, Launa was beside him, shouldering the hole farther open. Jack could feel his flesh burn. Behind him, Antia shouted. Pikes pushed more wood aside. Cloth ripped as knives cut more away. People fled on both sides of him.

Across the tent, one small flaming heap did not move. Jack took a deep breath and ran for it. Yanking off his loincloth, he beat at the fire and pulled flaming clothes off a little girl. He picked her up and raced for the other side of the tent. In the open, he gasped for air, then rolled on the ground to put out what fire he could.

Whimpers escaped tiny blackened lips. Jack searched, then caught sight of a stream. With this huddled lump of flesh, he ran for it.

Skidding to a stop beside it, he let the girl gently down into the cooling waters. He tried to brush aside more of the blackened cloth. It was not cloth. It was her flesh. Charred slabs of muscle came away, leaving bones exposed. Large brown eyes looked deep into Jack's, then closed.

Jack wept. Deep, racking sobs shook his body. He wanted to howl, to scream. Why? Why had this happened? He looked to the sky, to the flowing water, to the earth. The smells of springtime were overpowered by the stench of roasted human flesh. He had started a second fire; they had kindled a third.

Someone came, took the tiny body from the water. Launa stood beside him, helping him to his feet. Like a child, he followed where she led.

He found himself standing naked, the sun inflaming his seared flesh. Sara, Antia, Killala, stood with him, staring down at the murdered bodies of children, of the women who did it.

"Why?" Launa asked what Jack's entire body ached to know.

Killala knelt beside the girl Jack had pulled the lance from. "This girl was my friend in River Bend. We played together, dreamed of the men we would have when we finally knew why we wanted them." Killala shivered as she brushed back the dead woman's hair from her face. "The mighty man took her for his own servant. I thought she had it easy." She pointed to the woman who had led the others. "I think the chieftain's woman did not like that. She promised the lance would drink our blood, and drove it into this one's heart."

Killala stood and strode to where the wife lay in blood. "You ask why she did this?" She faced Launa and Jack. "She had a place at the mighty man's tent. Other women stepped out of her way, listened to her words." Killala looked hard at Jack. "You killed her man. Where could she go? Who would have had her at another campfire? And as for staying here— I have lived the life of a slave. I would die before they took me again. She was wise to choose death this time."

Jack stared at the body. How many in his century would accept loss of station and power? How had any person of power taken to the loss of control? Was power more important than life? Jack wanted to vomit.

Antia shook her head, face hard as flint. Then she turned her back and walked to her horse. "You and Jack must return to Tall Oaks. Many have died. We must lay them out for burial."

Someone brought Windrider to Jack and helped him mount. Antia led at a walk. Windrider followed. Jack twisted on his mount and rode from the camp looking backward. The sickness that had killed so many was etching itself forever in his memory. This was madness. This was how his world would end, six thousand years from now. What could he have done different?

THIRTY-FIVE

AS JACK RODE over the hill and down into Tall Oaks, his eyes rested on a gash newly ripped in the yellow earth. Across the fields, people collected bodies, carrying them toward the long, shallow trench that had been opened to receive them.

Jack wanted a bath. He wanted to wash the stench of blood and smoke and burned flesh from his body, his hair, his mind. He wanted a drink. He wanted to get drunk out of his mind. He wanted to go on a binge the likes of which he hadn't done since the desert. He turned his mount toward the river.

Antia blocked his path. "We gather where the earth has been opened." That was the last place Jack wanted to be. Numbly, he resigned himself to another funeral. His mind was dazed enough. As with Sandie's and Sam's deaths, he could ignore whatever those responsible for such things had to do and say.

The crowd beside the grave parted to let Jack and Launa through. Kaul with a bandaged arm, Taelon, Brege and Merik stood together. Launa walked Jack toward them. Kaul and Taelon wept. Brege stood dry-eyed. Merik stared dazed into the opened earth.

Jack looked down. In one long row, they lay. Tomas, Sisu, so many others of the town, lay on their sides, knees drawn up. The warriors lay on their backs, vacant eyes staring into the blue sky. Jack could not look at them. He stared into the sky. *Why?* he demanded of any God or Goddess who would listen.

"Where is Lasa?" Launa asked beside him.

Kaul shuddered as tears flowed more heavily. Taelon swallowed and glanced at his friend, then at Launa. "She is coming."

The People waited on She who Spoke for their Goddess. The sounds of their mourning rose and fell. Soft sobs were punctuated by wails of deeper anguish, quickly muffled as the grieving ones were clasped to other bosoms. Living flesh drew living flesh close, offering hope and warmth.

Jack drew in upon himself, willing his blood to ice.

A commotion drew Jack's attention from the silent sky. The People opened a pathway to the grave from town. Samath came forward, carrying the limp body of his son. Behind him, two women and a man helped Hanna. Samath reached the edge of the grave. A couple helped him lay his son in a vacant space. As he climbed out, his son's blood covered him. Hanna exploded with her loss, wailing her grief to drown out all else. Samath went to her.

She pushed him away. "You killed my son!"

She turned on Jack. "You killed my son!" Her shriek cut through all else. The community fell silent around her.

Jack looked at her. Nodding, he accepted his guilt for this death. He pinned her eyes with his. Would she accept her guilt, the guilt that came from her resolve to accept slavery and death freely from the horsemen? For a moment they stood frozen, eyes clashing in one final battle.

Then Hanna screamed. "My daughter comes!" Samath stood helpless as the others began the slow walk with the mother-to-be to the birthing sanctuary.

As Hanna reached the edge of the mourners, Jack caught sight of Lasa coming toward the grave. Hanna saw her too. Once again, she found breath to scream. "You have killed my son!" She need not have. Lasa's face showed no recognition. Hanna gave her one more glare, then turned away.

Lasa came to the grave haltingly, leaning heavily on

Glengish. In her arms, Lasa carried her child. The babe was quiet. Jack took two breaths before all air left him in a shudder. The baby did not move. Blinking back tears, he denied death one more victory, demanded that it give up this tiny prize. Then, with a choked gulp, Jack admitted defeat. This battle was already lost.

When Lasa stood at the lip of the grave, Glengish took the still form from her arms, stepped into the grave and laid it down. The woman could not have known where she placed the babe, but Jack did. To the right of the little one lay the red-bearded chieftain who had led the assault. To the left of the child lay a woman of the town. She had died with an arrow in her throat. Together the three formed a family in death.

Glengish returned to where Lasa teetered on the edge of collapse. Jack tried to take his mind elsewhere; he hated funerals. Today he'd had his fill of death.

Lasa whispered, "Jack."

His eyes snapped in focus on her face.

"A man led the attack on us. You and Launa have shown us the way to save our lives in trade for these." Lasa's hand swept the grave. "I will not have these buried by our ancient customs. A new time, hard and full of blood, comes upon us. It is for you, a man, to send these into the earth."

Lasa collapsed in a heap on the ground. Glengish searched in Lasa's robes, brought out bloody handfuls of moss, placed clean handfuls in their stead and held her down when Lasa would have stood again.

Jack waited until eyes turned from She who Spoke for the Goddess to him. So he who hated funerals would inter these dead. His mind raced through the rites he had sat through: Protestant, Catholic, Jewish. He remembered none of their words. He looked to the men and women beside him. These people did not deserve words borrowed from a distant future.

Jack slowed his racing mind, steadied his heart. Forcing his breathing to a measured pace, he centered himself on the ground beneath his feet, the people at his side. His soul reached out to touch them.

He began to weep. Not deep, racking sobs this time, but gentle tears that washed him clean of his deadly past, these people's lethal future. His mind softly touched the words and thoughts of his people, the lives they had shared with him this last year. From the depths of their living and loving, he found the strength to take a step forward.

"Launa, bring me red ocher, a bowl and water."

He waited, staring at the dead in front of him. Modern generals spoke of numbers for the cameras. Modern generals did not face the swarming flies, the circling birds, when they had won or lost their battles. Jack was not a modern general.

Launa returned, ocher and bowl in one hand, waterskin in another.

"Wash my hands."

Lovingly, Launa served acolyte to her captain. She poured the water slowly. He scrubbed at the blood, then turned with hands dripping to his people. "I can wash the blood of these people from my hands. But I can never wash the blood of those who died here from my heart, or from yours."

The People murmured their amen.

He mixed water with the ocher, plunged his hand in it, lifted it up as bloodied for all to see. "In blood, we come into the world. In blood, these have left us. Let them return to the heart of the Goddess, to know her love and joy, and to return again to us if she wills it." Jack had listened to the old ones share their hopes for an afterlife. Some believed death was a birth to a new life with the Goddess. Others hoped for reincarnation in another life here. Jack tried to pray with both.

Jack walked to the head of the trench. Naked, he stepped forward and slid slowly into the grave. Naked, he faced the dead.

Before him was Tomas. If the boy had practiced all winter with his pike, would he have remembered his lessons and lived today? Had the ride that saved Kaul and Jack's lives cost this man his own? Jack looked through tears into a face still shocked at his death wound. He sprinkled Tomas with ocher. "Return to the Goddess. Know her love and joy and peace."

Jack stepped to the next body, a grizzled old warrior with an arrow in his eye. Again he let drops of ocher fall. Again he said for all to hear, "Return to the Goddess. Know her love and joy and peace."

One by one Jack faced them, townspeople and horsemen, young and old, men and women. Each posed its own question to him. *What have you done? For what reason do I lie here? Is it worth it?* For none did Jack have an answer.

When he came to the woman, the child and the chieftain, Jack spoke slowly, paused long. There had to be a way to life that wasn't paved with death.

There had to be a way around all this pain and bloodshed. Blood begot blood. The earth swallowed up bodies, but it did not forget them. Blood would flow and flow until it swallowed the earth in its time. Jack had lost one world to blood. Now his new world flowed red. There had to be another way.

As Jack went through the second half of the grave, sprinkling and saying the words, in his mind another prayer repeated over and over. *There has got to be another way. There has got to be a better way.*

When each body had been faced, each blighted future offered some other hope, Jack struggled from the grave. Launa was there, her hand offering him a return to sun and sky and green from where he stood among the dead. He looked into her red-rimmed eyes and gave the command for their new mission.

"This is not the answer. There has to be a better way. We will find it."

THIRTY-SIX

LASA HUDDLED ON the floor, her knees pulled tight against her breasts. No child grew under her heart. She had delivered her daughter—dead. Lasa laid her head on her knees and wept. She wept for her child. She wept for the People who had gone into the ground this day.

And Lasa wept for the horsemen who now lay in a grave before Tall Oaks beside those they had come to kill. Lasa knew there was comfort there, that all the horsemen slept tonight in the grave and so many of the People lived to stand beside it, but she could not find it tonight. *So many have died! What had their lifeblood been traded for?*

In the dark, Lasa's eyes swept the sanctuary of the Goddess. It was as it had been for as long as she could remember. The changes spoken by the two soldiers were gone; the stoves, the wall hangings and mats that kept out winter cold were put away for the summer.

Across from where she huddled, the dais rose a short step above the People. The chair where sat She who Spoke for the Goddess stood next to the table that held the clay images of the Goddess, offerings brought by Hanna. She had thought a special call to the Goddess could avert today's bloodshed. It had not. Nothing could drive away the horror of this day.

Once, Lasa had thought images and burned offerings

could do anything. Once, the chair and She who Spoke for the Goddess had seemed otherworldly. She smiled, feeling again how wide her eyes had been when her mother brought her here when she had but six summers. The memories swirled around her of the celebration when her first moon blood flowed. Then Lasa shuddered, recalled the moment when wise Bellda, who had Spoken for the Goddess all of Lasa's life, declared that the blood no longer flowed for her. Another must be chosen to Speak in her place.

Lasa shook her head, trying to recapture the mad rush of feelings that swept her when Bellda picked her from among all the young women. Lasa had expected her friend Hanna to be the chosen one. The chair often passed from mother to daughter. Did Bellda see what Lasa had come to see? Hanna's sight flowed along narrow banks. Had Bellda seen what lay before the People? Lasa shook her head; who could have seen today?

Bellda had been gracious to the young woman she set in her place. She gave her Masin as a first consort. Wise old Masin, who had Spoken for the Bull as long as Lasa could recall. Lasa had not recognized the pain in Bellda's eyes, or Masin's as they parted. Now, Lasa knew how much it must have hurt Bellda to give up her consort. But the decision was wise. A new Speaker for the Goddess needs a wise Speaker for the Bull.

Before she first sat the Judgment Seat, Lasa had felt empty. Masin had taken her in his strong arms. "Listen, my young one. Listen to the words of the People. Listen to the words of the Goddess. Listen to the silence. You will know when to speak and you will know what words to say for Our Lady."

So Lasa sat the Judgment Seat for the first time, trembling inside. Now she knew the matter was minor, but it had seemed great then—where should the new woodlot be? One group of woodsmen said one place. Another would have it elsewhere. Death, rebirth and growth from the Goddess hung on these words.

The young Lasa saw much in her first decision. She listened hard to each word. She listened hard in the silences.

Would the Goddess speak for her ears alone? What would She say?

The words from the People were many. The words from the Goddess were none. Lasa looked to where Masin sat with the men at the far half of the longhouse. He gently shook his head, as did Bellda where she sat on Lasa's right. Lasa waited as the words of the People washed over her.

Then Bellda smiled. Lasa listened carefully to the words of the People. The words were no longer so different; both sides now spoke many of the same words. Lasa listened as the words grew more and more the same. Finally, when the two groups spoke with one voice, Bellda nodded. Masin nodded, and Lasa stood. She took into herself the Words the People had found and as her mouth formed each one and gave them back to the People, she knew they truly did come from the Goddess.

Over seasons, Lasa learned that Our Lady could speak with many voices. Until last year, she thought she knew every one of them. But what could one make of the voices from River Bend?

Lasa wanted to go to the chair, to feel its worn wood and reeds. Years ago, it had seemed from beyond the world. Tonight, it was nothing to her.

Her baby was dead. Kaul could give her no more children. She had nothing to give to the People. She wanted nothing. She was empty. She wept.

Kaul went from house to house, visiting those who had shed their blood. Normally, in a time of many dyings, Lasa did this, but no one begrudged the absence of one who had given birth to death. Brege might have stood in her mother's place, but now she also was in labor.

So Kaul saw that the wounded were cared for with help from Glengish. He brought mourners and comforters together. They were careful to look him in the eye. Yet often, their eyes slipped down to the price he had paid the horsemen.

In his ministrations, Kaul saw little of Hanna's people, and that was fine by him. For Hanna, he made an exception.

Several times he stopped at the mother's sanctuary and asked how Hanna and Brege fared. Brendi, the crone who stood first among the women who cared for the mothers at birth, curtly shook her head and went back to her work.

Kaul wondered what that wise woman who looked over all of them at birth thought of the deaths today. If she thought on it, she said nothing.

Late in the night a young boy dashed up to Kaul. "Merik has heard cries from within the birthing house."

Kaul trotted after him, but slowed as he approached the sanctuary. Merik was gone, probably within with Brege. The crone stood alone, wrapped in black like a crow. Brendi's skin shone in the moonlight with the sweat of her labors. She looked Kaul up and down with measuring eyes before she spoke.

"Brege is well, as is her daughter."

Kaul let the pent-up fears of the day escape in one long breath. The Goddess had seemed to forsake his family today. He was grateful for this one smile.

Brendi returned his joy with a knowing nod. "Hanna's labor was long and hard. Her son is exhausted from fighting his way into this world. He is small and feeble."

"He is whole?" Kaul voiced the common question, hating himself for the answer part of him wanted.

"He is a whole child," the woman whispered.

Kaul said a prayer for the baby. The omens were bad enough; there was no need for this child to pay in his flesh for worse.

The crone turned back to him. "The wind is changing."

Kaul felt no breeze on his flesh. The wind she spoke of was in the People's souls. "Yes."

"When the wind blows the hardest, only the oldest trees with the deepest roots may stand." Brendi fixed him with clear eyes.

"Yet an old tree may be too brittle to bend before the strong wind." Kaul respected the old woman's wisdom, but he feared where her words led.

The woman wrapped her cloak tighter and spoke in a bare whisper. "I have heard that Antia cut the head off the man who led the horsemen. They say she will take it to the horsemen."

Kaul had not heard this. There was no good in harming the dead.

"I have also heard from those who follow after Hanna that they did not do enough to stop the slaughter today. Now they wish they had stood between the two sides and stopped them from shooting their arrows."

Kaul scowled. Even now, did they not feel the heat of the horsemen's fire? He eyed the crone. Did she? He could not tell.

Her eyes searched him, from his bare groin to his eyes and maybe into his soul. "Someone else must Speak for the Bull."

Kaul stifled a groan; he had expected this. "Yes."

"Lasa must have a child and a new consort."

"There are those who would say that the People must have a new Speaker for the Bull . . . and for the Goddess." Kaul waited. Much hung on how the elders of Tall Oaks answered that question.

"It is not good for the People to have to listen to too many new voices. It is our custom to call only one Speaker at a time. We must call a Speaker for the Bull. Lasa is yet young enough to bear a child. It is not her time to step aside—but you must."

"Will the People listen to these words?"

The crone paced toward the sanctuary of the Goddess. Halfway there, she paused. He had followed her without a word, as she knew he would. "The People hear many voices after today. They do not know which one Speaks for the Goddess. They must have a voice that is familiar and that they respect."

Kaul nodded, his mind searching; then he grunted. "Merik will not want to leave Brege's side, but he can ride tonight."

"Good. I fear we will need Her words soon."

Kaul sought Lasa in the sanctuary of the Goddess. He found her huddled in the children's place. He held her while she wept. The solace and comfort traditionally offered did not fit times such as these. Kaul gave himself over to tears; the two wept as one. When exhaustion finally overtook them, they slept where they had wept.

THIRTY-SEVEN

A REDHEADED MAN, grinning through a slit throat, charged Jack, his lance leveled rock-steady at his heart. A laser beam shot from the tip of the lance, impaled Jack and burned the heart from his chest.

Jack awoke screaming, the smell of charred flesh in his nostrils. As he struggled to sit up, agony seared his back. Then Launa's cool hands were on his shoulders.

"Steady, honey. You're home. Everything's okay."

Jack's waking eyes took in Launa's worried smile, and their home behind her. He let his night terror out in a long sigh, then regretted it. The long breath he drew stank of a burned child. He gulped down bile. "I need a bath."

Launa said nothing, but carefully lifted blankets off him. As he struggled out of bed, she collected soap and a blanket, then held the deerskin door aside.

The sun was up; Jack figured he'd slept a night and a chunk of the next day. Launa set a slow pace, and Jack blessed her for it.

She didn't look too good either. Her hair was singed over her left ear; her left arm showed angry blisters. But she flashed him a smile.

At the stream, Jack sank into the water; its cold felt good on his burns. As he picked gingerly at his left ankle, a greasy ointment came off in patches. "How bad am I?"

Launa took a handful of soap and began washing him. "Your back is pretty much first-degree burns with a few blisters and second-degree spots." She took another handful and began massaging his scalp. He flinched.

"Sorry. You've got a couple of blisters up top."

Jack reached up, and she guided his fingers. He winced as he touched the first painful spot. She finished washing him, and he sank back into the water. The cool of the water turned ice cold; his teeth began to chatter.

Launa helped him stand and wrapped him in the blanket.

Jack avoided her worried eyes. "Stupid of me to want a bath, but the smell . . ."

Launa patted him dry. Jack tried not to flinch when she hit the wrong spots. "What's been happening?" Maybe he could distract himself with their tactical situation.

"You held together long enough for me to get you back home, then went into shock. Glengish gave you a drink that put you out, and showed me how to coat your burns. You kept going from hot to cold, so I spent the rest of the day taking blankets off and putting them back on you. Sometime last night you settled into a normal sleep, and I got some rest in the other bed."

"I'm sorry I woke you."

"I didn't sleep too well." Neither would say the word, but the nightmares had come for both.

Smoke curled from their chimney when they returned. They found Lasa's son Bomel inside feeding the fire, two large bowls of stew on the hearth beside him.

He stood as they entered. "I have food for you. Glengish says if you need more ointment I can bring it for you." His words wound down as he took in Jack's halted steps.

"Thank you. I am hungry. Launa, do we want anything?"

"I need more burn ointment. I want to coat you."

Relieved, the young man dashed out.

"I've got plenty, but he looked like he needed to do something for us."

Jack slumped beside the hearth and sipped the broth off his stew. It tasted good, but his stomach warned him to eat slowly.

Beside him, Launa nibbled at a spoonful. After a minute, she put the bowl down. "Dammit, we won. I mean, I don't think we ought to be drinking beer from skulls, but we ought to be celebrating. After the battle at the tree, we planted a wheat field and called it even."

"Don't think there're enough fields to plant."

Launa winced.

Jack took another sip. He did not want to think about yesterday, but there was something he needed to remember. The faces in the grave came back. "There has to be a better way."

"Yes. It can't get much worse than yesterday." Launa chewed a spoonful slowly.

"But how? In the desert, troops surrendered. These people don't. They're too committed or too desperate to quit."

"Maybe they don't know how to call it quits."

Jack swallowed on that idea. "Think we could give them a lesson on how to raise the white flag?"

"We did that yesterday, and they flunked the final." Launa grew very serious. "And you will not try to tell them how to do better next time. You won't lose what Kaul did. A year or two from now, when these damn implants wear off, I want to start raising some kids. We have a home for them now." Her hand reached out for his. She stroked the palm of his hand, about the only safe place to touch. It felt good.

He found himself quickening at the pleasure. He was alive. Suddenly, he wanted her. To hell with the burns.

Her eyes lit up as his interest grew. "How are we going to manage this?"

"I don't know, but we've always found a way."

"Are you awake?" Kaul's voice carried from outside. Jack woke slowly. He rested on his stomach. In afterglow, Launa had put ointment on his back. He'd drunk something and drifted off before she finished. Now his mouth was cotton.

Launa rolled out of bed. "We're awake. Jack, you want some water? Glengish said you'd be thirsty."

Jack took the offered waterskin. The wrapping around the wound on Kaul's arm showed red. He sat in the spare bed as

Launa took the skin from Jack and offered it to him. Kaul drank deeply and leaned back on the bed with a sigh.

"How journeys Tall Oaks?" Jack asked.

Kaul scrubbed at his face with his good hand. "The People live, thanks to you and a gracious Goddess—and to themselves."

"Will we feast tonight?" Launa asked.

Kaul shook his head. "I do not know. What songs would we sing?" The man looked tired and old to Jack—surprisingly old. The last months had aged him. Jack had seen this before. Food and rest would take care of the exhaustion, but could anything shake the years from his eyes?

"If we cooked a feast, maybe the People would discover the songs that were in their hearts," Launa offered.

Kaul winced and shook his head. "What is in their hearts? I have need of your wisdom."

Running feet stopped at their door. Bomel stuck his head in. "Kaul, we have need of you. Come quickly."

Kaul pulled himself to his feet. "I did not think it would happen so soon." He turned to Launa and Jack. "Walk after me."

They followed him. Bomel led them toward the Soldiers' Longhouse. There was a gathering around several mounted troopers. Jack spotted Antia, Sara, Cleo and Killala among those on horseback. The crowd was a strange mixture of First Legion and Hanna's people. Antia held a large jar. Someone on the ground made a grab for it, but Antia held it out of reach. People pushed and shoved. The horses shuffled their feet and nickered nervously. Most of the riders were not that skilled; if the horses got out of control in this press of people, things were going to get bad in a hurry.

"What is going on here?" Kaul's voice boomed above the noise. The crowd grew quiet and made an opening for the three. Jack moved to the nervous horses, patted one, soothed another.

Antia settled the pot in front of her on the horse. "I have a gift for the horsemen."

"It is the head of one of the horsemen," someone shouted from the back of the crowd.

Jack looked up at Antia. She opened the jar for him. He looked into the empty eyes of the red-haired man he had slain.

"Why do this?" Jack studied Antia. Hard, cold eyes stared back. What went on behind them?

Killala answered for the riders. "The Horse People take heads in battle. We have taken this head. We must show them we are warriors, too, and our land is not for the taking."

Jack nodded. "That is the way of the warrior—but is it the way of the soldier?" He turned back to Antia. "Last summer, you asked to be a soldier, not a killer like the horsemen. Will you now walk a different path?"

Antia glared at Jack. "And if I walk the path of the soldier, where does that lead?"

"To discipline and obedience." Jack spoke the words softly, but that stole none of the power from their meaning.

Antia rested her arms on the jar in front of her. "And who would I obey?"

Jack nodded. There was the soldier's eternal question. In obedience is honor; "Here we lay, obedient to their orders," said the Spartans' epitaph. But to whom or what is that obedience owed? There lies the dilemma.

"Me."

Jack's head snapped around.

Launa stepped into the space around Antia; the two women's eyes locked. There was none of the rawness Jack had seen in an idealistic West Point cadet. Here was the Launa who had led the escort back from the very gates of hell, the woman who planned her battle and fought it as it came. Watching her stance, the cast of jaw, the determined lips, Jack saw the general.

Antia's eyes slid away from Launa. "Yes, you will be obeyed. Who do you obey?"

"She who Speaks for the Goddess in Tall Oaks," Launa answered without a moment's hesitation. "The path you would walk will change the way the sun shines on all the People of Tall Oaks. It must be spoken of before the elders. Tomorrow, we will meet in the sanctuary and speak of it."

Antia nodded slowly, the way of the generations before her still powerful enough to stay her hand. She dismounted.

Jack let out the breath he had been holding for the last eternity. He was glad that was over.

The crowd opened again. It was Hanna they made way for. "It is good that you follow after She who Speaks for the Goddess in Tall Oaks. I Speak for the Goddess now, and I tell you there will be no heads taken anywhere from Tall Oaks."

Jack whirled to face this new threat. *Damn! How many constitutional crises can a town take in one afternoon?*

Launa words were soft, but showed no give. "I follow after She who has Spoken for the Goddess in Tall Oaks for many years. I do not see her here."

"Lasa cannot Speak for the Goddess." Hanna pointed to Kaul with a flick of her wrist and dismissed him with the same gesture. "Anyone who would let that Speak for the Bull is not listening to the Goddess. She chose her own path and has led us down it. If we truly had a Speaker for the Bull, none of what happened yesterday could have come to us."

At her words every muscle in Kaul's body tensed, as if slapped. Launa stepped between him and Hanna. "I follow Lasa. So long as she is the one the People have called out to Speak for the Goddess, I will follow her. We few here are not the ones to call another one to sit in her place." Launa turned, her eyes sweeping the crowd. "Tomorrow is soon enough."

Though Hanna's frustration was palpable, most of Launa's listeners accepted the wisdom of delay. The crowd dispersed. Soon Kaul stood alone with the two soldiers.

He sighed as his eyes followed Hanna. "A hunter seeks meat, but a stampede of cattle feeds no one. Too much comes at the People too fast."

Jack nodded; here was a test for the People as difficult, and maybe as brutal, as any battle. "Kaul, we talked for many winter evenings of what makes the people the People. Tomorrow, we may find the answer."

"Forgive me, friends, if I ask you to help the People in

their hunt. None of Hanna's words were unforeseen, although all were hard to hear." Kaul shook his head. "Last night I sent Merik to Wood Village to bring back Bellda. She is ill. Jack, will you bring her here?"

Jack looked down at his hands. The trembling had lessened; the stew had given him strength. "I guess Launa should keep an eye on our soldiers. I know who commands the legions."

She started to give him a one-arm hug, then settled for squeezing his hand. "How about we get more food in you before you hit the road?"

Stew bubbled on the hearth in the Soldiers' Longhouse. Jack ate half a bowl before Merik and Bomel appeared with Windrider and a half dozen remounts. Launa kissed him good-bye, then bent down to help him mount. He took her boost gratefully.

Kaul offered a linen poncho to cover Jack's burns. It would keep the sun from inflaming them. It only took a few minutes of riding for the light wind to blow dirt into the ointment; the poncho grated like sandpaper. Still, in a few days, he'd be fine. That was more than he could say for his town.

The People of Tall Oaks expected to live their lives as their parents had. When the People grew too many, some would pick up stakes and move a few miles farther east. It is easy to live in peace when there were unlimited resources.

Now they had collided with the horsemen—and bad weather was shoving the horsemen at them. Darwin may be yet to live, but his laws applied: Adapt or die. Jack spent the ride searching for ways he could help the People; it kept his mind off the pain.

They rode into Wood Village near sunset. Masin stalked toward them as they dismounted. The mixed emotions on his face were those for a friend . . . who brought a lover's death warrant. "Is it needed that she make this trip?"

Merik answered for them. "The needs of the People are great. The People may be no more when the sun sets tomorrow."

For a moment, Masin stood, eyes closed; then, with a sigh, he turned to Jack. "My consort is too sick to sit a horse.

We have built a raft, but the water is cold. How do we keep her warm?"

Jack followed Masin toward the river. *How did sailing ships keep a fire in the galley?* "Sand. We must keep sand between the heat of the stove and the wood of the raft."

Masin's eyes lit up. "Yes!"

Under torchlight, two men wove willow branches into a round, low fence as a woman stopped up the space between two logs with clay. A layer of gravel, then sand was held in place by the wicker fence, insulating the raft's logs from the fire.

Once Jack was sure of the design, he had Merik coat his burns and retired for the night. Others hauled the wood stove to the raft and lit a new fire.

Masin woke Jack before first light to inspect the installation. Coals in the stove already warmed blankets. As dawn came, Masin lovingly carried Bellda to the raft and laid her on a bed of furs. He covered her with warmed wool blankets. Masin poled the raft away from the bank and the current took them. Jack found an extra pole and added to the raft's speed. After a minute of watching him, Masin likewise began using his pole for more than maneuvering. Ashore, Merik led the horses.

The journey downriver went smoothly. Bellda was quiet, lying or sitting, bundled in wraps, eyes gazing vacantly. Only once did she show an awareness of her surroundings.

Toward midday, she motioned Jack to her. He had to bend close to make out her words. "You have seen the horsemen?"

"Yes."

"They do not follow the way of the Goddess?"

Jack swallowed his first answer. Unkinking his back, he stood up and stretched. His eyes roved earth and sky, searching for any answer but a straightforward no. He could find none. With a sigh, he bent to Bellda's ear. "No. The horsemen know nothing of the way of the Goddess. They follow another."

"Yes," Bellda hissed softly. "That is all my eyes have seen. I had hoped you might see more." Slowly she moved her head. Jack stared into dark eyes plumbing his soul. "And do you follow the way of the Goddess?"

Jack paused only long enough to take in a breath. "I am a stranger who is learning Her way. The path that opens before the People is as strange as I am. Yet I would have the People walk it as the Goddess would, not as I might."

Bellda gazed at him for a moment longer, then pulled her blankets close and lapsed back into herself. Jack returned to poling.

It was late in the afternoon when Tall Oaks came in view. Sara stood watch on the shore and raised a shout as they came in sight. A dozen people ran alongside the raft as Masin and Jack poled it to a landing. Sara and Merik had horses waiting for them, but Masin carried his consort in his arms.

THIRTY-EIGHT

JACK HEARD THE roar of voices from the sanctuary two
blocks away, but a screaming hush swept over the assembly
as Jack followed Masin and Bellda through the door. In a
glance, Jack knew, though the People were silent, everything screamed wrong.

No one sat in the chair of the Speaker for the Goddess.
Lasa stood near it, her skin mottled pale and scarlet with
emotions, her hands balled into fists.

Facing her, only a handsbreadth farther from the chair,
stood Hanna. Her body shook with tension; her breath came
in shudders. Her chin jutted out in haughty defiance.

The elder women did not sit on the benches along the
walls, but stood in clusters. The young women formed three
or four other groups between the older ones. Launa stood
near Lasa within a circle that included Brege and many of
the women from the legion. Several other young women
stood in another group with Antia and Killala.

There was no harmony, only sides being chosen for con-
flicts present and to come. Jack turned to where the men sat.
Their measured rows were now clumps—and Kaul's place
was empty.

Saying nothing, Masin carried Bellda to the Speaker's
seat and settled her on it. No voice objected when Masin
turned to face the assembly. For a moment his eyes swept

the room; then, with a slight bow to Lasa, Masin threaded his way toward the men.

Jack's eyes went to Kaul's place, the way a tongue searches for a missing tooth. Taelon sat next to the empty space. The crags of his face were a study in anger, but his eyes stared at the floor with empty despair. Taelon made space beside him for Jack. No one offered an explanation.

As Masin approached the men, his eyes searched them. Then he stepped into Kaul's place, turned and sat cross-legged. He showed no discomfort under scrutiny; his own eyes were fixed on Bellda. Slowly, obedient to Masin's gaze, Jack's eyes went to the wisp of a woman now seated in what he could only think of as Lasa's seat. She sat, hud-dled among her blankets, seemingly lost in the chair. Yet her eyes shone from their sunken sockets. They blazed with an intensity that demanded the allegiance of the People. And they gave it to her.

"Does anyone question the seat I have taken?" The room fell into a deeper quiet as Jack leaned forward to hear Bellda's rasping whisper.

Her eyes fixed on Hanna, Lasa gave the barest hint of a nod. Only when Hanna signaled in kind did Lasa give full expression to her agreement. Then, like dueling cats, the two lowered themselves to sit on the step of the dais. Jack watched them, as if in slow motion, give assent only so much as the other; each was ready to spring to her feet at the first sign of betrayal. When they finally settled in place, the other women took their seats.

War and its cousins, hatred and distrust, had come to the People. Jack felt like weeping for their lost innocence. In-stead, he bit his lip and adjusted his heart, dialing it in to twenty-first-century guile.

Bellda coughed, her entire body racking with each spasm. Masin started; his face was a mask, only his eyes showed the agony of a lover watching his beloved at the hour of death. How sick was Bellda? Much too familiar with sudden death, Jack had no experience with the death that seeps from toes to knees to heart. *Dear Goddess, the People haven't agreed on anything for six months. Don't take Bellda now.*

The wizened form in the chair opened her mouth. The entire room leaned forward to hear her. "Lasa and Hanna, you stand before the Goddess with the fire of angry words on your faces. Speak now, that She may find harmony for your hearts."

Lasa listened and nodded solemnly.

Hanna was on her feet in an instant, her finger pointing to Launa and Jack. "These strangers have killed our people, slaughtered the Horse People, and led my son to his death. There is nothing but darkness and anger in their way. No one who truly walks the way of the Goddess follows after them. They must be sent away before they cover all of us in blood."

Now Lasa was on her feet. "It is the lances of the Horse People who let out life's blood. These strangers whom we have welcomed seek only to show us the way to protect ourselves. With them, we will not be like sheep with no shepherd, to be slaughtered by wolves. It is the Horse People who know nothing of the Goddess and we who must find a new way to walk with Her. Hanna would have us killed like dumb sheep."

As Lasa stopped to snatch a breath, Hanna pounced. "Shepherds eat mutton, but no shepherd would eat every sheep in her flock. The Horse People are not so foolish as to kill everyone. Yes, they are strange. Yes, they kill. We have been told that they are hungry and flee a barren land. We have songs of people fleeing hunger when the rains do not come in their proper time. We all know in such times to share with our sisters. Instead of sharing, now there is blood and killing."

Now Antia was on her feet. "They killed first."

Hanna spun to face Antia. "Yes, they did. But they took many into their keeping, showing them the ways of the Horse People. They can gain wisdom from us as we taste the experience of their ways. We will be the better for it."

"You have not walked as a horseman would make you walk," Killala lashed out. "You have not watched sisters and brothers die under a horseman's whip."

"And would they have treated you so if these two had not

slain their brothers? Hear me. I will not have blood on my hands. I will not let you cover my children in blood as you did Hath. This I will say so long as I stand on the earth."

"And this I say so long as I stand before the People." Now Lasa turned to face the assembly. "My consort took words to share with the horsemen. You saw what they did to him." She opened her arms, not in blessing, but in pleading. "You saw the horsemen ride into the fields of Tall Oaks. They sent no one to sit in our council, to seek a path for their feet. No! They rode with lances leveled at our hearts." Both fists clenched. "Lances speak only the language of blood. The horsemen seek only our death and the death of our way. I say give them death when they come, every time they come." Jack did not miss the "I say." Lasa didn't Speak for the Goddess; she begged the People to follow her.

Before the People could answer, Antia hefted her pot with its grisly contents. "And I say let them know that it is death to come among us. Let them know in a language they speak that only death awaits them here."

"No!"

"Yes!"

"What else can we do?"

"Something . . . Nothing . . . Anything is better than . . ."

The assembly disintegrated into a confused babble. It was several minutes before the noise dissipated enough for one voice to be heard, but it did not matter. When people spoke in turn, they brought nothing more than their own emotions to the same two alternatives—resist or submit.

The hours passed. As in times before, a woman or man would rise and speak their heart. But this time it was different. Others shouted agreement or argued against them even as they spoke. Never had Jack seen people shouting in the sanctuary. But there was one island of silence.

Beside Jack, Taelon huddled in upon himself. He offered nothing, occasionally shaking his head when one of Hanna's followers spoke loudly. Once Taelon turned to Jack. "I never knew Kaul led such dumb animals. Have they followed the sheep so long they are no better? A hunter uses all his wisdom to hunt a deer. We know the cost of blood. We hunters know how to thank the Goddess for what She sends us. But these—what manner of people are they? What will happen to my people now?"

Jack had no answer, just a question. "Where is Kaul?"

Taelon shook his head and stared at the floor.

Beyond Taelon, Masin sat, leaning forward when his consort moved, catching his breath, forgetting to breathe when a coughing spell racked her tiny body. Jack, too, forgot to breathe.

But Jack had no answers. For a thousand years, the People had lived in simple anarchy; their problems were those of earth and water, life and death. Now they faced great threats, both from without and within. Under the pressure of Lasa and Hanna's conflicting visions, their simple ways were crumbling.

Kaul was wise to call Bellda back. If there was any hope for the People, it was in her frail body. Other days, Jack had seen the People slowly work themselves around to a compromise that the Speaker could articulate for the good of all. Bellda was the one person all would listen to.

But today, as hours passed, there was no change in the tenor of the voices. Those who had started out adamant for one path deviated not one inch. Jack rummaged through his training, sought in his soul for a middle ground. He had sworn on the graves of the dead that there had to be a better way.

He could see none.

As the light of the day failed, they were no closer. Men lit torches and the angry words raged on.

Sudden movement brought Jack out of his soul-searching. Masin was half on his feet; his eyes locked on Bellda. The Speaker had pitched forward in her seat, catching herself, but barely. Hanna and Lasa, united for once, were on their feet, holding her.

"Perhaps we should go to our homes for the night," Lasa offered. "Tomorrow will be soon enough. You must rest."

"There will be time enough to rest when this day is done," Bellda croaked; then she coughed and cleared her throat.

"Before the Goddess and this assembly, I have listened to

your words." The old woman's whisper became husky, throbbing with power. "It is our way to speak our hearts and to listen to each other, seeking in such words a single path we can walk together in the harmony of the Goddess." Every head nodded.

"Yet, that is not the only way for us." In a bare whisper Bellda went on. "When the fields are too few and the People too many, it is our custom to send some away to find more land. There are also times when two paths are so strong among a people that they cannot choose one for all. This is such a time."

The flow of words wound down as Bellda gasped for several breaths. A foot escaped her blankets; the flesh under her toenails showed purple. Death had already taken it. Bellda took one last gasp and struggled to her feet. On either side of her, Hanna and Lasa supported her.

"Hear your Goddess, Oh People.
There are two paths before you, and both must be
    walked.
Let those who would take up slings and bows
against the Horse People stand with Lasa in Tall Oaks.
Let those who will not be killers come to Wood Town
and there listen to the Goddess as Hanna Speaks for her.
Let my words pass from mouth to ear and from young to
    old
so that what we do here in the name of the Goddess
may be remembered."

Bellda slumped into the chair. Lasa knelt beside her, then waved for someone to bring a drink. Launa dashed for the back of the room. Hanna scowled at her mother. Resting closed fists on her hips, she spoke. "My children all have been born in the home of their mother and grandmothers."

"And you will have no more children." Bellda's whisper cut Hanna off. "The times are passing us by. We must go where we would not have gone. You have heard my words—remember them."

Hanna swallowed the rebuke, but went on. "Lasa has no

consort. How can she Speak for the Goddess with no man to Speak for the Bull?"

Bellda sighed, a deep racking sound that would have led to another session of coughing, except she did not inhale. When she could talk, her rasping whisper could hardly be heard where Jack sat, but no one moved or even breathed. Beside him, Launa froze in mid-stride, a steaming mug of herbal tea in her hand.

"How will you Speak for the Goddess, my daughter, you who have sent away your consort?"

"I will take another."

"And so shall Lasa. He who Speaks for the Bull will be one who can show the People a new path. Jack the Stranger will Speak for the Bull to the People of Tall Oaks."

Beside Jack, the mug slipped from Launa's hand to crash on the floor. In front of him, Bellda began to cough. In mid-hack her face froze and, despite Lasa's grasp, she slumped to the floor. In a moment, Masin was on his feet, dashing to his consort's side. He held her for a moment. She struggled to form a word, but she had no more words left in her. Masin pulled her limp body to his chest and wept.

Around him, others began to keen their grief. The community, so divided a moment ago, gathered as one to mourn the loss of this beacon to their united past.

Stunned, Jack repeated to himself the words he could hardly comprehend. The stranger will Speak for the Bull. Bellda had named *him* to Speak for the Bull. Never in his wildest thoughts had Jack considered the possibilities that now opened up to him.

He was the king! Feeling dizzy from the rapid changes, Jack tried to rein in his emotions. What did it mean for the mission for him to Speak for the Bull? He didn't really know.

His numb gaze wandered across the people around him. He could not share the grief they felt. They had known Bellda all their lives—he but a few short months. But he tasted loss. His gut went into free fall for the loss of the woman who stood next to him, frozen as a statue. Slowly Launa's eyes met his.

Jack stood. He wanted to reach out for her. He wanted to comfort her, to seek comfort from all that had torn at them since the horsemen first rode over the hill. He dared not.

"Captain." Launa's word was half a question, half a statement—all impersonal. That was the way it had to be. For Jack to Speak for the Bull meant also to be consort to She who Spoke for the Goddess.

"Yes, Lieutenant." Did the hopes for their mission and the billions of humans depending on them carry that high a price? Jack might not know all that it meant to Speak for the Bull, but he did know that to take Launa into his arms would be to cast aside everything Bellda had said. Jack waited for Launa to say or do something.

"I don't know what to say . . . sir."

"Launa. Lieutenant. I." Jack shut his mouth. There were no words to say what he felt, nothing in the Book to cover this.

Slowly, Launa drew herself up to attention. "If you'll excuse me, sir." The last word was mangled as she choked on it. Something damp splattered on the clay floor beside Jack. "Please, I have to go." Launa marched for the door.

Jack was too stunned to do more than follow her with his eyes. Someday, he told himself, he could return to her. Tomorrow, he might even reject the Speaker's staff. Holding onto that thought with both hands, Jack kept his sanity.

Tonight he did not have to say anything.

THIRTY-NINE

LAUNA MARCHED; SHE would not let herself flee like a routed army. In cadence, her body stomped down the street. She did not stop at her house—their home. *Didn't I mean anything to Jack? How could he leave without a last word, a final touch?*

The analytical part of her answered that conditions were more complex. She was tired and stressed out and still in physical pain. *Look at the situation from different perspectives.* Somewhere in her head a calm, sweet voice lectured her that things were not as bad as they appeared.

But the rest of her was screaming. *This isn't fair. This isn't the way you treat a hero. I put my body on the line. I fought the battle. I won. I deserve a warrior's reward. Instead, I'm getting the shaft.*

Launa reached the edge of Tall Oaks. Ahead of her was the stream where she and Jack, Brege and Merik had washed off the dirt from the field they had planted . . . and much more.

A wave of flaming rage swept over Launa as she halted. "They can't do this!" she screamed, yanking her knife from her belt. "I won my battle. I saved their damn lives." She buried her knife in a sapling. The blade refused to come out. Grabbing the young tree trunk with both hands, she choked it, whipped it back and forth, ripped it from the ground.

"Aaah!" The air fled from her as she slammed her new-made quarterstaff at four other saplings, mowing them down like stalks of wheat. "Fight me fair and square for Jack. But you can't, can you? You can't stand against me. One of you or a dozen're dog meat if you take me on hand-to-hand." That felt good.

Twirling her staff over her head, she spun around to face an old oak. Again and again she attacked it, slamming wood against wood until, with a loud crack, her sapling snapped. That didn't stop her. "You can't stop me. You can't stop *me*."

Launa finally slumped to the ground, racked by sobs, her staff reduced to little more than a fractured whip.

In all her roaming army life, she'd never expected to have a home, to meet anyone like Jack. Now she had. Now she knew what it was like to be in one sacred place, to have a man as companion, friend and lover. To have them for a moment, and then lose them to each other, left Launa worse than empty.

She should have lost that man when it wouldn't have hurt. He'd been a real horse's ass before the time jump. Last summer as the two of them struggled to put some kind of chain of command in place, he'd rubbed her the wrong way bad enough that she could gladly have traded him in for a nice, quietly affectionate local model. "But, damn it, I didn't. I chased that bastard to the mouth of hell. I fought my battle. Now, when I'm finally his equal, they can't snatch him away. Not," Launa choked, then finally gave herself up to sobs, "when I was starting to think of our children. Lasa can't have our children!" she screamed.

A while later, Launa had no idea how long, she realized she wasn't alone. Someone squatted at the water's edge; he must have been there all along. Were all the horsemen accounted for? Launa's hand searched for her knife. Just as she pulled it from the green wood that held it, a bit of moonlight found its way through the leafy canopy to reflect off a bandaged arm. "Kaul?"

"Yes." He stared into the water. "Why do you also weep?"

Launa had been raving in English. "Bellda has come and

she has died," she hiccuped. Bellda would have meant much to Kaul.

"Did she Speak to the People before?" Still Kaul's first thought was for the People.

"She spoke." Launa choked out the words. Kaul turned a worried face to her. Launa swallowed and went on. "Bellda invited Hanna's people to go to Wood Village. There Hanna will Speak for the Goddess. Lasa will Speak in Tall Oaks."

"That is good. Did she name a Speaker for the Bull?"

"Yes." Launa struggled to say the name. She could not. Still staring into the water, Kaul waiting patiently.

Launa swallowed hard. "Jack will Speak for the Bull."

"Oh, Launa." Kaul came to her, hugged her as her grief again racked her body with sobs. "I knew what fate awaited me, but you . . . to lose the man of your heart."

"It's not fair." Launa poured out her bitterness, in the language where the words existed, in English otherwise. Kaul listened through it all, gently rocking her back and forth. He said nothing, simply listened. The moon was high when Launa surfaced from her pain.

She shivered in Kaul's arms. His skin was cold; he wore nothing, not even his belt and knife. This night of all must be cold to him. Launa was still wearing the bikini bottom she'd fought the battle in. "There are blankets in my house."

Kaul nodded at her offer. He glanced back at the stream. Bits of moonlight reflected from it. "I had thought I had my fill of life, that everything for me was done. Yet, the water flows on and our lives flow. Never do we know what lies before us. The Goddess was gracious to send you to me this evening."

Launa wiped the last of her tears. "What good was I? All I did was load my troubles on you."

Kaul's face held a trace of a smile when he spoke. "You shared your grief and found my shoulder of use. Now you offer to share a blanket. Even when we lose what is dearest to us, we find there is still something we can do for another. That is enough reason to put one foot in front of the other, to breathe another breath, to live another day."

At her house, Kaul stopped as if he would wait outside for

the offered blanket. Launa pulled him through the deerskin door. "The night is cold. You have done so much for Tall Oaks. I will not leave you to sleep without a roof. You would not let me and . . . ah, Jack sleep under a tree. I will not let you."

Kaul went without a word to the bed beside the cold hearth.

Launa slipped out of her clothes and slid into her now too-large bed. The blankets and skins warmed as she lay straight as a board, marshaling her thoughts on the day, trying to ignore most of the reflections that came to her. Last night's nightmares had been bad; tonight's would be worse.

"Kaul, would you hold me? In the night, sights come . . ."

Without a word, he came to her bed and slid in beside her. His arm reached out to support her head, and she was grateful. The warmth of their bodies held some of the world's cold at bay.

Jack sat, empty as the broken mug beside him, as Launa marched away. The room was almost empty. Antia was one of the last to go. She clutched the jug with the horseman's head to her breast as if it were an infant. When she glanced at Jack, her expression chilled him.

Jack found himself alone with Taelon. "What do we do now?"

The hunter shook his head. "I feared worse, listening to the cackling of these geese. With you beside Lasa, perhaps my people will not become animals for the horsemen to hunt for fun."

Jack knew the words were meant to encourage him, but he was too numb to feel them. His mind was a whirl of questions and confusion. Where was Launa? Where was Kaul? What should he do? Did he want this? Could he refuse? If he did, what would become of him and Launa and their mission? He was spinning through the same questions when Lasa returned with Brege and Merik.

Taelon's frown was question enough for Merik. "Hanna did not want us at Bellda's side. Mother and Brege are still weak. It was good for them to leave."

"Where are Launa and Kaul?" Jack asked.

"Sara leads the watch tonight," Brege answered. "She saw both of them go into Launa's house."

Jack knew he should feel grateful that his two friends had found each other, but the twinge he felt in his gut brought more pain. So quickly Launa took in another. Jack had watched Launa and Kaul in the cave as he and the Speaker recovered. There had been a spark of something between them. But Kaul was . . . Launa would want more. Jack's mind boiled on, the stew of his emotions adding only more confusion.

Lasa went to the doorway leading to her private quarters. "Jack, you will need a place to sleep tonight."

Without conscious thought, Jack went to her. As she slid her hand into his, bleak emptiness covered her face. Was this the look women wore for thousands of years as political alliances sent them to beds not of their choosing? What did he look like?

In her room Lasa slipped out of her skirt with the efficiency of exhaustion. In a moment, she was in bed, the blankets pulled tight around her. Jack looked around; there was no second bed. There had been no need for a separate place for Kaul to sleep. Jack stood for a moment in indecision. Should he enter Lasa's bed . . . sleep on the floor . . . find a place outside?

Lasa rolled over to face him. With one cocked eyebrow she took in his confusion. Then, with a sadly crooked half-smile, she beckoned him. He got in the other side of the bed and laid himself out facing the wall, careful of his burns.

Three days ago, he'd won the first major battle of their mission. Now, without Launa, victory was ashes in his mouth. No, the ache in his gut was more than just her loss. With victory had come confidence that they *could* put all the pieces together. They *could* find a better way. He was not fool enough to think a single battle could guarantee victory in a 400-year war; still, he had felt it.

Now, he felt nothing. Before the jump, he had known he was a pawn in a game played by powerful men. But being a pawn was better than being a victim. Now he knew how the victims felt.

In this place and time, Jack had seen himself and Launa as the ones who changed what they had a mind to. Today the People had rubbed Jack's nose in just how little power he had. He and Launa were as much pawns now as before. Only now they played in a game with no rules. The anarchy of the People was giving way to an ugly chaos that promised only hurt and pain. Jack shivered, and Lasa reached over to rest a hand on his arm.

"It is too soon after a stillbirth for the Goddess to ask anything of you. Do not fear me, my loyal friend. Let us sleep close tonight. I must warn you that frightful and horrible seeings came to me in my sleep last night. If I cry out, do not fear for me. Kaul held me close, but I will not burden you."

"Such seeings may come to either of us. I will hold you when they come. That is the least we can do for each other."

Jack rolled over, took Lasa's hand in his and held it tight as they waited for sleep to come for them. Thus they were two souls, keeping the nightmares at bay.

FORTY

JACK STRUGGLED TO wakefulness, fleeing a confused dream. He reached for Launa. Beside him, Lasa moaned. Jack remembered where he was—and why. He rested a hand on her; she settled into a calmer rest. He let a painful breath out slowly through clenched teeth. Yesterday he had forgotten to coat his burns; they reminded him of his neglect.

Jack rearranged his body to ease the pain. Glengish would give him more medicine and coat him. He couldn't ask Lasa—she had enough problems guiding Tall Oaks. *Those problems are mine now.* The burden drove the air from his lungs; he gritted his teeth. Remember, every challenge is an opportunity.

But what were his responsibilities? It wasn't just the strange language that made so much of it unintelligible to Jack. For the last six months, he'd been busy planning a defense. He had no idea where the political and social land mines were. How long could he take to learn? His brain still felt like mush. *Dear Goddess, let me do it right the first time.*

Lasa rolled onto her back, glanced at him with a sigh. Her hand half reached for him, but fell to the covers before she touched him. "Dark visions came in the night. I felt your hand and thought it was Kaul's. It gave me comfort." Her lashes veiled her eyes. "I am sorry I am not your beautiful Launa."

What pulled at his heart the most, the trembling chin or the emptiness in her voice? Jack was defenseless. He reached for her, and Lasa fled into his arms. He rocked her gently.

"Lasa, both you and I weep for another. Must we accept the words spoken by Bellda? What would be the cost if I did not take Kaul's staff?"

Lasa pushed herself away from Jack to study him through teary eyes. "You would refuse? I know I am old and ugly, but for Launa you would bring down our town and all its people."

Damn—now I've got to cope with losing Lasa's respect as well as everything else. Jack shook his head. "No, that is not what I wanted to say. You miss Kaul; don't deny it. And yes, I miss Launa. Please, I do not know the ways of the People. Hanna left her consort. I heard Bellda, but I have seen Hanna disagree with you. Lasa, I am a child and must learn."

Jack took Lasa's face between his hands. Her eyes were still red with tears, and more tears pooled as he held her. "Lasa, you are not ugly. You are more beautiful than any woman should be who has gained your wisdom. You were beautiful when first I saw you. You were beautiful with child. You are beautiful today."

Gently, Jack kissed away her tears. His own tenderness kindled a fire in his loins. He moved to hide it. Her need was for closeness, not passion.

"You are a kind man." Lasa smiled, and Jack suspected he would never keep secrets from her. "Yesterday let many goats and pigs loose on the crops. Let us eat and see what the sun shows?"

Lasa eased herself out of bed. Jack saw dark blood on the bandage between her legs. Lasa blocked his view with her body as she checked the moss. "The blood is old. I no longer bleed. Maybe the Goddess does have more Words for me to Speak."

Jack slipped out of bed while her back was still turned and

hid his quieting erection in his briefs; they concealed little. The pain of moving quickly concentrated his attention elsewhere. He was going to have to see Glengish . . . soonest.

In the main room of the sanctuary, mush bubbled over the fire. Little Blossom quickly spooned out two bowls. She watched Jack and Lasa with the wide eyes of a child who sees her world changing and can make no sense of it. Jack smiled at her; she shifted closer to her mother.

Lasa eyed Jack over her bowl. "Someone must care for your burns."

"I will visit Glengish."

"Blossom, go to Grandmother Glengish. Tell her your mother asks her to share our meal and bring ointment for He who Speaks for the Bull."

The child was off, happy to please her mother, joyful at a chance to run.

"Do I Speak for the Bull?" Jack asked. "Is there a ceremony of naming?"

Lasa worried her mush with the spoon. "Yes, there is usually a meeting of all to decide upon a man. I think Bellda's Speaking has set that aside. And yes, there is a great feast, and the Bull speaks powerfully and often to the Goddess." Lasa paused, and Jack gulped. It looked as if Launa was finally going to get her orgy. *Can I even get it up with Launa watching?*

Lasa hastened on. "But I am in that time of pain. Many will question the wisdom of it, but I think we may do without the feast. Some of those who hold tightest to the old ways may still want the celebration. Their maiden daughters would give the Bull many chances to Speak. Would you like that?"

Now Jack really gulped—an adolescent dream, but a nightmare for him at the moment. Launa would kill him, and seeing him with a gaggle of young women would not help Lasa's morale. And if he didn't hold up his end of the ceremony, the omen to the People would be a disaster. What would Judith say? The old scholar would probably laugh her head off.

Jack was saved from further analysis by Glengish's arrival. Blossom started to ladle out a bowl of mush, but the healer went straight to Jack. The pain of her ministrations was a marvelous distraction from Jack's other worries.

"Have you heard any words from Masin this morning?" Lasa asked Glengish while she dabbed medicine on Jack's back.

"Hanna bickers with him. The woman has no harmony in her heart," Glengish diagnosed. "Masin would take Bellda's body to Wood Village today. Hanna would bury her here. I think Hanna would then stay here."

"Despite Bellda's Speaking!" Jack exploded.

"Yes." Glengish smeared a bad burn, and Jack did some serious teeth-gritting. The conversation went on without him.

Lasa stood up. "Blossom, get my skirt." While the child was gone, Lasa spoke in a whisper to Glengish. "And the rest of the People, how speak they?"

"With many voices. Those I talk to when I care for their wounds say they will follow you or Antia. Many men will follow after the Speaker for the Bull. Yet, among those who came late to the fight and those who walked with Hanna, there is doubt. Many do not want to leave their homes. Some are so filled with Hanna's vision that they will follow her to Wood Village, but I do not know what they will do if she stays here. It is as if the sun rose in the west. The People do not know which way to go."

Where had Jack heard that before? Blossom brought Lasa's skirt and she slipped it on.

Glengish finished. "You should have done something for those burns yesterday, but they are healing well. I will leave this pot for Lasa. She can coat you tonight."

Minutes later, Lasa and Jack faced Tall Oaks. Jack was surprised at the number of people about. Then he realized the morning was half gone. Down avenues, Jack could see farmers tending what was left of their crops; flocks of goats foraged on the hillside above the town. Work went on. Jack would ask Kaul for a briefing; he could ill afford mistakes.

Lasa stopped on the veranda only long enough to listen.

Then she and Glengish exchanged knowing glances and headed in the direction of loud voices. Five cross streets to the west, they found the source of the noise.

Masin stood with a linen-wrapped pack on his back. Hanna blocked his way. "She is my mother. She will rest beneath the hearth beside her mother and her mother's mother."

"She was my consort. She chose to live her last days in the home we built. I take her to Wood Village, just as she called you to go." Masin's voice was calm, but Jack heard the immovable rock beneath.

"You will not take her." Hanna's voice was sharp.

"She wishes to be washed by her old friends. They are at Wood Village. I take her there before her flesh is too stiff for them to do as she wishes."

"You cannot walk there quickly enough." Hanna spat.

"No, but he can ride," Jack took the opening to jump into the conversation. He doubted there was an angel in God or the Goddess's heaven dumb enough to do that. "Horses will speed Masin's journey. They can speed all who wish to go there. Let me give you a pony, Masin. Take a double hand of double hands of horses for your people's needs."

Launa, Kaul and Sara had just joined the group. Launa cast Jack a frown that shouted, "Just what do you think you're doing with my legions' horses, Mister?" Jack turned to Lasa, but spoke loud. "Horses eat grass. We have too many for Tall Oaks alone. Let us share with our friends. They will have need of the horses to carry goods and pull plows. People will eat better."

Masin nodded. "I never saw that, but yes, horses can pull plows. I thank you for the gift."

"You have too many horses because you kill too many Horse People. I will not have one of those beasts." But Hanna had been outmaneuvered. Now the argument was over horses, not Bellda's last resting place.

Sara dashed off; people were still arguing whether to accept Jack's offer when she returned with two horses. She had a blanket on one for Masin and a pack rack on the other. She and Masin lashed Bellda's remains tightly to the saddle.

Moments later, Kaul led five more horses into the crowd. Jack had not noticed, but there were five other women and men intent on accompanying Masin and Bellda. Kaul had.

With so many large beasts and people milling around, Hanna could not control the unfolding situation. Jack held his grin on a tight rein. You didn't smile in front of the loser when you were the winner. That had not changed in six thousand years.

When Masin and his party rode off, Hanna was nowhere in sight.

Jack checked the sun. It wasn't noon, and he'd done a good day's work. He accompanied Lasa as she finished her rounds. A small group went with them. Somewhere in the back, Jack glimpsed Kaul and Launa. Jack was glad of that. The four of them were still a team . . . even if relationships were a mad jumble.

Half an hour later, on the east edge of town, they found Antia. She had forty mounted troops—and the jar with Arakk's head. Antia looked straight at Jack.

"We go to show the horsemen that this is no place for them."

Jack glanced at Lasa, but her eyes were fixed on him. So this was to be his responsibility. No, it wasn't. These were legionaries, and the legions were Launa's command.

"Lieutenant," he called in English, "it appears that the legions you command have a disciplinary problem." He looked for her, found her in the back of the crowd. Their eyes locked. *What's it going to be, woman? Kaul showed that he's still part of the team. Are you still a player?*

Jack turned; the crowd opened a hole between him and Launa. There was anger in her eyes; for a moment Jack feared she'd turn on her heel and walk away.

Launa slowly drew herself up to attention. The anger never left her eyes, but she slowly paced off the distance to stand before him. Slowly, her hand came up in a salute. Just as slowly, Jack returned it.

"Okay, Captain. I'll handle this."

Pivoting on her heel, Launa faced her troops. Her hands went to her hips; she was the image of a drill instructor quailing out-of-line recruits. The mounted troops froze, as much as they could on their half-trained horses. Every eye was on Launa.

When she spoke, Launa put the sharp cutting edge of her anger into her voice. "Antia, you are a soldier of the legion, you will follow where I lead. I do not want to anger the horsemen. I want time to prepare for when next we meet them. I want them to wonder long what has become of this man you call Arakk. Let them wonder and grow fearful in their unknowing."

Jack listened, respect growing for her, even as he was glad Launa followed the old army tradition—venting her rage on the closest junior.

She had the tactical situation they faced thought through perfectly. Make the fog of war work for them for a change. We need to alert the rest of the defense. Horsemen could ride past Tall Oaks. Someone would have to go upriver and start building an alliance of fortified towns that could withstand the invaders for the next four centuries.

Antia was not buying. "*While* I was a soldier of the legion, I followed after you. I will be a soldier no more. I am of River Bend. I will return to River Bend. But first, I will take this head where it belongs."

Damn. Once Antia resigned, she was covered by the People's "No one can tell another" shit. Jack glanced at Lasa and Kaul. Could he get away with decking Antia? Probably not. Once more the two elders of Tall Oaks had assumed their wait-and-see pose.

Launa measured the situation. Stepping past Antia, she looked up to where Sara sat her mount. "Do you ride with them?"

The young woman nodded. "For Tomas's sake, I do. I do not wish to leave you, but I will."

Launa looked at the rest of them. Few met her gaze. Antia had half of Sara's scouts and Jack's dragoons, plus a score of her own pike cohort. It was a major drawdown on the legion's combat veterans, and Launa's recon assets.

Worse, Jack did not trust Antia. Hatred was no basis for sound policy. If she was out in front of him at River Bend, he would have to accept what she did in the name of the farmers. The more Jack thought about it, the less he liked it.

Launa walked through the mounted troopers. "Sara, where are your supplies?" she called from the rear.

Sara turned her mount to face her former commander. "We will hunt for food as we go. The scouts did that."

The riders opened a hole for Launa to face Sara. "People watching a river have time to gather food. Hands of hands of troopers riding fast across the plains have no time for that. You will starve before you find any horsemen. If you stop to hunt, the horsemen will leave you far behind. Sara, I thought you had listened better."

The young rider blushed. "I thought I did what I saw you and Jack do."

"You have a lot to learn about leading an 'independent command.'" Launa's English added to the confusion of her mounted listeners. "If you do something with a war trophy taken by my command, you will do it under my command. I will go with you, but we will do this like proper troops. I will not have those riding with me looking like a bunch of 'ragpickers.' We will draw supplies today and leave tomorrow."

Most of the troops dismounted. Launa stopped as she passed Antia. "No supplies, no spare mounts—where did you think you were going, a dance?"

Antia bristled. "We would take spare mounts as we passed the herd. He who Speaks for the Bull wants to give a horse to those who hid from the arrows. For each of us who stood in the line of battle, I would take two or three."

Launa threw Jack a look that should have melted him in place. If he had too many horses to feed when he talked to Masin, he had too many when he talked to Antia.

This situation just kept changing. Jack wondered if he'd ever get control of it. Now that he knew he wanted to hunt for a better way, he was too busy improvising minute to minute to do any planning. At least now, he had some time to catch his breath.

Kaul stepped forward. "The sending of a head taken at Tall Oaks to the Horse People should be accompanied by

one who Speaks for Tall Oaks. Lasa cannot ride, but He who
Speaks for the Bull can. Oh, Lady, I offer these words for
your heart."

Kaul and Lasa exchanged a glance that said more than he
and Launa could speak in an hour. But it told Jack nothing.

"Yes. Yes, wise hunter, He who Speaks for the Bull
should be there to Speak Tall Oaks' words. My consort"—
Lasa turned to Jack—"will you ride with these?"

Spending the next week with Launa wasn't Jack's idea of
a good time. Letting political issues—or worse, personal de-
sires—set military strategy stank to anybody's high heaven.
Launa's strategy was sound. Jack had expected support from
Lasa and Kaul. He'd gotten none. But unlike Kaul, Jack had
yet to learn how to disagree with She who Spoke for the
Goddess.

"If it is in your heart that I should, I will go."

FORTY-ONE

NEXT MORNING, KAUL rested his arm on Lasa's waist as they watched the riders cross the ford below Tall Oaks. Lasa smiled. "It is good to feel your flesh again. Will you come to my bed tonight? I have missed you."

"I will share your blanket with as much enthusiasm as I hope those two will share theirs."

Lasa looked after the departing horses. "He is a young man and has so much need. I can offer him so little."

Kaul snorted. "And I can offer her less."

"You old goat, do you think your ram is all a woman wants?" Lasa elbowed him gently in the ribs. "You are no more helpless and without tools with me than those two would be facing Horse People without their knives and bows. With bare hands and teeth, they would fight on. Should we all become like them?" Her voice trailed off in thought.

"I do not know, wise Speaker for the Goddess. I live each day as the sun rises. So long as the earth is beneath my feet, I will walk as best I can."

Launa rode at the head of the column. At the last moment, Merik showed up. He said nothing, just joined the expedition. Jack settled in with Merik as the rear guard.

Once on the plains, Launa spread the troop out in a line.

The dragoons who had fought with Jack gravitated to him on the left flank. Antia's now mounted pikes joined her on the right. Launa and Sara rode between them with the scouts. To Jack's eye, Launa did not lead a unit so much as three separate troops.

Launa led at a brisk trot. After two hours she ordered a break to change horses; in five minutes she had the troops back at the trot. The pace was not as grueling as a horseman might set, but it was a lot more than any of these riders were used to.

They halted that night beside a stream. While the rest made camp, Jack asked Merik to bathe and salve his back. It gave Jack a chance to find out just who really spoke for Tall Oaks. "Why do you ride with us?"

"If People go to River Bend, who will Speak for the Goddess and the Bull?"

Jack shrugged, and regretted it. Merik had been carefully applying the ointment, but Jack shrugged his finger right into a tender spot. "Don't the People of the town call the Speakers?"

"Yes, but if they come from another town, it is well if they go with the blessings of She who Speaks there. I suspect Antia wants to be named, but Brege thinks the People should have a choice. She is willing to go to River Bend. She thinks it wise if I go with you since she could not."

Jack was grateful for the company.

Antia lit a large fire, far bigger than needed. It threw a harsh light on the camp. Her pikes gathered around it to sing songs of anger and hate for the Horse People. Two dragoons contributed a plaintive hunters' song, full of longing for the women left behind. Antia did not let them sing another.

Where Jack pitched his roll, the dragoons did too. Launa and Sara spread their rolls to his left and most of the scouts joined them. The day's separation carried over into the night.

Once Launa had her element bedded down, she returned to the fire. "Antia, we must post a watch—four pikes. When the moon is here, here and here"—she worked her arm through the night sky—"let the four on watch wake four more."

"Why just pikes? Let some scouts and dragoons keep watch."

"Another night they will, but tonight the pikes do it."

Jack stood while Launa finished. When Launa spotted him, she came to him. With her standing agonizingly close, he whispered, "Do we need to talk?"

Launa took in a tight breath; she seemed to hover between the tough commander she had been all day and the lover he had known so long. She was still wearing only that string bikini. Jack wanted her in his arms. Then she came down on him like an angry colonel.

"Talk about what? We wouldn't be here if a certain king had gotten a decent policy adopted on how to handle the horsemen."

Jack winced, and looked for a rock to crawl under. With nothing big enough in sight, he tossed a few words out for cover. "I'm new at this job. Cut me a little slack while I figure out what it's good for."

"Right, and see what you screw up next time."

Jack was getting tired of this conversation. Was it screwed up, or just the screwing that bothered Launa? Jack bit back that remark. They had a job to do, and fighting her wouldn't make it any easier. He let out a long breath. "Well, if you want to talk about anything, I'll listen."

"You do. In the meantime, I've got a tough enough job leading this lash-up. You stay out of my way." She stomped off. Jack let her go.

Back in his blankets, Jack scowled. Once again they rode together, and once again she was madder than hell at him. Already Jack missed Launa—her mind a match for his, her commitment as hard and true, the familiar body he longed for. Jack wanted Launa for all the reasons a man could want a good woman—reasons a man realizes the most after he has lost her.

Damn, she was beautiful, and good—and good and mad. This was her command. He was just a politician along for the ride. *Remember that, Bearman. She calls the shots. You follow.*

With the dawn, Jack was munching cold biscuits and dried meat eaten at the trot. All day, Launa kept the pace fast. Two months ago, Jack had taken three days to reach the next river. Launa was there on the afternoon of the second day. She charged in without breaking stride. Antia followed Launa's lead—or dare.

Some of the troopers did not swim; Jack spent ten minutes urging reluctant cats into the water. He crossed last. Launa waited for them, then ordered the trot.

Jack had suspected they were close to a river. At the last break, Launa had switched to Star. Jack had chosen Windrider. He made a mental note—keep an eye on what horse Launa rode, because she sure wasn't going to warn him about anything. *How good can you read minds, Bearman?*

Camp that night was a silent affair; the pace was taking a toll. Launa assigned the pikes to the mid-watches. Scouts took the first watch, and four of Jack's dragoons got the last one.

As a bedtime exercise, Jack analyzed the deployment. He had never seen the people Launa named to the first and last watch talk to any of the pikes. The troop had divided into three separate groups; Launa did nothing to build unit cohesion. Normally, Jack would give poor ratings to any officer who allowed that. Here, it might guarantee who would guard Launa's backside.

What kind of trouble was Launa expecting? Jack could think of several—all involving Antia and dead horsemen. *Damn it, Launa, we really ought to have a staff meeting or two.*

Jack stopped himself. Why should Launa? Who could she talk to? Sara maybe, but if Antia was the problem, Launa couldn't expect a straight answer from her. Launa didn't have anyone she could trust to talk a problem out . . . except him, and talking was not what she wanted from him.

The next day's pace was just as fearsome. Several pikes began lagging. Merik spotted places where he had seen

herds last time—nothing this trip. Jack suspected he was riding some of the horses he had avoided three months back.

By sunset they had seen nothing but boring, empty
steppe. That night Launa drew the watch solely from Sara's
scouts and Jack's dragoons. It was Sara who told Jack he
had the last watch. Launa had the first and Sara would lead
the second. Jack wondered if he was to keep horsemen
out—or troopers in.

"We're getting close to the next big river," Merik said the
next morning. He pointed. "That clump of trees, with a rise
behind them."

Jack glanced at Launa. She was mounting Star; Sara readied Big Red. "Merik, pick your best remount. I don't know
what Launa is expecting, but she's getting ready for trouble."

Merik grunted. He had already selected his best.

FORTY-TWO

SARA RODE OUT front. She reached the low ridge fifteen minutes ahead of the rest, topped it, then wheeled around and retreated. Jack had a good guess what she saw.

Jack's body came alive as the smell of death rose around him. The steppe here was like the prairie where Launa and he had entered this age. The grass was heavy, bending in the breeze. The land would nourish horses and people. But it was the grass a thousand klicks to the east that drove people to kill.

Sara and her vanguard waited, far enough down the ridge so they were not highlighted against the skyline. Sara was good.

Launa signaled for an officers' call, and Jack rode with Merik up to the meeting. Antia brought Killala. Sara was the last to join. Launa sat her horse comfortably, but her hand rested lightly on her knife. Jack pitied anyone who crossed her. Antia and Killala halted a distance from the rest. When their eyes met, they smiled at some private joke.

Launa started the meeting with a commander's abruptness. "Sara, report."

"A very large herd is in the next valley. Two hands of warriors ride guard. The horsemen's camp is within sight. It is large. I think they have their women and children with them."

"How far away?" Launa asked.

"The herd is as far from the ridge as Tall Oaks is from the hills around it. The camp is off to the right and farther." *So, six to eight kilometers, maybe more. The horsemen would have plenty of time to react.*

"Thank you, Sara." Launa's gaze fixed on Antia. "We will form one line, pikes on the right, scouts in the middle, dragoons on the left. We will enter the valley at a walk. I want the horsemen to know we outnumber them. When the chief comes, I want all of you to join me. I will speak for the troops who took the head. Jack will speak for Tall Oaks. Any questions?"

Without a word, Antia turned her mount, and she and Killala galloped for the pikes.

Jack kneed Windrider closer to Launa. "Be careful," he offered.

Launa's eyes followed Antia. "Be ready," she answered. Jack wasn't the only one betting that Launa's orders would lose something in the execution.

"Stay close," Jack whispered to Merik as they rode back.

"Yes," Merik answered. Puzzlement showed in his eyes, but he'd seen and done too many strange things lately. His lips were a tight line; his belly pulled in tight.

Launa gave the hand signals to spread out in line and advance. Jack modified his deployment. He and Merik edged over to the right of the loyal dragoons, closer to the balance of the troop. Launa and Sara rode well ahead of the scouts. The horse herd they approached had a dozen warriors around it, but more were already riding out from the camp.

The troop was five klicks out when Antia made her move.

At a shout from Antia, most of the pikes and the half dozen scouts closest to them charged the horsemen.

Damn it, she's taking more heads, not delivering one.

"Put the dragoons between the horsemen and Antia's pikes," Jack shouted at Merik as he kicked Windrider. A quick glance back showed that Merik understood. He signaled the dragoons to charge at an angle.

Launa waved at Sara. Then, like him, she raced for Antia. Antia had stolen a march on them, but her troops were tired and mounted on local ponies. Jack and Launa rode for their erstwhile subordinate on horses born of six thousand years of breeding. The pikes were scattered. Jack had no trouble riding through them. As Launa pulled even with Antia, Jack came up behind the two.

Antia jabbed her lance at Launa. The lieutenant batted it away with the butt of her spear. Jack leaned over Windrider's neck and prodded Antia with the butt of his spear. Antia swung her lance around to get at Jack just as Launa swerved in and lunged for Antia's reins. With a hand full of bridle leather, Launa yanked. She and Antia's mounts made a hard left turn and almost went down in a heap. Antia and Launa were busy full time holding on to their mounts' necks.

Jack signaled the pikes to a walk.

Spread out by their mad dash and confused by what they had seen in front of them, most of the pikes obeyed. But Killala and three others headed straight for Launa.

Killala had her lance down and level at Launa. Jack took aim and hefted his spear. He missed, but the spear caused Killala's mount to shy. Half trained, it started bucking.

Killala dropped her lance as she fought to control her horse. Jack slipped from Windrider and quickly strung his bow. With an arrow half drawn, he stood with a clear line of fire at both Antia and Killala.

"Dismount. Now," Jack snarled, quick, tight orders bitten out with no room for disobedience. He nocked his arrow to settle any doubt.

Red-faced with rage, Antia went for her knife. Then she took the measure of Jack's glare—and his bow. She obeyed. Killala slowly slipped from her mount.

Launa glared down at Antia. "I do not know what you intended. We will talk later. I will lead the pikes. Jack, escort these two to the rear. If they do not obey, do what you must, but do not let them interfere. Antia, give me the pot."

Antia handed over the jar with Arakk's head; then the two women turned under Launa's stony gaze, mounted and led Jack through the line of pikes.

Jack glanced around to reacquire tactical awareness. Sara and Merik had the scouts and dragoons stretched out to cover the front between the pikes and the oncoming horsemen. Sara had slowed her detachment as soon as Jack brought the pikes' charge to a standstill. Now, with the pikes under Launa's command, everyone advanced together in two powerful lines.

In the rear, Antia and Killala spread themselves out. Jack pointed his arrow in Antia's direction and put tension to the bow. Antia glared, then signaled Killala to close in. The two rode in easy sight, but not so close that Jack had to worry they might hatch another stunt. They looked as if they had lost and knew it.

Launa halted a hundred meters ahead of the oncoming horsemen. She did not order bows strung, and none of the horsemen had their bows out. Jack kept his bow inconspicuous. Launa rode forward alone to meet the chieftain. An older man met her halfway. His long gray hair flowed free except for two braided forelocks.

Without preamble, Launa handed him the jar and backed Star away. The man only glanced in the pot, then fixed Launa with a bitter scowl. She sat her mount, returning his gaze with relaxed aplomb. After a long pause the chief said something. Launa did not look away. "Killala to the front," she shouted in English.

Antia turned to Jack, a raised eyebrow for a question.

"Killala, go forward to translate. Ride slowly." Jack adjusted his bow for emphasis. With a nod from Antia, Killala trotted for Launa.

Shokin, Mighty Man of the Stalwart Shield Clan, sat his pony. Behind him he could hear his sons getting the warriors in line. He did not dishonor them by glancing over his shoulder. He looked straight ahead and tried to make sense of what he saw.

It seemed that half of the riders in front of him had meant to charge his unprepared warriors and the other half had ridden between them and his warriors to stop the charge. Yes, Shokin would bet a good woman on that. When one who had made to charge him handed over a jug and was sent to the rear, Shokin knew his bet was safe. But why would a host that had two warriors for every one of his hesitate to attack him?

Shokin studied the woman walking her horse toward him. The stallion was large and well muscled. Shokin would gladly trade half a herd for that one; he would sire many. The woman's dress was like none of the Horse People. The scant affair she wore hardly covered her maidenhood, and her breasts bounced around for any warrior to see. No father or husband could allow such a display. Any warrior could take her and there would be much blood—or many horses would have to be paid.

The woman stopped in front of Shokin as if she were a chief. The knife in her belt would have made any chief proud. The quiver that hung from her waist held many arrows, and a bow that was too long to use from horseback. Shokin frowned, and then she walked her horse forward and shoved a pot in his hands.

Shokin lifted the lid. A glance told him it was Arakk's head. So the fool had not taken the stray horses he said were begging for a master. Shokin looked straight at the woman, but shouted. "Berok, come forward and listen."

Berok, the oldest son of one of Shokin's good friends, was nearsighted and useless on the hunt, but he was skilled with hands and words. He had learned many of the strange arts the captives brought to the camp last year, and many of their words.

The woman shrugged her shoulders and shouted something. From the back of the milling host, a woman rode forward. Behind him, he could hear Berok drawing near.

"What is this?" Shokin shouted at the two women.

The new woman said something to the chief woman. They exchanged words; then the new woman spoke. "That is the head of Arakk. He and all who rode with him are dead."

Behind him, Shokin could hear consternation and anger. Several of his warriors had friends or brothers who had ridden with Arakk. Shokin raised his hand for silence. He was obeyed.

"Many will want blood for blood."

"Let them come. They will have their own," the woman shot back. The chief woman's hand went to her knife. The other woman stopped. They exchanged words. Anger flushed red on her cheeks when next the speaker woman turned to Shokin.

"Launa, leader of the war host of Tall Oaks, puts these words in my mouth. None of the Horse People are to pasture their herds on the land between the river to the east and the river to the west. Let our peoples keep this land between us. If a double hand of horsemen are seen in this land, they will be named a war party and they will die. This we say and this we will do."

"I cannot say where other warriors' herds will pasture. I will take your words to the Mighty Men of the Horse People."

"Take them, then." The speaker was impatient for them to be gone, but Shokin was not finished.

"The man who came from the west to the winter camp this spring. Is he well?" Shokin could see that his words startled the speaker. The chief woman listened as a Mighty Man might. Shokin found himself liking this woman named Launa.

After a short exchange, the speaker said, "Kaul is well, and his arrows were in many of the warriors who fell before Tall Oaks. His arrows will feast on the blood of those who cross the rivers where they do not belong."

"His words were not of blood," Shokin parried.

"Your greeting did not match his words."

Shokin grunted; he had learned much. He would learn more when Berok shared what he had understood of the words between the speaker and the chief. Shokin would carry the words and the wisdom of this meeting to the summer encampment of the clans. There would be much to talk about.

Whatever questions the horseman asked and whatever answers Launa gave, Jack heard nothing. When they were done, the chief galloped back to his warriors. He shouted, and they all rode from the meeting site. Soon they were driving their herd to the east. Jack had spent the last year fearing the horsemen's lances, yet today the Horse People were an anticlimax. Antia had come closer to drawing blood.

Launa returned to her troops. "About turn," she ordered.

"Pikes, turn," Antia called, and the pikes wheeled. Jack wasn't sure who they obeyed. They probably weren't either.

Antia kicked her mount to a fast trot and the rest followed. Jack stared open-mouthed. He and Launa were alone where moments ago several forces—Jack still wasn't sure how many—had been on the verge of slaughter. He kicked Windrider to a gallop. Half a klick away, Launa urged Star to a catch-up pace.

Launa watched her departing command with puzzlement. She had gauged Antia almost to the minute. The princess Jack had rescued was turning into a witch as hate devoured anything soft in her. Launa remembered a modern woman— Marilyn, the Green Beret, preparing with Jack and her for the time jump. Marilyn's anger at a male-run world had led her to guile, then murder, and finally to her own death. Antia was well down that path.

At least Jack had not muffed his lines. It would have been nice to debrief with him, refine her estimate of Antia. But, damn it, she wasn't a cadet anymore; she had her command. Beside, she didn't need a politician looking over her shoulder. *Right, politician; call it anything but Lasa's lover.* And a politician who hadn't been able to get a sound military strategy adopted.

She glanced over to where Jack sat his horse alone. *God, slow the world down so I can put my life together.*

Launa turned to face the dust cloud the troop was raising. Antia was up to something, and Launa hadn't the foggiest idea what it might be this time. She'd better catch up.

After the first rest break, Launa's once divided troop mingled as one, except for a silent bubble surrounding her and Jack. He kept to the far right flank. Sara had Launa's remounts waiting for her on the left. She settled for that flank and watched as riders relaxed after their brush with the enemy.

"What were you up to, charging in ahead of us?" one of Sara's scouts asked a pike—one of the women Jack and Antia had rescued at River Bend.

"We were putting on a show for those bloodthirsty ticks. Make sure they never bother us again. What did you think?"

"I don't know. It looked awfully confusing for a while." The scout seemed only half convinced. Launa glanced at Antia. The woman rode in silence. As Antia listened to the false interpretation of her plan, a smug half-smile crossed her lips.

The pike continued. "We put fear into them, didn't we? You saw them run. I love the sight of horsemen's backsides."

Everyone could agree on that. Slowly, then more quickly, the thought of the near atrocity Antia had attempted was replaced by the common joy of success. They all felt they had put the fear of the Goddess into the Horse People.

Launa shook her head. She knew people rewrote history, but she'd never been around when they did. Then her gut knotted. These people were going to River Bend! This was their first communal experience. It was drawing them together, making them a people unto themselves. And it was a lie!

And worse, the people who had been there, seen with their own eyes Antia's attempted attack, were letting it happen. When these people got to River Bend, what would Antia have them doing? Launa's blood ran cold.

They camped that night on the banks of the Dniester. Antia had a great fire built. Even before the sun was down, she began dancing around it. First Antia sang of the rape and slaughter of River Bend, but quickly she passed on to her escape from her captors. Launa's eyes grew hard at what now was missing—any mention of Jack's part in her rescue. Antia's song grew faster, louder as she turned to the defense of Tall Oaks. Again she gloated over the death of the Horse People. Again only her deeds were sung. But the refrain caught on with all who joined her in an ever widening circle around the fire. Shouts of "Death to the Horsemen—Death to everyone" rang out.

Sick at heart, Launa walked away from that fire. In the few minutes of daylight left, she sparked a second fire. Jack appeared with a large armful of wood, dumped it and quickly disappeared to search for more. Several dragoons wandered over.

"Can we join you, Lady?" one asked.

The other glanced over his shoulder and quickly added, "I no longer see going to River Bend as a good path."

Launa sent them into the twilight for more wood. While she was alone, Merik came to squat beside her. "Do not let my path sadden you. The People of River Bend will need someone to Speak for the Goddess and the Bull. Brege wants them to remember us when they name the Names of Choosing."

Launa patted his shoulder. Maybe Antia wouldn't get her way. Gladly, Launa sent Merik back. Hatred fueled that fire; there was need of something gentle and nurturing around it.

Jack and the others returned. Launa measured the wood pile and judged it sufficient. She had warmed meat while they were gone. She placed it between biscuits with bits of cheese. The dragoons looked at the concoction with puzzlement, but ate.

Jack grinned and took a bite. "Good hot sandwich, my lov . . . Lieutenant." He looked away to cover his mistake and moved to the opposite side of the fire.

The noise from the other fire made sleep impossible, but Launa sought the comfort of her blankets early. She wanted Jack in them, but not just for one night. Jack was close, but he might as well have been on the other side of time.

Launa had chosen Jack knowing there was a rough as well as a good side to him. But never had she thought he could put her behind him, certainly not so quickly. A small voice deep within her asked what she would have done if the tables had been turned, if the People had asked her to walk away from Jack.

Launa didn't want to listen to that voice; she had no answer. Instead, she listened to the shouts from the other fire. Hatred and anger she could understand. Anger made it possible to stay in her own blanket. Maybe she would need to hate, too. Blinking back tears, she prayed hatred would not be necessary; she loved Jack. Could the day ever come when she didn't?

Next morning, the other camp slept in, exhausted from the party. Launa roused her four at first light. Without looking back, they rode straight for Tall Oaks at an even faster pace than they'd kept on the way out. The dragoons rode between Launa and Jack, keeping silent. There was much to do when they returned; Launa spent the ride planning.

FORTY-THREE

A SICKNESS GATHERED in Kaul's belly as Jack and Launa crossed the river into Tall Oaks. The dragoons riding between them might have been a fence with no door. They did not even glance at each other as they turned their remounts over to the dragoons with thank-you's and smiles that held no pleasure. With slumping shoulders Jack walked for the sanctuary and Lasa. Launa charged past Kaul and disappeared into her house.

Kaul had hoped this journey would give his friends time to mourn their loss and celebrate their love one last time. The shadows of a future that darkened Jack's eyes had once more swallowed Kaul's two friends. What ugliness lurked in the tomorrows of the People that it could so haunt these two kind souls? Kaul followed Launa, beseeching the Goddess for a path to help them all.

Inside, Launa had tossed a wicker basket upside down, emptying it on her bed. A pouch fell on the floor, spewing its contents. A small bar of metal gleamed like none Kaul had ever seen. But it was the pouch that held Kaul. The pattern worked into its soft leather was like none other. Here was power, strange and distant. Sliding from the sack was something like a block of wood with large straight markings. Launa stooped hastily to grab them and put them back in the pouch.

Kaul spoke to fill the silence. "You journeyed well?"

In a nervous rush, Launa shared the story. Her hands flitted from sack to sack, arranging them, then rearranging them in piles on her bed. So Antia had tried to stack up more bodies. "Her path will lead to brambles with no fruit," he said.

Kaul's one smile came when Launa shared Merik's words. Brege was a wise woman from a wise mother. The girl he had bounced on his knee had become a farseeing woman. Kaul's eyes misted with the tears of a father proud of a child grown to wisdom. His years were not wasted. "That is well done. We will blend Antia's bitterness with others who are soft and nurturing."

"Yes," shot back Launa. "There are many towns upriver. I will invite the young women and men who yearn for a journey, for open land. Let them come to River Bend and stand between the horsemen and those who follow the Goddess. Antia's bitterness may yet season a stew worthy of the Goddess."

"Will Jack go with you?"

Launa scowled, then turned away. "Jack is Lasa's consort. He has no time for what I do. I will go. Let him stay."

Kaul heard the pain she could not hide. He went to her, put his arms around her. "You love that man, whatever bed he sleeps in. The People called him from you with no time for a dance of parting. That was poorly done. I had hoped you and he might make your own dance while you rode the steppe."

"He is Lasa's. I would not touch what must be at her side." Launa's eyes overflowed with tears, but she pushed Kaul away.

Hands helpless at his side, Kaul struggled to let Launa's words into his heart. She spoke of Jack as if he were a cloak given to Lasa. This was no way to speak of one who must find his own way to walk with the Goddess. Kaul had not grasped what Jack meant when he spoke of "slaves." Then the horsemen knives showed Kaul how a man might have a heart of mud.

He searched for words to comfort. "Jack is consort to

Lasa. But he was consort to you until Bellda called him from your side. He cannot be brushed from your heart like flies from ripe fruit. You should not have to turn your face from him as from one dead."

"But he *is* dead to me." Her words flew like a slinger's stone. "He is Lasa's. What if I took him for a night?"

"Lasa and I would share your laughter." Kaul watched all color drained from Launa's cheeks. "Jack is consort to Lasa and Speaks for the Bull. We all pray that the Goddess will grant them a long and giving life together. But none of the People will deny what the Goddess has given you nor share anything but joy when you recall it. And if recollections should lead to more memories, such happiness comes from the Goddess."

Breath exploded from Launa. All the anger, pain, desire and duty that had bound her heart for the last week exploded with it. *What have I done? What could I have done?* Launa swiped at tears she had held back—tears from an emotional dam she need never have built. Then she sighed. "Go, Kaul. I will ride out tomorrow. Ask among the People if any will ride with me."

Kaul stepped off the short distance to the door, eyes staying on her, then turned and left.

Alone, Launa collapsed on her bed, letting the tears fall. Did these wonderful fools think one more night in Jack's arms would somehow make up for the missed years ahead? Launa wanted to scream at all of them: *Save yourselves.*

On the bed, trinkets, tools and weapons of a dead twenty-first century surrounded her. Something hurt her back. She reached behind and pulled Maria's book from underneath herself—Maria, a simple Mexican cook on a CIA ranch. Yet Launa had pledged herself more to Maria and her hugs than to the President of the United States.

Memories of Maria's smile gently pulled Launa back to duty. Her fingers traced the hand-tooled leather with Indian and Mexican symbols painted on or worked into its surface. When she pulled the book out, her second lieutenant's bar came with it. She held the book in one hand, the cold metal bar in the other.

Since her thirteenth birthday she had yearned for that rank insignia. For three years at West Point she had struggled for it. At the President's bidding, she had been commissioned a year early. She had worn her butter bars exactly once—to receive the President's orders. Now, she was here, six thousand years before the rank of Second Lieutenant, United States Army, meant anything. If she succeeded it might never mean anything.

But to her, it was duty, honor, country. It meant putting her body between death and those she loved. It meant a lot to an idealistic young girl. That girl was gone. Now the woman, combat veteran—and, for duty's sake, cast-off lover—was on her own. She could do nothing, or she could do what duty required. Doing something had always been Launa's first choice. She would feel better with a horse under her and miles between her and Jack.

She tossed the gold bar in the air. It glinted in the light as she caught it. It did not belong here. The tactical situation around Tall Oaks could come unhinged at any time. She should do something about this anachronism and the book she held in her other hand.

The metal would be hard to destroy, but if she buried it, time would disfigure it. The book was easier. The wood stove beckoned; she could burn it to ash.

Launa leafed through the pages. The pictures of flora were beautifully detailed. Beside each plant was a list of remedies made from it. Scientific notes followed each traditional entry, dryly commenting on the actual value. Even those notes were dated. Launa found the title page: Philadelphia, 1902. It did not belong here any more than her rank insignia.

But there was a difference between the two. The butter bar bestowed rank and power that had no meaning here. The book gave knowledge to heal and soothe. That knowledge was needed among the people Launa had grown to love.

Launa took a stick from the fireplace and dug in the dirt beside her hearth. The hole she made was not deep, but it was enough to bury a second lieutenant's gold bar. The book went back into its pouch. She would take that with her. There was too much she had to learn before she could destroy all it held.

The sun was high; Jack shaded his eyes to follow Launa. She traveled with Kaul and eight archers. Jack had sent them with ten spare horses each; the towns upriver would have horses for plowing—and scouting. Jack rotated his tense shoulders; already he missed that soldier at his back.

As Launa's small detachment passed from view, Jack scanned the hills. Again, with no orders from He who Spoke for the Bull, the men of Tall Oaks took care of the pasturing of the sheep, goats and horses. Just what was his job? A few months from now, after Lasa recovered from the miscarriage, he knew what his duty was. But for now, what did these people expect from him? In the army, you look things up in the manual. Here they grew up knowing their roles. How could a stranger find his place?

A lone rider splashed across the ford at the east edge of town. Jack raced for the main avenue. He arrived just as Merik was dismounting in front of the longhouse. In the shade of the veranda Lasa sat with Brege while she nursed her daughter.

Merik went to Brege, kissed her and received his daughter into his arms. He held her, bounced her and, without giving her up, spoke to his wife. "Oh, Lady, I address you as Speaker for the Goddess in River Bend and call you to join our people as soon as you may travel."

Lasa stood, smiling at the news and her daughter. "Let us feast in celebration." Hunters rode out, confident the afternoon would be long enough for their longbows and horses to bring back fresh meat. The cooks began preparing what was in their larders.

Jack joined the gathering around Lasa as Merik continued. "Antia wanted to be named Speaker for both the Goddess and the Bull. She says she will never take a consort. There were some who would accept her that way, but more shook their heads. The council went long into the night with everyone speaking their hearts. It was Sara who first asked if Brege had not been called by the Goddess to stand at River Bend between the horsemen and the People. Was it not Brege who fought at the tree and brought Tall Oaks the song that rang in our hearts? Did she not fight beside us and bring forth a daughter on that very same day?"

Merik spoke with eyes so overflowing with pride that Jack wondered how Merik could find words for his mouth. Antia leading the point of the spear had terrified Jack. Brege and Merik standing point between Tall Oaks and the horsemen would let him sleep at night.

"Antia is not happy," Merik finished, "but the council made the call to Brege and me. It is done."

Brege took their daughter back and offered her a breast to suck. When she turned to Glengish, it was the Goddess who spoke. "We have no one with your wisdom of herbs. Will you join us and speak your wisdom at our council?"

The hunter woman sucked on her few remaining teeth for a moment, then turned to the man who led the hunters from the cave many rivers away. He spoke in answer to her wordless question. "I would like to be closer to our old hunting grounds. Maybe now the horsemen have left them. I will go with you to hunt around River Bend. Many will go with us."

Jack accepted the fragmentation of his town with mixed feelings. He did not like losing Glengish and Kaul on the same day, yet the hotheads at River Bend were getting allies that he could trust to keep Antia on a short leash.

Only time would reveal an answer. Jack sighed. Time was his enemy and his ally. The only thing straight around here was a lance, and nothing ever stayed the same.

FORTY-FOUR

THE FEAST WENT long into the night. For the first time, Jack heard songs of victory. The People celebrated more their liberation from slavery and death than the defeat of the horsemen. The songs were rough made, and often out of step with the dance. They would not live in the People's memory like the songs of old, but they were a beginning, and they could be rewoven.

Over the next days, small groups trekked off to River Bend; Jack didn't keep count. Sometime before the next full moon a trickle of people began to pass through Tall Oaks on their way to River Bend. Launa's recruiting effort was bearing fruit.

Jack lost himself among the People, flowing into their gentle life. Crops needed hoeing. Sheep and goats had to be taken to different pastures. He who Speaks for the Bull had many duties. He discovered his power was not that of an officer of the king to tax and execute. Rather, he stood first among men and women who knew what needed doing and went about their daily business with an enthusiasm and commitment to life. Only when one's actions rubbed against another's did he find himself listening, cajoling, encouraging. The power of the Speaker inflicted no pain, no suffering. Jack found within himself a new power, one that nurtured rather than drove. He came to like it.

It was easy for a man to lose touch with time. Each summer day held the same warmth, the same duties, the same rewards. One afternoon, Lasa called him aside.

"It is warm. Let us bathe in the river."

Jack had nothing demanding his attention. Lasa had been showing more and more concern for him lately. Now that his burns were healed, her massage often drained his body of the tensions of his on-the-job training.

"Last night was the dark of the moon." Lasa's words rambled on as they strolled to the river. "That is the second one since the battle."

Jack recalled a full moon lighting his fingers as he nuzzled Launa the night before the battle. It had been a long time, and the mere memory quickened him.

Jack almost missed a step. It had been six weeks after Sam's birth that Sandie had met him at the door in her sheerest negligee. Visions of his first wife, Launa and Lasa swirled in his head—the women of his life. One dead, one sent away, one beside him. After six weeks, the needs of his body were strong, but was it fair for Lasa to share his mind's eye with so many?

Yet Lasa was no virgin. Bellda had given her Masin, and they had conceived a son. Lasa had chosen Kaul, the love of her youth, and now Ballda had again given Lasa a consort . . . Jack.

He let Lasa wash him. Then he washed her and let his ministrations lead where he knew they should. He was no novice in the ways of pleasing a woman, and he gave Lasa the full measure she deserved. The afternoon passed with no one disturbing them, and when the Bull finally spoke to the Goddess, Jack found he had come to know Lasa's body, every valley and curve of her. And it was Lasa he made love to, no ghost, no banished lover. When Lasa's passion consumed her, it was Jack's name she called.

Over the next several weeks Jack lost track of many things. The men gave him knowing smiles when too late he remembered he should have checked on new pastures. They had done it already. Jack guessed there were few secrets in a town of three thousand. But one secret Lasa made sure he learned first. Over breakfast one morning, she carefully lifted each breast. The other women sharing the meal with them watched her. The one in black who cared for the birthing hut slid over to touch them after Lasa finished. Finally she nodded.

Lasa turned to Jack. "The Bull is strong in you. I believe I caught the first dance."

It took a moment for Jack to follow Lasa's meaning. Then he grinned, remembering watching Sam grow, knowing he had made a child. The thought of the new life they had made raised a hunger in Jack. He wore nothing but his belt; there was no hiding his desire.

Lasa opened her arms and spread her legs, beckoning him with a smile. The other women did not even turn away. Now Jack knew what it meant to be the Bull speaking to the Goddess. There was nothing here to hide. He wanted Lasa. He wanted to celebrate the life that grew in her. He went to her, took her with all the strength one brought to the love of a Goddess. He was where he belonged, and the People celebrated with him.

That afternoon, as Jack helped bring in a herd of goats, two couples came down the trail from upriver. Jack hailed them; the number of people passing through on their way to River Bend had been down lately.

"Is this River Bend?" one of the women called.

"No, this is Tall Oaks. You are welcome for the night, or for a day of rest. River Bend is an eight- to ten-day walk. I am Jack who Speaks for the Bull," he said as he fell in with them.

"Kaul and Launa praise you and your, ah, battles." The word came hard to the man's lips.

"How are they?" Jack swallowed hard, trying to slow the racing of his heart at Launa's name. After all, he was Lasa's consort. They had a child on the way.

"They are very persuasive. They and the trader, Nak."

"Nak passed through your town?" So Launa had gotten

the old trader's attention. He must be telling of the rape of River Bend from here to Greece.

"Yes," one of the women added. "I knew we had to do something. We could not just sit, waiting for them to come for us. But others did not see that path."

"I am glad you saw it. We will need many."

Suddenly, the four of them stopped walking; uncomfortable, they looked at their feet. "There were more of us when we started," one of them mumbled.

"What happened?"

"On our way people joined us. They follow after a woman . . . Hanna. They sang different songs. They invited us to go to Wood Village and hear Hanna's words."

"Did you?" It was not just the cool of the approaching evening that chilled Jack.

"Yes, we listened to her. It is a terrible thing to kill another person. Many of our friends either stayed there or returned to our town. We alone chose to go on."

Jack shook his head, anger rising. So Hanna had not forgotten them. But all this was not these people's fault. They were his guests and deserved hospitality. "Let us feed you. You will eat tonight with many who stood against the horsemen when they came to Tall Oaks. Listen to their stories and songs." Jack led them into Tall Oaks. This day that had begun with celebration was not ending well.

A lathered horse stood outside the sanctuary. Jack's temper cut in full blast. He'd taught his people better. You ride a horse into a lather, you take care of it first. As he reached the longhouse a boy raced out and made to lead the horse off. Jack grabbed the kid's shoulder. "Did you ride that horse?"

"No, O Speaker. A woman rode it. I will care for it."

Jack turned the visitors over to the cooks and stomped into the sanctuary. No one should leave a horse soaked like that.

Then he froze. Sara was talking in a whisper to Lasa. Death hung over Lasa's eyes. Suddenly, the horse was not that important.

Lasa looked up when she saw Jack crossing the room.

Sara stopped talking. Lasa pursed her lips, then turned back to Sara. "Tell Jack your story from the beginning."

Sara nodded but did not meet his eyes. In a rush of words, she spoke to the packed earth floor. "Antia asked to lead a troop onto the steppe to make sure the horsemen left the land between the rivers. Brege called the women into council and we decided no. Glengish's hunters would roam that land and what they saw, they would tell us. Antia was not happy, but she accepted the wisdom of the council. Or so she said. The next day, she and many of the pikes went hunting. They went south, but they were gone for more than a hand of days. When they returned, they stayed among themselves. The next time they went hunting, they took a few more. Each time, a few more."

"Where did they hunt?" Jack asked.

Sara looked up at Jack; tears rimmed her eyes. "Last time, they invited me to the hunt. Out of sight of River Bend we turned, rode north and crossed first one river and then the next. We found a herd with three hands of warriors around it. Without a thought, Antia charged them. The lucky ones died in the battle. The others died, but more slowly." Sara ended with a shudder and turned her face away from Jack.

"So Antia is taking heads." Jack suddenly felt very tired. This was stupid; they had a war to fight, and Antia was playing with the enemy—an enemy deadly as any snake these people knew. From the look in Sara's eyes, Antia's play was vicious.

Sara turned back to Jack. There was none of the tough soldier in her now. "Antia does not take heads. She takes what they took from Kaul."

Jack saw the nightmares behind Sara's eyes, but he had no time to comfort her. "Shit." There would be no mistaking these raids for one from another horse clan. Antia was leaving her fingerprints.

"We have other problems, too." Pacing back and forth, Jack briefed Lasa and Sara on what he'd learned from the pilgrims. "So while Antia stirs up trouble with the Horse People before us, Hanna does her best to keep anyone from helping."

Lasa's hand went to her belly. She was a mother and thought first of her child. "Are Brege and Merik in danger?"

Sara shook her head. "Antia has taken less than one in three with her on her hunts. She would not harm the Speakers. Even those who hunt with her would not dare do such a thing."

Jack considered the risk to Brege and Merik, found it acceptable for now, and dismissed it. As he weighed his problems, the herdsman sloughed off him, like a new skin too weak to withstand the harsh rays of an angry sun. With each breath, his back grew straighter, this mouth tighter, harder. Jack was a soldier, an Apache warrior, bred for war. Lasa watched him; he saw his metamorphosis reflected in her concerned eyes.

"The horsemen will come for us. Let us call the People together." Part of Jack relished the change. He packed away the nurturing side of him, buried it deep, wondering if he'd ever find it again.

Lasa's lips moved. Did she want to gainsay him? She nodded. "Send a rider to Taelon. We will meet tonight."

Lasa surrendered the council to Jack as soon as the name of the Goddess had been invoked. Jack stood and painted the threat before them with broad brush strokes. The assembly listened in silence. Point by point, Jack outlined what needed to be done.

Taelon would mount his hunters, and throw them out as a screen to give the town early warning and a supply of meat. The old hunter grunted and silently accepted his orders.

The youth tending the sheep would be given horses and would keep a lookout for horsemen. If they spotted any, they would ride for Tall Oaks; the sheep would fend for themselves. That drew murmurs but no argument. The legion would drill. The horsemen could be expected to attack before the snows came. Jack finished his operations plan with details of his own assignment.

"I will ride upriver to find Kaul and Launa. We will revisit each town, seeking people to join us. I should return before the moon is again full. When we are as strong as we can be, we will meet Antia face to face."

No one disputed the wisdom of his words, but Lasa would not look Jack in the eye.

FORTY-FIVE

LAUNA DIDN'T LIKE the feel of this town; the hairs on the back of her neck bristled. Meticulously, she studied the buildings and surrounding terrain. Something was wrong.

They had left the last town three days ago. Thirty or forty recruits set out for River Bend as Launa led her small detachment farther west. She'd left a stallion and a mare pregnant by a modern horse. That was her policy; she was now short ten horses. But with the horse, a new way of life had come to five towns.

This town was a large one, up a river valley in the foothills that the map in Launa's head called the Transylvanian Alps. Fir trees and green meadows covered the hills rising on both sides of the river. In many places, rock showed through in majestic outcroppings. When Kaul pointed them up a tributary that ran under one of those rocky points, Launa's combat instincts kicked in.

She saw the town long before they came to it. Like Tall Oaks, houses spread out from a central plaza, first in reasonable order, then in a jumble. There was no wall. Croplands surrounded it. Green pastures stretched out from them. Cliff Town looked about the size of Tall Oaks.

"Where are the herds?" Launa asked.

Kaul twisted on his mount, surveying the hills with a frown. "I do not see any."

Launa raised her hand, and the column halted. The troops formed a rough circle, eyes covering all directions. It had been hard for her to get across that danger might come from any direction, but the lesson was taking root.

Launa studied the town. There was little movement in the streets—too little. Above the town, near the cliffs that gave it its name, black smoke that had been billowing from a chimney suddenly turned white. "Looks like someone just doused a fire."

Kaul stroked his beard. "Why would someone do that?"

Launa's West Point-trained mind could think of many. Since Kaul's farmer mind could not, Launa grew more edgy. She considered ordering her troop to dismount and string bows, then thought better. If she was going into combat, she wanted her bows in the best shape; the natural sinews stretched when strung too long. There were plenty of complications to the ancient combat picture. "Let's move out, but keep our eyes open."

An hour later they were within a longbow shot of the town and Launa again called a halt.

"Where are all the people?" Kaul asked.

"I don't know, but let's be ready to leave in a hurry. Half of you switch mounts. The rest string bows." While Launa moved her blanket to Star and got him ready for a run, Kaul strung his bow, never taking his eyes from the town. When she finished, they swapped duties. With his back turned to her, he whispered. "People watch us from doorways and behind houses. This is not like the People."

Launa grunted agreement; she'd caught sight of spears and bows even as she changed mounts. Nothing developed while the rest of the troop finished. Launa felt better facing the unknown once her unit was prepared to run like hell.

"Do the People have any way of showing other people that they come with no anger in their heart?" She asked Kaul.

"Before last summer every heart we saw was empty of anger."

"Right," Launa sighed.

The standoff continued. When Launa had had enough, she

handed her bow to Kaul and stalked down the path into town. At twice normal bow range, she stopped and squatted on her haunches. For a long minute she waited, catching glimpses of eyes in the shadows of open doors or heads quickly ducking around corners of buildings only to disappear immediately. Then a lone figure detached itself from a shadow and walked toward her.

The man was Launa's height and looked to be her age. He walked with a grace and presence that reminded her of Kaul, but he held a spear at the ready. His clothes were as scarce as Kaul's, just a belt and knife. Launa eyed the knife. The blade was not dull stone or obsidian. The sun caught the dagger. It gleamed copper yellow.

Adrenaline pumping, Launa made ready for anything. The trader Nak had visited the last town. He had sung them the song of the rape of River Bend. Many had remarked on the knife Launa had given him, but Nak would not trade it for anything. Was that Nak's knife? How had this stranger come by it?

Launa laid her copper knife in front of her and stepped back as the man approached. She kept her right hand near the bronze blade that hung from the back of her belt.

The man stooped and, without taking his eyes from Launa, picked up the knife. He studied it for a moment, then placed his own blade on the ground where Launa's had been and took three steps back to study her knife more thoroughly.

Launa quickly picked up his blade and retreated two steps as she examined it. The knife was copper, and new. Smaller than the ones they'd brought through time, it was more roughly made. Launa gulped; she was probably holding the first indigenous metal weapon on earth. Finished, she held the knife out hilt first.

"I am Launa of Tall Oaks."

The man gave her back her knife as he recovered his own. "I am Dobrovnish, first son of She who Speaks for the Goddess in Cliff Town. Are you the Launa of whom Nak sang?"

Score one for Nak, a regular Paul Revere. "Yes."

"Have you met the horsemen again?" Dobrovnish eyed the horses behind Launa.

"The horsemen came to Tall Oaks this spring with lances and bows. None of them now live."

"And you ride their horses." The townsman smiled. "That is good. I wish for our People the same power to face the horsemen and put them in their graves."

He raised his hand. At the signal, young men and women, spears and bows at the ready, broke from cover. "Come, friends, meet Launa of Nak's song. She has much to tell us."

Launa assessed the deployment. It was poor; archers and spear-carriers mixed together with no eye for mutual support. Still, the horsemen would not find them easy prey. Here were people Launa would not have to recruit. Here, all her time could go into training. That was good, but first, Launa had to find out where the copper knife came from.

The fire glinted off Dob's copper arm bracelet, a match for the one Launa now wore. Again she held his knife, turning it over in her hand, letting the light play on it, telling the tale of its manufacture.

The smoking building up the hill was the foundry, if you could call it such. Two small furnaces, no more than a cubic foot each, were heated by blowing through reeds. The copper didn't melt but coagulated into large chunks. Once the mess cooled, the slag was broken up with stone hammers and droplets of copper picked out. Warmed again, these were beaten into bracelets, or the moon-shaped earrings Launa saw around the fire.

After Dob saw the knife at Nak's side, he hammered several droplets together into a single blade. Now other jewelry was being beaten into weapons; Launa was surrounded by committed allies with technical knowhow. She should be glad.

Instead, it was her worst nightmare. If the Kurgans captured this town's artisans, they had the beginning of a military-industrial complex. As much as she loved the people of Tall Oaks, the safety of Cliff Town was now more important.

Kaul hunched across the fire from her. The drawn look on

his face told her the realization had hit him too. His gaze rose from the hissing embers to fix Launa. "We must give these people your wisdom."

It was nice to have a second opinion. She wondered what Jack would say. No time to ask; she turned to Dob.

His eyes were fixed on her. They brimmed with commitment, and respect, and maybe something deeper that made Launa tingle. She would let time reveal that—if they had time. "Tomorrow I will show your woodsmen how to fashion the longbows we carry. You can bring down deer at five or six of your bow shots."

Dob nodded. "Or horsemen."

Launa liked this man's focus. "I will show you how to use long and short spears to fight the horsemen, and where to stand so many people may work as one. How many will walk with you?"

Dob held up both hands; ten times he spread them. "A double hand of double hands will walk with you at tomorrow's sun."

One hundred, Launa counted. A good start.

Time passed quickly in drill and work. Two more furnaces were built, and extra shifts hammered away at the cliff face. Dob and his sister Sadira were popular. No one rose to challenge She who Spoke for the Goddess and He who Spoke for the Bull when they cast full support behind their children's effort.

Maybe it was the visual impact of Kaul, helping craftsmen, working beside miners, blowing on the furnaces, showing hunters how to use the new bow. Always smiling, always helpful; Kaul never covered the scars the horsemen's knives had given him in their assembly. His flesh screamed its testimony for all to see.

Still, there were those who could not find it in themselves to kill another. While their neighbors prepared, this gentler half quietly worked extra hours at the mine, longer hours at the hunt, doing what they could while others did what they would. Launa was grateful not to face another Hanna.

Launa turned over the spare mounts, all ninety of them, to

Cliff Town. The horses let the hunters range farther afield and bring in more meat. Dob had his own use for the horses. One night he asked Launa if she would like to see what he had done.

Next morning, they rode out alone. The summer air was warm, making the shade beside the river pleasant. Many nights, Launa had talked beside the campfire of battles, strategies and tactics. This morning she listened while Dob talked about himself. Launa's heart was light as her new friend told what it was like growing up in these hills, learning to farm and hunt and work metal. When she dodged his questions about her youth, he did not press her. Inevitably, talk turned to what lay ahead.

"When I listened to Nak's song, my heart was heavy. Could such a thing happen to our people? That night, in a dream, I saw one of our fastest runners tending his sheep. He looked out over the valley and saw the horsemen. Fast as a rabbit, he ran to us. Though my mother and father fled with many of the old ones into the hills, I did not run. With my sister and many young ones beside me, we stood with our bows and spears."

"Did you win the battle in your dreams?"

"I awoke. Maybe I did not know what would happen next."

Launa looked away; Dob's heart was gentle. Killing would not come easy, but he would do what he must. She liked that about Dob. She was finding more and more that she liked about him. She didn't want to follow that thought too far. "So you set up watch posts?"

"Yes, and one of our fastest runners did race into town shouting that he had seen two hands of horsemen. We made ready to greet horsemen such as Nak had sung of. I am glad it was you. After listening to your words and watching you drill our people, I see how poorly we were prepared to fight for our lives."

For several more hours they rode downriver; Launa enjoyed the company. When they reached the last hill, Dob led Launa up a path. In a meadow, sheep and a horse grazed under the watchful eye of four youths. Dob waved to them and dismounted.

"Come with me." Dob led the way through trees farther up the hill until they scrambled out on a rocky ledge. The view was unlimited for a hundred kilometers.

"You could have seen our campfires for two or three nights."

"Yes, with the horses, we can have that many days warning."

"And we passed several places where an ambush would have cost raiders much."

"Yes, 'defend forward' you say. But I think Cliff Town should be defended even more 'forward.' I want to go with you. Together we can fight at River Bend. Let us stop the horsemen before anyone else pays the price Kaul has."

Launa looked eastward. Out there was River Bend, Tall Oaks—and Jack. Dob put an arm around her. "I will stand beside you wherever you battle for the People."

FORTY-SIX

JACK MUSTERED BOTH legions. They stood in what would
have been a field of buckwheat, if it hadn't been trampled in
the battle. To his troop's back was the mound that covered
the dead.

Jack took their measure; there were many holes. Cohort
commanders like Brege, Antia and Kaul were missing. Their
seconds in command filled their place. There were holes in
the ranks, too. Troopers were at River Bend or Wood Village. Before Jack could say anything, people started shouting, calling friends from the most shrunken units to join
them, filling out their ranks. Wordlessly Jack watched as the
legion of Tall Oaks reformed itself. Then he laughed. "You
are not leaving me much to do."

The legion laughed with him.

Jack did make some changes. He wanted four cohorts
each of pikes and archers. He kept the two axe cohorts. All
afternoon the legions drilled. Jack joined the ranks of a pike
cohort as it practiced keeping a contingent of axes at bay.
Pike in hand, still Jack's mind spun, listing the hundred
things he needed to do. He did not pay attention.

Das lead the axes. He weaved and twisted; suddenly, he
was past the unpointed tips of the practice pikes. The flat of
his ax came down. It would have hit Jack, but the little girl

who held the wicker shield in front of him deflected the blow.

"Jack, where are you? Have you flown off to where commanders go?"

Jack joined in the laughter and waited until it died. "Das is right. When you carry a pike, your eye must always be where the point of the pike is. Do not make my mistake."

Thanking the eight-year-old who had saved him from a knocking, Jack gave up his place in the cohort. Das was right, his mind was elsewhere, and he should follow it.

Jack stayed with the troops until full dark. Lasa was waiting for him by the fire when he returned to the sanctuary. He briefed her on the day's events as she massaged the knots out of his shoulders and back. With death wrapped around him like a cloak, it was hard to celebrate life. They did not make love.

The next day went much like the first. Sara organized a score of archers and named them Second Dragoons. She would command the anvil for the next horsemen's assault. Since no clansmen had survived the last attack, Launa's old battle plan should be good for a second run.

Jack had no reason to stay.

At supper, Jack asked for nine archers to ride with him. He had a hundred volunteers. For the sake of Tall Oaks, he left the best behind.

That night, Lasa came to him. "Brendi is sure. The Goddess has given a life to our keeping." Jack held her for a long time that night. He wanted to love her, to celebrate their child again. He could not make it happen. The child within her was now a task, a burden for him. For its life, he would kill many. He shared their bed that night with visions of slaughter.

Jack rode out the next day with mixed feelings. The troops he left behind would protect his child and Lasa while he was gone. He wondered what kind of man he would be when he returned.

One of Taelon's hunters, Jinu, served as guide for the troop. Jack rode fast, pushing his soldiers almost as hard as

Launa had ridden those who went with her to deliver the head. But he wanted this small force ready for a fight. Horsemen might be sidestepping around Tall Oaks. He did not know what lay ahead of him as he rode west.

For two days Jack saw nothing but plains and wild herds. Jinu proved himself a competent second in command as well as a skilled guide. That left Jack time to think. He did not like what he thought about.

Was the change coming over him the right one? This was the way he had been taught to train for battle—put the mind and body on automatic. That way, when you hurt or were hurt, you did not feel the pain. Jack knew pain was coming, but was there another way? He had promised Launa and every god in heaven that he'd find a better way. Was he any closer to it?

On the third afternoon, Jinu pointed and said, "Spring fish camp. You fed us well there."

Jack wondered how close they were to the drop point as they changed horses. He remembered a pond with a waterfall. The memories warmed him; it was better to think of that time than what his mind had gnawed at all day. Jack aimed his troops up the trail Taelon had first shown Launa and him.

Maybe two hours of daylight were left when Jack trotted over the ridge and into *their* valley. The lone tree still stood on its rise. The pond nestled in a clump of trees with the stream lazily flowing down from it. Where Jack and Launa had camped, smoke rose from six fires. The low sun glinted off metal.

Jack reined in his troop. A herd grazed between him and the camp. Two riders walked guard among the horses. Jack tried to count the mounts, but they appeared and disappeared too quickly behind gentle rises.

Quickly, Jack ran a threat analysis. Six fires could mean as many as sixty horsemen. They had some sort of refined metal, copper most likely. Did they have the technology, or had they stolen or traded for it? Unknown.

Could Jack take them? Most likely, if they didn't have longbows. Should he risk attacking? Metalworking was critical intelligence. Feeling as if hell had invaded his personal heaven, Jack ordered the dismount.

"String your bows and check your arrows. If it looks like a fight, I will order the dismount." Eager young faces obeyed. Jack felt the burden that was his alone as he mounted Windrider.

Jack led at the walk. The riders tending the herd spotted them and raised a shout as they rounded up their charges and got them moving toward the camp. A few ponies took off on their own; the herd guards were smart enough not to give chase.

Jack counted fifty or more people running out from the camp. A few of them made for the herd, but most formed a line under the watchful eyes of their sergeants. Three people talked among themselves in front of the line.

As Jack got closer he took the measure of the bows. Several looked as long as his own—*metal and longbows.* Outnumbered five or six to one by a force he had no technological edge over, he was in deep trouble.

Jack brought his troop to a halt 400 meters from the opposing line. For a long minute the two forces eyed each other across the plain. The sun was in his eyes, and Jack had trouble making out his opposition. He suspected the evening twilight was not yet dusky enough to hide him. At least if he ran, the pursuit would be short.

No one did anything. Jack studied his men—young, nervous. "Dismount," he ordered.

"Form line, prepare to receive a charge. Jinu, take the spare horses and keep watch behind us."

Jack's archers spread out in line. They jabbed arrows into the ground in front of them; whoever charged first would pay a high price. *So this was how Colonel Custer felt,* Jack snorted. He was outnumbered, dismounted and open to being surrounded.

Jack scanned the area nervously. Only fifty were in sight, but a horde could be hiding behind any of the folds in the land. Launa and Lasa would never know how he died. *Damn! What a screw-up. Why didn't I back out of this mess as soon as I saw it?*

For a long minute Jack sweated, trying to figure out what to do next. Nothing suggested itself.

"Jack, that you?" Launa's voice and English took a moment to register.

"Yes" was all Jack could get past dry vocal cords.

"Thought so from the deployment. Bring your troop in, Jack, and meet the First Cav of the Cliff Town National Guard."

Jack took a moment for his legs to stop shaking, then remounted his troops and led them in. Launa gave him an off-hand salute. He returned it as he drew up in front of her and what looked like her command element—Kaul and a young man.

"Evening, Lieutenant." With Lasa pregnant, he'd better remember his place.

"Fidon, find these people a place to bed down and get them some food," Launa ordered. The man threw Launa a smart salute and led Jack's troops off.

Launa turned back to Jack. "Captain"—it sounded like Launa was going to make it easy on him—"may I present Dobrovnish." The handsome young man beside Kaul held his hand up in greeting. Jack did the same as he slid off Windrider.

Launa continued. "Dob is firstborn of the Speakers in Cliff Town. When he heard Nak's song, he began preparing for the horsemen. His eye is good, and it is well that we came slowly into Cliff Town." Launa flashed the young man a smile.

He returned it with quiet self-assurance. But the way his eyes fell on Launa sent a lurch through Jack's heart. He was clearly a man Launa admired, and the attraction in his eyes for her was obvious. Jack knew he should be happy for her.

Jack let his eyes wander over the busy camp. The pond glinted invitingly in the low sun. Launa had picked a good place to camp. Had she intended to add more memories? Jack forced his mind back to Launa's story; he was a married man with a child on the way. Launa handed Jack a copper knife. He turned it over in his hand. The heft was different.

"This comes from Cliff Town. They've been smelting copper for two generations. When Nak showed them one of our knives, Dob started making his own. Dob saw that the horsemen must not gain this knowledge even before we arrived. He is one canny soldier."

Jack heard a lot more in Launa's words than just a situation report. "So you gave them the bow."

Kaul nodded. "We must build a wall between the horsemen and what Launa calls the mines of Cliff Town if we are to walk away from the tomorrows that stretch before us."

Jack agreed. He was about to surrender Windrider to a waiting soldier and ask about supper when he noticed Star nearby. He glanced at the horse, then back at Launa. She did not meet his eyes, but stooped to pick up the pouch that rested at her feet—Maria's book. "I needed to think. I was going up to the tree to read a bit before the daylight failed."

"The tree is a good place. I bring news of Tall Oaks."

"I figured you did." Launa quickly mounted Star.

As Jack swung himself up on Windrider, he spoke to Kaul. "My words are for your ears also." The older man offered Jack his hand. Jack pulled him up behind him.

At the hill, they dismounted. Launa took a moment to stare out over the plain. Jack's eyes followed her gaze; somewhere out there, three miles away, was the drop point where they had entered this millennium. Jack turned to Kaul. "Lasa is with child."

He wanted to kick himself for blurting it out, but Kaul's reaction showed only his love for the woman. "She must be overjoyed to be blessed so quickly. She is lovely when she carries a gift from the Goddess. This is good. Care for her." Kaul enveloped Jack in a bear hug.

When the hug broke, Launa offered her hand for the traditional handshake. Jack took it. "I'm glad for you both." Launa's voice was flat.

Jack swallowed words he could not say. This should have been his and Launa's child. If their world had not given her the implant and they had borne a child, would these people have taken him from her? Jack would never know.

He shook himself and turned to Kaul. Quickly he described the latest developments.

"Damn!" Launa snapped upon finding her recruits were being intercepted. When Jack finished, she scowled. "Just what we need, Hanna behind us and Antia pissing off every horseman from here to China. What do we do?"

Jack outlined his plan to recoup what recruits they could. Then, with an army at their back, try talking some sense to Antia. "The People of Tall Oaks do not want a fight, but they know what Antia does brings death to them all. They will not let her walk her own path. The tradition has its limit."

A sonic boom cut Jack off. He and Launa turned as one to face the steppe. Just where Jack would have bet was their drop point, a shimmering light hung in the twilight.

Again in the presence of the twenty-first-century, Jack put out an arm for Launa, his only touchstone to the future. She did not flinch away.

His eyes on the light, Kaul came to stand with them. "That is the door to your home, just as Launa described it to me?"

"Yes," Launa mumbled.

"Your people are calling you home," Kaul whispered.

"It can't be." This was supposed to be a one-way trip. Jack's heart battled with his head. He wasn't sure which part of him wanted what.

"Is your work here done? You have planted the seed. Dobrovnish and I have listened well to Launa's words. We can lead the legion."

Jack shook his head, trying to clear his thoughts. He wanted to scream "Yes." He wanted to shout "No." He wanted to flee back to a world where he was just one of many, not the one on whom all history turned. Where did his duty lie? He held tight to Launa. "What do you think?"

She did not take her eyes off the shimmering. "Judith said we should let the Old Europeans help us find the way. God knows they've usually done things their own way."

Jack took a deep breath of evening air and let it out slowly. How often had he been a mover and shaker? More often he'd just been along for the ride. Someone up-time was calling this shot.

Launa sighed. "Maybe we have done all we need to do. Maybe for us to do more is to risk what we've already done."

Jack wanted to agree. "Lasa carries my child" was the only answer he could make.

Kaul squeezed his arm. "I have helped Lasa raise four children, and one of them was Masin's. I can raise another."

Launa broke from Jack's hug. Holding the pouch with Maria's book, she mounted Star, then turned to him. "You coming?"

Slowly, Jack's gaze swung from Launa to Kaul. Had he once more conceived a child he would never see take its first step? How many times could his heart be ripped out? Each fiber in his body made its own separate decision, protesting, agreeing, as Jack walked to Windrider and mounted. "I'm with you, Launa."

She kicked Star; they raced for the shimmering gate. With each stride, Jack changed. Light as the wind on his face, he embraced freedom.

Halfway there, Launa started laughing. Jack couldn't help it; he laughed with her. They had done it. They had accomplished their mission. They were going home.

FORTY-SEVEN

LAUNA KEPT HER eyes on the shimmering light as they rode. She had planned to go to the tree, say good-bye to her memories of Jack and commit herself to Dob. His eyes, his words told her he was hers. Here the woman chose the consort, and it was time she started living that way. Dob had listened intently to the short course she had given him and Kaul on strategy and tactics. He had the savvy and eye of a good field commander. He would make a good partner for a soldier.

Then Jack showed up, and her heart was in her throat. She knew who he was long before she hollered. How could she miss the way he sat Windrider, the stoop of his shoulders as he understood what he faced? Her deployment must have really scared him.

Launa urged Star for more speed. So Lasa was pregnant. Launa knew that was what had been expected of Jack. Still, the news had been a kick in the gut. Launa had wanted to run down the hill, throw herself in Dob's arms, take him by storm. Before she could take a step, the gate opened.

Launa prayed she was doing the right thing. The folks at Livermore had said this was a one-way mission—no return. Yet, the gate was here, calling them back. She and Jack must have done their job. Launa blocked all questions. They had fought their battles. They had shown these people what was possible. She and Jack deserved a chance to be themselves now.

Launa leaped from Star. Standing in front of the shimmering, she felt like a kid before a glowing Christmas tree. She waited for Jack. Reaching out, she grabbed his hand, pulled it to her breast. God, it felt good to touch him again.

Laughing like children, they ran for the light. She paused at the shimmering. "You want to do this?"

"Yes." His answer was so low she wondered for a moment if he really meant it. He stepped forward; she followed him, pace for pace. Together they entered the sparkling air of the gate.

Launa tried to remember what the last trip had been like. The sphere appeared smaller; there was no room in this one for horses. She clutched Maria's book close to her breasts. It held a warmth all its own. The light was softer, not glaring white.

Launa took a shallow breath; the air was cold, but there was no acrid taste this time. She pulled Jack to her. The warmth of their bodies held the cold at bay. The touch of his hands on her skin, the feel of his muscled arms around her, brought tingling to her that had nothing to do with the time gate.

Still, cold seeped into her muscles; her legs cramped. There was none of the last trip's bone-numbing vibration. Again, Launa wondered how long the journey would take. Just when she thought she could stand it no more, the light began to change. The shimmering became constant. Then suddenly, it was gone.

Launa stood in a lab at Livermore.

But it wasn't her Livermore Lab. The cream-colored walls of the bunker were now earth tones, green and brown. The lab equipment that had gleamed severely in whites and chrome now was coated with a wild hue of colors.

And the bunker wasn't underground. The walls had windows giving her a view to the east. Marching up the hill were row upon row of windmills, each one turning briskly; more were being built. When last she'd seen that hill, one of the few remaining windmills had wound down to death. Today, one came to life.

Even before Launa saw the people, she knew she had not come back to the same world she left.

Then a woman stepped forward. "I'm Judith Lee."

Launa recognized the anthropologist who had been her friend and briefer at a CIA ranch. Now Judith was dressed in khaki shorts, but her embroidered white blouse still matched her hair.

Behind her could only have been Brent Lynch. A white beard hid his face, but who else would have worn a polka-dot kilt with plaid socks? His tank top bore a pattern of African tribal art.

Behind these two, Launa recognized several of the scientists at a control console. Standing with them was Samantha Tanner. The skimpy red mini she wore wasn't an inch longer than the tennis skirt Launa had worn in gym. The half-sized bikini top that supported her breasts hid nothing. Some things apparently had not changed.

Launa snapped to attention. Beside her, Jack followed her cue. "Lieutenant Launa O'Brian, United States Army, reporting the return of the Neolithic Military Advisory Group. All Present. Mission accomplished." Launa saluted.

Samantha scowled at the technicians. "What the fuck is the United States Army?"

Launa broke from her military pose and whirled to face Jack. He reached out for her, and she leaped into his arms. "Mission very definitely accomplished," she rejoiced.

Jack swung her around. "If they don't know what the hell an army is, I bet they never heard of war either."

Brent joined Judith. "I think I understand something of what they said. You can trace the words back from their roots in the Latin and Old High German. But what is 'hell'?"

Launa watched the expression on Jack's face change. She turned to face Brent. "In six thousand years, the followers of the Goddess haven't decided between heaven or reincarnation?"

"No," Judith said. "There are many who hold with both."

Launa's whole body trembled as she suppressed a laugh. "I wonder what the Pope thinks of that?"

Judith cocked an eyebrow in puzzlement. "And why should that bother her?"

Jack laughter filled the lab as Launa sighed. "We definitely aren't in Kansas, Toto."

As they ushered them into a conference room, Jack started asking questions. "How did you know when to recall us?"

The woman in the white smock frowned. "Recall you?"

"You're Dr. Harrison, I believe." Jack had only met the woman three times.

"Lady Harrison," the woman corrected him with a quick nod. "You know me?"

"Yes. In my world, you helped Dr. Milo build the time machine."

The woman cast a quick glance at the pudgy man beside her. "Scholar Milo is on my team." Jack got the drift. This was no male-dominated world he and Launa had forged.

Samantha overrode the discussion with a question to Launa. "How did you come to enter our power bubble? Where were you? You seem to know what you have done. Tell us what we have done!"

Before Launa could answer, a young woman entered carrying a small dog. What was a dog doing here? Jack remembered the troubles the disappearance of one small mutt had caused in their first test of the time machine. He frowned and elbowed Launa to get her attention. They both eyed the pup.

"Muffin?" he called.

The woman set the dog down and the animal came to them, wagging her tail. Jack reached for her collar and held the tag where Launa could see it with him.

"L.A. tags." Launa grinned. "You've come a long way."

"You know the dog's name?" The young woman marveled as she took the dog.

"Our time machine was first tested by sending a dog named Muffin back five hundred years. She disappeared and we weren't sure the machine would work for us," Launa answered.

"We were running an experiment," Lady Harrison explained. "Everywhere else they got one result. Here, we got something different. When we put through almost fifteen megawatts yesterday, this little dog showed up. Today, we were up to nearly eighteen megawatts, the highest levels ever recorded, and you appeared. What will we find tomorrow?"

"Nothing, I suspect. We three are the sole survivors." And Launa began the story of a world that had sent the soldiers forth to change its own history.

Jack stared numbly out the window. Things were going slowly. Like Kaul, these folks were very accepting, but they were having a hard time accepting what they heard.

And Jack needed time to digest just how much had changed. The North Columbian Department included the United States as well as Canada and Mexico. A Christine Colon had led the expedition in 1492 that finally brought the Western hemisphere into the global economy. Jack was getting used to minor modifications like that. Other things were harder to adjust to.

Jack had no problem listening quietly while the women asked Launa questions and she answered them. But several times Launa had asked Jack for help remembering.

Jack had yet to finish an answer. Samantha talked over him every time. Jack remembered female officers complaining about old colonels ignoring them in meetings. Now he knew how hard it was to sit on that anger.

Launa made a point of asking Jack to describe the battle at the tree. Samantha cut Jack off with a curt, "We don't need to know the details of primitive conflict management." This Samantha could take a few lessons from Lasa on how to conduct a meeting. Then Jack frowned; the Samantha from his other world had needed the same lessons.

Samantha called a break and took Launa aside with Lady Harrison to talk about quantum mechanics. While they conferred, Judith asked Jack to finish his account of the battles.

Jack was surprised at how fast he covered the two defenses. If war really was unknown to these people, Jack didn't want to tell them any more than was necessary.

He found himself staring at the coffee cup that had appeared in his hand some time earlier. He thought Brent had brought it. He wasn't seeing a drink. He was back six thousand years ago staring at dirt running red with blood. He shivered.

"What does it feel like?"

Jack came out of his reverie.

Brent repeated himself. "What does it feel like?"

Jack stared at the man. How could he comprehend what is was like to walk a primitive land with six thousand years of history on your back? Could any of these people grasp how it felt to look into the face of another man who wanted your blood, when billions of lives depend on your living? How much about his own world did he want to tell these people?

Jack looked from Brent's face to Judith's, then back again. "How do I feel? I should feel like I've done a damn good job."

Jack pushed himself away from the table, stretched out his legs and arms, let every muscle in his body tense, then willed them all to relax. Finally he sighed. "Maybe sometime, about a week from now, I'll feel great. Right now, I feel as if I'm wrapped in cotton. An hour ago, I was getting ready for a battle I expected to die losing. It turned out to be Launa's troop, and I was just starting to relax when your gate opened up." Jack shook his head again. "But there's more to it than that. We were two or three months away from the first snowfall, and I figured we'd have to fight one, maybe two battles between now and then. I was gearing myself up for that."

Brent nodded.

Judith stared hard at Jack. Before he could go on in that vein, she changed the topic. "Tell me about your twenty-first-century family."

Jack scratched his ear, thought for a moment. "Where to start? My father, Sam, died in the Vietnam War in 1972. I don't imagine you had a war over there at that time."

"We haven't had a violent, organized conflict in two thousand years," Judith answered softly.

Jack shook his head again, trying to let that soak into his skull. "Launa and I really did it."

Judith smiled and went on. "Did you know your grandfather?"

"Grandfather, let's see." Jack had to struggle to remember grandfather's given name. "Oh, right, John Walking Bear. I was named after him. When I visited him summers on the San Carlos Indian Reservation, everyone just called him grandfather."

Judith's green eyes lit up. "When you said your name was Walking Bear, I wondered if you were related to the John Walking Bear I know."

Jack sat bolt upright. "He lived outside Phoenix."

Judith's grin widened as Brent sat down at a keyboard and screen. It was bigger than the ones Jack remembered.

"Is that a personal computer or a terminal?" Jack asked.

"Personal computer?" Judith echoed the question; then it must have clicked for her. "Oh, heavens, no. All the terminals are networked to the main data file servers. They're all linked together, too. This way everyone has access to all the same data. Why would anyone want an isolated computer?"

Jack shrugged off the question as Brent excitedly pointed at the terminal screen. "You said your father's name was Samuel and your name is John."

"Yes."

"Your grandfather is alive, living with your father on the Santa Carlotta Cultural Diversity Preserve." Brent spoke so quickly it took a moment to register. He paused for a moment before he finished. "They live there with Johnny Walking Bear."

"Does your computer say anything about Sandie?"

"Sandie?" Brent echoed.

"My first wife." Had he gone from having no wife to having three? Time travel could complicate a man's life.

Brent worked the terminal, the screen blinked, then the old archeologist shook his head. "She was killed four years ago in a car crash." Brent turned to Jack. "A baby died with her."

Jack turned away. Some things didn't change.

Brent reached for his arm. "I'm sorry."

Jack shook his head. "It happened four, no, five years ago for me, and much has happened since. It's an old pain."

"Sweet Goddess." Judith covered her mouth with her hand and looked Jack up and down. "I know you. You're Johnny. I can see him in you now. You looked so different, so determined, I couldn't see the resemblance. But you're little Johnny."

Judith rushed on, as if trying to wash away the sorrow with new joy. "I know your grandfather and father and Sam's boy. I can arrange for you to visit them. Would you like that?"

"Yes," Jack mumbled, struggling to come to terms with what he had heard. He could meet himself as well as the dead father he had never known. "Where do they live?"

Again, Brent did something to the terminal and a map appeared. "The Preserve is just outside Phoenix."

Jack stared at the map on the screen, trying not to frown. His eyes traced the boundaries of the Santa Carlotta Cultural Diversity Preserve. They were the same as the San Carlos Indian Reservation he had visited as a child.

"Diversity Preserve?" Jack echoed, inviting Brent to go on.

"Yes. Less sophisticated cultures must be protected from the more successful mainstream culture. A mother must look after her children."

Jack nodded, afraid to trust his voice to answer. *God, don't let that mean what it could mean. I'll never be able to talk these people into sending me and Launa back to make another try at world-changing.*